//
The Warrior

The Warrior

Ben Tousey

Northwest Publishing, Inc.
Salt Lake City, Utah

The Warrior

All rights reserved.
Copyright © 1995 Northwest Publishing, Inc.

Reproduction in any manner, in whole or in part,
in English or in other languages, or otherwise
without written permission of the publisher is prohibited.

This is a work of fiction.
All characters and events portrayed in this book are fictional,
and any resemblance to real people or incidents is purely coincidental.

For information address: Northwest Publishing, Inc.
6906 South 300 West, Salt Lake City, Utah 84047
JC 1.16.95
Edited by C.D. Allen

PRINTING HISTORY
First Printing 1995

ISBN: 1-56901-297-0

NPI books are published by Northwest Publishing, Incorporated,
6906 South 300 West, Salt Lake City, Utah 84047.
The name "NPI" and the "NPI" logo are trademarks belonging to
Northwest Publishing, Incorporated.

PRINTED IN THE UNITED STATES OF AMERICA.
10 9 8 7 6 5 4 3 2 1

To my mom, Sharon,
for all her support.

To my sister, Anna.

Prologue

Universe after universe, galaxy after galaxy, they stretched out for eternity. Teeming with life they whizzed through space with an awesome beauty that was virtually impossible to comprehend; unless of course you were fortunate enough to see it for yourself. There were giant planets, so large that it took them days to make one complete rotation, and small planets that could almost be mistaken for moons. There were planets that had as many as two dozen suns, or moons, and planets that had but one. There were big planets and small planets, and everything in between. Every one of them made their way through their respective galaxies and solar systems with a grace and beauty that seemed to sing into the space around them.

There were giant universes that housed solar systems and galaxies, and stars and suns sent their light and warmth into the universes around them. Comets the size of stars made their way through the maze of space and matter. Asteroids floated passively by, and light bounced and played off the dust in the empty space. Despite all the movement of comets, asteroids, planets, moons, and everything else that shared these universes, everything moved smoothly and quickly, and nothing interfered with anything else. Everything worked in perfect order.

The planets hummed as they spun around their suns, the stars whistled, and meteors chirped playfully as they bounced their way through space. Everything worked in perfect harmony with everything else.

In the midst of all this splendor, an ocean of sparkling blue water seemed to appear out of nowhere. From a distance it looked like it was on a flat plane and the surface was just a few centimeters above the bottom, but up close it was like walking into a three-dimensional movie. The colors were so bright and vivid that they seemed to bounce off the water. The water was dark blue, mixed in with shades of green and a little touch of white. The colors would cascade off the water and through the air as the waves would crest and then recede.

The waves lapped and played and bounced off each other, then they would rise off the surface of the ocean, slap each other joyfully, and recede back into the water.

In the water lived every species of fish and marine life known to man, and it also carried some species never before seen on any other planet. They were indigenous only to this ocean. And there was no food chain here. All the marine life played and lived together in perfect harmony with one another.

Down through the middle of this ocean a massive roadway, miles wide and made out of solid gold, made its way through the water. The gold in this highway was pure and white, and it shined like glass. It made its way from the very edge of the ocean, right through the ocean's center, and then inland.

Several miles in, the water lapped up against the shore. In some areas massive cliffs jutted above the shoreline, and other areas met the ocean with a rolling and soft plain that gently sloped up and away from the water. In this plain a river approximately two miles wide emptied itself into the ocean. The highway made of gold split in half a few miles offshore, where the river had built up a magnificent delta, and then continued its course on land, divided so that it ran on both sides of the river. The color of this river was somewhat different than that of the ocean's. It was white and silver, with sparkles of metallic blue and gray mixed in with it.

As the road and the river continued inland, the terrain began to take on many changes. Miles beyond the plain a mountain range rose up out of the countryside. This mountain range ran parallel to the shoreline throughout most of its spread. In some areas the mountains were so high that it was almost impossible to see the top.

The highway and the river ran through this chain of mountains, where a pass seemed to make its way from one side of the chain of mountains to the other. The river ran between giant cliffs and cut into the rock, creating breathtaking mountain scenery at dizzying heights. The road wound its way through the mountains with the river still running through its center hundreds of feet below.

Despite the size and ruggedness of the terrain, it was not threatening. Instead, it offered a steady, solid pathway through the mountains.

Further down the road, the mountains dropped off into a deep valley, and the river and the road joined each other on the same level again. In this valley was a city that none could describe. A massive, walled city that stretched a thousand miles in every direction. The foundation of the city and the city walls were made of twelve different precious stones, each one layered one on top of the other. Huge gates of uncut pearl hung without hinges on every wall, open so that all who would could enter.

Just as the mountains broke off into the valley, thousands of feet in the air, the road branched off and began to descend down toward the city. Built like a suspending bridge, it gradually descended until it became level with the floor of the city.

The road split into several smaller highways just outside the city. They ran the parameters of the city and entered through the gates on every wall on all four sides of the city. Opposite the first highway was another golden highway, and they both approached the city and split to move around the walls.

The river continued to flow down the middle of the highway, right into the center of the city. In the heart of the city, massive buildings, skyscrapers, beautiful bridges, lakes and rivers, beautiful freeways, palaces and mansions, and other beautiful structures unfolded one by one, revealing the most magnificent city ever seen. Everything that one would see in most major cities could be seen in this city. Only these structures were made of diamonds and rubies and emeralds and other precious gems. Pure light bounced off every building and structure and mixed with light bouncing off other structures, until it looked like the aurora borealis in the middle of the day. The light, and these colors, could never be described to anyone who hadn't actually seem them first hand.

As the road entered the city, it was joined by other roads, also made of gold. They wound their way around the city, thousands of miles of roadway all paved with gold. Then they were joined by road after road, as they rose into the air and moved in and out of each other, sometimes as high as the skyscrapers themselves. They all moved together, the structures and the roads.

Then right in the middle of the city, everything stopped. The roads once again dropped down to ground level and moved back into four roads, one from each gate.

This was the center of the city, and it consisted mostly of a giant plain made of pure crystal glass, which was transparent, yet at the same time reflected everything over it. It enhanced the light, and then added to it to make the whole city shine like the sun. Despite its being glass, it was not fragile. On the contrary, it could carry the weight of the world and still hold more. Nor was it slippery. It was smooth, placid, and peaceful. The sea stretched about a hundred miles in diameter.

In the middle of the sea of glass sat the throne of the Great Emperor. His throne was tall and majestic and surrounded by shards of light, shards that looked like fractures of a rainbow. They shot out from the throne in every direction, shooting through the air and bouncing off other shards of light, bouncing off the structures of buildings and off the sea of glass itself. The glass plain reflected every little shard, magnified it, and then seemed to double it and send it back into the air. Then the process repeated itself again. There was so much light and color that the air itself seemed to be alive.

This was the home of the Great Emperor and of every one

of his servants and followers.

The Great Emperor loved beauty and went out of his way to be surrounded by it; and truly, there wasn't anything as beautiful in existence as this city.

The Great Emperor was also a kind and generous ruler, and everything he had, he graciously offered to all of his servants, everything except his throne and his rule. Those went undisputed. The city of the Great Emperor was open to all. The whole of creation was welcome through his gates. With one exception.

1

Below the throne of the Great Emperor, in the midst of all the splendor and wonder of his kingdom, spun a swirling mass of darkness very much like a black hole. It was small in comparison to the rest of the celestial splendor that stretched out in every direction, but it loomed ominously over all creation.

The blackness swirled slowly around, pulling itself and the darkness within it deeper and deeper into itself. No light could enter, and nothing could leave. It held a firm grip on the darkness. This was the one and only dark spot in the whole of creation.

Within the black hole, at its very core, lay a lonely little universe all to itself, a universe isolated from all existence, and the splendor of the cosmos around it. Deep in the heart of that universe, a small dark planet spun quietly in its orbit around the sun. Although it was one of many planets in this particular universe, it was still a small and lonely planet in that vast and lonely universe.

Despite one sun to light the planet, there was still a supernatural darkness that seemed to surround this universe so intensely that it kept the darkness lurking constantly behind the light. It was the supernatural darkness that created the black hole in the heavens.

No one was allowed in, and no one got out. The only beings to enter this hole in the cosmos were those specifically chosen by the Great Emperor. Once they were chosen, they underwent extensive training before they were to have any involvement in the unfolding of events that took place beyond that black hole. Although nobody was allowed in, everyone in the Great Emperor's kingdom was allowed to watch the saga. They could all see the events unfold as if they were there, but that was their only involvement. They were spectators only, while the Great Emperor worked out his intent. Of those that were allowed to enter the black hole, the most notable visitor was the Great Emperor's son, the Prince of Light.

The only planet sustaining any form of life at all in that universe was known as the Darklands. The Darklands was a small planet in comparison to the rest of the planets in that universe, and was capable of sustaining only a few billion people at a time. As it would seem, already this planet was far beyond capacity. Things had become so crowded, and the problems of the planet's surface had become so great, that the little planet groaned under the weight and the strain of its predicament.

The residents of the Darklands had no concept of the universe that surrounded them, and they knew nothing of the black hole that locked them in and held them prisoners. Nor were they aware of any existence beyond that black hole. They had become so accustomed to the darkness that surrounded them and their universe, that they were completely unaware that anything else might be out there at all. The darkness that hid all this from the Darklands was the same darkness that threatened to destroy the planet altogether. Every resident knew of the potential danger, that they and their planet hung on the brink of destruction, but because this thought was so terrifying, they accepted the darkness and the solace and comfort it offered them. As long as they didn't see the danger, they could feel safe from it.

But despite this darkness, there was a small light somewhere on the planet's surface. A single light, a light the size of a firefly. It flickered only for a second, and then vanished. Although this light was small and only a flicker, it carried the intensity of a twenty megaton nuclear warhead. Only a little flicker, it was, ironically, so intense that it could completely destroy all existence in one single blow.

Several miles above the planet's surface, cloaked in the supernatural darkness, was a massive, multilevel structure that covered nearly half of the planet's surface view. It hovered there with all of its windows and doors and other openings pointed directly toward the planet itself. This structure looked like a maze of tunnels and caverns and rooms, all carved out of some rocklike material. There were large conference rooms and file rooms. There were strategy rooms, rooms with floor-to-ceiling maps of every square inch of the Darklands, marking not only topography and land mass, but population and affluence as well. In this room were files of all leaders of the Darklands, major personalities, and the key players. Also from this room, strategies were marked out, battles planned, and human weakness was tracked and exploited.

There was one room that stretched out for miles and looked like a giant control room. From this room, observers monitored every resident of the Darklands and recorded their every movement and then sent the information away to other observers and behaviorists who studied the documents and used that information to discover new ways to annihilate and exterminate humanity in the most gruesome ways they could.

There were rooms for everything, including rooms that housed some of the highest ranking generals in the known universe. Powerful beings, with a supernatural power so strong that in a single blow they could destroy nearly half of the planet's surface at a time. They used this power to keep all of the Darklands under their thumb and to make sure that chaos and violence reigned on the planet.

Although this structure all but surrounded the Darklands, cluttering up the universe around it, The fortress was transparent and could not be seen by the planet's residents.

It was from this structure that Draygon, the self-proclaimed ruler of the Darklands, looked out on the planet. Since there was no one strong enough to challenge him, his rule went undisputed. He was a ruthless being who cared nothing for life and humanity or even the survival of the planet. Sometimes called the Prince of the Air, he lived and ruled from this fortress above the Darklands. Thousands of years ago he had stolen the Darklands from the Great Emperor and the residents of the planet at that time. The Great Emperor had given it to them as a gift, and they in turn handed it over to Draygon. The Great Emperor allowed Draygon to rule this planet for a time, but he remained involved in the planet's evolvement as well.

Draygon resembled a man in many ways, but he was much bigger, at least a head or two taller, and he was so hard and cold that his eyes had sunk far back into their sockets and they could no longer see anything but his purpose to destroy all of the creation that was currently under him. The hate on his face seemed to distort it in such a way that it would be unbearable for any human to look upon him. Fortunately, very few humans were ever given that chance. Nowhere else in the whole of creation was there so much hate evident in any one being.

Draygon was the epitome of hate and evil and terror.

Under Draygon were millions and millions of soldiers of various ranks and positions in the order of Draygon and his army. Hideous creatures who roamed the planet preying on helpless victims, holding them in the darkness. They served under Draygon to enforce his cruel reign, and also to wreak havoc themselves. They manifested themselves in all manner of ways, by creating strife between men, by using natural disasters to destroy humankind, and on the higher levels, to create war amongst nations, to give power to cruel governments to hold their subjects in complete terror for their lives, and many other things that are too numerous to mention. They all worked to bring about destruction of the Darklands and the Darklands residents in every way they could. This was their sole duty under Draygon.

Draygon called an emergency meeting of his top officials, generals and lieutenants of the highest ranking. The most powerful and hideous beings in the universe all assembled in one place. They sat around a large, flat, stone table, watching Draygon. Draygon stood in front of a large screen that could illuminate and focus on any part of the Darklands that he commanded. It could select small areas, or it could bring into focus the entire planet. At any time he could bring up an area, a person, or a group of people—anything on the planet's surface that he wanted to see. To the left of this screen, outside of the fortress, could be seen the planet itself, spinning quietly, unaware of anything that was happening around it, barely aware of what was happening on its own surface.

Draygon stared first at the screen, and then at the planet itself. The rest of his generals and lieutenants watched him in silence, an intense silence that nobody dared to break. Nobody knew why he had called this emergency meeting, but it was only the second time he had done so. The questions of what and why screamed in the heads of everyone there, but nobody dared ask. Draygon only continued to stare intently at the surface of the Darklands. For a long time he said nothing, then eventually he spoke.

"He's out there." That was all he said, but those words brought a wave of terror that swept through the entire assembly gathered around the table.

Draygon had seen the little light, the light of the firefly. He had watched it flicker only for a split-second, and then disappear into the darkness again.

Draygon never said *who* was out there, but he didn't have to. Everybody knew whom he was talking about.

The silence in the room was tense. Nobody moved; nobody spoke; they barely dared to breathe. For Draygon to actually come out and say the words, "He's out there," meant that the magnitude of the situation had gone beyond words.

They all waited breathlessly to hear what Draygon would say next, but he said nothing for a long time. So long a time that even the slightest movement caused every one of them to jump.

Draygon continued staring into the darkness.

"I sense it," he said again, finally breaking the silence. The suddenness of his words, with the tension in the room, caused everyone there to jump. The sound of his voice had startled them out of their own private thoughts. "He's been silent all these years," Draygon went on. "Still. Planning his strategy. But now, he's beginning to move."

One of Draygon's most powerful generals spoke up.

"Sir," he said, "we've sealed off the Darklands so tightly that no one could get in. We've set up watches around every parameter. We have not seen him, and he hasn't penetrated our defense at any time...we would have known if he had."

"He didn't *just* penetrate the Darklands." Draygon turned and faced the others at the table. "He's been here all along. That's how he works. He remains silent for long periods of time. He disappears, and he plans and schemes. I saw him leave. But he didn't leave. He left part of himself here. I should have known."

Another general broke in.

"Sir, if he is planning something, how are we going to counter? The last time we thought we had overcome him, he turned our own plan against us."

Draygon's face turned cold and violent. He made a choking motion with his hand, and the general grabbed his neck and gasped for air. Draygon pulled his hand down and the general's face slammed into the table. Draygon continued to move his hand up and down, and the general's face continued to move up into the air, and then to pound back down onto the table with a terrible force. Despite the general's attempts to stop the beating, he could not. He flung his arms desperately in the air, trying to gain some form of control. Then Draygon violently swung his arm to the side, and the general glided through the air and landed on the floor several feet away. Draygon crossed over to his general and grabbed him around the throat and lifted him into the air like he was a rag doll.

"You will never speak to me of that incident again!" He glared. "Is that understood?"

The general nodded weakly. Everyone else agreed emphatically, out of fear for their own necks. He looked around at the others, then let go of the general, whose body fell to the floor like a piece of clothing with nothing inside. He quietly pulled himself back up off the floor and staggered back to the table, still gasping for air. He secretly hoped that Draygon did get what was coming to him, but he dared not mention that. He hated Draygon, but many years ago had decided he would take Draygon's side when he rebelled against the Great Emperor, and now there was nothing he could do. He was under Draygon and would be for a long time. There was no way out of that decision.

Draygon looked around the room. Nobody moved. They all sat there in terror. He looked them over one by one, and they could feel their faces giving them away.

"What are you not telling me, Cobran?" he asked his highest general.

General Cobran swallowed hard, then spoke in a shaky voice.

"Sir," he said, pulling out a file, "we have noticed a lot of activity going on in a couple of different places. We've noticed increased support and protection around at least three young men in the Darklands. Two in Darklands City, and the other in the Fortress of Light." He paused for a moment. "We didn't want to tell you just yet because we weren't sure if it meant anything."

"How much activity?" Draygon's voice was threatening.

"About triple the usual activity," Cobran whispered in a shaky voice.

Draygon glared at him the same as he had glared at the other general. His eyes burned hotter and hotter.

"About triple! The activity of the enemy triples over three young men, and you tell me nothing about it? Have you learned nothing from the past? Do you not remember what happened last time?"

"Yes sir," Cobran answered, "But there wasn't enough evidence that anything of the same nature was happening in this case. We weren't sure if this meant anything just yet."

Draygon's eyes turned cold with hate. He looked Cobran directly in the face, and then he swung his hand in the air. Cobran flew to the ceiling and hit with such a force that the entire structure shook. He gasped in pain as Draygon held him there tightly. Then he let go of Cobran and moved his hand in a circle. The air around him began to swirl. A whirlwind began to form around him, and he screamed in pain as it sucked him away into the Pit of Utter Darkness, a pit that consisted of nothing but darkness and pain.

Without saying another thing, Draygon took his post back at the window, searching the darkness for the flicker of light. This time there was no flicker. Only darkness lay there. Silence and darkness.

2

In the heart of the Darklands, Darklands City stretched out like a sea of concrete and modern structure. A giant metropolis, and a magnificent city that covered nearly a hundred and fifty miles from one end to the other. Centrally located in reference to the rest of the Darklands, it sat about twenty miles inland off the Nefacarious Sea.

The Nefacarious Sea was the largest body of water on the Darklands, and it was fed by thousands of rivers and tributaries. The largest river to empty into the sea was the River Thromins (pronounced *trow-mins*). Twenty miles inland, up the river, lay the heart of Darklands City.

The River Thromins moved quickly as it hurled itself into the sea and carried so much water that when it hit the ocean, it created a ten-foot wall of water where it met the Nefacarious

Sea. All this movement of water and currents created winds that constantly blew down the river and out to sea. These winds could be very dangerous at times, sometimes reaching speeds that would capsize even the larger boats.

The river had also built up a delta that stretched miles and miles into the sea. On this delta many unique plants and other forms of vegetation grew. Fish and other unique and bizarre marine life floated and swam amongst the vegetation. Some of these creatures were harmful to humans, but they preferred saltwater, so they very seldomly made it up the river. No humans could live there in the delta as the ground was too unsteady.

The River Thromins had become a garbage disposal to many of the residents of Darklands City, and those who lived along the river and some of its tributaries would carry the garbage and deposit much of it on the delta. The Delta Thromins, as it was called, looked like a dump, littered and cluttered with all the debris from the city.

To make it possible for ships to enter and leave the river that led to the port of Darklands City, the city had built a dike down the center of the river at the point where it met the sea. Workers constructed the dike partly of concrete and steel, but they were also able to use parts of the delta itself as a natural dike. They dug and cleared out the area used as a waterway into the river, stacked the trash up higher on the existing delta, and opened up a channel for ships to pass unharmed by shallow ridges or reefs or the ten-foot wall of water that constantly loomed over the opening of the river.

Further inland, inside the city, beautiful bridges spanned the river, connecting the north side of the city with the south side of the city. The river was lined with them. Suspension bridges several feet in the air spanned the great river below them, moving ever so slightly with the air currents that flowed in and out with the river. There were also floating bridges that floated atop the river's surface and opened and closed for passing ships. Double-layered bridges allowed twice the traffic to pass.

In the downtown area, massive skyscrapers reached high into the air, so numerous that they seemed to go on forever. Darklands City boasted some of the tallest buildings in the world and held the prestigious honor of having the Darklands' highest building. It stretched one hundred ninety-six stories into the sky. The view from this height was dizzying. From this building, the City Building, one could see anywhere in the entire city and the surrounding countryside. It was truly spectacular.

Darklands City was considered by many to be the most beautiful city in the world.

Millions and millions of people flocked there looking for a better way of life, looking for the pot of gold at the end of the rainbow, looking for that elusive "promised" land; Darklands City seemed to offer it all. It offered independence, freedom, a new beginning, action, adventure, excitement, and almost endless opportunity. People flocked in by the droves from all over the planet, looking to the city as a better way of life, to be a part of all this beauty and splendor in the most beautiful, affluent, and powerful city in the history of the Darklands as a planet.

Only things were not as they appeared.

In the heart of downtown, a police car turned the corner and drove slowly up the street. Its headlights were off, and it drove silently. The car was painted black so that it would blend in with the night, and therefore go unnoticed. A few feet down the street, three vagrants sat huddled together in a dark corner, trying to keep warm.

One of the vagrants sat with his back toward the street, looking into the fire.

"You know it isn't safe to sit with your back to the street, Numbsie," one of the vagrants told his friend.

"If they're going to shoot me, I'd rather not see them do it," Numbsie mumbled back.

"But what about the gangs?" his friend retorted. Then he took on an ominous whisper. "What about Wildy?"

"Wildy's the least of our problems," the third vagrant

chimed in. He took a long drink from his bottle, then looked deep into the fire.

"What do you mean, Willie?" his friend turned his questioning to him.

"Our real enemy is this city!" Willie took a long look at the streets in front of him. Numbsie suddenly turned around to see if Willie was looking at anything in particular. Willie wasn't, so Numbsie returned to his position with his back to the streets.

"The Promised Land," Willie continued, almost to himself. "That's what they called it. The Promised Land. People flocked to Darklands City by the droves, looking for that pot of gold at the end of the rainbow, only to find out the gold is dirt clods with gold paint. Once you're in, there ain't no getting back out. And the city. The city don't care. The City Building. A modern spectacle of human achievement. Cost over a billion dollars. You know how they paid for it?" Willie went on without even waiting for an answer. "They paid for it by cutting back on the salaries of the city employees. They paid for it by cutting back on benefits to the jobless, and the homeless, and the sick. They paid for it by raising taxes so high that no citizen of the city could buy food or clothes. They spent all their money building their big beautiful bridges, their beautiful buildings, their big beautiful mansions far away from the real world. They left the rest of the world to starve. The only thing they care about is their big fat salaries and their huge holdings. Violence has overcome these streets, and poverty and hunger and disease run rampant. People can't even afford to take care of themselves, and the city refuses to take care of anyone else but themselves. Wildy's doing us a favor. He's getting the city where it hurts!"

Willie took another drink from his bottle.

Numbsie looked up at his friend. "You'd have to be pretty bitter to talk like that. You know yourself that Wildy wouldn't do no favors for no one."

"Bitter?" Willie asked. "Bitter? Before this damned city got a hold of me, I used to have a place to live. But the city raised my property taxes, and I had to sell it. I had a small business to help support myself, but the city took it over when I couldn't pay my bills because they had robbed the rest of the city so that they couldn't come to me. Bitter? I hope Wildy tears this city apart!"

Willie took the last drink from his bottle and threw it against the wall of one of the buildings.

As they were talking, the police car drove quietly around the block and stopped about a block away, and the two men inside looked hard at the vagrants.

The driver looked over at his partner. "What do you think?" he asked.

His partner drew his gun and readied it. "I think it's time to exterminate some pests."

"Why don't we check it out first before you kill them?" the driver asked.

"They know the rules," his partner replied.

The car started up once again and raced down the street. The partner rolled down his window and fired several rounds at the three vagrants. Sure enough, he hit his targets, and the men fell dead. The driver radioed headquarters, reported the incident, and requested assistance. Then he turned the car around and headed back to the sight where the vagrants were. The police officers sat in the car with their rifles ready. Then the passenger opened his door and stepped out of the car.

"Maybe you'd better wait until back-up gets here," the driver cautioned him as he stepped out.

"I'm just going to take a look," his partner said, approaching the bodies. First he surveyed the area, checking around the buildings and alleys, making sure there was no one there.

The driver stepped out of the car, but stood in the doorway with one foot still on the floorboard. His partner kicked over one of the bodies and studied him.

"Yup," the partner said, "it's just a bum."

At that moment, almost as if they came out of the night, several street kids surrounded him. Two of the kids grabbed the first officer from behind and held him firmly there, while the others surrounded him.

The driver of the car quickly jumped back in the car and locked the doors. He jammed on the gas to get away from the scene. Two shots were fired, and the bullets shattered the back window and lodged themselves in the back of the head of the driver. The car spun out of control, then crashed into another parked car. After that, there was no more movement from the car. The driver was dead. His partner watched in horror, then tried to break away from his captors.

"Where you trying to go?" one of the kids behind him asked.

The police officer said nothing.

Then the group parted and another young kid approached the officer. His appearance showed that he was definitely a dangerous person. He stood five feet ten inches high, and his arms and legs were bulky and defined. He was stocky, which made up for his height. And he was fierce. His eyes alone expressed that. They were cold and bitter, and out for destruction. He approached the police officer, who could only stare at the boy as he approached.

Sweat broke on the officer's face, and his breathing went shallow. He was afraid, but he tried desperately not to show it.

"Wildy?" the officer whispered.

"That would be me," the boy smirked as he did a mock bow.

The police officer was really frightened now. Nobody had ever seen Wildy and lived. He was the terror of Darklands City. The officer made another desperate attempt to break free, but the people behind him were very tough.

"You killed a bum," Wildy said.

"I was just doing my job," the officer pleaded.

"I think you like your job," the boy continued.

"It's just a job," the officer said. "They knew the rules."

"What rules?" Wildy asked.

The officer struggled. "The rules."

"What rules?" Wildy spat, pulled out a switchblade, and

held it up to the officer's chin.

"Anyone out after dark is to be killed. No questions asked," the officer said, not wanting to anger his attackers.

Wildy turned to the people behind him. "Well then, I guess we know what we have to do," he joked.

The rest of the company laughed at the joke. The police officer begged for his life. "Please?" he begged. "Please let me go."

"You know the rules," Wildy jeered. Then he slit the officer's throat with the switchblade. The rest of them watched and laughed as the officer bled to death.

The officer could feel his life floating away from him, and there was nothing he could do. They still had him firmly in their grasp, and they held him there as he grew weaker and weaker. He began to sink in their arms, and he could no longer hold himself up. Soon the helplessness overwhelmed him, and he cried.

As soon as he was dead, the back-up patrol that his partner had called for arrived.

The group took the officer's body, and as soon as the other police cars got close enough, they hurled the body onto one of the cars, then ran off. The police jammed on their brakes and jumped out of their cars, firing several shots into the darkness. There was nothing left there. Only the body of the officer—and silence. The others had just disappeared into the darkness. One officer picked up the body of the dead officer and placed it in the back of an ambulance that traveled with any back-up call-ins, just for procedure. The other three bodies were examined and checked for identification. When it was discovered that they had no identification, they were thrown into the back of a garbage truck where they would be taken to an incinerator where their bodies would be disposed of.

The City Building downtown was Darklands City's most beautiful and luxurious, with no expense spared in the making. Willie was right that the building cost so much to construct that Darklands City almost went bankrupt. In order to pay for it, the city cut back on the salaries of city employees and aid to the homeless and jobless, then increased taxes so high that even some of the wealthier citizens found themselves bankrupt trying to foot the bill...but it was Darklands City's pride and glory.

The top floor of the City Building, floor one hundred and ninety-six, housed the most posh room in the entire building. The room was the size of a small house, with dark blue carpet at least an inch thick covering the floor from one wall to the other. Large, expensive paintings hung on the walls, and life-size sculptures that cost millions of dollars in and of themselves dotted the floors and shelves around the room. It was here that about thirty of the city's highest ranking officials sat around a large oak table.

These people were the most powerful men and women in the city and throughout the Darklands. They sat around the table watching video images rushing past them on a giant screen hanging from the wall. The lights were down, and in the darkness the screen showed them pictures of their city and the events that were shaping it.

The city council hired private cinematographers to go throughout the city, inconspicuously taking pictures with their cameras and learning everything they could about what was going on out there on the streets. They got as close as they could to the underlords that ruled the city streets to discover who they were. There was also another purpose, and this was the main purpose that these people were out there: to capture on video the face of the one man that plagued the city like a disease, an elusive young boy known only as Wildy. Everyone in Darklands City knew his name, but no one had ever seen his face. Those who did were killed shortly after their encounter with him. So to photograph him, the city paid several freelance cinematographers a lot of money to go undercover and find and photograph Wildy. There were those who did manage to get close to Wildy, but their bodies would eventually turn up later, with their cameras dismantled and lying next to them. The film chamber was always opened, the film emptied and disposed of.

Some cinematographers managed to get footage of the city, and somehow they managed to find a way to get that footage back to the city officials. The film had been edited together, and that was what the officials were watching this night.

The screen showed a city overwrought with violence and poverty. It was hard to believe that this was the same city that each one of these officials saw every day. The pictures were graphic. They showed people dying on the streets in their own waste. They showed murder, rape, robbing and looting, and rioting, and it was all happening out of the control of the city and its officials.

The movie stopped, the lights came up, and the screen rolled itself back into the cylinder hanging from the ceiling. For several moments nobody said anything. They sat mulling over in their heads what they had just seen. Eventually one man spoke, the mayor of Darklands City. He was a tall man, and somewhat menacing in stature. He had dark hair which seemed a little uncontrollable and tended to look like it was about to fly away. This gave him a somewhat ghoulish appearance. The city council knew him only as Mr. Myer. He sat at the head of the table and presided over this meeting.

"Ladies and gentlemen," he said, "as you can see, Darklands City continues to grow steadily worse. If things keep going as they are going..." He paused to think about that. "Then I shudder to think what might happen next." He leaned into the table and looked around at everyone else sitting there. "We've got to do something drastic."

"How much more drastic can we get?" one lady, Mrs. Perkins, asked. "We already have some of the most drastic laws in the world. Especially our curfew laws. Can we get any more drastic than that?"

"Apparently it isn't drastic enough," Mr. Myer said coolly.

"Not drastic enough?" Mrs. Perkins shot back in surprise.

"The minute the sun goes down everyone is to be indoors. Period. And anyone caught outside after dark is to be shot. No questions asked. I don't see how we could get much more drastic than that."

"It's not a question of *how* drastic," Mr. Myer informed her. "It's a question of what it takes to make this city safe for its residents. And as of this point, this is what it's going to take." Mr. Myer looked around the room, studying the faces of everyone there. Then he continued, "If we are to keep this city under any form of control, we have to take a tough stance against anything that might undermine our authority. We're dangerously close to losing any control we might still have. Until we do something about these street gangs...and until we find Wildy..." Mr. Myer's voice trailed off when he mentioned Wildy's name.

The gangs Mr. Myer referred to were one of the prime reasons for this emergency meeting. The gang problem had turned Darklands City into a war zone. At one time there were several gangs throughout the various parts of the city, all fighting for turf, but slowly at first, then very suddenly, they were all swallowed up by one of two gangs.

Reduced to two gangs, it was like having two countries against each other. Now that there were only two gangs left in the entire city, things had gotten worse instead of better. Both of these gangs were bitter enemies, caught up in a vicious rivalry and bent on the complete destruction of the other.

These two rival gangs had become the mightiest gangs in the region, and most experts believed that it possibly applied to the rest of the Darklands as well. They ranked in numbers that were only estimated because there could be no official count. They came and went before anyone knew what had happened, and they left death and destruction in their wake. Although there were no accurate counts, their estimated numbers amounted to nearly a thousand in Darklands City alone. Then they franchised, so that many other gangs going by their names cropped up in most of the major cities throughout the rest of the Darklands. With that in mind, officials guessed they might be approaching a nearly a quarter of a million members strong, both male and female, around the planet. Of course it was only a guess, because not even the members of the gangs themselves knew how large they had become.

The fierce and bitter rivalry between these two gangs had all but destroyed the city. Nobody knew when or where either gang would strike next so they were unable to prevent an attack, and nobody had the manpower to stop an attack once it had begun. Every branch of the armed forces had been called upon to help with this problem, but they too were all but defeated. As a result, an emergency curfew was put upon the city, and all residents were ordered indoors exactly as the sun began to set, and all stores and businesses were closed, and everything else shut down and boarded up for the night. Nobody was to leave again until the morning of the next day. That was the law, and anyone out after dark ran the risk of being shot by the authorities. That was their policy. Anyone they saw after dark, they shot, no questions asked.

The city was in a state of emergency.

The leader of one of the gangs was Wildy, and Wildy led a gang called the Venomites, which he had led for many years. Legend had it that he had grown up in this gang since he was an infant. Despite many battles and many attempts on his life, his rule over the Venomites was undisputed. He had trained and developed his fighting skills to such a point that he was now powerful and hard—unstoppable. He himself was responsible for the deaths of over a thousand of his enemies through the years. He was a legend in the city, feared by everyone—the law, the civilian, the Darklands' leaders, and even members of his own gang. Any other gang that might be going up against him also met the challenge with a great deal of anxiety. Throughout Darklands City, Wildy was one of the most feared and hated men of all time, a reputation he cherished and fought hard to keep.

The Slasher was Wildy's archenemy. He was also very

good, and his gang was powerful, but he did not have the experience or the cunning of Wildy. Slasher was cocky beyond words and never considered the consequences of his actions. He had led his gang recklessly, and he took many unnecessary chances. This had also given him a reputation as a terror in the Darklands. He became the leader of his gang, the "infernal," by killing off the former leader as they were battling another one of the smaller gangs. This act almost cost them the fight, but when it was over, the Slasher claimed rulership of the infernal, and nobody challenged him. Slasher was also responsible for killing large numbers of people— some his enemies, some people he just felt like killing. For him, killing was a sport, something he did for fun, not only for territory, profit, or any other kind of gain. It was a game for him. He really loved to torture his victims and to kill them in the most gruesome ways he could think of. He thrived on other people's pain.

As Mr. Myer addressed the city officials, a page boy quietly entered the room and approached one gentleman named Rhend. The page boy handed Rhend a note. Rhend took the note from the boy and read it quietly to himself. When he finished with it, he handed it back to the boy and then motioned him out. The page boy left, and Rhend quietly and inconspicuously rose from his chair and also left the room. Once out of the room, he turned down a hallway and into a small broom closet, where he was met by a young street kid named Borgie.

"Slasher says it's up. We go tonight."

"How come I wasn't informed of this earlier?" Rhend questioned him.

"Look!" Borgie told him. "We do it our way, or we don't do it."

"All right," Rhend conceded. "But remember who's funding this little excursion."

"No problem." Borgie slapped Rhend on the shoulder. "Just remember, we want the money by morning, or your guys are next." He then left the broom closet and headed out of the building. Rhend watched him go. He was worried about Slasher. Slasher and his gang were Rhend's best investment, but it was hard making Slasher do only as Rhend instructed. He had a lot riding on this battle, and it was imperative that Slasher win. This battle could be very dangerous, and Rhend wanted them to be more prepared before they actually went out and fought Wildy, but Slasher did what he wanted, when he wanted.

Rhend took a deep breath and leaned back against the wall. For months now, he had been trying to prepare for this. He knew that it was chancy sending Slasher to fight Wildy, but he had to try. He had to get Wildy out of the way. He and Wildy had been at war for years now, and Wildy was costing him serious money.

Rhend was into everything. He had so many illegal operations going that nobody could count them, and Wildy threatened every one of them.

The war started when Rhend sent out some of his men to Wildy's gang to coerce them to join his company. They would do his legwork, his running and smuggling, and they would offer Rhend and his agents protection. Rhend offered to pay Wildy handsomely for his part, but Wildy refused. Rhend would not be refused, so he tried to get rough with Wildy and the Venomites. He took out a contract on Wildy.

Wildy found out about the contract, and one night he crept into several of Rhend's warehouses and set fire to them, and in the process he killed hundreds of Rhend's men and cost Rhend millions of dollars in lost merchandise and lost business. Then Wildy crept into Rhend's own personal residence, past his tight security, and into Rhend's own bedroom. He put live snakes in his bed, and then crept back out. The snakes weren't poisonous, but they did scare Rhend nonetheless.

That was the beginning of the bitter war between Rhend, the Venomites, and their leader, Wildy. From that moment on, Rhend relentlessly looked for any way he could to get back at Wildy. So when Slasher came to power, Rhend worked out a deal with him. Rhend would finance them and, in return, get them ready to destroy Wildly. Starting this war was yet another attempt on Rhend's part to do away with Wildy.

Rhend decided that there was nothing to do at this juncture than to just wait. He had a lot riding on this battle. He wasn't sure that Slasher going up against Wildy at this point was the best idea, but Slasher had made up his mind. There was nothing more Rhend could do from here. He walked out of the broom closet and back down the hall. As he did so, another messenger approached him.

"Sir," the messenger said, handing Rhend the note. Rhend looked at it. The minute he saw it, he spat vehemently and cursed Wildy. He dismissed the messenger and joined the others back in the conference room. He quietly entered the room and took his seat. Nobody had noticed him leave or return except Mr. Myer, who said nothing and pretended that he also saw nothing.

On this night, as with every night, the city streets were quiet. All the shops and buildings were locked, chained, and boarded up tight for the night. Anyone who happened to be unlucky enough to be out on the streets that late hurried cautiously to their destination, or looked around for a safe place to hide until morning, continually glancing behind them to see if they were being followed. Even the transients kept themselves hidden. All were in fear for their very lives.

It was a night lit only by the faint glow of a few remaining neon lights that had not been broken out by vandals or other violence on the streets. Around the corner of one of the city skyscrapers, almost as if on cue, the Slasher and his gang marched down the middle of the street, where they were met by Wildy and the Venomites.

Wildy faced the Slasher in the middle of the street, and the two gangs lined up behind their respective leaders, switchblades, bats, chains, knives, and various other weaponry in hand. They faced each other, poised and ready for battle. This was the first time these two gangs had ever come face to face like this. There had been many skirmishes between individual gang members, but never in the history of either of these two gangs had they come together in an all out war. Now it was time, time for one man to own the city, and the other to back away with his tail between his legs, or die trying to defend his turf. It was time to settle this score conclusively and remove all competition.

Wildy was the first to speak.

"You're on my street!" he shouted over to the Slasher.

"It's not your street anymore!" the Slasher shouted back. "Haven't you heard? We're the most powerful gang on the streets now, and we're moving in."

"You were never the most powerful anything!" Wildy shouted. "So now I'm gonna have to move you out." Wildy knew his opponent, and he knew that he was not about to let this creep rule his city. He determined that even if he died, Slasher would die as well. He screamed out the battle cry and rushed toward the Slasher. The others followed, and the war began.

All around Wildy the bodies began to fall, some members of the Venomites, and some members of Slasher's gang. Wildy had a couple of slashes in his stomach, one down his wrist, and a couple of stabs in the chest, but he was fighting as hard as ever.

He found an opening in the Slasher's stomach, and drove his switchblade home. When the Slasher doubled over, Wildy slit his throat. The Slasher's body fell to the ground, and Wildy drove his head deep into the pavement with his foot. Then he stood on the Slasher's body to pronounce his victory.

"Now you don't own anything anymore!" Wildy proclaimed. "Now I own this city." He laughed triumphantly and jumped up and down on Slasher's body. "And you can tell your master, Rhend, who is the stronger here!" Then he kicked Slasher's body.

As he enjoyed his victory, all those members of his and the Slasher's gang who had survived the ordeal ran past him in sheer terror. There were still hundreds of them left, and instead of fighting each other they were running together to get away from something.

"What's happening?" Wildy asked. "Where's everybody going?"

"Get out of here, Wildy," someone shouted back at him. "There's some bad dudes headed this way."

"No problem," Wildy shouted back. "We'll take 'em."

"Not these guys, Wildy," the guy shouted back, then he ran out of view.

Wildy stood alone on the dark streets, he and all the bodies that had fallen in the fight. Off in the distance he could hear footsteps. Many footsteps. Faster and faster they approached. Louder and louder they grew. Then they turned the corner and came into view.

The sight of them was terrifying. This was not just an army, but an army of the most hideous and grotesque looking creatures Wildy had ever seen in his life. Giant batlike creatures and snakelike creatures with the body and face of a serpent, standing upright on two legs, with arms off to the sides of their bodies. Those that did have human forms had faces so twisted and distorted that they hardly looked human at all. Leading the whole army was the most powerful-looking being Wildy had ever seen in his life. He had cold dark eyes filled with power and hate. His body was massive and strong, but the most terrifying thing about him was such an air of hatred that it threatened anything and everything around him. Just his mere presence seemed to suck the life out of Wildy.

The soldiers were on a killing spree and their swords were covered in blood. They killed everyone they came in contact with. Those gang members who had survived the initial battle were now being hewn down mercilessly by this new rival in the war. They completely eliminated most of the members of the two gangs. They laughed and joked and played with their prey like a cat plays with a mouse. They ran in and out of buildings, looking for any form of life and killing anything in their way, including man, woman, child, and animal. They had a keen sense of smell and managed to sniff out every person on the streets, no matter how securely they had hidden themselves. These beings also destroyed house pets and wild animals that roamed the streets. Then they placed their bodies in the most hideous positions they could. Along with the killing, they kicked out lights, broke windows, destroyed buildings, and looted stores. Wildy could not believe what he saw. Never before had he seen such destructiveness. Not even from his or the Slasher's gang.

The creatures approached Wildy, and for the first time in his life, he was terrified. He turned and ran.

One of the guards ran Wildy down and dragged him back to the leader, with Wildy kicking and fighting and trying desperately to get out of the beast's grasp. Then the beast held Wildy directly in front of the leader, and a couple of other guards moved in to help contain Wildy.

"Who have we here?" Draygon asked in almost a sneer.

"Some street kid," one of the guards replied, as if making a joke.

"So this is the punk that all the fuss is being made over," Draygon observed.

Wildy assumed this being was talking about the fuss in the Darklands, with the police, the armed services, and other authorities, but before he could comment, Draygon continued.

"Don't you know the streets aren't safe at night?" Draygon asked Wildy.

Wildy struggled again to break free, but the guards were holding both of his hands behind his back. Instead of being intimidated by this, Wildy became more defiant.

"They're safe for me," he sneered back. "I own them."

"Well then," Draygon was calm and cool. "It looks as if your reign of terror is over."

"I don't give up without a fight."

Wildy made a sudden jump that threw his captors off guard. As soon as he got out of their grasp, he grabbed his switchblade. He swung at Draygon, but Draygon merely put out his hand and stopped the knife. The blade went completely through the hand, but it didn't seem to affect him at all. He casually pulled out the knife like he was taking off a glove. There wasn't even any blood.

"As you can see, Wildy, fighting won't do you any good." Draygon said this as casually as if he were making a simple statement.

The guards behind Wildy had regained their hold on him. They grabbed Wildy and held him so tight that there would be no way he would break loose this time. There were three guards on him now. One on each side, and one holding him by the hair.

Draygon looked into Wildy's eyes. Wildy had never seen so much hate in his life, not even in the eyes of his most fierce rivalries. Because of the intense hate, Wildy was not able to hold Draygon's gaze.

"Does that surprise you?" Draygon asked. "That I know your name? I know more about your miserable life than you do, and unlike you, I'm not playing some child's game."

Wildy stared back at Draygon. "You're not so tough."

Draygon put his face into Wildy's face. "Tough enough."

He stood back up and threw Wildy's knife on the ground. Then he looked over at one of his generals.

"Kill him," he told the general. Then he went back to Wildy. "You've served your purpose, but I don't need you anymore. As of now, I'll get someone else to take your place."

He looked down at Slasher's body and shook his head.

The guards grabbed Wildy even tighter and pulled him down to his knees. There would be no escaping now.

The general whom Draygon had spoken to took out a large sword. It was black and cold, and the edge was jagged instead of straight. It had little shards of metal sticking out from the blade, and it was thirsty for blood. An ugly grin came over the general's face, and he began to rub the sword along Wildy's throat to taunt him. As the sword went across Wildy's throat, it cut it and nicked it with the little shards sticking out from the blade. Wildy swallowed hard. He could see the other guards drooling and licking their lips. They looked like a pack of wild dogs moving in for the kill. The general raised his hand and brought the sword down.

As suddenly as the general brought the sword down, it flew out of his hand, slicing him across the palm and cutting the hand completely off. Then the sword flew through the air, and through the center of the rest of the army of creatures. It took out several other limbs and appendages of many of the other beings gathered there as it passed through the crowd. The general screamed in pain and bent down to pick up the rest of his hand and put it back together.

In the middle of the confusion, a small light about the size of a firefly, only a thousand times more intense, and so fast that it left a trail of blazing light behind it, flew in and among Draygon's army, scattering them in every direction. It flew right between Wildy and Draygon, then exploded into a bright shard of light, causing everyone, including Draygon, to fall back, though Draygon quickly regained his composure.

Through the spots in his eyes, Wildy saw a figure like he had never seen before. It looked like a man, but not like any man Wildy had ever seen in the Darklands. The man was at least a head taller than any other man, and judging by his figure, he could take on anybody he pleased. Every muscle in his body was tuned to perfection. He wasn't huge, but he had the most well-developed muscle structure Wildy had ever seen. He also had an air about him that was even more powerful than that of Draygon, only this was something different, and Wildy didn't know how to identify it.

The man also had a strong jawline and a powerful face. His hair was long, and his eyes... When the spots cleared out of Wildy's eyes he was able to look into the stranger's eyes. The stranger's eyes were full of emotion. Every emotion Wildy had ever felt he could see reflected back in those eyes. The eyes were strong and hard like the eyes of a warrior, yet kind and gentle like the eyes of a lover. And they blazed like a fire, burning with such intense heat that it burned white. But the most amazing thing about him was that he seemed to be made of light. A different type of light, but light nonetheless. It was almost pure white, yet it had in it every color imaginable. It seemed almost as if there were nothing else there, only the light in the shape of a man, and his form lit up the night. Wildy could see clearly now the faces of those around him, especially the face of Draygon. There was such a contrast between this man and Draygon, and the creatures in Draygon's army.

At first Draygon looked terrified, but slowly his face began to take on the same defiance and hate that Wildy had seen earlier.

"The Prince of Light!" Draygon sounded both angry and afraid, but his defiance was coming through loud and clear. "I didn't expect to have this confrontation so soon."

"I am now the 'Warrior,' Draygon." The man seemed completely unmoved by Draygon's attitude. "I am here to restore to my father his lost kingdom."

His voice was almost frightening. It seemed to use all frequencies of sound at the same time, from low frequencies to high frequencies, and everything in between. The lower frequencies of his voice rattled and rumbled everything in the area as they passed through buildings, the ground, and everything else that was in their way. The higher frequencies bounced off things, and jumped around in the air, creating a sharpness and crispness in the voice. The middle frequencies filled up the space and made the voice full and alive. Wildy didn't know whether to be afraid or to feel hope. The one thing he did know was that the guards who were holding him were trembling just as much as he was, but as time passed in the presence of this 'Warrior,' they began to grow more and more defiant. Wildy, on the other hand, couldn't take his eyes off this being. He felt something, but he'd never had feelings like this before, so he didn't know exactly how to identify what it was he was feeling. All he could do was stare at the man.

Draygon continued to question the Warrior.

"So why all this over some street kid?" he asked.

"He has a high calling," the Warrior said, holding Draygon's gaze. Draygon, on the other hand, was unable to hold the Warrior's gaze for very long, but he still continued to question the Warrior.

"Him?" Draygon asked. "This kid? This criminal? This murderer? You do see the bodies lying just under your feet, don't you? Who do you think put them there? He's nothing by Darklands standards, let alone by your high standards." Then he added sarcastically, "Your Holiness."

"He is of far more value than you recognize."

As he spoke, the Warrior's eyes burned hotter and hotter, and Draygon could no longer look at him. Draygon made one last desperate attempt to win this argument.

"But he's a resident of the Darklands, and he's been working for me all his life. That makes him my property... Or have you forgotten?"

The Warrior cupped his hands and held them out in front of him, and they filled with blood.

"And have you forgotten the Fountain of Blood?"

As he said this, he threw the blood onto Draygon. The blood left little traces of red light as it flew through the air, but none spilled, and there was nothing left in the Warrior's hands. Not a trace, not a drop. When the blood hit Draygon's face, it made a sizzling noise and he cried out in pain.

"I hate the Fountain of Blood!" Draygon screamed almost as if he had gone insane.

The Warrior turned to the guards holding Wildy. "Turn the boy loose," he said.

One of the guards holding Wildy grabbed onto his hair and pulled his head back. Then he put his foot in Wildy's back, and, pushing with his foot, he pulled on Wildy's hair. Then he let go, and Wildy fell on his face to the ground. The guard grinned an obnoxious grin like he had gotten away with something awful. The Warrior looked completely calm and said nothing for a moment. Finally he spoke.

"I can remain tolerant of only so much," he said, and then

he held his hand in a clutching position. The guard behind Wildy screamed in pain and grabbed at his face. Wildy looked over his shoulder in time to see the guard fall to the ground trying to stop some sort of pain in his face. The Warrior held his hands above his head.

"My patience is wearing thin," he said. "Take your rebels and begone...quickly!"

As he said the word "quickly," there was a short, sudden rumble, like a clap of thunder. Then the rumble seemed to move through the air like a wave. Wildy could feel the ground shake and he saw the skyscrapers of the city tremble as if they were in the middle of an earthquake. Draygon and his army quickly scurried off, leaving Wildy alone with the Warrior.

For several moments, Wildy didn't dare move. He just lay there on his face, not knowing what to do. He could feel the Warrior's eyes staring into the back of his head, and finally he couldn't take it anymore.

He cautiously picked himself up off the ground, his eyes continually on the Warrior. Neither of them spoke a word; neither of them broke eye contact. In Wildy's case, he couldn't take his eyes off the Warrior. They seemed glued to him. Something about those eyes seemed to pull at Wildy, right in the soul of this being. Quickly Wildy snatched up his switchblade from off the street and held it toward the Warrior.

"I'm afraid you'll find that I too am impervious to your weapons." The Warrior showed no sign of emotion, and did not blink or break eye contact with Wildy.

The switchblade was wrenched out of Wildy's hand and fell once again to the street. Wildy turned and ran, but he could still feel the Warrior's gaze behind him. Even though his back was turned, he could sense the sadness in the Warrior's eyes, and he turned around again to face the Warrior.

"Who are you?" Wildy asked. "What do you want from me? Why did you save me? Why did you let me run away?" Still the Warrior said nothing. "Why are you here?"

"You were in need," the Warrior said at last.

Wildy couldn't tell if the man's mouth was moving, and

he couldn't tell where the sound was coming from, but all of a sudden the Warrior's voice seemed to come from all around him, and even more disconcerting, right inside of him.

The Warrior's eyes looked directly into Wildy's soul, and they saw a part of Wildy that the young man had never acknowledged. As he looked back into the Warrior's eyes, he saw his own soul being reflected back in them.

"How did you know?" Wildy asked, staring at his own soul.

"I know many things." The Warrior's voice sounded quiet, and not the least bit threatening.

"So why did you save me?" Wildy asked in a whisper. It was almost as if he was afraid of disturbing the mood of the moment. "What do you want from me?" Then he suddenly became suspicious. "Whatever it is, don't think I'm going to do it for you just because I think I owe you one."

The Warrior looked up into the sky and studied the darkness.

"I must go now," he said.

"Where are you going?" Wildy asked.

"The power of darkness is falling fast." The Warrior looked very serious. "I must raise up an army and rescue all those who will be rescued from the coming storm."

Then slowly and quietly, unlike the way he came in, the Warrior began to fade out of sight.

"Wait a minute!" Wildy called out to him when he realized what was happening. "I want to talk to you... Will I ever see you again?"

"If you desire it," the Warrior answered him.

"How will I find you?" Wildy asked.

The Warrior had faded away, and Wildy searched the air looking for some trace of him, but there was none. All was quiet. Then suddenly he heard the voice of the Warrior.

"You will search for me, and you will find me when you search for me with all your heart. I will be found by you."

"Where do I search for you?" Wildy shouted into the air. But this time there was no answer.

"Who are you?" Wildy asked again, mostly to himself. *Oh what do I care anyway*, he thought. He started walking away from the spot, but something kept calling him to follow.

"Follow what?" Wildy shouted angrily into the sky. "Follow what? He said I have value! What did he mean?"

For several minutes Wildy stood in the middle of the street and tried to make sense out of everything that had happened that night. This man was like a magnet. Somehow he had pulled at Wildy with such a force that even someone as hardened as Wildy could not turn away. Wildy had seen his own soul, and this man knew where it was, and deep down inside of him, Wildy wanted to see it again.

While he was contemplating all this, he heard a car silently approaching, without any lights. Wildy knew the only people out tonight would be the police, so he hid behind one of the buildings. The car spotted the bodies and stopped. Instantly there were police cars everywhere, and police were searching every nook and cranny of the area. Wildy was without the rest of his gang and knew that he would be no match for the police, so he moved out of there as quickly as possible.

This turned out to be the bloodiest fight Darklands City had ever encountered. It would go down as the fight of Darklands City's history. The authorities would be pulling bodies off the sidewalks and out of the streets and gutters and the alleyways for days after this. The social, economical, and physical damage to the city was also immeasurable.

Mr. Myer was jarred out of sleep in the middle of the night by the sudden vibrations of the room and the sounds of glass and dishes falling to the floor and breaking. He jumped out of bed and looked around. As suddenly as it happened, it stopped, and everything was silent. He thought he must have imagined it. It couldn't have been an earthquake. It happened too quickly. But he couldn't explain the glass and dishes lying on the floor. He started picking up the debris, and the telephone rang. He picked it up, and it was the police chief calling from his car to announce that a critical emergency meeting had once again been called, and that he would be arriving very shortly to pick up the mayor and transport him to the meeting.

Mr. Myer put on some clothes and waited for the police chief. When he arrived, he escorted Mr. Myer out the door. Just outside the door, they were immediately met by an onslaught of microphones and cameras and television cameras, and behind them all, reporters, all wanting to know what happened that night. He gave them the usual, "We are doing what we can," and, "We'll get to the bottom of this as soon as possible," and, "We still have control in this city," and, "Everything will be all right, and everyone should go home where it's safe, and lock the doors," as he pushed through them to the car waiting for him.

In the car, the police chief briefed him and explained to him what they knew about the events of the night, starting with the earthquake and ending with the street. As they approached the downtown area, Mr. Myer was surprised by what he saw. Hundreds of bodies still littered the streets, along with glass and rubbish, and many of the contents of local stores and businesses that had been looted. The streets also swarmed with police and other emergency crews, doing everything they could to clean up the mess. Because of the debris, the bodies, and all the onlookers, Mr. Myer and the police chief had to leave the car and walk the rest of the way to the City Building. Several police officers escorted them from the car to the building. They had their hands full, trying to ward off angry citizens who were threatening harm to the mayor and demanding answers. The mayor looked around him in amazement. What had happened this night? It looked as if there had been an all-out war on these streets.

Once again Mr. Myer was high atop the City Building. It was there that he and the rest of the officials were filled in on all the details, such as they were, about what took place that night. They had captured some of the gang members of both sides and were holding them in a special containment cell of the city jail, but as of yet they could say nothing. Most of them were too frightened to even speak. They just sat in a corner, or anywhere else that they could be alone, and trembled. And every time they did seem to remember anything, they would shake and scream. When officials question them, anything that they did say made absolutely no sense. They kept babbling about hideous creatures, supernatural beings, and other strange phenomena. The police didn't know how to take this.

Whatever had happened was quite severe. The power was out throughout two-thirds of the city and over a million people were without electricity. The hospitals were completely full of people with serious wounds—knife wounds, gunshot wounds, heart failure, accidents from stumbling around in the dark, people overwrought with hysteria, and the list went on. The problem was so bad that people were dying in the waiting rooms. The city called out every licensed medical practitioner and mortician within a two-to-three-hundred-mile-radius of Darklands City to help deal with the people and the bodies. Those victims that had no family, or money for a proper burial, or any form of identification, were simply counted and burned. The city was taxed beyond its capacity.

The anger generated toward the city officials and their inability to control the situation had reached a crescendo. Thousands of people marched around the City Building to demonstrate their frustration. They screamed, yelled, and threw things, and in the heat of their anger, they turned on each other, creating even more of a hassle for law officers and medical staff.

Mr. Myer looked around the room at the city officials. He stared coldly over at Rhend. "This is all your doing," he said. "You set this whole thing up."

Rhend looked at him through emotionless eyes. "There's no way on earth those two gangs could have killed each other off like that, unless there were more of them than we think," he said coolly.

"You know yourself there has never been a legitimate number count on these gangs. It's all been guessing!" Mr. Myer screamed.

The police chief also informed the council that they had recovered the body of Slasher, but not the body of Wildy.

Mr. Myer turned and looked out the window. "You've only recovered the one body?" he asked.

"Yes sir," the police chief responded.

"Then Wildy must still be alive," Mr. Myer sighed. "Maybe he'll be regrouping. Whether he is or not, we'll have to treat it as though he is until we know for sure. As for the Slasher, someone else is bound to take advantage of this situation and step in and take over. Or our worst fears may come true. Wildy may rule those streets undisputed." He continued looking out the window. "I wish I knew what happened out on those streets tonight."

Then the police chief approached Mr. Myer again and whispered in his ear.

"Another one of Rhend's warehouses was attacked earlier tonight. We think it was done earlier in the afternoon, before the battle, and we're sure Wildy was behind it."

Mr. Myer said nothing, but continued looking out the window.

Soon the secretary entered the room, bringing with her several folders filled completely full of legal and other documents. She handed the folders over to Mr. Myer.

"Here are the files you requested sir," she said, then left.

Mr. Myer looked over the documents and threw them down on the table. Somebody had been tampering with them, probably the secretary.

"I know you're behind this," he accused Rhend a second time.

Rhend said nothing, but returned Mr. Myer's cold stare.

Mr. Myer could never prove anything, but he knew that Rhend had been funding Slasher's gang for years. Now he suspected that Rhend had probably been behind this whole fight, that he possibly even instigated it.

Mr. Myer had seen many a profile on the Slasher, and, based on those reports, even he wouldn't have taken on Wildy unless he had good reason to do so. Slasher knew what Wildy was like and wouldn't have gone against him without some incentive. There was one thing that Slasher liked more than killing people: money. And beyond that, killing for money. Slasher would do anything for it. For enough money, Slasher might even go against Wildy.

Mr. Myer also knew of the bitter feud between Rhend and Wildy. Rhend never told any one of his war with Wildy, and his determination to stamp him out, but it was common knowledge to everyone there. Even the media knew of it, but they never reported it.

Mr. Myer glared at Rhend. "You started a war!" he screamed. "Thousands of innocent people died because of you. Do you care nothing for that?"

"Don't you make any accusations against me unless you have proof!" Rhend screamed back. "I didn't start anything."

Mr. Myer looked out the window over Darklands City. It was mostly dark now because of the power outages. No lights were lit, except far off in the distance. Downstairs he could hear sirens, the breaking of glass, and people screaming.

"Your muscle is gone," he said to Rhend while continuing to look out the window. "Your empire has collapsed. You tried to finance this war to increase your own position, but you've failed. And I know that with enough time, I can prove that." He walked over to the phone and called in security. "So until I do, you are under arrest."

He motioned the security guards to take Rhend out of the room. Rhend screamed and cursed and yelled obscenities and threatened Mr. Myer, but Mr. Myer said nothing more to Rhend. Everyone else at the table watched in silence. They were glad that Rhend was being put away, but they were even more glad that it wasn't them doing it. Slasher may have been dead, but they still didn't know who might be left of Rhend's network, and none of them wanted to risk doing what Mr. Myer just did.

Mr. Myer himself wouldn't have done such a thing under normal circumstances, but this was his chance. This little mishap had given him an edge in the power game, and he decided to take it while he had the chance. He also had the security guards pick up the secretary on charges of obstruction of justice and hiding evidence. So while the security guards and the police hauled Rhend and the secretary out of the room, Mr. Myer took his place back at the window. He heard the screaming, the fighting, and the violence of the streets below him.

"Brace yourselves," he said, looking out the window. "It's going to be a long, hard fight to regain control of this."

Tye was a young storekeeper in downtown Darklands City, and he lived with his father above their little store. Both he and his father were asleep when the gangs began to assemble, but late into the night he heard the screams in the street below that jarred him out of sleep like a terrifying nightmare. Things like this happened often in that part of the city, and he didn't often get a good night's sleep because of them. But tonight something was different. Tonight it sounded like a massive battle cry.

Instinctively, he jumped out of bed to make sure all the bars were secure across the storefront windows, and all the locks were tightly fastened. They were. All but a couple of them. He went to fix them when suddenly somebody grabbed him around the neck and slit his throat. He fell to the floor, bleeding profusely. He tried to stop the bleeding by holding his hand tight around his neck, but he continued to bleed. He sat there in the dark and watched as several people looted his store. He lay still, knowing that if he made a move, these people would be back to finish him off. He was afraid and tried not to think about the fact that he was going to die at any minute.

He fought hard to stay awake, but his eyes were getting heavy, and he was losing a lot of blood very rapidly. Soon the intruders were gone, and he could move without fear of them returning. He fought and fought, trying desperately to get up from where he was. Only now, because of the loss of blood, he could not pull himself up off the ground. He cried to himself and settled back against the wall. There was nothing he could do but wait. The blood collected in a puddle around him and soaked him and his clothes. Now he could not move at all. He broke down and let himself cry.

Then he suddenly began to hallucinate. He saw several people running away, followed by several hideous creatures coming down the street after them. These creatures were just like something he might have seen in his nightmares. They were hard for him to describe, and in his state he really didn't notice a lot of detail, only that they were terrifying. They also brought about that feeling of terror and helplessness that he had so often had while sleeping, when he would dream that some horrible creature was chasing him, and he couldn't run or get away from it—no matter how he tried, he could never gain any ground. That's how Tye felt now. His entire body was numb and paralyzed, and he felt like he wasn't there, like he was only watching the whole thing from somewhere up above himself. He tried to run, but he couldn't move even a muscle. He couldn't get up from where he had fallen, and he couldn't even whimper for help. Even his tears were unable to flow. He watched helplessly as the creatures took body after body and diced them up into several pieces, mangling them in the most gruesome positions Tye had ever seen. They destroyed man, woman, and child, and even the animals on the streets. One of the hideous creatures passed right in front of him, but for some reason didn't see him. He was glad for this, but he wasn't sure why he went unseen.

Then he saw a beautiful white light approaching the middle of the group. It was small like a firefly, but it shone brighter than a star. It circled the group a couple of times, exploded into brilliant colors, and took on the shape of a man, the most incredible man Tye had ever seen. He could not take his eyes off this man. He stood head and shoulders above everyone else, and it seemed like Tye could see right through him. Then suddenly he looked right a Tye. At least that's what it looked like. Tye didn't know what to do. But he couldn't move anyway, so he sat there, holding his neck. He looked into the man's eyes, mesmerized by what he saw in them. A small white light shown from somewhere deep within them, and like a pool of water, seemed to dance and sing. This didn't make sense to Tye. How could a white light sing? He didn't have much time to contemplate that question, though, because soon everything went black.

When he awoke, everything around him was still black. There was no sound, no light—nothing. Tye lay there and didn't move for several minutes. Again he began to cry. He didn't know what was happening to him, and death was too much. *What next?* he wondered.

He noticed his hand in something wet and sticky. He brought the hand up close to his face, and in the faint glow of a light from somewhere, he could see that his hand was in a pool of blood. Probably his blood. He quickly moved out of it, jumped up, and looked around.

I'm standing, he thought.

A quick glance around the room revealed that he was still in his father's store. He pinched himself to see if he could feel anything, and he could. He walked around the room and touched things. He could pick them up. He tried to walk through one of the walls and nearly broke his nose. He dug through a couple of drawers in the counter and found a flashlight. The batteries were still good when he turned it on, and he beamed the light around the room. Sure enough, it had been looted. Not a shelf was left standing, and almost everything that could be taken, had been. They had even gotten into the safe and had stolen all the money. Money that he and his father were saving so they could get out of Darklands City... his father... Tye suddenly remembered his father. He ran upstairs and into his father's room. His father was lying quietly on his bed.

Tye approached cautiously, calling out to his father. Surely his father would have heard all the racquet going on downstairs.

"It's me, Dad," he whispered. "You can relax now. They've gone." But there was no movement or sound from his father.

Tye's heart was beating hard in his chest. He approached the bed and looked down. The sheets and blankets were soaked with blood. Tye bit his lip. He couldn't move. He didn't know what to do. He stood there, wanting so badly to pull the covers off the bed, but he was afraid of what he might find. Eventually, not knowing became worse than knowing, and with a quick jerk, he pulled them off.

There on the bed lay the body of his father, diced to pieces, and his bed soaked in blood.

Tye screamed and ran out of the room. He ran down the stairs out of the store and into the street, the image of his father still burning in his eyes. He had to sit down just to keep himself from falling. He sat down on the curb and stared out into the darkness.

Then suddenly it occurred to him. *I am still alive. But how?*

He knew that he too had been stabbed, yet he had to be alive. None of his dreams were ever this vivid. He put his hand over his heart, and sure enough, it was beating. He took in a deep breath. Then he put his hand over his neck. There was nothing. He pinched it a little, played with it a little. He was still alive, but how?

Something caught his eyes. It was that figure of light he had seen before, the one that broke up that group of horrible creatures. Only this time he was alone. Tye looked into his eyes, and they were crying. Without this man saying a word, Tye knew that he was hurting for him, and that he was feeling Tye's pain. Tye stood up and looked at him.

"Why me and not him?" Tye asked. He didn't know how he knew that this man would know what he was talking about, or even have the answer, but for some reason he felt as if the man would know.

"Each person is given only so much time," the man said. Tye couldn't tell if the man's lips moved or not. "You have been granted a reprieve."

"Why?" Tye asked.

"Why is not an easy question to answer," said the being. "Ask not *why*, but look for ways to take that which is given to you, or taken from you, and make of them what you can."

"What do I do now?" Tye asked.

"Watch and wait, be prepared."

"Prepared for what?" Tye asked again.

"You will know when it happens. In the meantime, go—to a place that I will send you. There you will meet with me, and you will know the power of my blood. And you will be freed from the pull and the domination of the Darklands."

Tye looked at him with a confused look on his face. The man noticed this and reassured him.

"Do not be afraid," he said. "Only believe."

Something convinced Tye that he could trust this person. But he didn't know what had convinced him, or why. As the being stood there, Tye suddenly remembered something that he really wanted to say.

"Thank you," he blurted out. "Thank you for the…" He put his hands up to his neck.

"You are welcome," the being said. "But you have much anger and much hate built around your life of tragedy. That is easily understood. But soon you will learn to forgive, and you will be free."

Tye didn't know if he wanted to forgive. He had hated Wildy and the Slasher for years. That was his way of life. How could anyone forgive something so incredibly horrible?

He had gotten so caught up in these thoughts that when he finally came back to where he was, the stranger had gone. He called out to him, but there was nothing. But somewhere deep inside of him, he could feel something leading him, something pulling at him from inside, and he began to follow.

3

Wildy banged his shin on a stump. He jumped back to grab his leg and fell backwards into a patch of stickers. He spat out a stream of obscenities and continued to hobble through the forest. He was really beginning to regret leaving the city.

Weird people are one thing, he thought, *but God only knows what's out here.*

The undergrowth was getting thicker, and it was becoming increasingly difficult for him to make any progress. This, and the intense darkness, made travel that much harder. Wildy wasn't used to black darkness. He was from the city, and there was always some form of light, light either from a neon light, or lights from buildings, or even the light of the fires of the transients trying to warm themselves in the cold.

There was always some form of light in Darklands City. But out here there was nothing. Even the moon had buried itself behind a thick cloud covering.

Wildy wasn't sure why he had left the city in the first place. It wasn't necessarily the police. He had learned years ago how to avoid them. It was something else. This Warrior person, or whoever he was. Who was this guy that he could take someone like Wildy and pull him completely out of his environment and put him out in the middle of an even more hostile environment than even Wildy was used to?

It was something about the Warrior's eyes. His eyes had found and exposed Wildy's soul, and Wildy's soul desperately wanted to be discovered, to be shielded, and for some reason, it thought that this Warrior could do that.

Wildy had never been out of the city, and he had no idea how to survive out in the forest, but he was stronger than most, and his determination would help him immensely during his journey. Despite all that determination, though, there were things out here that he knew nothing about.

A wolf howled in the distance, and Wildy jumped. It was a sound he'd heard before, but never in the wild. It sounded so haunting out there in the middle of the night.

As he pushed his way forward, he kept trying to push the nagging questions to the back of his mind and focus on what was ahead, but no matter what method he used to distract himself from them, the questions kept coming up. Questions like, *How do you know you can trust this person? After all, he didn't say much, and when you tried to question him he disappeared. What if you aren't able to find him? What if he turns out to be just like Draygon?* The harder Wildy tried to suppress these questions, the louder they became. Before long, he reached a point that he could not take any more. His frustration level had jumped dangerously high.

"Forget it!" he shouted as another tree branch slapped him across the face. "This guy doesn't care if I find him. For all I know, this is just some sort of game these people are playing with me. Or maybe I'm being set up. More than likely

I'm some sort of guinea pig, or a patsy for these people."

He turned around to go back the way he came, but as soon as he turned around, somewhere in front of him he heard something growling and snarling at him. At that moment the moon peaked out from behind the clouds, and a shimmer of moonlight dimly illuminated the forest. In this moonlight, Wildy could see two red eyes staring at him, and he could make out teeth and fangs of what looked like a mad dog. He pulled out his switchblade.

"Come at me, mutt," he whispered, not wanting to disturb anything else that might be hiding in the shadows. "It's you and me, so let's do it."

Almost as if they recognized Wildy's dare, several other dogs joined in. Slowly they began to push Wildy back. Several pairs of eyes stared him down. They snarled at him and bared their teeth. Every one of them was ready to attack. They were drooling and snarling, looking at Wildy like he was their next meal.

"At least one of you is going to die before you get me," he said, more to himself than to them.

As he stared down the dogs, a thick black shadow moved between him and them—a shadow that seemed more like a black nothingness than anything else. It had the shape of a large, humanlike figure, but it was empty and dark inside, like a vacuum. And the darkness was so terrifying that the hair on the back of Wildy's neck stood straight up. A cold, clammy sensation passed over him and his skin broke out into little bumps all over his body. The dogs howled in terror and ran off. Wildy, on the other hand, could not move. He stood there, frozen in the spot that he was standing in. The fear that had suddenly seized his body paralyzed it so completely that he could barely breathe.

The shadow moved away, and the night was quiet again. Nothing moved. There was no sound. Not even the wind was stirring.

Wildy was breathless with fright.

"Who's there?" he whispered. Hoping on one hand there

would be no reply, but on the other hand, wanting to know what that shadow was.

Still nothing moved.

"Who or what are you?" he asked again.

Again there was no answer. Still frozen, Wildy tried to think about what he should do next. Then suddenly a branch snapped behind him, and he panicked and ran.

He ran and ran, constantly looking behind him to see if anyone or anything was following. He was sure that something had to be out there, but he didn't know what. He thought it had to be something terrible to scare those dogs like that. Of course, with limited amounts of information, his imagination was bound to take over and create all kinds of scenarios. Wildy's went crazy.

He tripped over stumps and large roots growing out of the ground, he got caught in thick underbrush, and he ran into trees and low-lying branches. He nearly scraped the skin completely off his arms and legs. Many were the times he would rip out low-hanging branches just because they happened to be in his way at the time. His sides ached, his lungs burned, his stomach constricted like he would throw up, and he could barely breathe; but still he ran, blind with panic. Eventually, as happens even to the strongest of men, Wildy's body could no longer keep up with his fear.

He came to a small clearing in the trees which he noticed to be a cemetery with several large headstones scattered carelessly about. Under the headstones were small mounds of grass and dirt where the earth had been dug up and replaced.

Wildy was breathless and tightly clutched his sides gasping desperately for air, trying to get enough oxygen into his lungs. His chest heaved and heaved, and despite any amount of breathing he did, it just didn't seem to be enough. He felt as if his chest were wrapped up in some type of metal cable, so tightly that he could not expand it. His body cried out desperately for oxygen, but there was none. He leaned over the side of one of the tombstones and threw up. Then he got up and walked around a little, hoping to relax and calm his body down. He knew that if he sat down or lay down at that moment, things would be even worse. Once again he leaned over the tombstone and threw up. When he could finally breathe, he sat down on one of the headstones and placed his feet on the mound of dirt below it.

Then suddenly two hands came up from the grave and grabbed Wildy around the ankles. In terror Wildy struggled with the hands, slapping them and pounding them. He even tried cutting them with his switchblade, but he could not free himself of them.

As Wildy struggled with the hands, he could see several of the hideous creatures from earlier that night emerging from the graves around him. Every single one of them was hungry for blood. His blood. Like the dogs, they were also drooling, snarling, and looking at Wildy like he was their next meal.

Just off to one side, Wildy watched as a coffin began to rise up out of the ground. Once the bottom of the coffin reached ground level, it stopped. The lid opened, and Draygon sat up and stepped out of it. Wildy didn't know what to do now. He was so frightened that he could hardly move.

Draygon gloated over his catch. "Welcome, Wildy," he sneered, "to your final resting place. I see you're standing on your own grave."

Wildy struggled like a madman to break free from the hands, but no matter how he fought, he could not break their grip. Draygon and the others continued to taunt him.

"You can't escape death, Wildy," Draygon teased. "Every man must die. Now it's your turn. Pity you'll never find the Warrior now, since you won't be leaving this graveyard."

The hands began pulling Wildy down into the grave. Wildy screamed for someone to save him, but the only response he got were the sneers and jeers from Draygon and his minions. When Wildy had sunk about waist deep into the dirt, he grabbed onto the headstone to try and stop himself, but the headstone broke off and Wildy continued to sink deeper and deeper into the ground.

Directly above them in the sky, unnoticed by anyone, a

horse galloped toward them. The horse was pure white with white wings that seemed to stretch forever from the tip of one wing, to the tip of the other. It had a long flowing mane that flapped in the wind behind the head of the horse, and its tail seemed to sweep the stars in the sky as it passed them. It was obvious that this horse was a battle horse just by its build. Its legs were large and muscular, and the muscles in the legs seemed to transcend into the muscles of the back, shoulders, and neck of its body. It was a magnificent and powerful creature. It stood about eight feet tall, and it left a trail of light behind it as it galloped across the sky at a speed that exceeded the speed of sound. It looked almost as if the horse's whole body consisted of nothing but pure white fire.

The rider on the horse had long white hair, and it trailed behind him, flapping in the breeze like the mane of the horse. His eyes blazed like red hot coals and his countenance gleamed like the northern lights. He also had a large sword made of fire tied to his side. The horse and rider rode through the night sky and into the graveyard unobserved by anyone there. Once they touched down in the graveyard, a cry of terror went up through the crowd of beasts and creatures, and they ran in every direction, trying to get out of the way. Those who didn't move fast enough were hewn down by the sword of the white-haired man.

Wildy was up to his chest in the dirt, and the hands continued to pull him deeper.

The horse stopped between Wildy and Draygon, and the rider jumped off the horse and ran to Wildy. He grabbed Wildy's arm at the shoulder and pulled him out of the ground, and stood him on his feet. As soon as Wildy's feet came to the surface, the white-haired man cut off the hands that were still holding fast on Wildy's ankles. Then the white-haired man lifted up his sword high above his head. His hair flew wildly around his face, and his voice bellowed as he laughed into the air. The sword seemed to catch fire in the man's hands and roared to life. Wildy looked at him for a moment, then passed out.

• • •

It was daylight when Wildy woke up, and the sun had already risen quite high in the sky. Wildy woke up slowly at first, but as soon as his eyes opened he jumped up to his feet and quickly looked around. The graveyard was quiet now, and there wasn't a trace of anything unusual. He turned slowly in a circle, expecting to see the crowd and the scene from the night before, but everything was quiet.

What a nightmare, Wildy thought. *This isn't me!*

He was angry, and he shouted up into the sky: "I'm not doing it anymore. I'm not wandering around in the woods being attacked by wild animals, or chased by some giant shadow, and I'm not going to wind up at the bottom of some grave without being given the chance to die first. The city I can handle, but you people are out of control. All I can say is I'm out of it! Do you hear me? Out of it! I don't need no Warrior, and I especially don't need all this! What do you care whether or not I find you? Huh?" He shook his fist in the air and stood there, half-expecting an answer. After what he'd been through the last night, it wouldn't have surprised him. But there was no sound. A light gust of wind rippled the grass in the cemetery, but other than that, nothing happened.

Wildy picked up his switchblade from off the ground. "I'm going back to the city where it's safe," he said. His voice was quieter, but the anger was still there.

Then he walked around the parameters of the graveyard, trying to remember which way he came in, but he could not. He had been in such a hurry, and it had been so dark, that he hadn't even thought to check where he was or how he had arrived. He continued walking aimlessly through the cemetery, from corner to corner, hoping that something would spark some sort of recognition. Nothing did.

Great, he cursed. *What do I do now?*

4

Wildy realized there would be no going back. He didn't know where *back* was, and he didn't want to stay there. He wanted to put as much distance as he could between him and that graveyard before nightfall. He thought he spotted a small trail leading away from the graveyard, so he decided to follow it, hoping it would take him somewhere.

The trail turned out to be barely a trail, and it was obvious that no one had been down this way in years. It was so densely covered with gnarled and twisted tree roots, with broken and fallen branches, and with thick underbrush that Wildy could barely tell where the trail began or ended. He had almost no idea where he was going, or if he was even on the trail most of the time. Toward evening, he reached another clearing, scratched and beaten and bruised from the underbrush and tree stumps and low-hanging branches that he had been battling all afternoon. He was extremely hungry, and his mouth was dry from thirst. So when he entered the clearing, the sound of a brook was a welcome sound indeed. He found the little stream just outside the clearing. It made its way down a little hill, then pooled up at the bottom before it continued its journey out of the clearing and back into the underbrush.

Wildy decided to set up camp there. He could stay close enough to the underbrush that it might protect him, yet he had the clearing so he could see anything that might be following him.

He took a long drink from the brook and then bathed in the stream. While bathing, he discovered that the stream was full of fish, and with much perseverance, was able to catch a couple for dinner. He lit a fire and cooked the fish on a rock that he heated in the coals.

By the time he finished eating, it was dark.

After eating, Wildy wrapped himself in his coat and went to sleep. He was used to sleeping in awkward places, so this was nothing new to him.

Later that night—Wildy didn't know how much later, but it must have been the middle of the night because it was pitch black outside—he suddenly woke up with a start. The fire had burned down to mere coals now, and they shined an eerie light throughout the campsite. He didn't know what it was that had wakened him, whether it was a sudden sound, or a motion, or whether it was a bad dream, but something had jarred him from sleep. He thought he sensed some presence out around the camp. He pulled his switchblade out of his boot and sat up against a stump and looked around.

A few feet away from the fire, a figure walked out of the bushes and stood like he was watching for something. This figure had his back to Wildy, and he seemed to be staring intently into the brush.

The stranger had hair down to the middle of its back, and from the back Wildy couldn't tell if it was a male or a female. He guessed it must have been a male because of the shape of its upper body. It was tall and muscular looking; its torso tapered off in a sort of V. It also appeared to be made of light; yet Wildy could not see through it. He knew it wasn't the Warrior, although it seemed to resemble him in many ways. The most notable likeness was his form, and the light substance of his body.

"Who the hell are you?" Wildy shouted at the figure. The figure said nothing, but merely turned and looked at Wildy for a moment. Then he put his finger to his mouth to motion Wildy "shush." Yet he made no sound. Then he looked over at the fire and it went out. He turned again and looked back into the woods. He stood there, silent and motionless, for what seemed like hours. Wildy didn't know what to do, so he just sat there and watched.

Then suddenly, in a split second, the figure shrunk down into nothing right on the spot where he was standing. Wildy jumped up and looked around, but he couldn't see anything in the darkness. At that moment something jumped at Wildy from the bushes. Wildy saw the form, but could not make out the details. It looked like a deformed cross between a human being and a doglike animal. With thick black hair all over his body, growing out of its nose and ears and eyes as well. Its face was gnarled and twisted, its eyes seemed to be unevenly placed in its head, and it had large fangs that protruded from its upper and lower jaws. Behind it, it left a trail of drool and slobber as it hurled itself toward Wildy. It let out a long, shrill howl that seemed to cut right through Wildy's soul. Wildy held out his switchblade, but he knew that it wasn't going to do him any good.

At that moment the beast leapt over the spot where the figure of light had been standing. When he did, a large shard of light shot up from the ground and pierced the beast in mid-air. The beast screamed in pain as the shard of light ripped and shredded it into several pieces. Then it exploded into the air and not one trace of him could be found anywhere. Immediately after that, the light transformed back into the figure Wildy had seen before. He turned and looked at Wildy, who was trembling so hard that he could barely stand. The figure looked back over at the fire, and the fire lit itself into a roaring blaze. Wildy could feel the heat almost immediately, and the warmth felt good in the cool night; he had been so cold with fright. Then the stranger turned, walked into the woods, and disappeared.

Wildy sat back down by the stump and leaned with his back against it. Facing the fire, he sat there, not daring to move, and especially not daring to go back to sleep.

An hour had passed, and Wildy was still afraid to sleep. He jumped at every sound, and whenever his head nodded, he would quickly jerk himself back awake. His eyelids wanted so badly to slam shut, his head started spinning and turning inside, and his body cried out desperately for sleep, but he did not dare. He sat there, doing everything he could to keep himself awake.

He heard another sound. He listened again. It was still there. He sat up even straighter and listened harder. It was the faint sound of little wings just in front of him. He looked over and saw a beautiful white bird, no bigger than a hummingbird, flying with grace and delicacy toward him.

She landed just a few feet away from Wildy's feet, and looked up at him. She gave him the most peaceful look he had ever seen in his life. Wildy was glad to see her, probably because of the peacefulness about her, which was such a contrast to all the turmoil of the last few days and the loneliness now that he had nobody around him to talk to any more. Maybe he sought the comfort of some other living creature nearby—a creature that was real and gentle, not some supernatural monster. For whatever reason, the company was quite calming to him.

"Hi, little bird." He spoke softly because he didn't want to frighten her away. He was glad for her company and didn't want to lose it by doing anything too sudden or loud.

"You sure are pretty."

She hopped a little closer; he got a better look at her in the firelight.

"You look so calm," he whispered again. "You must have missed what just happened here tonight. Or what's been happening to me lately."

For some reason, perhaps because of his most recent experience, or just because he needed to talk to someone, or even something, he opened up to the bird and talked to her like she was his closest friend. He told her about what happened to him in the city, what happened to him in the graveyard. He told her about the Warrior, and how he just appeared into Wildy's life, and then disappeared. He told her that he was afraid that he left the city for nothing, and that whatever it was he thought he was following didn't exist. He felt a well of emotion spring up inside of him as he talked to her about what he saw in the Warrior's eyes. But he didn't cry. Not even in front of the bird. He was afraid he told her too much. Afraid that the one person who had gained his trust might turn on him. He couldn't get those nagging questions out of his head. What if he was lying to Wildy? What if Wildy had misunderstood this Warrior, and he had never been intended to find him? Wildy talked over all of this with the little bird. It was somewhat therapeutic for him.

"I wish I knew what was happening to me," he whispered more to himself than anything else. "I came out looking for the Warrior, but it looks like I'm never going to find him. Maybe he doesn't want me to find him... I don't know." Wildy sat still and looked out into the night. "Whatever I do, I don't dare fall asleep. Not now, maybe not ever again."

He suddenly shook his head like he was trying to bring himself back to reality.

I'm cracking up, he thought. *I'm sitting here talking to a bird.* Then he looked back over at the bird. "But you are such a peaceful bird."

The bird chirped. It wasn't a loud chirp, but a soft and quiet, peaceful chirp that sounded like several birds at once.

"You're also the best-sounding bird I've ever heard," Wildy said to her.

The bird chirped again. Then she flew to the stump and

perched near Wildy's ear and began to sing the most beautiful song a bird had ever sung. It sounded like a choir of birds all chirping in harmonies with each other. It was soft, low, soothing, and tender.

Wildy smiled as the song soothed every muscle in his body and brought about a peacefulness that seemed to wash over him like a hot bath, and within a few minutes he was fast asleep.

The bird continued singing early into the morning, but Wildy didn't wake up again for many hours after that.

When he did wake up, she had gone.

5

The Fortress of Light was a shabby, run-down little fortress hidden deep in the heart of the Darklands. It sat atop a hill for all to see, but it seemed relatively unaffected by the hustle and bustle of everyday life in the Darklands around it. High wooden walls ran around its parameter so that nobody from the outside could see inside the fortress. This was the home of a group of people who called themselves followers of the Prince of Light, and these residents used the fortress to hide themselves away from the rest of the Darklands. They believed that one day the Prince of Light was going to come and rescue them from the horrors of the Darklands, and until he did, they would lock themselves in this fortress to protect themselves. They determined they would stay there until the Prince of Light returned and delivered them from the clutches of Draygon.

This particular fortress was small in comparison to most fortresses, but its residents lived under the illusion that they were strong. Strong enough that they could hold out any would-be enemy, including Draygon and his forces. Draygon knew of their existence, and at any moment he could have crushed them, but he chose to let them continue in their illusion, partially because as long as they were locked away they posed little or no threat to him. The last thing he wanted them to do was to start considering their own weakness and turn to the Prince of Light for strength, so he left them alone. To move against them could have started them thinking, and as long as they weren't thinking, they were no threat to him.

A large wooden door cut out of one of the walls opened into a giant courtyard that completely surrounded the outside of the fortress. The floor inside the courtyard was made of stone that had been carefully cut and pieced together with mortar. Due to weather and age, the mortar had begun to crack, and the stones had worn down. Along the outside wall overlooking the Darklands, large stained glass windows, about two per wall, carefully camouflaged the outside to anyone who might look out through them.

Despite the care taken in the construction of the fortress, maintenance had been far from consistent. The courtyard was dirty and dingy and littered with dirty clothes, empty cans, boxes, papers, and other debris scattered along the floor. Paint was cracking and peeling off the walls, leaving them scarred and blotched. In the center of the courtyard along the inside wall, directly across from the main entrance, were large double doors that hung lazily on their hinges, leading into the main section of the fortress.

A sign above these doors read, "All Welcome," but very few people had ever gone in far enough to see it. Those that were already in never left, so the sign went unnoticed. Although the residents of the fortress denied it, membership was very exclusive. Any new or potential member was carefully screened as to their potential, then indoctrinated into the protocol of the fortress, and then instructed to sever all ties to the outside world. They were then given a very rigorous schedule of activities and duties within the fortress, and a series of rules and regulations they must follow to prove their loyalty to them and the Prince of Light.

Wildy pushed open one of the large doors. Once inside the courtyard he looked around. The surroundings seemed odd to him. He wasn't sure if he should continue in, or turn around and leave. The sign proclaimed boldly that this was the Fortress of Light, and he decided that he may as well look inside. He saw the double doors, and the sign above them in small letters saying "All welcome." He pushed open one of the doors and was immediately greeted by a very strange man. He was an older man of average height, but he was very thin, and he had a strange, animated, cartoonlike walk. He wore a gray suit with a white shirt and a bold red tie. On his face he wore a large plastic smile so big that it seemed to Wildy that the man's mouth stretched over the whole of his face, and stopped at the ears. He approached Wildy smiling, then looked him up and down. As soon as he got a good look at Wildy, the smile slowly went away. He stared at Wildy for several minutes, then cautiously extended his hand to Wildy to shake.

"Hello," he said, pointing to a large white badge on the lapel of his suit jacket. "My name is Greeter. Earnest T. Greeter." Then he began to go on, talking to himself more than anyone else. "Been standing here for years. Years and years. Hardly seen anyone come through those doors. Always wanted them to, but they never did. But here comes someone. Right here at the door. Looks different, though." He suddenly remembered Wildly. "So how may I help you?"

"I'm looking for someone," Wildy told him.

"Looking!" Greeter's eyes lit up. "Looking. My friend, you've come to the right place. We were all lost once, but now we're found."

"I'm looking for the Warrior." Wildy continued trying to see around Greeter and into the fortress.

Greeter's eyes suddenly turned very cold, and the smile

left his face again. He glared at Wildy.

"You're one of those radicals aren't you? I thought so. I could tell by the way you were dressed. Look at that hair." Then he went back to talking to himself. "You can always tell by the hair. That's a dead giveaway. That long hair is a sure sign that something's wrong with a fellow." Then he looked back at Wildy and addressed him. "Sorry, but your type isn't welcome here. You're going to have to leave."

He tried to close the door, but Wildy managed to get his shoulder, head, and one leg through the opening and hold the door open.

"I need to see if he's here," Wildy urged. "It says 'Fortress of Light,' and he's made of light."

"Absolutely not!" Greeter retorted. "Your kind is not tolerated here. We don't want any radicals. You'll just have to look elsewhere. We have no warriors here."

He tried to push Wildy out of the door, but Wildy became angry and threw the door open. He grabbed Greeter by the nape of the neck and threw him against the wall. Then he took out his switchblade and held it up to Greeter's throat.

"Listen here, pal!" Wildy said as close to Greeter's face as he could stand to get. "I've just had the worst day of my life—several of them, and all of them right in a row, and I'm not in the mood for this crap. It's very important to me that I find this person. Now, for your sake as well as mine! Your sign said 'All Welcome,' and that would include me."

Greeter gulped hard and looked into Wildy's eyes. They looked like the eyes of someone who could and would do something crazy with a switchblade. Wildy looked violent, and Greeter didn't want to get hurt, so he led Wildy into the main hall of the fortress, with Wildy's switchblade in his back the whole time.

Once inside the fortress, Greeter led Wildy into another large hall. At the back of that hall opened up yet another long hallway that led to virtually anywhere in the fortress. The hallway was circular, and it circled the parameters of the fortress. Door after door dotted the walls along the hallway, all leading somewhere in the fortress. In every corner of the fortress, staircases leading up and down branched off from the rest of the structure, and beyond that, other hallways branched off of them.

Wildy and Greeter took one of the inside doors that led down another hallway and around a corner; they seemed to Wildy to be following the hallway they had just come from. Wildy couldn't help but think that he was in some sort of maze, and he took great care to remember every turn and every move they made. The hallway emptied out into what seemed to be a large meeting room. There were seats along three of the sides of the room, and steps through the center of those seats that led down to a large platform. The platform was elegantly decorated with large plastic plants and beautiful glass fixtures. Large, beautiful chandeliers hung from the ceiling, and strange symbols that Wildy didn't recognize decorated the walls. Off to one side sat a large conference table with many chairs around it. It looked to Wildy like this was the meeting place of the entire fortress.

Several people were milling about the area, all of them deeply involved in some sort of a project. Whatever this project was, Wildy could not tell, but every one of them acted as if whatever they were doing, it was incredibly important. They ran from one side of the room to the other, they checked on each other, and talked with each other like they were out of breath. But despite all this activity, Wildy couldn't get even an inkling of what they might be doing. So he watched them. They looked busy as they chatted with each other and hurried about the room as if the entire fortress depended on them and their work. They were like chipmunks dashing frantically about, trying to find the nuts they had hidden last fall. *What a strange place*, Wildy thought.

His thoughts were soon interrupted by Deacon Bouncer, who greeted them once they were inside what seemed to be the inner sanctum. Deacon Bouncer was a large man about six feet, two or three inches, with a large belly and a thick black mustache that seemed to grow almost down to his lower lip.

He wore a large cheesy smile full of teeth and had extremely bad breath. He met Wildy and Greeter at the door.

"Hello, Greeter," he boomed in the biggest, friendliest voice he could muster. "Who have we here? Haven't had a visitor in a long time."

"This young man would like to come in and look around," Greeter said coldly.

"Certainly," Deacon Bouncer replied. "Where would you like to sit?" he asked Wildy. "Will that be clapping or non-clapping?"

Wildy didn't understand the question so he merely stared at Deacon Bouncer, trying not to be overcome by his breath.

"Drinking wine or not drinking wine?" Deacon Bouncer continued, getting more and more impatient.

Wildy still didn't understand Bouncer's questions.

"Well speak up, boy," Deacon Bouncer pushed. "Where would you like to sit? What are you into? Cosmic revelations? Wondrous works? Divine powers? What special divinations are you into?"

"I'm not into anything, damn it!" Wildy shouted in frustration. "I'm just looking for someone! That's it!"

Deacon Bouncer looked coldly down at Wildy, but his stare didn't intimidate Wildy.

"My, my," Deacon Bouncer shook his head. "Do I detect an attitude? I think I do." He then folded his arms across his chest. "Well your type is not welcome here unless you're willing to do something about that attitude." Then he made a shooing motion with his hands, like he was trying to get rid of a dog. "So until then, shoo! Shoo! Scat!" he pressed Wildy, and his breath almost overpowered Wildy.

This made Wildy furious. He threw Greeter out of the way and flashed his switchblade at Deacon Bouncer. Deacon knew how to handle punks with knives, so he moved in for Wildy's wrist. Wildly, of course, was one of the best, and he'd shredded the Deacon's coat before the deacon knew what had happened.

"You're good," Wildly sneered, "but not good enough.

Next time I draw blood."

He backed both the men against the wall, then tried to find his way out of the building. He'd had enough. *There's no way the Warrior would be here*, he thought. These people were too out of it. They were nothing like the Warrior. He was much more connected than this.

As he was about to leave through the door he came in, Wildy bumped into Rusty.

Rusty looked about Wildy's age, about Wildy's build, but he was very different from Wildly in personality. Rusty was soft-mannered, well-disciplined, and friendly. He had short hair and was dressed somewhat conservatively. He was also very intelligent and liked to use his mind more than his hands. Rusty read constantly, ravenously devouring every form of information he could get his hands on. However, when it came to real life experience, Rusty had little. All he really knew about life was what he had learned through books.

Rusty was reading a book when he walked around the corner and ran headlong into Wildy, who was trying to exit the building. Rusty dropped his book on the floor, and Wildy's switchblade almost went with it.

Rusty quickly apologized to Wildy and then picked his book up off the floor. He and Wildly looked eye to eye for a brief moment. Rusty recognized immediately that this person wasn't from the inside and his appearance frightened him. He saw the switchblade in Wildy's hand, and his first impression of Wildly was to move away from him as quickly as possible. He looked wild, angry, and lost. Rusty suddenly realized he was staring, quickly apologized, and opened his book back up. Wildy turned back toward the door to leave.

As soon as Wildy turned around, an invisible hand touched his chest and gently pushed him back into Rusty. Rusty and his book once again plummeted to the floor. This time Wildy picked it up and handed it to Rusty and apologized. Again they looked eye to eye. When Rusty saw Wildy's eyes this time, he saw something that he hadn't noticed before. Something that looked like a little light flickering just behind the cornea. Again Rusty realized he was staring and looked away.

"I'm sorry," Wildy said again.

Again he turned to leave. Only this time two unseen hands pressed tightly against his chest and kept him from moving forward. He pushed and he pushed, but he couldn't budge. Although he couldn't see the hands, he could feel something pressing against him, and angrily he pushed even harder. The hands released slightly so that Wildy fell forward, then they pushed him back so that he fell backwards onto the floor.

Rusty watched Wildy's odd behavior, not knowing what was happening. He assumed Wildy had taken leave of his faculties and started backing away. As he was backing up, he felt something on his back that wouldn't let him move any farther. He looked around to see what it was, but there was nothing there. He fought harder to break away from the force, but he could not. He was getting scared now. Nothing like this had ever happened to him before. He wondered if possibly this wasn't what was happening to Wildy. He wondered if maybe Wildy was some sort of magician, or a warlock, and he became even more frightened. Then the thought crossed his mind that a magician or a warlock would not be able to penetrate the fortress. Yet he could not deny that something strange or magical was happening.

Wildy jumped up, cursing and swinging his fists into the air at the unknown force. Then he looked over at Rusty.

"I didn't do it," Rusty whispered, now desperate to break the force that surrounded him and run away.

"I never said you did," Wildy said in a frustrated voice. "This sort of weird stuff has been happening to me a lot lately. My life has become one long nightmare. Ever since I ran into this..." He searched for a word that would adequately describe the Warrior, but thought better of saying too much. "Person."

"What's his name?" Rusty felt the force weakening. He hoped to find out what had just happened without coming out and saying anything that might upset the person he was talking to.

At first Wildy wasn't going to say anything, but he looked into Rusty's eyes and saw something he'd never seen before. He didn't know what it was, but he decided that if this guy turned out to be any trouble, he could take care of him without a problem. So he answered Rusty's question.

"He called himself the Warrior," Wildy told Rusty.

Rusty thought for a moment, trying to see if he recognized the name. Wildy searched Rusty's eyes and face hopefully, looking for some spark of recognition.

"I don't recognize the name," Rusty said at last.

"So what else is new?" Wildly asked in frustration. He was slowly losing hope of ever finding the Warrior. "Nobody's ever heard of him. I don't even know anything about him. He just appeared out of nowhere one night, and then he disappeared. I know absolutely nothing about him, yet I'm desperate to find him. And since I've started looking for him, every weird and horrible thing that could happen to any one person has happened to me. Things that you would never believe were possible."

"What makes you so sure you're going to find him?" Rusty asked cautiously.

"He said I would," Wildy told him. Out of sheer desperation, Wildy opened up just a little to Rusty. "I don't know why I remember so clearly, but I couldn't forget if I tried, those last words he said before he disappeared. His *exact* words were: 'You will search for me and you will find me when you search for me with all your heart. I will be found by you.' That's it, then he disappeared. And that's all I know about him."

Rusty felt the strength leave his body. His hands shook, and his knees knocked together. His hair felt like it was crawling across his scalp, every pore in his body burned with electricity, and his heart literally leapt inside his chest.

"I know those words," he said weakly.

Hope filled Wildy's heart.

"What do you mean?" he asked.

"I think I know who you're looking for," Rusty stammered the words. He could barely speak. His mouth was dry, and his head was spinning. He couldn't believe what was happening to him.

"Who?" Wildy pressed.

"The Prince of Light," Wildy answered.

Wildy said nothing; he only gave Rusty a blank stare, so Rusty continued.

"The Prince of Light spoke those words many years ago. It's recorded in the sacred books. The Prince of Light is the son of the Great Emperor, the ruler of all life, of all existence. He's the one everyone here is waiting for. He promised to deliver us out of this world and take us to the world of his father. A world of incredible beauty and perfect happiness. I can't believe it! You've seen him! No one's seen or heard from him in thousands of years, and out of the blue he comes to you."

By now, Rusty was talking so fast that he almost couldn't keep up with himself.

"Do you know what this means?" he asked, finally stopping to take a breath.

Wildy shrugged and shook his head no.

Rusty was so full of excitement he could barely keep his feet on the floor.

"This means that he's here. At last the Prince of Light has come. He's here among us someplace. He's going to deliver us."

Rusty ran into the room and jumped up on one of the chairs and tried to get the attention of everyone else.

"Everyone...listen!" he shouted.

Once he had everyone's attention, he proceeded to tell them the exciting news.

"I've got great news," he told them. "The Prince of Light has come. He's here, in the Darklands." He pointed to Wildy. "This guy has seen him. He's talked to him!"

Deacon Bouncer walked over to where Rusty stood, and looked him in the face.

"Who's seen him?" he asked Rusty.

"This guy has," Rusty said again, pointing to Wildy.

"Has he?" Deacon Bouncer asked in a sort of condescending tone. He went on without even looking over at Wildly. "It just so happens that I met this young man earlier, and I know for certain that the Prince of Light would have nothing to do with him."

"But I know he has," Rusty pleaded. "I know it."

"How do you know?" Greeter chimed in with the same insincere and condescending tone in his voice.

Rusty was frustrated. He had lived in the fortress all his life and had always been very studious. He studied hard, respected his elders, tried always to be reliable and dependable, and had never made claims or said anything that he couldn't back up. His only crime was that he dared to ask questions. He had gotten used to them not listening to him, ignoring him, but it still frustrated him to no end. Rusty had a thirst for knowledge; he was curious. He found himself constantly asking questions, and in an environment like this one, asking questions was the wrong thing to do. To ask questions regarding anything might be construed as defiance against authority, rebellion, or just plain ignorance. But Rusty couldn't help himself; he was curious. He went on a rather arduous search for what was and what was not. He had become intrigued by so many things. In his mind many questions raced around and jumped up and down looking for answers. Questions such as, *What is right, and wrong? How do I know the difference? Who defines right and wrong, and who makes up the rules? Why do my family, my friends, and the leadership of this fortress behave toward me as they do?* So he went on a quest for this knowledge, and he searched out every avenue he could to get his answers. Of course this type of behavior does not make one trustworthy to any group of leaders or followers who are content to go on without ever disturbing the routine of their everyday lives, or to people who are frightened by truth, and therefore create their own truths to make up for it.

What really frustrated Rusty at that moment was that nobody there was the least bit inquisitive about what he just said, and why he said it. Didn't anyone feel the way he did? Couldn't they see it, couldn't they tell? Every time he heard the name of the Prince of Light, or now, the Warrior, he literally felt his entire body tingle. Yet these people were just staring at him like he had gone round the bend. They didn't even bother questioning him as to why he might think that the Prince of Light was in the Darklands. He knew that Wildy had met the Warrior. He could tell just by looking into Wildy's eyes, now that he knew what it was he was looking at. How could everyone here, who claimed to be followers of the Prince of Light, not even know his calling, or sense it in some way, like he was sensing it? So he continued trying to convince them.

"When this guy quoted to me what the Prince of Light said, I literally felt my heart jump inside me. I felt my body tingle. My hair started to crawl. That's never happened to me before. He's calling us to follow, I can sense it."

The only response Rusty could get was the blank stares of everyone in the room. Greeter said that Wildy wasn't anything but a common criminal, and Deacon Bouncer kept insisting that the Warrior and the Prince of Light were not the same person. He said that Draygon sent Wildy to seduce them and lure them outside the fortress to their deaths.

"But he quoted the Prince of Light," Rusty insisted. "How could he do that unless he had somehow come in contact with him?"

Deacon Bouncer remained unfazed.

"Let me remind you, Rusty," he pointed out, "Draygon can quote the Prince of Light quite fluently. We all remember the stories of how he tried to lure the Prince of Light to worship him by quoting the Great Emperor. He even came as a messenger of the Great Emperor himself."

Rusty thought about this, then looked over at Wildy who had been standing off to the side, watching the whole thing. They looked eye to eye for a moment. Then another thought crossed his mind. *If Draygon was to send someone to infiltrate, why would he make it so obvious?* When he asked this question out loud, the others all jumped in and tried desperately to deprogram him. They reminded Rusty of all the times that he asked questions about things that didn't matter. They warned him that because he questioned everything and never took their word for anything that he had put himself in a vulnerable situation. Then they warned him that if he didn't listen to them, he could wind up seriously deceived. What really hurt Rusty, though, was a comment made by Deacon Bouncer who said that this was just another one of those tangents that Rusty was constantly going off on.

Wildy watched for a while, and then he became so angry that he couldn't take anymore.

"I don't believe you people!" he screamed. "You wouldn't know the Prince of Light, or the Warrior, if he bit you on the face."

"Now you just listen here...," Deacon Bouncer spat venomously as he approached Wildy.

"No, you listen here...," Wildy said into Deacon Bouncer's face. He could smell Deacon Bouncer's breath, and he wanted to cut out his tongue just for spite. "You're all so sheltered here in this dreamland you call a fortress. You have no idea what's going on out there in the real world. You wouldn't know the difference between Draygon and the Prince of Light. Well I do. I've met the Prince of Light, and I've also met Draygon."

Rusty felt chills run up and down his spine, around his scalp, and throughout the rest of his body. He got goose-bumps on his arms the size of boils.

"You've met Draygon?" he asked Wildly.

Wildly nodded.

"And this may come as a surprise to you," he said, addressing the rest of the group, "but you're not as safe here as you think. You're not safe at all. Draygon could crush you in an instant. I know that for a fact. And I'm not going to be here when he does." With that, he turned to leave.

"Where are you going?" Rusty called after him, jumping down off the bench.

"It was nice meeting you," Wildy said. "I'm glad that there's at least one person in this world who believes me and knows what I'm talking about. You're the only sane person I've met since I left the city, but I'm getting out of here. This place is a loony bin. I'll find the Warrior, or the Prince of Light, or whoever he is—the real one—if it kills me." Then he added to himself, "Which is more than likely the way it's going to happen."

Rusty ran after him.

"I'm going with you."

"Look, I appreciate what you tried to do," Wildy told him, "But this is something I've got to do...alone."

"But I'm the one who knew who he was," Rusty reminded him. "I can help you find him. I know I can."

"How do you know?" Wildy asked.

Rusty thought about Wildy's question.

"I don't know how," he said at last. "But I know I can. I know who he is. I've read about him, I understand the holy books, I've heard the legends about him, and I've done everything I could to know more about him. I've grown up with this stuff all my life. I know I can help you."

Greeter moved in and tried to stop Rusty from following Wildly, but Rusty would not be swayed. When the others realized that they couldn't stop Rusty, they all moved in on Wildy. They decided that Rusty's rebellion was due to Wildy's demonic influence, so they closed in on him.

"You're not going to get away with this, you demon you!" Deacon Bouncer spat venomously at Wildy.

Wildy grabbed Rusty around the chest with one hand, and held the switchblade to his throat with the other.

"That's right," he spat back. "I am a demon, and if any of you take one step closer your friend here will be dead. Now get out of my face."

The others cleared a path for Wildy. As Wildy passed the others, they told Rusty that this is what they meant, and that he should get away from Wildy as soon as possible and get back to them.

"I don't believe you," Rusty gasped. He was holding Wildy's arm and trying to breathe because Wildy had wrapped it so tightly around his neck. "The Prince of Light is here, and you won't believe it."

As soon as they left the main section of the fortress, and were in the outer courtyard, Wildy let go of Rusty.

"I'm sorry," he apologized. "But I needed to get out of there."

"Well it was a little drastic," Rusty replied, "But no harm was done..." He put his hand to his throat to see if everything was okay. "I don't think," he added as an afterthought.

From behind them, a voice spoke.

"It's so boring in there," the voice said. "That's why I like to come out here and look out the window just to see what's going on out there."

Wildy turned around to see three young people—two guys and a girl—standing in front of one of the large floor-to-ceiling stained glass windows, just staring outside.

When Wildy heard them talk about looking outside, it was almost too much for him to take. He snapped. He grabbed one of the guys by the shirt, kicked out the glass with his feet, and held the boy so that they could see eye to eye.

"What is it with you people and these games you play?" Wildy shouted, shaking the boy so hard that he could barely stay on his feet. "If you like it so much out there, then why don't you just go out there and check it out for yourself? Without the window or a wall to protect you!" Then he threw the boy through the window.

As soon as the boy fell through the window, a gunshot thundered through the air, and blood splattered all over the girl. A body fell through the window and landed on the floor, half in, and half out of the courtyard. The girl screamed and ran into the arms of the other guy standing there, who had said and done nothing. After that, both of them backed slowly and quietly against the far wall.

Rusty looked down at the body, then he squatted down and cautiously touched it. This was too much for him, and he ran to one of the corners and threw up. He then turned from that corner, walked a little way down the courtyard, leaned with his back against the wall, and slid down it until he was in a squatting position. He sat there, merely looking into the emptiness of the room, running his fingers through his hair with one hand and tightly clutching his stomach with the other.

Wildly watched him for a moment, not knowing what to do. Finally he went over to Rusty.

"Look," he said, "maybe it's not a good idea for you to come along."

"I've never seen anything like that before," Rusty confessed.

"That's what it's like out there," Wildy told him. "And if you don't know your way around, this is what'll happen to you. And there's no way I can watch out for you and me both. We'll both get killed."

Rusty said nothing, but gripped his stomach even tighter.

Someone tapped Wildly on the shoulder. He jumped up and turned to face the stranger like he was ready for a fight, but the stranger neither jumped back, nor flinched, nor recoiled. He merely stood there with an expressionless face.

"What do you want?" Wildy snapped.

"You are looking for the Warrior." The man spoke these words simply, like he was making a statement. All the while he continued holding Wildy's gaze.

"Yeah?" Wildy asked suspiciously. "What about it?"

"You will find him at the Fountain of Blood," the man said, not taking his eyes off Wildly. Wildy was getting uncomfortable with this guy and with his staring. "When you arrive," the stranger went on, "you will wash and be sealed in the blood."

"So where do I find this Fountain of Blood?" Wildy asked. He started getting cockier with this guy every minute, but the man said nothing more to him. Instead, he brushed past Wildy and squatted down next to Rusty. He gently put his hands on Rusty's shoulders.

"Be strong and courageous," he whispered to Rusty. "Do not be afraid; do not be discouraged. The power of the Warrior will be with you wherever you go."

Then he breathed on Rusty. His breath was like sweet cologne, and as Rusty breathed it in, it coursed through his blood like oxygen. It calmed his stomach and soothed his head, and it seemed to bring strength and power and courage into every muscle of his body. The most amazing thing about the man's breath was that it seemed to awaken Rusty's spirit. He felt his spirit come alive inside of him. It started out like a gurgling and churning in his soul, and then it began to swell up until it had reached Rusty's height and width. Once it was alive, it began to call for the Prince of Light, and if Rusty thought he had desired to know more about him before, now he could think of nothing else.

Then the stranger stood up and gently pulled Rusty to his feet. He looked once again deep into Rusty's eyes and said simply, "Go."

Rusty instantly felt like someone had tied a strong but thin cord around his heart and that cord was gently pulling him toward something, and he knew that he had to follow it. Then the stranger turned and walked out of the building.

At first Wildly was mesmerized by the scene before him, but the sound of the door closing suddenly snapped him back into reality.

"Wait," he ran after the stranger. "Where do I find the Fountain of Blood?"

The stranger disappeared. Wildy ran over to the window and looked out.

"Where did you go?" he screamed into the air. Then he angrily pounded his fist against the wall. "What is this game everyone's playing with me?"

He took a step and tripped over the body on the floor. In anger, he picked it up and threw it out the window. Then he looked out the window himself and yelled into the air. "Will someone please tell me what the hell is going on?"

Not even waiting for an answer, he stormed through the

window. Rusty followed him out without saying a word.

The young man and the girl with him waited until everything had quieted down, and then both went out through the broken window looking for their friend.

"Michael?" they called. "Michael?"

6

The atmosphere in the Fortress of Light had suddenly become very disturbed and intense. A deep sense of something ominous settled in the fortress following Wildy's abrupt arrival and departure. Wildy's presence shattered the quiet little world of the Fortress of Light, and an emergency meeting had been called to discuss the day's happenings.

The fortress elders gathered around the large conference table, and Greeter and Deacon were among them. At the head of the table sat Dr. In, the self-proclaimed, self-ordained leader of the fortress. It was he who made all the decisions as to what was of the Prince of Light and what was not. He called himself their spiritual leader and their teacher, and everyone there was expected to put their trust in his interpretations of the holy books.

The rest of the residents and lay people of the fortress gathered around the elders at the table and watched the debate taking place with great interest. Nobody dared to admit it, but they had all become very afraid since Wildy left the building.

One of the elders there was a very old and wise lady. She had not been present during the episode with Wildy and Rusty, but she had been filled in by both the lay people and the fortress elders. Though she heard many versions of the story, through her wisdom and cunning, she was able to devise what she felt might be a fairly accurate version for herself.

The wise elder looked around the room, and then spoke very cautiously. "I believe it is entirely possible that this boy may have seen the Prince of Light."

"Are you crazy?" Greeter screamed. "The Prince of Light would never desecrate himself by being even remotely associated with the likes of that hooligan. He pulled a knife on me."

"And he threatened to kill Rusty," Deacon Bouncer added.

"But nobody really understands what happened or why he turned on Rusty. There are several conflicting stories about what happened with the boy and the knife," the wise old elder rebutted.

"He confessed to being a demon!" Deacon Bouncer screamed out.

"He *was* trying to get out of the fortress," another elder put in.

"All the same," the wise elder went on, "the Prince of Light has been known to go directly to the rif-raf and street people, without appearing to his so-called followers. He cautioned us that we might not always recognize him in the way he chose to present himself to us unless we were very observant."

Another elder joined the debate. "The Prince of Light promised the last time he was here, *thousands* of years ago," her emphasis was on the fact that the Prince of Light had not been seen or heard from in at least that long, "that when he came back he would come directly to us."

The wise old elder's patience was wearing thin.

"He made no such claim," she said. "He said only that when he came back he would come to those who would receive him. How do we know he didn't come to us in the form of this boy?"

"He said that he would come and deliver us from Draygon," another elder blurted out.

"There is still much confusion as to the way he will deliver us. We know only that we must be vigilant and prepared for anything."

"You're a heretic!" Deacon Bouncer yelled over to the wise elder.

"And you're blind!" she retorted.

One elder sat and quietly listened to everything being said, but he himself said not a word. His heart was heavy, and his eyes moistened with tears, but he would not allow himself to cry. He was torn between defending Rusty, a boy he knew deep down would never just go off on an impulse unless he really believed that what he was doing was the right thing, and protecting his high reputation as one of the most respected elders of the Fortress of Light. So he sat and listened to the debate, often drifting in and out of his own private thoughts. He wanted the voices inside of him to stop yelling at him to come to Rusty's defense.

The voices grew louder and louder, but he kept silent.

Nobody knows what would have happened had the fight been allowed to continue, but they were suddenly cut short by Dr. In trying to get their attention.

"Ladies and gentlemen!" he shouted over the noise. As soon as everyone quieted down, he started his deliberation. "I think it's only proper to say that this young man was not acting under the Prince of Light, but was instead a plant from Draygon to deceive us so that he could break in and destroy this fortress. He did not bear the physical markings of the Prince of Light, either in is attitude or appearance. His hair was long, his clothes were that of a common criminal, and his attitude was that of a deviant and a rebel. The Prince of Light warned us that this sort of thing would happen shortly before he returned. Fortunately, only one was deceived. A very dear friend," he glanced at the silent elder at the other end of the table, "but it is better that one should die for the people than the other way around. Our knowledge of the holy writings tells us that the Prince of Light could, in fact, not have appeared to this young boy for the very reasons I have just mentioned. The Prince of Light warned us that many people would come in his name, and under false pretense, only to trick us and then destroy us. But have no fear, our fortress is strong, and we can resist Draygon. This was merely a close call."

The wise old elder shook her head. "If this fortress is so strong," she asked, "then how in the world did he get in here in the first place?"

Dr. In glared at her. "We let our guard down," he said angrily. "From now on we must be even more cautious of who we allow into this fortress. Greeter thought he was doing the right thing, but we know now that he was not. But we shall extend to him our forgiveness."

"You're very kind," the wise elder spoke quietly, almost as if she had conceded. She knew that the fortress wasn't strong enough to hold out Draygon, but she could never get people to listen to her. For many years she had tried to convince the people that they were not safe, and that instead of playing safe, they should be preparing for the coming storm. But the people went on about their business, and nicknamed her prophet of doom.

So now she conceded. She was too tired to fight. She knew that something was happening in the Darklands. She could see the signs. Strange events were taking place, and unlike her constituents, she made it a point to be informed of the outside world. Things were getting desperate out there, and that could only mean one thing. She sensed that Wildy's presence in the fortress was an omen that things were going to take a serious turn for the worse, but she would say no more to those around her. It was obvious they would not heed her warning. The arrival of Wildly was a sign, and she felt inside that she should prepare to depart this life. She was old and tired, and she knew that she was not strong enough to face the coming struggle. Her only request of the Prince of Light was that he would be gracious to her and give her a peaceful end.

Those thoughts were suddenly interrupted by the conference room doors being flung open. Draygon and his men entered the room, surrounded the table and herded everyone in the room into the middle of the circle. Sudden terror seized everyone in the group, and the elders at the table jumped to their feet to face Draygon. This was the second time an outsider had intruded into their quiet little hideaway.

Despite the confusion in the room, Draygon was calm, cool, and deliberate, but underneath all that poise, he burned with anger.

Dr. In stood up to face him.

"What do you want?" he asked.

The lay people gathered around the table were quietly looking for a place to hide and slowly trying to back away to someplace where they could be out of the way of the hideous creatures.

Draygon said nothing as he looked around the room, unmoved and uncaring about the uproar he and his men had just caused. His evil and cruel eyes seemed to be searching intently for something, or someone.

"I understand you had an unwelcome visitor," he said at last.

"I don't know what you're talking about," Dr. In replied.

"Don't you think that I know what's going on in here?" Draygon interrogated.

Dr. In approached him slightly. "You're with Draygon aren't you?" he asked.

Draygon looked him straight in the eyes. "I *am* Draygon."

A sudden panic seized everyone in the room, and a short burst of fright emanated from their mouths as they began to crowd each other to get back against the doors. But the guards had surrounded the place very tightly, and nobody would be able to leave. Everyone there looked to Dr. In to save them. He said they were strong; he said they could withstand Draygon. So they all watched and waited. Nobody knew what else to do.

"Get out!" Dr. In screamed. "I command you in the name of the Prince of Light...get out!"

Draygon didn't move, he didn't say anything, he only stared at Dr. In.

After a moment, a sneer crossed his face.

"The same Prince of Light whose messenger you just dismissed as one of mine?" he asked. He was enjoying making Dr. In pay for his ignorance, and he made every moment count. He hated Dr. In, not just because of his ignorance, but because of the way he constantly threw around the name of the Prince of Light, using it to make demands and threats toward Draygon. Even though he had no power, Draygon hated his arrogance, his pomposity, his stupidity, and worst of all, his total disregard for who Draygon was. Draygon basked in the terror he threw into Dr. In's tidy little world and derived immense pleasure out of it. It was time for revenge. So he went on.

"The same Prince of Light you just finished telling everyone in this room wasn't in the Darklands?" His voice grew angrier as he spoke. "The same Prince of Light whose name you didn't even recognize. I have taken all I can out of this group of people. Your arrogance, your pomposity, your defiance of authority. For centuries I have allowed you and your ancestors to lock yourself away in this little shack you call a fortress, to live under some false illusion that you were followers of the Prince of Light, and that you could order me around simply by throwing out a name. Well my patience is at an end with you!"

Dr. In's voice reached a high-pitched scream as he tried desperately to get Draygon out of the fortress. "In the name of the Prince of Light," he screamed, "I command you!"

Draygon was unimpressed. He simply turned and faced Dr. In. "The Prince of Light doesn't seem to be responding," he said. Then he looked over at one of his generals. "Kill him."

The general ran Dr. In through with a sword, and Dr. In collapsed to the floor in a pool of blood. A scream went up through the crowd. Women fainted dead away, children screamed and cried, and the men tried to somehow hold themselves together. The wise old elder sat down in her chair. She knew now why Wildy had come, and that the warning had gone completely unnoticed. But she was ready to go, and she knew that was what would happen next. Then suddenly something came over her, something beautiful and calm, and she knew that she would depart her life in peace. The Prince of Light had granted her last request.

Draygon looked over at his men. "Kill everyone of them. Search this fortress and find that boy. He must die in front of me. Is that understood? And if he's met and teamed up with the other boy, then find both of them.

Draygon didn't know about Rusty and Wildy's meeting, but he knew about all the attention Rusty had been receiving by cohorts of the Prince of Light. Once his followers admitted to him that there was triple the activity over these two Darklands residents, he set out to destroy them. But as with Wildy, it appeared he might be too late. The Warrior had gotten to them first.

So the bloodbath began. They all tried to escape, but they were run down by Draygon's men, who seemed to enjoy their task and performed it with such glee. They got great joy out of chasing their prey, toying with them, and running them down and torturing them. They killed children in front of their parents, and parents in front of their children, husbands in front of wives, and wives in front of husbands. They started with the lay people, so that all the elders could watch their little toyland collapse. Rusty's father, the one silent elder, watched all of this in horror. Rusty was right. The Prince of Light had been calling them. It was a warning. But it was too late, and he hadn't listened. Then the sword hit him, and there was nothing left. Soon Draygon's men were done with their job. They left absolutely no one alive. Dead bodies lay discarded on the floors and the furniture of the building. The wooden floor of the fortress was now blood-red, and the bodies of the people who thought that they were safe from any attack of Draygon were now mangled and lifeless throughout the building. Every square inch of the fortress was searched thoroughly but there was no sign of Wildy. Draygon's messengers brought back word that Wildy was nowhere to be found in the entire building.

Draygon thought it over. "The two boys have paired up. This must have been his plan. They're gone from here, and now he's put a hedge around them...but they cannot hide forever."

"Do you think they found the fountain?" one of his soldiers carelessly asked.

Draygon glared at the soldier, and then took a sword and diced him into pieces. "It's possible," he said, "but that doesn't mean it's over." Then he turned and left.

7

Mr. Myer sat and looked out over Darklands City from his office high atop the City Building. The lights were off, and from where he sat, things seemed so quiet. They didn't seem even half as bad as he knew they were.

It had only been a few days since the massacre on the streets, and the city was still reeling from the damage and destruction. Updated reports were coming to him about every half-hour. Just one floor below him, in a special session, the city council was still in session, and had been round the clock since the crisis. Nobody was getting any sleep, food was being catered to them by any means possible, and for all their work, solutions were lax in coming.

The hospitals remained crowded and unable to deal with the vast amount of those in need of their services. There was no power yet to most of the city, and the downtown area still looked like a war zone. Most sources of food had been destroyed, and the water was contaminated. The bottom line was: Darklands City was broke. They had no money to deal with the situation at hand. They went far into debt constructing the City Building, then they spent too much money paying for expensive accessories, and now they were paying the city council members exhorbitant salaries. They couldn't pay to restore the power; they couldn't pay to clean up the streets; they couldn't pay to take care of the hospital situation; and they couldn't pay the military or the law officials to keep order.

Mr. Myer's popularity had been on a downward spiral for several months because of the economic problems the city was facing, and this brought it to its all-time low. Things were so far out of hand now that he had no way of winning public trust again. He knew that while he sat in his office trying to come up with solutions of his own, the city council was downstairs plotting to take advantage of this situation to promote each one of themselves to power. Mr. Myer would have been there to defend himself, but he knew that they could never arrive on *who* would take his place as a new leader, and while they fought and bickered and argued, he had a little time to think and come up with a plan of his own.

He contemplated the money problems of the city. Without the money, they wouldn't get the power back on, they wouldn't be able to clean up the streets, they weren't going to get the hospitals functional, there would be no school, and nobody would be reporting to work. The city was on the brink of financial destruction. Even so, the most frightening prospect was that Darklands City might lose its prestige as the Darklands' greatest city, and its standing as the Darklands' most powerful governmental authority. With the Darklands in such a domestic dilemma, a great opportunity awaited any other power to move in and take advantage of the situation. Another thought that concerned Mr. Myer was his position, his wealth, and his power and prominence in the high-class financial realm—everything that he had worked for all his life. Everything that he had spent years collecting and gathering, and making his own. These were not easy things for him to walk away from.

Meanwhile the frustration of the people of the city continued as demonstrators and rioters crowded the streets of the city below. They smashed in windows, vandalized shops and stores, and burned buildings. (Some of the buildings were being burned so that the people could have warmth, and some of them were being burned out of anger and hate.) They knocked over statues and sculptures, and they blocked roadways so that nobody (especially those who could afford to) could leave the city. They opened fire on anyone who represented authority, and they even fought each other. They destroyed anything in their path.

As Mr. Myer ran through all this in his head, a voice suddenly brought him back to the quiet room. He recognized the voice, but he didn't know how he got in there, since all the doors were locked.

"It looks like this is the end of your career," the voice said quietly.

Mr. Myer snapped out of his thoughts and turned his chair to see the man from whom the voice was coming from. He recognized the man. The man had never really identified himself to Mr. Myer, only that his name was Max. Mr. Myer had met Max on several occasions at high-function gatherings, but he had never liked him. Who Max worked for, nobody really knew, only that they were very powerful people, and that nobody wanted to get to close to them. For this very reason Mr. Myer had done his best for several years to avoid him. Yet now Max was in the room, sitting just across from him.

"How did you get in?" Mr. Myer snapped as he got up and crossed over to check the lock on the door. It was still locked. "How did you get in here?" he snapped again.

"It doesn't matter how I got in," Max answered. "None of that is important. I want to talk about your career."

"I don't want to talk about my career with you."

Mr. Myer was a little disheveled at having Max in the room with him, all alone, so he crossed back to the door to leave. The door was still locked, and he could not unlock it.

"Whether you want to talk about it or not, we've got to talk."

"What about?" Mr. Myer asked.

"For starters," Max told him, "it's over."

"Look!" Mr. Myer snapped. "I don't need you—"

"I'm not here to rub your face in it, and I'm not here to create contention between us. I'm here because I think I can help you."

Mr. Myer wasn't sure he wanted Max's help. He knew that Max was a very powerful man, and he didn't want to get involved with someone he knew so little about. For instance, who did Max work for? Why was it that nobody knew who they were, yet everybody lived in terror of them? What did they want out of him for all their help? He crossed back to his desk and sat down.

Max continued speaking, and it was almost as if he read Mr. Myer's thoughts.

"It's like this," Max said, "Darklands City is almost in ruins right now, and it's only a matter of time before the rest of the Darklands follows after it. You have no money to save yourself or your people. Major companies around the world have invested in your city and country, and now it lies on the brink of disaster. If Darklands City falls, and you know this, the rest of the world falls. You've done much in trying to keep peace among all other powers on this planet, and without that, the rest of the world will collapse into utter chaos. Then you will lose everything—your prominence in the rest of the Darklands, your power, and worst of all, you're going to lose your beautiful mansion, your money, and your position as mayor of Darklands City and all the perks that go along with it, and quite possibly your life. Worse yet," Max said in a much more serious tone, "you may even lose the Darklands."

He was watching Mr. Myer's face closely, and he knew

that he had struck a chord, so he continued on that note.

"I'm prepared to offer you some help."

"What kind of help?" Mr. Myer asked.

"It's very simple," Max said. "We are prepared to give you all the assistance you need to bail out Darklands City. Especially your economic difficulties. You come through for the people, you help them out in their moment of extreme crisis, you become a hero to them. You gain their trust and they re-elect you. You keep your very illustrious position as mayor of Darklands City, you own the city council, and you keep your beautiful house, your perks as the mayor, and all your other possessions that you've become so attached to over the years."

"And what do you get from all of this?" Mr. Myer asked.

"I think you know," Max said. "The Darklands. We become power of the Darklands. In return, you get everything you've wanted. Your position, your possessions, and your good name in the Darklands. You answer only to us, and in all other situations, your word is law."

Mr. Myer stood up from his desk, angry and upset.

"You want me to sell Darklands City?" he screamed.

Max was unmoved by Mr. Myer's display of emotion. He remained calm and held Mr. Myer's stare.

"It boils down to this," he said, "if you turn us down, you will be thrown off the city council and impeached from your position as mayor to appease the people of Darklands City. You yourself know what's going on downstairs. It's just a matter of time before they come up with a way to get rid of you. And when they do, you'll lose everything, and the person that takes your place will gain it all. He'll live in your house, he'll have your servants, and he'll have your possessions, your job, and your money. It's quite possible that Rhend might be the person that takes your place."

Rhend's name shot through Mr. Myer's head like a cannon. Rhend was the last person Mr. Myer wanted in any position of authority. Especially now, after he had thrown Rhend in jail. Having him take the place of mayor of Darklands

City would be disaster. Mr. Myer knew that Rhend would never kill him outright; instead, Rhend would torture him to make him pay for what he did. Mr. Myer steadied himself, and sat down.

"What we're offering you," Max continued, a little softer now, "is the security you've been wanting for both you and your city. You can't do it without us, and we'll get it anyway. It's up to you."

"Who's us?" Mr. Myer asked quietly.

"That's not important," Max assured him. "You will be dealing directly through me. We'll work through you, and to all those people out there, you will be the hero."

"All right. Fine," Mr. Myer conceded. "Whatever you want."

Max pulled out a contract from his coat and set it on the desk in front of Mr. Myer. Mr. Myer looked it over, signed it, and slid it back to Max. It was done. Darklands City, and eventually the entire Darklands, had been sold to some unknown entity. Mr. Myer tried to convince himself that it was all for the good of the city and the Darklands as a whole, but it all boiled down to reasons that Mr. Myer could keep his position, his house, his job, and his position in the city...and the world.

Max took the contract and set it back into his coat pocket.

"A large sum of money will be deposited into the city's bank account first thing in the morning. Congratulations, Mr. Mayor."

He held out his hand to shake Mr. Myer's, but Mr. Myer simply waved at him slightly and disappeared back into his own little world. He didn't even see Max leave. When he thought of this, he got up and crossed over to the door again. It was still locked. He wished then that he would have paid closer attention to how Max left.

He sat back down at his desk and looked out the large picture glass window. *First thing in the morning,* he thought. *What's going to happen from here?* Although the thought crossed his mind, he didn't really care anymore. He had what he wanted.

8

The going had become extremely rough, and the boys had to fight harder and harder for less and less ground. They had begun ascending a large mountain that seemed to loom over them like some dark shadow. It reached high into the clouds, so that the boys could not see the top. It also seemed to tilt just slightly, like it was leaning over them, stretching out for miles in every direction. It appeared as if there was only one way around the mountain, and that was a little pathway that led right up to the top of it. Wildy took a deep breath, looked over at Rusty, and began the climb. He was exhausted from the journey thus far, so the idea of a climb this late in the day did not appeal to him. They talked about making camp at the base of the mountain over night, and then attempting it in the morning, but neither one of them wanted to be at the base of this mountain overnight.

Huge boulders jutted across the path, and at times the path itself was almost impossible to find. Night was falling rapidly, and cold thick clouds covered the mountainside. A light, freezing mist sprinkled their faces, yet they could not stay at the bottom. On one side of them a massive wall of rock and granite sheered straight into the air to the summit of the mountain, and on the other side of them a cliff dropped hundreds of feet to a deep chasm below. Yet for all this, the boys could not wait until morning. Something was driving them up that mountain, and, at all cost to their own lives, they had to go.

An eerie feeling hovered over the mountain and seemed to bring about a deeper chill than the air around them. Rusty couldn't help remembering every horror story he had ever heard as a child growing up, and every nightmare he had ever had, and every monster or horrific creature that had ever waited for him before in the dark of his room; and they all haunted him now. Somehow he expected to find them just behind every boulder, ready to pounce on him the minute he passed by.

Wildy had gotten used to this sensation from his recent experiences over the past few days, and so kept getting more and more suspicious. He constantly checked behind him, looked around him, and glanced around every boulder before he would continue any further, so tense was he that he hardly dared to blink for fear that something might materialize in that split second his eyes were shut.

Neither of the boys said anything, but they knew each other was feeling the same sensation of almost debilitating terror that seemed to make its home on this mountain.

For some unknown reason, Wildy suddenly jumped up on a boulder and checked his feet. This movement nearly caused a heart attack in Rusty, who out of instinct and fear did the same.

"I can't stand it!" Wildy said panting. He looked over and saw Rusty watching him. Rusty's face reflected his own fear. "I'm just checking for headstones," Wildy mumbled.

"What?" Rusty asked.

So Wildy told him the story of what had happened to him the other night in the graveyard and of his encounter with Draygon and his men.

"I wish you wouldn't have told me that story," Rusty said, now becoming more fearful than ever before. He knew that someday he might have to meet Draygon, and he hoped that if he did it would be with the Prince of Light close by.

Neither of them moved for several minutes, until it became just as frightening to stay put. They didn't know what to do, stay or go, but the longer they stayed in one place, the more their feet seemed to be willing to leave without them just to get away from there. The only other option available to them was to get up to the top of the mountain, and they chose to continue on. It seemed a little easier to deal with the fear of moving than of standing still. Somehow they almost got the idea that if it got too bad, they might be able to outrun it.

When they finally reached the top, they came to a large floor made out of rock, sanded down and cemented together to make a smooth surface. The rock plain stretched out several yards in all directions and appeared to be the very top of the mountain itself, and, except for the path that the boys had followed up, there was no other way onto the floor. On three sides were sheer cliffs that even the most prominent mountain climber could never in his or her wildest dreams conquer.

In the center of the plain sat a large, concave, stone table, curving up just high enough to give it a bowl shape. The table was about seven feet long, about four feet wide, and tilted down just slightly at one end. At that end, the edges of the bowl dropped down to form a small outlet for water to drain out of the table. Surrounding the table, just under the bowl, a gutter ran completely around the outside of the bowl, tilting in the opposite direction of the bowl, and allowing the water to spill onto the rock plain itself. At the bottom of the gutter, another gutter opened up in the stone floor itself. This gutter ran to the end of the stone plain, then dropped off where the floor dropped into the vast expanse of the gully below.

The clouds had lowered themselves so that they sat several feet below the mountain's crest. It was late into the night by the time the boys reached the top, and in the bright moonlight it looked like the mountain was an island, surrounded by a sea of white fluffy cotton. The clouds rolled and swirled and spun their way around the mountain, and sometimes a fingerlike wisp would crawl across the stone floor.

The moonlight also cast a frightening glow on the stone table. In the middle of all this surrealism, the table seemed to take on a life of its own. It sat there in the center of the rock plain, completely silent, completely motionless. A steady dripping of water could be heard flowing from the table, into the gutter, and then out along the stone floor and over the edge of the mountain. The air up there was extremely cold, and the boys shivered as they stood and stared at what lay before them. Nothing disturbed the still night. A freezing breeze would whip up occasionally, but other than that, nothing else moved.

Terror seized Wildy and Rusty and held onto them tight. Wildy would never have admitted it, but he was very glad at this moment that Rusty was with him. He had never in his life been afraid like this before, and he had plenty to be afraid of. He panted hard as he stared at the table, like he had just run a five-minute mile. In Darklands City, when he was afraid, he could wrap himself up in his anger and hate, and fight it out, but that would not be the case here. Here he had been stripped for the moment of everything he had ever used as defense. Anger, hate—everything he had run to instead of facing with real emotion—was gone. With all these defenses gone, there was nothing there to protect Wildy's soul. He stood in agony as his heart and soul lay before him, defenseless and vulnerable, a condition that Wildy had never been in, from the time that he was old enough to do something about his life. Emotion pushed at him from the inside, and there was nothing there to stop it. He felt like someone had ripped open a scab the size of his body, and he was bleeding profusely. Only his blood was the emotion that flowed out of him like water when a dam breaks. No matter how Wildy tried, he had lost control of himself from that moment on.

Wildy knew that he was staring down the brink of the most terrible thing he would ever experience in his lifetime, even more terrifying than any encounter he'd ever had with Draygon. That stone table seemed to threaten him like no threat he had ever had before. That stone table could destroy him. It could take his very soul, and with little or no effort whatsoever, throw it away to a place where the only emotion it would know would be the torment of utter loneliness. He could see his soul now. He could see it struggling desperately to free itself from the dark caverns of his inner being, he could see it writhing and dying, he could see it as it really was, as it had been for so many years with him, and there was nothing he could do to save it.

He looked back at the stone table. *What does it want, and why is it there? Why can't I just run off the mountain?* But the table wasn't about to let him do that, and Wildy knew it.

To Rusty, the table was a giant, cold, and unfriendly tomb. He felt like he was staring death in the face. Rusty had never seen death, except for the one body at the Fortress of Light. But this death was different. The death that he saw here was even more frightening than any other type of death he knew of, in that it was the complete separation of everything that Rusty held dear, and there was no hope of ever seeing life again. It was an eternal death. A death that had no hope of life afterwards. For so many years back in the fortress, Rusty cried out for life, he searched for it, he dug for it, he had devoted his whole life to finding it. He searched and searched for the purpose of his life. Something that would mean something to him, something that would help him face his own life. Rusty had lost hope and given up to despair a long time ago, but he would never admit that to himself. Now he too stood before this stone table stripped of every defense. He looked his hopelessness straight in the face, and for the first time in his life he had to admit that there was nothing he could do about it. Like Wildy, Rusty hated this feeling. He was completely vulnerable. He was exposed and helpless, with the sense that he was going to die.

Rusty knew also that he would not be allowed to run from this place, but he didn't know if he could face it. His heart pounded so hard that his chest hurt and his sides ached from how hard he had to breath to keep up with his heart. His throat was dry, and he could hardly swallow. Back at the fortress, he had never been afraid because there was always someone around him, but now he was alone, except for Wildy, but even then, he was completely alone. For whatever it was that table wanted, it was between Rusty and the table, and like the death that Rusty faced, he had to go alone. He started wondering if coming with Wildy was such a good idea after all. But the problem was now, and good idea or not; he had to deal with this table. He could not turn back.

Neither boy moved. Rusty decided he would simply stand there as long as he could. Then suddenly he noticed that he was just within arm's length of the table, and he didn't know how he got there. He knew he hadn't moved, he knew he couldn't move because every muscle in his body refused to do so.

"What happened?" Wildy screamed. His voice seemed so loud in the silence that he immediately pulled it back to a whisper. "What's happening, Rusty?"

Rusty could hardly talk because his voice was trembling so much. "I don't know," he whispered back, again not wanting to disturb the silence.

He glanced behind him and noticed that there were several yards between where they were now and where they used to be. Rusty knew this was the work of the table. He had heard many legends growing up in the fortress. Legends of supernatural things. Things that lured mortals, things that would literally seize control of anyone unfortunate enough to meet up with them, things that would destroy any mortal they encountered.

Now that he and Wildy were alone, every one of those horrible stories ran through his head bigger than life.

Wildly cautiously reached out and touched the edge of the table. The minute he did, some force immediately threw him into it. He screamed and thrashed around, trying to get out. Rusty turned to run, but his feet wouldn't go anywhere. They were frozen to the floor. Suddenly a thought crossed his mind. *You have a choice,* he thought. *You can run, or you can face what's in this table. You must choose.* Rusty wanted to run, but something told him he needed to face it. So he turned around and touched the table. He felt some force throw him in like a straw being hurled through the air by a hurricane. Then as quickly as it began, it was over, and Rusty was inside the bowl of the stone table, and what he saw there made his blood curdle.

Laying in the table Rusty saw the dead body of who he knew must be the Prince of Light. He had never seen him before, but he knew who it was. His body had been ripped and shredded by many beatings and extreme abuse, and what little bit of skin he did have left clung loosely to his broken frame. Yet despite that he was dead, he continued to bleed profusely. The blood seemed to ooze out of his body in quarts and fill up the bowl of the table. Then it ran out into the gutter, through the stone floor, and out over the cliffs.

The Prince of Light looked beaten and broken, like the most pitiful thing that Rusty had ever seen. Yet Rusty could see on his face that he somehow looked peaceful and victorious. It was this look that suddenly tipped off Rusty as to where he was. He knew now that he was at the Fountain of Blood. And what they thought was water that they heard flowing through the gutters and over the cliff was not water at all...it was blood. The Warrior's blood.

Wildy also recognized this body. The body of the being that had appeared to him on the city streets so seemingly long ago...the being that saved his life and called him away from the world he knew and was familiar with, out into a strange and terrible world that had threatened him every step of the way. It was the being that had somehow found his soul, and then showed it to him. It was the being that Wildy had left everything for and devoted the rest of his life to finding, and now this being was dead.

He went into a frenzy. He started screaming "What's happened? What's happened to him?" He tried to take the body out of the table, but he couldn't lift it any higher than the top of the bowl itself. The more he struggled with the Warrior's body, the more entrenched he became in the Warrior's blood, until he was completely covered with it. This was the one who found his soul, this was the one who showed him his soul, and this was the one his soul would do anything for. This corpse laying in this bowl. Like a dam breaking, all his hopes and newfound dreams were blown away. He sat there, bare before the Warrior, with nothing. Rusty tried to calm Wildy by grabbing him and trying to hold him still. While trying to calm Wildy down, Rusty himself became covered with the Warrior's blood.

Once Wildy finally did calm down, he grabbed the body of the Warrior and pulled it close to his chest and held it there. The body seemed so fragile, and so frail. It was a wonder that it didn't fall apart while Wildy and Rusty struggled with it. Wildy looked down at it again. He had seen many people die, some of them friends, members of his own gang, some of them enemies, but none of them affected him the way this did. He never allowed himself to be vulnerable to anyone. But the Warrior caught him completely off guard. He became so intent on finding the Warrior, that he forgot to really build up any kind of defense against him. So now here he was, and this body in his lap revealed emotions that he had never had before and never would have allowed himself to have. His heart ached so that he thought he would come apart. He hated this feeling. He hated loving someone like he suddenly discovered he loved the Warrior. And he hated losing the only person that he ever really loved, and he hated discovering love and losing it within minutes.

He held the body tightly and rocked it back and forth.

Once Wildy was calm, Rusty leaned back against the slope of the bowl on the other side of the Prince of Light's body. He looked into the face. It was the most tender and loving and hard and sad face that he had ever seen. He wanted so bad to see that face with life behind it. He wanted to talk to the person behind that face. He knew that it would be full of wisdom, that it would comfort him, that it would build him up, and give him hope.

Then he looked down at the hands. They were strong and big. Rusty couldn't help but notice the size of the hands. These were hands that looked like they had a lifetime of hard work behind them. They looked like hands that could break or crush steel, yet hands that could hold a baby, and caress, and express compassion, and bring comfort. Rusty took the hand and held it in both of his hands. He held it up and looked at it, and then began to cry. He didn't want Wildy to see this, so he turned his head and wept quietly to himself. He laid down on his back alongside the Prince of Light and looked up at the moonlight. It was cold outside and he could see his breath, but there was still heat left in the blood and he was plenty warm. He watched small patches of steam ascend from the troughs into the air. He put the Prince of Light's hand in his and held it there.

Rusty had heard about the Fountain of Blood in the fortress, but they had never explained it like this. They never told him about the impact it would have on him. They never told him about the emotion, or the pain. Most of all, nobody ever told him how beautiful the Prince of Light was. Even dead.

"He said he was going to save us," Wildy whispered, "to save the Darklands."

"This was the only way he could save us," Rusty whispered back.

"By dying?" Wildy asked. "What good is he dead? How can you save anyone when you're dead?"

Rusty thought about that. Things were all so different now that he was here. The fortress, the Fountain of Blood, his own life. It was nothing like the legends, and answers didn't come so easy to him now as they once had.

"Did Draygon do this?" Wildy asked.

Rusty nodded.

Wildly thought about the last time he saw the Warrior...how he dominated Draygon and all his men.

He laid the body down again and thought back to the night he met the Warrior. He thought how odd it was that this Warrior hadn't asked anything of him. He saved him from Draygon and let him go. Wildy knew the Warrior let him go. He thought about all the hell he had recently been through trying to find the Warrior. He had lost count of the days since he left the city. He thought about being chased by unseen shadows, scared out of his mind nearly every night, and experiencing just about every weird and horrible thing that could happen to any one person in any one lifetime, trying to find some guy who identified himself only as the Warrior. Now that Wildy thought about it, the Warrior never identified himself to Wildy at all. It was to Draygon that he spoke his name. The Warrior said that Wildy would find him again, but he didn't say Wildy would find him like this.

Rusty began to recite the legend of the Fountain of Blood. He wasn't really talking to anyone in particular, he just went over the story now that he was there. It seemed only fitting.

"Thousands and thousands of years ago," he began, "nobody really knows how long, the Great Emperor ruled every universe and every world throughout eternity. His rule was undisputed. Under him were millions and millions of beings, most of them probably a lot like us, only they all did his bidding. Yet as powerful as he was, he was fair, and he believed in justice. So everyone was happy. Nobody got sick, nobody had anything wrong with their bodies, nobody got hurt or hurt each other, and nobody died. Everyone there live in perfect harmony with everybody and everything else. They didn't have to sleep, they didn't have to eat or drink, there was no time, and they could go anywhere they wanted in the Great Emperor's domain within seconds. They could travel faster than light. They could do anything they wanted.

At that time Draygon was one of the most powerful

beings in the Great Emperor's court. He served directly under the Great Emperor and his son. He had power, wealth, and beauty. So much beauty that nothing in eternity could compare. But for some reason, this wasn't enough for him. As incredible as this place was, he found something wrong with it. His problem was that everyone served the Great Emperor and not him. He became power hungry. He decided that it wasn't enough to be just under the Great Emperor; he wanted to be the new ruler of all creation. So he set about quietly gathering followers. He started casually, subtly bringing up questions regarding the fairness of the Great Emperor and placing doubt in the minds of all his followers. He didn't say too much at first, just enough to make them wonder what he was talking about. In the beginning, nobody knew what to think. These people had served under him for millions of years (as far as they knew because there was no time), and they had never seen a rebellion before. They didn't even know what one was. They'd never even heard the word 'rebellion' before, nor had they ever questioned the Great Emperor before. This was all so new to them. But slowly, over time, and then more quickly as the problem began to escalate, there came a division in the Great Emperor's kingdom, and the problem grew steadily worse. There was arguing and bickering, and contention broke out as these beings began to fight with each other. Draygon had succeeded in starting a conspiracy in the Great Emperor's kingdom, a rebellion that he actually thought he could win. Because he was fair, the Great Emperor allowed him to get away with this. He had based his kingdom on justice and fairness, and he wanted everyone that served him to do so because they loved him, and not for any other reason. So, he let the problem go on.

Soon things got so bad that there obviously wasn't enough room in the Great Emperor's kingdom for both Draygon and his followers, and the Great Emperor and his followers. Something had to be done. So they went to battle and the Great Emperor threw Draygon out of his kingdom. The battle was intensely fierce, but Draygon did lose. He and all his cohorts were cast out of the Great Emperor's domain and into the darkness.

Looking for a place to rule, they came here, to the Darklands. Only they weren't called the Darklands then. It was a beautiful planet, and the Great Emperor had given it as a gift to one man. He had total dominion over all creation, over everything that lived on the planet. But along with giving this man the planet, he also gave him a choice. A choice as to who he would follow. Now that Draygon had rebelled, the Great Emperor provided for this man a choice to disobey him and join Draygon. It wasn't an easy choice, as this man had only one place on the entire planet that he could not go. That was it. As long as he obeyed those simple instructions, everything would be okay.

But the man went into the forbidden place. It was there that he met Draygon, and Draygon deceived him, and he sold the planet outright to Draygon. That's why he's here. Not that he has any rightful claim on the planet, but that he tricked a man to get it. As a result, the planet was isolated from the rest of the Great Emperor's domain, and Draygon was given a place to rule. That's how we became the Darklands. At one time we used to be a planet of light, like everything else in the Great Emperor's dominion, but Draygon put us in darkness. Now we are the Darklands. What this man really did was sell himself and his descendants to Draygon and to Draygon's form of government. That meant that Draygon had a claim on him, and us, and that nobody, not even the Great Emperor, could help him. Because of the Great Emperor's fairness, and justness, he could not reverse what had been done. The man had sentenced him and all his descendants to die under the cruel reign of Draygon.

But the Great Emperor did not want us destroyed, so he worked out a plan. According to the laws of fairness and justice, there was one way to turn things around and to stake a claim on these people, and quite literally, buy them back. The laws of fairness and justice said that for crimes such as this, the perpetrator must die. Draygon had introduced death into the Great Emperor's domain, so someone else must die to reverse the pattern. An innocent person had to die for the guilty. So to claim back the planet, he initiated the Fountain of Blood. He knew that one of us could never reach the standards of fairness and justice, so he and his son worked something out. His son would take our place, and he would die. And since blood is the essence of life, then by losing that blood, and spilling it out upon the ground, he would essentially pay for the right to intervene in our lives, give us hope, and rescue us from Draygon, relinquishing Draygon's claim on us."

Rusty thought about the story he had just told. "Such an insignificant little planet in the Great Emperor's domain, yet for some reason he and his son were willing to go to great lengths to save it."

Wildy looked up at Rusty. "The Warrior," he said, suddenly realizing who Rusty was talking about.

Rusty nodded.

That would explain why he threw that blood on Draygon back in the city when he mentioned the Fountain of Blood. He was staking his claim on Wildy, and Wildy didn't even know it. This thought almost completely threw Wildy out of the bowl. *How could he love that much?*

Looking down at the body, this was the first time Rusty had ever seen what kind of love it took to do what the Prince of Light had done.

The wind had begun to pick up, and as much as they wanted to stay, the boys decided that it might be a good idea to get down off the mountain, knowing how mountain storms could be. Slowly they climbed out of the fountain and crossed the stone floor back over to the path. There was no forcefield holding them in anymore, and they could leave easily. Once outside of the warmth of the blood, the cold air hit them like an iceberg.

The mood was heavy and sad as they descended the mountain, a completely different mood from the one going up. There was no sensation of fear and terror now, only a sadness and a heaviness that seemed to leave an ache in the heart that nobody could explain away. A pain that went beyond tears and seemed almost so heavy that the boys could hardly walk.

The clouds had broken up, and the moonlight lit the way down the mountain so that the pathway could be seen clearly now. The wind didn't seem to be reaching this side of the mountain, but it was still very cold, and even though it was downhill, the going was difficult. With the chill in the air, the heaviness of their hearts, and their clothes still soaked in the Warrior's blood, it seemed almost harder going down than it had going up.

As they neared the bottom, it slowly began to warm up, but the boys hardly noticed it, they were so wrapped up in their own private thoughts.

When they were close to the foot of the mountain, they passed a man in a cape, sitting on a rock with a hood drawn over his head in such a way that his face could not be seen. The boys would have passed him without even noticing, but he spoke to them.

"You are strangers here?" he noted, and his voice startled the boys out of their thoughts of grief. "Looking for someone?" he asked again once they were focused.

"We found him," Rusty responded politely.

He didn't want to talk; he just wanted to be left to himself. Talking seemed like so much work right now, and it required too much energy. Energy that he didn't really have, or want to extend. But on the other hand, he didn't want to be rude either.

"Then why is he not with you?" the stranger persisted.

This frustrated Rusty a little. He didn't want the guy to start asking a lot of questions. He didn't want to talk to anyone, and he especially didn't want to answer any questions about the Prince of Light. He simply wanted to bury himself away in his own private thoughts and walk in silence, mulling over his most recent events. But again, he tried not to be disrespectful.

"Please, sir," he said, "it's been a difficult day, and neither of us feel much like talking. Please understand."

"The one whom you seek is not as you suppose," the man said again after a long pause.

"What?" Rusty asked him. This time he was really frustrated. Couldn't this guy take a hint? Didn't he hear what Rusty had just said?

The stranger looked them both in the eyes. "Him whom you presume dead."

Wildy had run out of patience. He didn't know this stranger, but he was entirely too inquisitive, and Wildly, like Rusty, just wanted to be left alone. *And how did he know so much in the first place?* Wildy thought.

"Look," Wildly snapped. "I just saw him there. In his own blood. Whose blood do you think we have all over us?"

"Mine," the stranger said quietly.

Both boys froze in their tracks and stared at the stranger. Rusty had that feeling again. The one where the skin on his neck would start crawling over the skin on his head, all trying to get out of the way of something. He felt as if his hair must be going in about thirty directions now because of the way the skin crawled around on his head.

Slowly the stranger removed his hood, and at once, the boys recognized him.

Wildy fell on his knees, and Rusty threw himself on his face in front of the Warrior, screaming, "You're alive!"

The Warrior lifted Wildly to his feet.

"You have been washed in the Fountain of Blood and are cleansed," he said. "You are no longer the property of Draygon or the Darklands. You are free to choose your life. No longer will you be known as a murderer and a thief, but from now on you will be a son of the Great Emperor."

Then he squatted down and lifted Rusty to his feet, took his face in his hands, and looked him eye to eye.

"Now you have seen me, Rusty," he said gently. "You can look on my face. You will know me, and I will be known by you."

Rusty looked into those eyes. Those tender and compassionate eyes, which teemed with life and love and wisdom. Then the Warrior held his hand out to Rusty.

"This is my hand," he said. "My hand is the hand of strength, and it will save you. The hand of hope, and it will comfort you." Then he continued, "Look on my face. I do love you, and I will console you, and I will generously bestow my wisdom upon you. From now on you will no longer search for life, for you have found it. From now on you will search the depth of my father's kingdom, and you will find it."

Rusty wept again, and the Warrior held him.

"I have so many questions," Rusty sobbed.

"And in me you will find the answers," the Warrior told him. "But not all at once."

Then he reached behind him and pulled out a sword. A sword made not just of steel, but of steel and light. It glowed in its sheath and vibrated with some sort of electrical energy as the Warrior held it there. He pulled the sword out of its sheath and held it up in the air. The moonlight hit it and sent beams of light all over the countryside. He spoke to Wildly, and the expression on his face was very serious.

"This is your *new* weapon," he said. "You must learn to use it and rely on it at all times of conflict. Do not be found without it!"

The warning seemed very stern and very serious. He took the sword, put it back in its sheath, and handed it to Wildly. Wildly took the sheath and tied it around his waist. The Warrior then pulled out another sword just as beautiful and just as powerful and handed it to Rusty.

"Rusty," he said, "this is your first weapon. Do not be afraid, only believe. This sword will deliver you by my power. Use it. Do not be afraid. Know that I will never leave you or forsake you. I will be with you always. Fear not."

"I don't understand," Wildy asked. "What's this all about?"

"You have been washed in my blood," the Warrior said. "And therefore you have broken ties with Draygon and have become a child of the Great Emperor. We are at war with

Draygon, and you have become his enemies. Do not be found without your swords lest Draygon come and find you vulnerable."

Rusty asked, "So what are we to do from now on?"

"Go," the Warrior said. "Find all those who will join you, and wait for me. The swords are not for offensive use, they are to defend yourself. Do not start battles, but do not back down from them. Learn to use your weapons well."

"Wait for you to do what?" Rusty asked.

"To ride against my enemies," the Warrior said. Then he disappeared.

"He did it again!" Wildly shouted. "He just took off."

Rusty knew that he was in for the time of his life. Never before had anyone acted toward him as the Warrior had, and he felt that the Warrior had confidence in him—something that those at the fortress never showed toward him.

"His ways are so odd," Rusty mumbled to himself.

Suddenly they heard something growl behind them. This growl seem to belong to a large catlike animal, and it sent the hair on the back of their necks straight up in the air. They looked around, but could not see anything.

"He picked a fine time to leave," Wildly whispered.

Since the noise came from behind them, they decided to head straight forward, and that's the direction in which they ran.

9

Rhend threw the newspaper down on the cot and pounded on the walls of his jail cell. He was furious. Every page of the newspaper sang the praises of Mr. Myer. Somehow he had managed to find the funds to pull Darklands City out of its most calamitous crisis up to date. Due to Mr. Myer's diligence and perseverance, he found a way to return power to the city, which in turn meant that hospitals would be able to take care of the residents of Darklands City, schools and business would be opened again, and the economy would begin climbing. Somehow he found the money to repair the buildings and the city structures. The most incredible aspect of it all was that he mobilized the police force in such a way, that any form of rebellion within the city could be completely squelched. All in just over a week.

The newspaper article read almost like a fantasy novel, and Mr. Myer now had complete power over Darklands City. This meant that he owned the city and the city council. Nobody, or nothing, could stand in his way now.

Rhend looked around the room. It had been a week and a half since Mr. Myer had him thrown in there, and with his sudden success, Rhend knew that there was no chance of him getting out soon. He threw the paper down in a fit of rage, walked over to one of the walls, and kicked it out of frustration. He then grabbed the bars of his cell and screamed as loud as he could. He wanted to find a way to release all of the sudden anger, but there was no way that he could possibly vent the intense anger he was now feeling.

He grabbed one of his cellmates by the nape of the neck and threw him against the wall. The cellmate tried to stabilize himself, and in the process, accidentally slapped Rhend across the face. This angered Rhend even more, and he beat the man until he was bleeding. Three of the other cellmates stepped in to help their friend out, but only found themselves at the other end of Rhend's fury. One of them grabbed Rhend and threw him against the wall, while the other two held him there.

"Look," the cellmate said, "none of us did anything to you. I don't know what your problem is, but it isn't ours."

Rhend stared at him for a moment, and then spit on him. This angered the cellmate enough that, while the other two held him against the wall, he proceeded to punch Rhend repeatedly in the stomach and across the face.

"I don't know who you think you are on the outside," the cellmate screamed between punches, "but in here you're nothing! You're nobody!" And with that, he gave Rhend one good kick which knocked Rhend off his feet. Then the cellmate picked Rhend up by the nape of his neck and threw him back on his bed.

Rhend lay there in great pain, bruised and bleeding. Every movement brought him new sensations of pain, and every breath came in shallow spurts, so breathing became laborious.

As he lay there on his cot, he seethed inside with anger and plotted revenge. That's all he could think about the rest of the night.

Meanwhile, the four cellmates made their way to the other side of the cell where they talked in whispers. A guard came back to see what happened, but by the time he arrived, the fight was over, and everyone had gone on to their own side of the room. He looked around carefully, and then went back out of the room. Rhend watched him go, and then turned toward the wall and fell asleep.

Later that night Rhend was awakened by someone calling his name ever so silently and shaking him ever so slightly. Even though the movement was slight, it still sent waves of pain riveting through his body. He rolled over, ready to fight, but the voice stopped him.

"It's okay," the voice whispered.

Once Rhend's eyes adjusted to the dark, he could see the face behind the voice. It was Borgie, the Slasher's own right-hand man.

"Borgie?" Rhend questioned

"Yeah, it's me," Borgie responded.

"Where have you been? What's been going on? How did you get in here?"

"I'll tell you when we get out of here," Borgie whispered back.

They were just about to leave the cell when Rhend asked Borgie if he had brought a gun. Borgie had, so Rhend demanded to borrow it. Borgie didn't want to let him, because he was afraid the noise would tip off the police that they were breaking out, but Rhend insisted. So Borgie handed him the gun. Rhend took the gun and walked over to the sleeping cellmate who had earlier beat him. Rhend placed the gun in his mouth. This woke up the cellmate, and he looked up at Rhend. His first response was to jump up, but Rhend pushed the gun further into his mouth. So far, in fact, that the man gagged on the barrel. The cellmate laid his head back on the pillow and tried to act calm.

"Remember me?" Rhend whispered to him. "I'm the guy you thought you could push around." Then he spit in the cellmates face again. "What are you going to do now?"

The cellmate looked up at him and pleaded through the gun for Rhend to let him go. Rhend took some evil pleasure out of this and spit on him again.

"There's nothing you can do about it!" Rhend gloated as he drooled on the man. "No matter how you beg."

Borgie urged Rhend to hurry. Rhend looked down again at his cellmate, who had started crying.

"Ooh, I love to see a grown man cry!" Rhend gloated again. Then he pulled the trigger.

The sound of the gun going off woke up everyone else in the cell. They all jumped up and saw their friend dead, then they backed against the wall, trying to get away from Rhend. Rhend wanted to shoot them, but the gun blast had now alerted everyone in the building of something gone wrong, and Borgie was pushing him to leave. Rhend took a couple of wild shots into the air, and they ran out of the building, shooting anyone who got in the way. By the time they were out of the building, seven people were dead. Including Rhend's cellmate.

Once out of the jail, they ran off into the city to the hideout of the last remaining members of both Slasher's and Wildy's gang. Compared to the numbers that used to be in these groups, there were only a relative few of them left. Rhend looked around the room. He recognized some of the members of Wildy's gang.

"What's going on?" he asked.

Borgie explained to him that they had banded together the night of the battle on the streets to try to protect themselves from the creatures that ran throughout the city. They told Rhend about the night of the battle. The battle intended to be fought between two rival gangs, but was crashed by an unexpected army. They told him about the creatures, and how they came out of nowhere, killing everything in sight. Once these creatures had gone, they had so many other obstacles to face now that they had been fragmented; they stayed together to try to save themselves. After the devastation on the streets, they had to stick together to keep at least one of the groups alive. And Borgie had become the new leader.

After they were through telling their story, Rhend sat still as could be and said nothing. After a few moments of silence, he aimed his gun and shot one of the members of Wildy's gang. Everybody else screamed and hit the floor. Then he targeted another one of Wildy's group and shot him as well. Borgie ran to Rhend and grabbed his hands and someone else took the gun away from him. Then they held Rhend still.

Rhend screamed and cursed, trying to break free. "What are you trying to do?" he screamed. These are our enemies! Have you gone crazy?"

"We can't shoot them," Borgie screamed back at him.

"Why not?" Rhend asked.

"Because we were told not to," Borgie said.

"Who's the idiot that told you that?" Rhend screamed.

"That idiot would be me," came a voice from across the room, somewhere in the corner.

When they heard that voice, everybody suddenly cleared away from Rhend and made a pathway for the man to approach.

"I didn't know you were here," Borgie whispered. "I'm sorry. He just went crazy."

The man looked at Borgie. "You won't be held accountable for a man like Rhend."

"Thank you, sir," Borgie sighed, moving away from the man.

The man approached Rhend and stared at him for the longest time. Rhend, not wanting to be outdone, continued staring back at him. But eventually he had to break eye contact.

"And don't forget that you broke eye contact first," the man said.

"Who are you?" Rhend asked. He was angry that any man would be able to stare him down, and he resented the power that this man had over Borgie and all the others. These were people that he had working for him, therefore he should be the man they feared.

"We're not in competition," the man said, almost as if he could read Rhend's thoughts. "I am superior to you. I am *your* leader, and you will remember that."

That statement really angered Rhend. How dare anyone call themselves superior to him? Rhend lunged at the man in anger, but was immediately thrown against the wall. He looked around to see what threw him, but he couldn't see anything. He didn't know how this could happen, as the man was several feet away and everyone else in the room had cleared the area that this stranger was in. The pain Rhend felt earlier had suddenly doubled in intensity from just a few hours ago.

"Remember that pain," the man said again, "because whatever those men did to you in jail is nothing compared to what I'm going to do to you."

"How do you know about that?" Rhend asked.

The man said nothing, but only looked at Rhend.

"You have no right treating me like this in front of my people," Rhend spat at the man.

"They are no longer your people," the man retorted. "They belong to somebody else."

Rhend looked around the room. Nobody was disputing the man. They had all come together—two groups of people who hated each other enough to die trying to kill each other, and who, only a few days ago, had tried just that. Then he looked at the man who seemed to have brought these two groups of people together. The man with so much power. He asked, "Who are you?"

"My name is Max, and that's all you need to know." He approached Rhend even closer. "I sent Borgie to get you out of jail."

"Why?"

"Because we want Wildy."

"How do you know he's still alive?" Rhend asked, but the

man said nothing. His eyes did communicate that he knew something.

"I can't believe it!" Rhend shouted, slamming his fists against the wall. He wanted Wildy dead more than anyone in the Darklands, and the idea that Wildy was still alive really frustrated him.

"But why me?"

"Because you want him dead more than we do," Max answered.

"And who is *we*?" Rhend asked again; and again, Max said nothing.

"And another thing," Max said. "We know how badly you want to take revenge on Mr. Myer. He's off limits to you. You cannot kill him."

That statement really angered Rhend. He pinned a lot of hopes on just that notion, and now he was told that he could not. Max could see how badly Rhend wanted to diffute the new rule, but Max would not change his word. He did, however, have some good news.

"We have reinstated you onto the city council, but you must remember that any misbehavior on your part will result in immediate termination—of your position, and possibly, your life."

"Is that a threat?" Rhend spat.

"Take it however you like," Max responded. "Take it as a threat, or a promise, or just the result of wrongful negligence." Then he turned and left the room. Everyone sat there in silence, including Rhend.

After a few moments, he looked over at Borgie and glared.

"You betrayed me," he said.

Borgie was notably nervous, but he said nothing. He looked back around the room.

"Come on," he said to the others. "We got work to do."

10

Unseen by any human eye, a red horse rode across the sky and in a complete orbit around the planet Darklands. The horse's hooves sounded like thunder in the clouds as they passed overhead, but nobody from the planet saw him. The rider of the horse carried a silver sword, which he swung several times around his head. He then hurled it down toward the ground. The sword moved so fast that it created a powerful wind in its wake which spread wider and wider and roared over the hills and valleys, reaching the four corners of the Darklands. Just before the sword hit the ground, it swerved and ran parallel to the planet, running in a complete circle of the globe, sailing over land and sea, mountain and valley.

As it flew over the sea, the force of the wind behind it created a wake in the water so powerful that the water literally split behind it and shot up in a twenty-foot wall of water on either side of the sword and followed it to the banks of the shore. When the water hit the shore, it was moving so fast that it went several miles inland before it ran out of power and lashed out on the land like a combination of tidal wave and cloudburst. It was like the ocean simply fell out of the sky onto the ground below, flooding and destroying and sweeping away everything in its path.

As it sailed across the land, it created tornadoes and violent winds which catapulted everything in its wake away from it, and threw it up and out into the sky where it dangled defenselessly until it hit the ground.

Once it had finished its orbit, the sword shot back into the air and returned to its owner. The rider of the horse had the power to take peace from man, and in its place, to give men the power to slay each other. When the sword returned to him, his work was done, and the sword carried with it peace and left behind violence and war. Then he and the horse thundered back into the sky and beyond the solar system.

At each of the four corners of the Darklands, one of four beings stood, each one massive in stature and in build. They had powerful arms and legs, and their hair was long and disheveled as they were the beings whose job it was to hold back the winds of extreme trouble and turmoil from the Darklands. They fought day and night with the winds and had done so for thousands of years. They were neither male nor female, and there was no distinction between the four of them. They all looked exactly the same.

They saw the rider and the red horse, and the sword as it hurled through the air. When the wake from the force of the sword hit them, it hit them so hard that they immediately released the winds that they had battled with these many years. The winds screamed and wailed, elated to be finally free. They hurled themselves at one another with such a devastating force that when they touched each other, there was a crack, and the force of those winds coming together caused the entire planet to shake and rock nearly off its foundation.

11

Tye sat down at a patio table outside a little cafe. He sipped a nice cold glass of water and studied his surroundings. He was in a small village nestled deep in a valley. The mountains around them were very tall, reaching high up into the sky. Instead of gently sloping hills, the terrain around him was sheer and rugged. Giant cliff walls jutted around the parameters of the valley. Just a few feet from his table, a river ran through the village and downstream toward the two cliffs. The cliffs formed a narrow outlet where the mountains allowed just enough space for the river to pass through, as well as a small path that travelers could use to enter or leave the valley. This path around the river and one other way over one of the treacherous mountain paths were the only ways into and out of the village. It was for this reason that there were not many visitors in the quiet little town called Volkstag.

Tye spotted a newspaper on an empty table just a few feet away, so he picked it up and took it back with him to his table. It had been several weeks since he left Darklands City, and he was incredibly curious as to how the events there were transpiring. He had also hoped that there would be some explanation of the massive earthquake, the windstorm, and the other strange events. He was alone when they happened, and they had terrified him so much so that he couldn't move for several days.

The paper he had picked up was a couple of days old, because news and events in the Darklands were slow in reaching Volkstag. The front page continued to read about the near devastation of Darklands City several weeks ago, and for the first time, Tye was given some information of what had happened that night. He was able to read the details and understand that it was all about the gang war and the fight for turf. He didn't see any mention of the strange creatures, but then he didn't really expect to. That was not the sort of thing a respectable newspaper would print. Which was odd, because it was these creatures that did most of the tremendous damage to Darklands City.

Reading about that night also brought back a flood of emotion for Tye—emotion that his journey thus far had kept him preoccupied enough not to feel. He started to experience again the pain of losing his father.

Seeing the story all laid out in the papers like this also brought back a collage of pictures, and each one of those pictures carried with it some horrible emotion of the night that he nearly lost his life—the night that he found his father butchered in his own bed. Tye fought back the tears, not wanting to cry in public. To avoid this emotion, he thrust himself full force into his reading.

All the damage ended up being blamed on Wildy and the Slasher. The paper pointed out that the Slasher was dead, but that it was believed that Wildy might have survived, and that he might still be at large and regrouping his forces. The news was that Darklands City officials had recovered Slasher's body, but since they could not yet find Wildy's, they had to treat the situation as if Wildy were alive and possibly planning another attack on Darklands City like never before.

The news frustrated Tye. He had hoped against hope all through his trip that Wildy's body would be the one recovered. Of all people to die in this massacre, Wildy was the one who deserved it most. It was good that Slasher died, but why not Wildy? Then Tye thought it might have been possible that perhaps Wildy could have died, and his body simply hadn't been recovered yet, or that Wildy might have been killed by someone else trying to escape. And if that didn't happen, perhaps he would be hunted down and killed for the bounty, which the paper said had been set at an extremely high price. Regardless of what might happen, until Wildy's body was actually found, Tye could not be at ease.

He hated Wildy.

Further on in the newspaper story, Tye read about the massive power outages, about the crowding of the hospitals and shelters, and how many people had been turned away from them because of the lack of room, facilities, and ample help. He also read that the death toll was so high, that they couldn't even keep count anymore. He read about Darklands City's near bankruptcy, their lack of supplies, and their starving residents. Of course the officials of the city held to the notion that they had everything in control, and that things weren't as bad as they seemed. But the papers said nothing of the earthquake and the windstorms.

Then he turned the page and saw a picture of Mr. Myer, and Max shaking hands. The caption above the picture read "Mayor Myer finds a solution to Darklands' Problems." When Tye saw the picture, goose bumps the side of golf balls suddenly popped out all over his skin. Something about this whole set-up caused him extreme anguish, but he couldn't figure out what.

He became so caught up in reading that, at first, he didn't notice the elderly lady at the other table staring at him.

Eventually, though, he began to sense the eyes, and he glanced up and looked around. When he looked up, the lady who had been staring suddenly looked away. Tye tried to play it cool and pretend he didn't notice, but he kept catching glances out of the corner of his eye of her looking at him. He would look over occasionally to see if she was still staring, and sure enough, she would be. But any time she thought Tye might be looking back at her, she would quickly turn away. This was making Tye more and more self-conscious by the minute.

He had been out of the city for many days and had survived by living off the land. (He was used to this, because he and his father would go hunting and camping many times when he was a young boy, long before they got trapped in Darklands City.) He had been away from civilization for a long time, just he and the wilderness. He had followed the river, and it led he to this village. He caught his food from the river, he drank from the river, he bathed in the river, and he camped near the river. So he suspected that the only reason this lady could be staring at him would be that he looked a little ragged, or that he was a stranger in this little town. The signs were evident that his clothes were not holding up so well under the strain of the life he'd been living recently, and he hadn't shaved in a long time—he probably looked a little unkempt. But whatever her reasons for staring, Tye was getting tired of it.

Soon the lady worked up the courage to approach him. She pointed to the seat across from him.

"Do you mind if I sit here?" she asked.

At first Tye was hesitant, but he agreed. She sat down and looked at him for another minute.

"You're from the city, aren't you...Darklands City?"

Tye was a little stunned. *How did she know that?* Was it something about the way he was dressed? Or did most strangers come from Darklands City?

"I'm sorry to be staring, I'm not usually like this." She extended her hand to shake his. Tye shook it. "My name is

Anna," she said. She looked at him as if she didn't know if she should go on, but decided she had better. "I'm a prophetess."

Tye gave her a peculiar look. He had met several people like that in the city—people standing on street corners, screaming to all passersby that the world was going to end, that their doom was certain and that they were all helplessly lost. Tye didn't like these people, so he became very tense at Anna's announcement.

Anna must have sensed the tension because she quickly clarified her statement.

"I know what you're thinking," she said. "You're thinking of those lunatics that stand on street corners and scream and accuse and verbally abuse passersby. But that's not a real prophet. That's some maniac with an ego problem. These people don't realize that a true prophet is *slow* to speak, *quick* to listen, and slow to get angry."

This was something Tye had never heard before. Especially from someone who called themselves a prophet or a prophetess. It was very refreshing, and Tye started to warm up to Anna.

"Did you meet someone in the city?" Anna suddenly blurted out.

Her question caught him off guard.

"Someone that gave you a gift," she went on. "A very precious gift. And along with that gift, a call, to a certain task...but as of yet you're not quite sure you know what that task is?"

Tye's head was reeling. What else did she know? Who was she really, and what was she up to? Tye didn't like anyone knowing that much about him, especially someone he didn't know well.

Anna looked into his eyes.

"I sense much sorrow in your eyes," she said softly. "Much sorrow and much bitterness. You are churning with emotions. Deep emotions that seem to keep you uneasy inside."

"Stop it!" Tye yelled. "I don't know who you are, but you

can just take a table someplace else. I would like some peace and quiet if you don't mind."

"I'm sorry," Anna apologized as her eyes filled with tears.

Tye responded as almost any guy would at seeing a woman cry. He quietly apologized to her. He really was sorry that he had blown up at her, and he was really sorry that he made her cry. He never intended to hurt her; it had been a natural reaction to her getting so personal.

Anna cried quietly to herself so as not to offend or hurt Tye. She looked carefully at him and said one more thing.

"I'll go. I'm really sorry. I did not mean to cause you more pain. It's just that when you sat down, I instantly felt in my own body all these emotions, and images began to come to me, images of horrible creatures, frightening to the very core of my being. Images of a gentle stranger, images of you talking to someone. Someone that became very precious to you the instant you met him, but as of yet, someone that you do not really know. I also saw someone hurting you, and I saw something else that I can't make out. It seems to be you. Many years ago. There's someone else with you, a young girl. She is screaming with fear. Then she's being dragged away by someone or something. That's why I asked all these questions. I wanted to check this all out to see if it was me, or if these emotions were coming from you, and that there was a reason that you were here. A reason for which I suspect is of the utmost urgency. Even though at the moment I don't think you realize the nature of your calling."

"Who are you?" Tye asked quietly, fighting hard to hold back another sudden surge of emotion and a reservoir of tears that felt as if they were pushing at his eyes trying hard to find an escape route.

"I am Anna," she said, and gently reached across the table and took his hand to comfort him. "A prophetess... I sense a lot of activity around you. A lot of supernatural activity. You have some very powerful forces at work in your life. Forces that can neither be seen nor heard by the human eye and ear, but that are very much real nonetheless."

Suddenly Tye lost control and began to sob uncontrollably. Anna took his hand and they walked down by the river where they could have a little more privacy. Tye told Anna all that happened in Darklands City, and how he wound up in Volkstag, in the middle of what seemed like nowhere. He told her of his father's massacre, and of his hatred toward these street gangs, and especially toward the two major gang leaders. And at the top of his list, he hated Wildy.

Many years ago Tye met Wildy face to face. When he was a young teenager. He was probably the only person to do so and live. He and his sister were walking home from school one day and they saw Wildy and his gang approaching them. Tye and his sister tried to run away, but Wildy and his gang ran them down, beat Tye almost to death, and kidnapped his sister. Tye never saw her again, but he could guess what might have happened to her. Many nights he would lay in bed, and his imagination would run away with horror stories of what they might have done. Night after night, nightmare after nightmare, he could almost see her face, and sometimes in his dreams he would hear her screaming. He could never forget that day. These pictures terrified him, and the nightmares woke him up frequently during the night.

Tye's confessions shocked him. He had never talked about the incident for many years, and he had all but forgotten it. He buried it deep, trying to get away from it, but here he was spilling his insides about this whole incident to some total stranger.

He told Anna about him and his family moving to Darklands City when he was very young because his father was seduced by the idea of a better life in the city. Once they got there, his father invested everything they had into a little store, hoping that it would be a profitable business. Instead, they were constantly robbed and looted. Most of these burglaries were being done by Wildy's gang and the Slasher and his gang. Tye was one of the few in Darklands City to see Wildy's face and live. He had seen it a few times, and he never understood why Wildy didn't kill him, but for some reason he didn't. The one thing that Tye remembered most about Wildy was his eyes. He could never forget the hate and the coldness in Wildy's eyes. Most of all, he could not get over the way Wildy glared at him the day he stole Tye's sister.

Once inside the city, Tye and his family were all trapped because they had no money to leave. They had to live up above the store. Soon life in the city began to get worse and worse. Financially the city went further and further into debt, taking with it most of the residents of the city as well. Tye's family was among those people affected. As things went downhill economically, the streets became more and more unsanitary. Tye's mom took ill one day, and because they didn't have the money for treatment, she soon died. She had eaten something that had been contaminated, and before the rest of the family could do anything to help her, she was dead. Tye was a little boy at the time, but that was another incident he could never forget.

First his mom died, a few years later his sister was stolen away, and the latest in his story of tragedy was that his father was massacred the night of the Darklands City war.

When he talked about Wildy, Tye's voice became hard and cold and bitter. It was easy to see why he hated Wildy, and the more he relived his past experiences, the stronger that hatred grew. He hated Wildy more than any other human being alive.

Anna took his hand. "There is much pain inside of you," she said. Then she stood in silence for many minutes, allowing Tye to work through the emotion that had suddenly surfaced. Shortly, though, she sensed he was ready, and she asked again. "What of the stranger? What did he say to you?"

"I don't know who this person is," Tye confessed. "Only that I was killed...or I thought I was killed. I really don't know. I know that sounds odd to you, but my throat was cut, and I bled and bled. I couldn't move, I had lost so much blood. I'm sure I had to have been dead. Or at least really close to it. But the stranger said that I had been saved. And somehow I knew that he had the power to do that. I knew that he was no ordinary person just by his appearance. And when he talked to me, his voice seemed to come from inside of me and all around me. Then, when he was done talking, he just disappeared."

That's when Anna told him about the Prince of Light, and of the battle between him, the Prince of Light, and Draygon. She told him how that the prophecies, as she understood them, seemed rapidly to be coming to pass. She told him that she believed that the stranger was the Prince of Light, and that Tye had been given a high calling by the prince, and that he had been led to the little village of Volkstag.

"But why?" Tye asked.

"I'm not sure," Anna said, "but I think we can find out."

They talked long into the night, and when they were done, Anna offered Tye a place to stay. She had a small guest house in the back of her home, and she offered it to Tye for as long as he needed.

"It's no accident that you're here," she told him. "I think that possibly the Prince of Light has brought us together for some reason. That's why he let me in on your pain, and he allowed me to experience your hidden emotions."

Throughout the days that followed, Tye worked for Anna. He took care of household chores, mended broken windows and doors, and helped Anna get back on her feet. She was an old woman and was not able to do many things. Tye's presence in her house turned out to be advantageous for her.

Tye also took an acute interest in Anna's knowledge of the Prince of Light, the Great Emperor, and the history of the Darklands. He would spend hours listening to her, going over the holy writings with her and learning from her. He struggled intently to understand her and attain her wisdom.

12

Rusty and Wildly finally slowed down enough to catch their breath. They were both worn out and exhausted from hours of intermittent running and hard walking. Whatever it was that they had heard near the Fountain of Blood seemed to stay right on their trail, despite all their efforts to outmaneuver it.

The sun had just come up over the mountains and was generously beginning to distribute its warmth and light over the countryside when the boys reached a little wooded area. Rusty sat down on a stone, took off his shoes, and rubbed his feet while Wildy walked around the area, cautiously looking around. He still suspected that something was just behind them in the bushes. Rusty thought to himself, *We must have walked about a hundred miles last night; that is, after we quit running that hundred miles.*

Wildy was puzzled as he looked into the bushes. "I tried to shake that thing; I tried every trick I know, but it stayed right on our tail."

Rusty swallowed hard. "Did you shake it?" he asked. "Please tell me we managed to shake it."

"I'm not sure," Wildy answered. "In the city I could lose anything, but this thing is something else. No matter what I did, I just couldn't lose it."

They sat there quietly for a long time, not knowing what else to do. Nothing moved for about an hour, so they decided that whatever it was might have given up on them or left to get some rest itself.

The small clearing they were in turned out to be a meadow with a river running through it. Hot and sweaty, and still caked in blood, the boys decided they could jump into the river for a quick bath. The water and sunshine felt good, and when Rusty thought about the last night in these surroundings, he couldn't help but wonder how he could have gotten so scared on that mountain. The things of the last night seemed so far away from him now. They took turns standing guard. Rusty took guard while Wildy bathed, and when he was done, Wildy kept guard. Rusty found it a little hard getting the blood out of his clothes, and it had been on his skin so long that it almost didn't come off.

"I can't get this blood off," he told Wildy.

"It'll come off," Wildy told him. "Sooner or later."

"How do you know that?" Rusty asked him.

"I've had a lot of people's blood on me. I used to be in a gang, you know."

"Have you killed a lot of people?" Rusty asked him.

"A few," Wildy answered.

Rusty swallowed hard. He was just getting to know this person and wasn't sure he liked hearing that Wildy had killed people.

Then Wildy told Rusty of some of his exploits in the city, and what it was like to be one of the most hated and feared gangs in the area. Rusty was impressed and wondered how anyone could kill another human being. He wondered, *What would it take?* and *What it would be like to kill somebody?* But as they were talking, Wildy thought he heard something in the bushes.

"That thing's never going to go away" Rusty complained. "Just let it eat us."

Wildy suddenly disappeared into the bushes. The sudden movement frightened Rusty, and he jumped out of the water and threw his pants on. He called after Wildy in loud whispers and looked around frantically, trying to figure out where he had gone to, but Wildy didn't answer. Rusty didn't know whether to run or stay put.

Soon enough Wildy did come out of the bushes holding another boy around the neck, with a switchblade at his throat. The boy's name was Michael, and he looked about the same age as Wildy and Rusty. At the moment, though, Michael didn't look real good. He looked like someone who had seen some very rough times.

"I found this guy lurking in the bushes," Wildy said, throwing him to the ground.

Michael looked around. "I just had to make sure it was you," he said, getting back up.

"What are you doing here, Michael?" Rusty asked him.

Wildy got a little confused. "You two know each other?" he asked.

"I didn't know where else to go, Rusty," Michael said. "I saw you two walking, so I decided to follow you."

"That's a great way to get yourself killed!" Wildy said, and he grabbed Michael by his shirt front.

"I didn't know what else to do," Michael said. "I've been scared. Everywhere I go, I hear them. I hear them following me, I see them at night, stalking me. I just know they're going to catch me. Last night I tried all night to get away from them, but no matter where I went, they were right behind me."

"Who's behind you?" Wildy asked, letting go of Michael. "What's going on?"

Michael looked at Wildy.

"Remember back at the fortress when I was standing in front of the stained glass window, and you threw me out of it?"

"That was you?" Wildy asked.

"When I fell out the window," he said, "I heard a shot and ducked. Something hit me on the head and I must have been knocked out, because when I came to, I was at the bottom of the hill, just lying there on the ground. I saw something like an army walking up the path to the fortress. As soon as I saw them, I felt large hands grab my feet and pull me into the bushes. I tried to fight them; I grabbed at them, but there was nothing there. I clawed at everything I could grab hold of, hoping that it would hold me back, but they were stronger than I was, and they pulled me in like I was nothing. As soon as I was in the bushes, the hands let go of my feet. I laid there for a minute, and then I felt a heaviness on my chest. I tried to move but I was paralyzed. I tried to scream out for help, but I couldn't yell. Something had a hold of my tongue and I couldn't make a sound.

"I don't know how long I was like that, but it seemed like hours. Eventually, I felt the handlike thing come off my body, and the pressure released. I could move then, but I was too afraid to. So I laid there for a while longer. Then I couldn't move because of the fright, so I waited some more. I figured I would stay there until morning, when I heard something move behind me, so I got up and ran as fast as I could back to the fortress."

Michael bit his lower lip, and tears began to moisten his eyes.

"When I got there..." The memories of that night began to flood over him, and he was unable to stop his tears. "I've been so busy trying to get away from those things, I'd forgotten how much this hurt."

Michael's behavior caused Rusty to get concerned.

"What happened, Michael?" he asked. "What happened at the fortress?"

Michael went on. "When I got to the fortress, I found..." He paused, bit his lip, and finally blurted out, "Dead."

A strange sensation hit everyone in the group. Wildy felt like he had just been slugged in the stomach.

"Dead?" he asked.

"They'd all been slaughtered," Michael said. "In the most hideous way imaginable. When I went in I saw all of those people laying there. Twisted and mangled, hardly even recognizable. The place stank of blood, and of other smells that I couldn't place. When I saw all those bodies, I ran. I didn't know where I was running to, but I ran. I thought they were after me because something's been following me for two or three days. No matter where I go, this presence has been behind me. That's how I ran into you."

"Something's been following us too," Wildy said.

Rusty walked toward some reeds near the river and stared into the water. Then he looked back at Michael.

"My family?" he asked.

"Everyone."

Rusty felt like every bit of life had been instantly sucked out him, like every ounce of strength had been drained out of every muscle in his entire body. He couldn't stand up anymore. His body seemed to almost float down to the ground as he collapsed into a pile there. He sat there staring into the water, almost as if he wasn't even there. For the first couple of minutes, he couldn't even cry.

"I left without really saying a word to anyone," he said to no one in particular. "I was so excited about seeing the Prince of Light that I didn't even think about saying goodbye to my family. I didn't get to say goodbye…ever." He buried his head in his hands and wept bitterly.

For several moments nobody said anything. Wildy walked around the outside of the clearing, trying to make sense out of what was happening. He didn't understand. Why would the Warrior allow this to happen? Was this what he meant when he said that they were at war? What happened, and how were they supposed to respond?

"Don't you care at all for anyone?" Wildy whispered up toward the sky where he thought the Warrior might be.

Michael was the one who seemed to be able to put it all into words. "I don't understand," he said. "Everything was normal a few days ago. I was talking to them. I never thought this could happen. They always told us we were strong and could never be penetrated by an enemy... I wonder who could have done this..."

"It had to be Draygon," Wildy said, more as an afterthought than anything else.

Michael walked over to Wildy. "It couldn't have!" he said strongly. "The Prince of Light would never allow him to do anything like that. Never!" He looked over at Rusty. "Right Rusty?"

For a moment Rusty said nothing, but then added quietly, "It had to be him."

"No!" Michael screamed. "We're followers of the Prince of Light. We're infallible, we're unshakable, we're strong, we are—"

"Idiots," Rusty broke in.

"What?" Michael screamed.

"It's a game, Michael," Rusty screamed back, standing up to face Michael. "We've been playing a game. We locked ourselves away from the rest of the world in some beat-up old fortress and we told ourselves we were safe because we were followers of the Prince of Light. We thought we could just throw around the name of the Prince of Light and get whatever we wanted. That just by the flip of our tongue and the drop of a name, we could take on any of our enemies. So we spent all our time making our fortress nicer and more exclusive. We added beautiful decorations and gave ourselves every luxury we could get hold of, but we forgot that there is no safe place from the Darklands and its problems. Nowhere. Not even in the Fortress of Light."

This wasn't easy for Michael to hear, and it made him very angry. "We are children of royalty!" he screamed.

"Then why didn't the Prince of Light come to us?" Rusty screamed back at him. "Why did he have to go to someone on the street? For godsake, Michael, we didn't even know his name when Wildy came looking for him... it was just a game to us."

"It wasn't a game," Michael said.

"Then what were you doing in front of the window?" Rusty asked him. "Seeing just how close to the outside you could get without getting hurt? We went to great lengths to avoid it, but we all got hurt."

Michael quieted down a little. "Why didn't he at least warn us?" he asked.

"Aren't you getting any of this, Michael?" Rusty was frustrated that Michael wasn't seeing what he was seeing, that Michael wasn't able to piece this thing together for himself. "Why do you think the Prince of Light sent Wildy to the fortress? If we had been paying attention, we'd have known that it meant something was happening. It was a sign. A sign that we passed right over in our stupidity. We were going to war. Where do you think Draygon's going to strike first? Who does Draygon hate the most? He hates the Prince of Light. So it only makes sense that he would get rid of all proclaimed followers of his right off the start. As for the Prince of Light, who do you think paralyzed you and dragged you into the bushes to save your life? I wouldn't be surprised if it wasn't the Prince of Light that's been chasing us all night, and that it was his way of getting us together, so that now we just happen to run into each other..." He looked helplessly toward the sky. "All I want to know is why couldn't he save my family?" He screamed out "Why them? Why?" Then he fell onto his knees and put his head on the ground and wept some more.

Michael went down on one knee and placed his hand gently on Rusty's shoulder. Then he put his head in his other hand and he wept also. They remained that way for several minutes.

"At least he's left us with each other," Michael said through the tears.

Wildy walked away from the rest of the group and looked out over the river. It seemed so quiet, so undisturbed, so untroubled by anything. It didn't seem bothered by the loss that the others had just discovered. He envied the river, wanting to be free just like that, if only for a while. Life had become so radical lately, and he wasn't sure he could take much more of it. He had gone through more in the past few weeks than in his whole life as a gang leader in the city.

"I don't know if you can hear me," he said quietly into the air, "but I just have to talk to you. It was you who chased me the night of my calling. It was you who saved me that night in the graveyard. You saved me from those dogs. You were that terrifying shadow that passed between me and them. You were behind me and Rusty getting together. You're the one who told me about the Fountain of Blood. You might even have been the little bird that sang me to sleep. All this time, I thought I was alone, that you had left me on my own. That you were just playing a game with me. Yet you were always somewhere, in ways I just never realized. I don't know what to say. Maybe you needed to do it like this. Maybe I wouldn't have followed you if you had done it any other way, but if you could please tell me how to make sense out of what's happening to me right now...I'm not used to feeling. Especially like this. I don't know what to do with all these emotions."

He stared into space. Nothing moved in the silence. Eventually he turned around, gathered some wood, built a fire, and caught some fish out of the river. After breakfast, Michael took a turn to bathe in the river.

They ate in silence during that meal. Nobody knew what to say. A lot of tears were shed by Rusty and Michael, and for the first time in his life, Wildy actually felt his heart go out to somebody. Wildy himself felt the sting and the pain of loss. These feelings were completely new to him, and he didn't know what to do with them. They made him uneasy, and he found it hard to sit still, so he took a walk.

On into the late morning, exhausted from running all night, and spent from mourning over the tragic news that had just reached them, they all fell into a deep sleep out in the sunshine.

13

The boys slept all day and long into the night. The fire burned out late in the afternoon, but nobody noticed. Later that night, about the middle of the night, as the moon was once again full and bright, something stirred in the bushes only a few yards from the campsite. Several people wearing long black robes, with hoods covering their faces, made their way past the boys to a ritual sight just a few yards past the campsite, completely unaware of the boys' presence.

Wildy woke up first and looked around. When he saw the procession of black-robed people, he quickly laid his head back down. He had no idea who these people were, whether they were friend or foe, but after all he had been through, he knew it wasn't a good idea to take any chances. Rusty heard the stirring and also looked up, but Wildy quickly grabbed his head and forced it back into the dirt. This, of course, didn't make Rusty very happy, but he didn't dare put up a fight. Once he quieted Rusty, Wildy reached over with his other hand and slammed Michael's head down on the ground just to play it safe.

Michael was not as accustomed to these strange occurrences as Rusty had become, so he put up a bit of a fight and almost gave them away. But Wildy continued to drive his head further into the ground, and Michael soon gave up simply because he couldn't take the pain.

Once they were quiet, they could hear the rustling of the bushes, and the sound of someone passing close by them. Even after the rustling had ended, none of them dared to move. They waited in the silence until they didn't hear anything for a while. Then Wildy carefully took his hands off the heads of the other two and got up on his hands and knees and looked around.

"Who do you think it is?" Rusty asked. "I mean, who do you think they're with?"

"I don't know," Wildy whispered, "but there's something going down. It can't be too good; it's not often that good things happen in the middle of the night...or in the middle of nowhere."

The three of them crawled to the edge of the clearing and looked into the bushes. Rusty fastened his sword and sheath around his waist. Although Wildy picked his up, he didn't put it on. Michael, of course, didn't have one, but he wouldn't have had an idea of what to do with one, anyway.

They spotted a small trail where the grass had been trampled down by several people walking over it, and they followed. It took them through the meadow and into the forest. Several yards into the forest, they came to a clearing where the trees had been cut down to form a perfect circle. The circle spanned only a few yards and looked like it could only contain about a hundred people. The boys walked around the outside of the circle until they came to a hill that overlooked the area below them. From there they could see a large altar in the middle of the circle, and on that altar large torches burned on every corner. The altar was made out of large stones stacked on top of each other, about seven feet long and four feet high.

Tied to the top of the altar was a young girl who appeared to be about the same age as the boys. She had been stripped of all her clothing, and she had no protection against the sharp stones under her back. She struggled with everything she had inside of her to break free, but she had been tied down so tightly that she could barely move, much less get away from them. All she succeeded in doing was ripping and shredding her back and the backs of her legs. As she struggled, she cut deeper into her flesh, and her blood soon trickled down the stones and down the side of the altar.

At the head of the altar stood what seemed to be the high priest. He wore a scarlet sash around his waist, and his hood was pulled back to reveal a massive scar across his forehead. In his right hand he held a dagger. The blade on this dagger was not straight like most daggers; instead it had many jagged edges and curves in it, apparently to cause great pain to its victim. He held the dagger high up in the air and danced and chanted around the altar.

A dimly lit fire burned a dark red in the middle of the coven, and a pentagram had been around it. There were also candles set up just about everywhere else in the coven, and small fires burned near the corners of the altar.

The fire illuminated the girl in such a way that the boys could see the terror and the pleading on her face. The light from the fire cast an eerie glow on her that sent pangs of fear and pain to the hearts of all three of the boys standing there.

They spoke in whispers, trying to understand what it was that was happening. Wildy had never before in his life seen anything like this, and Michael never paid attention to anything of real substance in the fortress, so he was about as ignorant as Wildy. Although he didn't know what was happening, Wildy was getting used to this feeling of fear that seemed to be surging through his body. It seemed almost a daily occurrence, but he still didn't like it. He remembered it on the streets of Darklands City, in the graveyard, near the Fountain of Blood, and the other night running from the presence behind him and Rusty. And now he had it again. What he hated most about this feeling of terror was that it was always followed by some horrific event or some terrible circumstance that would challenge the sanity of even the strongest human mind. So he braced himself, hoping to be ready for whatever might be coming.

Rusty immediately recognized what was going on, because of his reading and his studies in the Fortress of Light. He recognized that this girl was going to be a human blood sacrifice to Draygon, and he told the others this. "Draygon has a ferocious appetite for blood," he told them, "and these people offer living blood sacrifices in exchange for more of his power."

Wildy thought about the oddity of this. *He'll destroy them*, he thought. He asked Rusty about this.

"Eventually he will," Rusty said. "But for now these people help him do his destructive work."

"Then let's go," Wildy said.

"Go where?" Rusty asked.

"Let's go get the girl."

Rusty stood there for a moment. "Are you crazy?" he asked. "They'll kill us."

"What are you talking about?" Wildy asked. "He doesn't have as much power as the Warrior."

Rusty knew this to be true, but he also knew that, despite this fact, Draygon was still very powerful.

"We're working for the Warrior now," Wildy went on. "How can we lose?"

That's when Michael threw out another thought: "That's what they said back at the Fortress of Light."

Rusty walked a little way away from them.

Wildy gave Michael a couple of backhands on the chest. "Way to go!" he said. Then he crossed over to Rusty. "That girl down there is going to die," he said.

Rusty knew that, and he wanted more than anything to be able to help her, but he really was scared. He didn't dare admit this to Wildy, but he was. He had never had to fight anyone before, especially someone who worked that close to Draygon. He thought that the only reason Wildy must not be afraid was because he didn't know who Draygon was. But that was not true, and as soon as he thought about it, he dismissed it. Wildy did know who Draygon was, and Rusty knew that. But what he didn't know was whether he, Rusty, had what it took to be a follower of the Prince of Light, now that he saw what being a follower really entailed. He thought back to the Prince of Light's words back at the fountain. He had specifically told them not to start any battle. How were they going to reconcile that?

While he was locked away in these thoughts, a huge blast of smoke over the altar yanked him back to the situation at hand. He and Wildly and Michael watched these new events happen from their hideout up on the hill.

Out of the plume of smoke, a huge, hideous demon appeared. He loomed high above everyone else, suspended in the air above the altar. He looked around at everyone in the coven. The boys shrank down, fearing he might see them. They watched and listened intently, hardly daring to breath for fear that even the sound of their breath might give them away.

Finally the demon spoke.

"I bring a message from our feared and powerful leader, Draygon," he told them. "His archenemy, the one who now calls himself the Warrior (he said *the Warrior* with utter contempt and a sneer in his lips) is again in the Darklands. Do not fear; he has been defeated already. But he has turned loose certain renegades, certain vigilantes. These boys have become a nuisance to us, a thorn in our side, and they must be dealt with at all costs. But their bodies must be brought before Draygon. It would make an excellent sacrifice to your cruel and ruthless leader. The one who brings back their bodies will be generously rewarded."

Unobserved by anyone else, several fighters began to surround the parameters of the circle. These beings were huge. They had shoulders and arms and legs like that of lifetime body-builders. They stood at least eight feet tall, and some even taller than that. Their faces were strong and powerful, but cold as a stone, and they were painted with war paint. They were dressed in black, but their clothes were tight around them to allow maximum movement, and the material was of a strong, resistant fabric that was virtually unpierceable. They had the same swords that Wildy and Rusty had been given, but of a much larger version, one that would fit them and their size.

These warriors appeared around the outer parameters of the group, but they said and did nothing. They watched in total silence, standing so completely still that they looked just like the night. If someone were to look directly at one, they could easily mistake it as just a shadow in the darkness.

Meanwhile, the drama continued in the middle of the coven as one of the followers questioned the demon.

"Oh master," he said, "where will we find these boys?"

"Not far away," the demon spat. "You will find them just outside the coven. Bring them to me."

Wildy turned to Rusty.

"They know we're here," he said.

"Let's get out of here," Michael spoke as he turned to leave.

They turned around only to face another hideous demon.

"Hello, boys!" it sneered.

Several other demons joined in and began closing in on the boys, forcing them closer and closer to the center of the coven and to the altar. Rusty realized he no longer had a choice as to whether or not he would fight. If he wanted any kind of chance at all, he would fight.

Wildy pulled out his switchblade.

"I don't know about you guys," he said, "but I'm going to die fighting." He threw his sword on the ground to concentrate on his switchblade.

"Wildy, use your sword!" Rusty screamed at him.

"Nothing doing," Wildy screamed back. It was too big and awkward for him, and he was used to his switchblade.

He tried to fight the demon with the blade, but the demon grabbed the blade and threw it on the ground.

"Your weapons are worthless," the demon at the altar shouted out. Then he called out to the others. "Prepare them for sacrifice; Draygon will feast on blood tonight!"

Suddenly something came over Rusty, and he unsheathed his sword and held it high in the air. He shouted, "We stand here in the name of the Prince of Light, the mighty Warrior, the son of the Great Emperor who has conquered you and your master."

There was a rumble through the clearing, and a crack, and everyone fell back several paces. Human members of the coven began to vomit violently, and a strange blast of air swept through the crowd. To the boys it was sweet and refreshing, but to everyone else, it was nauseating.

As Rusty held the sword in the air, it suddenly seemed natural in his hands. But the swords in the hands of his opponents were just as natural, and they had much more experience with them than Rusty had.

As if by some signal, the warriors standing outside the coven unsheathed their swords and ran into the circle, screaming and fighting. Their style was fierce, and their skill was unmatched by anyone there, human and demon alike.

One of them moved in behind Rusty and grabbed his hand, and held it, and helped him fight. Although Rusty could feel the warrior's hand, he never really had time to turn around and look to see what it was that was moving his hand.

When the fighting broke out, Michael was completely unarmed. He was not given a sword like the other two. "What am I going to do?" he asked. "I don't have anything to fight with."

At that instant, one of the warriors deposited a sword in his hand.

"Whoa," he mumbled to himself.

He felt the blade of a sword slice him across the chest, and he would have been wounded worse, but another one of the warriors stepped in front of him. The blade hit the warrior on the second blow, and the warrior drew on the demon and sliced him into several parts. Michael just stared in disbelief. He did not see the warrior, but he did see the demon diced into so many parts.

The place was chaotic. Nobody knew what was going on. Swords and knifes were flying, and blood was spilling. Everything happened so fast that nobody had time to think about what to do next. Rusty lobbed off one man's head, and it fell to the ground. The body followed close behind. Then he attacked and went after one of the demons, who screamed and ran into the darkness.

When Wildy saw the kind of success Rusty was having with the sword, he reached for his also. One of the demons saw Wildy reaching for it, and he kicked it out of Wildy's way. One of the warriors grabbed the sword off the ground and threw it back at Wildy. After Wildy caught the sword, he looked around to see who had thrown it, but it was hard to see anything in all this chaos, and he couldn't spend a lot of time thinking about it.

The warriors went head to head with the demons, and the boys took on those from the coven. Soon the demons were running off in fear, and everyone in the coven was dead. Their bodies scattered on the ground. Nobody knew if anyone had escaped or not, but nobody there was alive. The warriors cleaned their swords and placed them back in their sheaths, then left the campsite unnoticed. One of the warriors placed a sword on the altar next to the girl and left also.

This was Rusty's first battle, and now he and Wildy had something in common. He looked at the bodies, and his stomach turned sick inside of him.

"I've never killed anyone before," he said.

"You get used to it after a while," Wildy told him.

"I don't want to get used to it," Rusty responded.

Rusty cut the girl loose from the altar, took one of the

robes off the bodies of one of the coven members, and covered her with it. When she was free, she took the robe and ran off into the woods away from them, and wept and wept. For a while nobody said anything to her. They just left her alone. But eventually, Rusty went to her.

He approached her cautiously, not wanting to alarm her. As he approached her, she looked up at him, and he could see fear in her face.

"Who are you?" she asked. "Please just let me go. I won't tell anyone, I promise." Rusty was moved by the tears running down her face.

"We're not going to hurt you," he told her. Then he started searching for a way to answer her question. He didn't know what to tell her that wouldn't frighten her much more than she already was. "We're with the Warrior," he continued, "and we just happened to be here when this whole thing happened. It was quite by accident."

The minute Rusty said Warrior, the girl jumped up and started backing away. Rusty searched for something else, something to comfort her.

"It's not what you think," he told her. "The Warrior doesn't want to hurt anyone. On the contrary, he wants to rescue the Darklands and restore them to his father."

"Who's his father?" the girl asked.

"His father is the Great Emperor, the ruler of the universe. The Warrior has another name—it's the Prince of Light."

When the girl heard the other name, the Prince of Light, her strength left her and she collapsed into a heap on the ground. Again she wept. This time her whole body shook so that she could hardly contain herself. Rusty went to her and placed a comforting hand on her shoulder.

"Oh, thank you, thank you," she cried.

"For what?" Rusty asked.

"For saving my life," the girl replied.

"That's okay," Rusty said and held her close. Then he picked her up off the ground and walked her back into camp. When they were back with the others, Rusty set her down on a rock and, with the help of Wildly and Michael, completely demolished the altar. Rusty noticed the sword on the altar and took it over to the girl.

"What's this?" she asked.

Rusty wiped his own sword off on the clothes of one of the corpses and put it back in its sheath. "It looks like a sword."

"Where did it come from?" Wildy asked.

"It was laid on the altar," Rusty answered.

"One just appeared in my hand," Michael told them.

"Whose swords do you think they are?" Wildy asked.

Rusty looked the sword over. "It bears the same markings as ours." He looked over at Michael's. "Let me see yours." He looked it over. "Yours does too."

"What do you think it means?" Wildy asked him.

"I don't know," Rusty answered, "but I think we had visitors tonight. We had to have."

"These swords are something," Wildy said. He picked up his switchblade from off the ground and looked it over. Then he compared it with his sword. "I guess I won't be needing this anymore," he said. "I've found something that works a whole lot better." He tossed the switchblade away.

Rusty noticed fresh blood on Michael's shirt and had him take it off. Michael had a gash that ran from his upper chest down past his stomach. The skin had fallen back, and it was bleeding profusely. Rusty grabbed another robe off another one of the corpses and took it down to the river. He soaked it in water and cleaned Michael's wound. Michael winced from the pain, and Rusty went through several pieces of borrowed clothing to get the wound clean. Then he wrapped another piece of cloth tightly around Michael's chest. He set Michael down next to the girl. Wildy also had a few miner wounds, and Rusty attended to them as well.

Then Rusty got to the girl. She had wounds on her back, on the backs of her legs, and on her shoulders. They were dirty and infected from the rocks and dirt. Rusty tried to be extremely gentle with her, as cleaning these wounds put her in great pain.

"So what's your name?" Rusty asked her.

"Akeshia," she answered. He touched her back with a wet cloth and she winced.

"What in the world are you doing out here like this?"

"I got caught off guard," she said through clenched teeth.

"What do you mean?"

"You see, I used to live in the Fortress of Light. That's why I knew that I could trust you when you mentioned the name of the Prince of Light. When I first saw you, I couldn't trust you. I was terrified. I had a feeling around you like I had never had in my life. Something surrounds you, something frightening. A certain sense of power emanates from you. Now that I know who you are..." She paused and bit her lip. "I believe you really have met the Prince of Light."

"But what got you out here?" Rusty asked.

Then Akeshia told him her story.

"I was always curious about what was on the outside of the fortress. So I used to stand in front of the windows and stare and stare and stare. I would get as close to the outside as I could without getting caught. People were always warning me how dangerous this was, but I wouldn't listen. Then one day I got brave enough to actually go outside. After I had been out there a while, I met a guy. He was the most incredible guy I had ever met. So smart, so sensitive, so good-looking. At first I felt kind of bad for hanging around him but I kept the relationship on a very formal basis. I kept telling myself that eventually I would coax him into the fortress. But instead, he wound up coaxing me out. Before I knew it, the fortress was just a memory. It wasn't until much later I found out he belonged to this group. He tried to get me to join, but my old convictions wouldn't allow me. I knew better. No matter how far away from the fortress I was at that time, I could not bring myself to join forces in any way with Draygon. So I refused, and I wound up here."

"Well, the fortress is gone now," Rusty told her. "Draygon destroyed it. You and Michael and I are all that's left. And I have a suspicion that all other professed followers of the

Prince of Light are fighting for their lives just like we are."

She looked at them. A wave of shock hit her. "Oh my god," she said, and started crying again. "What's going on? What's happening?"

Michael's head was swimming. He was still trying to put everything together. "In the fortress," he said, "they never made Draygon out to be as bad as he is. They always blamed him for everything, but they treated him like just another bad guy. Someone that we could order around in the name of the Prince of Light. No one ever told us how really bad or really awful, or how really powerful he is."

Rusty handed Akeshia her sword.

"What's this?" she asked.

"I think it's a present from the Prince of Light," he told her.

"A second chance," she whispered. She took the sword and looked it over, and once more she began to cry. "I guess it's finally happening. We're finally going to war."

Rusty finished with Akeshia's back and gently pulled her robe back over it. He thought about her statement about war. They had been told about a time when the Prince of Light would return, and just before that the Darklands would be thrown into a time of utter chaos. Evil and destruction would reign supreme, and all those that refused to succumb to Draygon would find themselves locked in a battle for their very lives. But at the time it all seemed so far away. Now here it was, staring him in the face. And the thought of what might happen to them terrified him. All the emotions of the evening began to pour over him like molasses running down a tree, thick and overpowering. He went over to the river to sit and think, and to try to find a way to control the overwhelming sense of fear that had suddenly washed over him. "Is this it?" he asked, looking up into the sky. "Is this really the end? What will happen to me? What's going to happen from here?"

14

When news of the battle at the coven reached Draygon, he was furious. He rounded up every one of his soldiers who were there that night, had them beaten severely, and then he placed them in a dark dungeon filled with pain and torture, a place he had reserved for all insolent and disobedient forces. They would sometimes be there for decades, even centuries before they were released back into service again.

Then, Draygon raged through the heavens, wreaking havoc with the elements, causing severe disruptions in the Darklands weather. He created a huge whirlwind in the plain below the mountain, which blew over large boulders, threw over trees, and nearly leveled some of the smaller mountains and hills. He was desperately searching for the boys. The seas swelled far above their shores, and a mighty wind blew on the

Nefacarious Sea like a hurricane of enormous proportions. The earth trembled and roared. Nothing was safe from Draygon's fury.

He flew around the globe, his eyes searching the planet's surface, looking for the rebels. His anger burned hot, and he was obsessed with the thought of destroying them. He had no mercy, and anyone or anything that happened to wind up in this path would perish.

He came to land on the top of the mountain near where the incident with the coven had taken place, and he looked out over the valley. He saw the coven, but there was nobody there. The Prince of Light had put a covering over them, and he could not see through it. He screamed in anger and swung his arms high in the air. Instantly a torrential rain began to fall. Then he opened up his mouth and spewed out a wall of water that went roaring down the mountainside. He hoped that the boys would be in the pathway, and that the water would find them.

The boys saw the wall of water coming toward them down the mountain, and they knew that they would never get out of it's path. Wildy wanted to run, but frozen in terror and indecision, they just stood. He and the rest of them watched the water come. Right before the water reached them, the ground opened up and swallowed it right in front of the boys.

Wildy panicked. "What's going on?" he screamed over the roar of the water and the earth.

"I don't know," Rusty screamed back.

Suddenly the earth began to shake, and the mountain above them began to tumble. Huge boulders fell around them, one on top of the other. Landslides went thundering down the mountain on all sides of them. When the ground stopped shaking, the place where they were standing was the only place that hadn't changed. The countryside around them looked like it had suddenly been shifted to a completely different country. Large portions of the mountain fell into the river and created a dam of stone and rock, backing up the river and creating an instant reservoir. What once was a lazy, carefree river was now a massive lake, getting bigger and bigger as the water continued to pour into it. There was an outlet just a few yards from where the boys were standing that let the water out, only now it was a large, wild waterfall cascading hundreds of feet below them. They themselves ended up standing in a large cavern, with ground and rock above them, and the grass they were standing in before had become the floor of the cave.

They all looked at each other in sheer terror.

"It's started," Rusty said at last.

"I can't believe it," Akeshia whispered hoarsely.

"What's started?" Wildy asked.

"This is it," Rusty said. "The end. The Warrior is returning. All the prophecies pointed to it, and it's really happening. And we're right smack in the middle of it."

"I don't think I like the sound of this," Michael said, his voice trembling.

Wildy sat down against the new stone wall and ran his hands through his hair. He was exhausted. Life had suddenly become so strange for him over the past few weeks, and this news wasn't hopeful at all. He laid his head back against the wall of the cave and stared at the wall in front of him.

As he stared at the wall, it suddenly began to move. Then it rolled down the hillside into the river below. Wildy got up and walked out to look over it and see what was below. Suddenly a strong wind came up behind him. He saw a giant funnel cloud, like a tornado descending down, and before he could get away, he was caught up in the middle of it. The funnel pulled him higher and higher into the sky and violently tossed him around from one side to the other. He tried to scream out, but he couldn't be heard over the roar of the wind. His entire body was paralyzed and he was helpless against the storm.

Then the cloud lifted back into the sky, and Wildy was glad it was gone. The peace sounded so beautiful, and he just wanted to absorb it, until he suddenly realized he was suspended in midair, and there was nothing to hold him there.

And he began to fall. Faster and faster he fell, while the ground rushed up toward him. He felt a horrible tingling sensation in the pit of his stomach. By now he was just feet from the ground when he felt a horrible jerking sensation. He sat up in the cave. He was breathing hard and sweating like he had just run a marathon. He looked around at the blackness, and thought to himself that it was just a bad dream. But it felt so real.

He got up, walked outside, and sat down on a rock near the lake. The moon was shining bright and he could see his reflection in the water. He hadn't seen himself in ages and was surprised by the face that looked back up at him. The face had softened considerably. It looked much older, wiser, and more experienced. And for the first time, Wildy was able to look into his own eyes. They looked deeper, like there was more substance behind them—not the hate that he had been so used to seeing in them. That hate was slowly dissipating, and something else was taking its place. A soft white light. Perhaps some small glimpse of his soul was shining back at him through his eyes. Then suddenly he noticed that another face was looking back at him along with his. He jumped and turned to face Rusty.

"You shouldn't sneak up on a guy like that."

"I couldn't sleep," Rusty said.

"You either?" Wildy mumbled. "Bad dreams?"

"The worst. I keep dreaming of earthquakes and violent wind storms. I woke up feeling frightened and out of breath."

"Me too," Wildy said. "I don't know which is worse—not getting any sleep, or sleeping and having dreams like this."

"It's a tough call," Rusty said as he looked into the water. He too could see a noticeable difference in his face. It looked stronger, more determined, and less naive. He could see courage and strength looking back at him. He also noticed something else behind his eyes: more depth, wisdom, and peace. The Prince of Light was being true to his word and imparting his wisdom onto Rusty. This thought gave Rusty some comfort in the midst of the chaos.

Neither of the boys said anything for several minutes. They just stared into the water while their minds chattered on and on, thinking thoughts that neither of them had thought in a long time.

"I remember when you came into the fortress," Rusty said at last. But his voice was so soft that it was almost as if he were talking to himself. "When we ran into each other. I was scared of you. I had never seen anyone like you before in my life. But before you know it, I'm running with you. I never dreamed that you and I would be paired up like this. I always thought I would grow old and die in the fortress, that the Warrior would never return in my lifetime. Oh, I always hoped he would, and that I would have some big part in it, but I had also had another hope that I would be protected, someplace secure and safe. Yet now it's happening; the whole thing is winding down, and here I am. Me, and an ex-gang leader. Right in the middle of the most violent time in the Darklands history." He shook himself to shake off the feelings of impending fear and doom.

Wildy sat in silence for several minutes, taking in everything that Rusty said. "I never thought I'd get much older...," he answered. "I mean, when you're on the streets, you don't tend to live too long. But I've never been afraid of death. Death is like the ultimate rush. So you just hang on to what you have. The trick is not to lose anything you've claimed until you die. And that was my life. But then the Warrior dropped into my life, and nothing's been the same since. I've seen some horrible situations before, and have even been a little scared before, but I have never in my life seen what I have seen lately. For the first time in my life, I know what real fear is. I know what it's like to have sheer terror seize your entire body and hold it so tight that every muscle aches with excruciating pain. I know that now. But I have also felt what it's like to love someone, care for someone, and that's something else I never experienced on the streets. I have to say, I have lived more in the past few weeks than in my whole life."

"I hear you there," Rusty whispered, almost to himself.

Rusty realized for the first time that he was no longer playing a game or living in a story, but now he was living real life. This was it. Life as he had never experienced it before. Again he looked into the water.

"Do you ever miss your parents?" he asked Wildy. He didn't know if this was a good question to ask, but he had been curious about Wildy's parents since the beginning. He wondered, as is natural for someone like Rusty, whether or not Wildy had completely rebelled against them, or if his parents were the type that didn't care about their children.

"I don't know who my parents are." At first Wildy sounded angry, but then he softened. "My mother threw me in a dumpster when I was born. Apparently she didn't want to have a son hanging around. I think she was a whore, but I can't be sure. Anyway, some street kids found me and took me in and raised me. I was raised in this gang, by the leader himself. He taught me how to fight, how to steal, and how to watch my back at all times. And when I got old enough, I took it over from him." He suddenly looked at Rusty in a very serious manner. "I've never told anyone this...," he said with a slight threat in his voice.

"Don't worry," Rusty assured him. "I'll never tell anyone. I promise. Besides, I don't even know if I'll live long enough to ever get the chance to mention this to anyone else."

"Now you're getting a feel for what it feels like on the streets," Wildy told him.

"I'm glad I don't know what that's like," Rusty said.

"This is worse," Wildy told him. "Trust me."

There was silence again, and then Wildy spoke. "What about your parents? What were they like?"

Rusty was quiet for several minutes.

"You did like them, didn't you?" Wildy asked.

"Of course I liked them!" Rusty's snapped. "You're supposed to like your parents!"

"Who told you that?"

"It's in the ancient writings—children are to love and obey their parents!"

Wildy was picking up some strange emotions from Rusty, and he didn't quite know what to think.

"You didn't love them?" he asked.

"I just told you I did," Rusty exploded at Wildy.

"Then what's your problem?" Wildy asked.

Rusty stared at Wildy for a moment, and then apologized.

"I'm sorry," he said. "I guess I'm just not sure what to think about them at the moment. When I first heard they were killed, I was hurt beyond belief. But this time away from them and the people at the fortress has been like I was let out of a prison. My dad used to constantly control me and badger me, make me do anything he wanted me to simply by constantly throwing that obedience thing in my face. He never allowed me to do anything for myself; he had to dictate my life to me."

"He was one of the high elders in the fortress, well-respected by everyone there, but alone, when it was just he and his family, he was a violent and cruel man. All he cared about was his reputation, and he would never do anything that would violate that. Nor would he allow us to. And if standing up for his son meant risking his ever-loving reputation, guess what won out. That stupid reputation. All I wanted to do was to find out why we believed the way we did, why we took so many of the things we believed for granted, and why we didn't at least question the legends and stories handed down to us and see for ourselves what might be. I couldn't reconcile some of the things I was reading in the holy writing with some of the things that we believed without question. So I would read everything I could get my hands on and try to reconcile some of them. But everyone in the fortress accused me of being rebellious and stubborn, and of leaving the faith. They said I was getting into the areas of demonic teaching and that my father ought to have more control over me. All I wanted was answers. But we were not to question the leadership of the fortress."

"So my father, to protect his reputation, would punish me severely for daring to put his good name on the line. He forbade me to read any more books, and I was never to ask any more questions. I was never to question the beliefs established by the early founders of the fortress ever again. And instead of coming to my aid, my mom only watched and submitted to him. She let him control us, and she let him destroy our lives."

"Well, now he's dead. He got what he deserved..." Rusty started to cry, but he didn't want to cry in front of Wildy, so he said nothing and bit his lip so that he could stop.

Wildy was sympathetic to Rusty and wanted to let him know that he thought nothing less of Rusty for crying, but he didn't know how to express this. So he kept silent.

"Since we found out about the massacre," Rusty continued slowly, "I've been feeling guilty for feeling the way I do about them."

Rusty's words sent a chill through Wildy. He'd never expected that Rusty, a mild-mannered, quiet, and gentle person could carry this much emotion. He seemed so easy-going, like he never really had any problems. "It's just games," he said quietly, looking out over the newly formed lake.

"Just games," Rusty whispered back. "Games that cost us our lives."

15

A sudden news bulletin flashed throughout the Darklands and across Darklands City, warning everyone along the coastal regions and within a hundred miles of the coast to quickly take cover. There was no place to go and no time to get there. The best they could hope for would be to find shelter within the next few hours.

Over the Nefacarious Sea, the air suddenly started to move. It quickly began to swirl and blow, pulling in on itself as it did. Soon the winds were moving nearly two hundred miles an hour. As the storm developed, it grew in size and intensity. In just a matter of hours, the storm went from a tropical storm to a full-blown hurricane. Inside of the hurricane, swells of water forty to fifty feet high rocked back and forth and jumped and pounded as they reeled in the fury of the wind. As it moved throughout the Nefacarious Sea, the hurricane sent before it tidal wave after tidal wave, moving out in every direction. They traveled hundreds of miles across the ocean, building up volumes of water as they went. The storm itself covered approximately one hundred and fifty miles in diameter, and there was nothing in its path capable of surviving its ferocity. Early into the evening, it slammed onto the shore just about a hundred miles north of Darklands City.

Despite the distance of the hurricane from Darklands City, its effects on the city were devastating. The tidal waves made their way down the coast and into the delta of the River Thromins. Once inside the river, they maintained intensity as they worked their way upstream twenty miles to the port of Darklands City and further. When the tidal waves hit the city, all of the beautiful floating bridges that spanned the river were washed away, along with buildings, homes, and people. Tons of metal and steel, glass and lumber, and other rubbish were pushed up and carried several miles upstream where the tidal waves finally lost their power to push any further. Then, as soon as it lost its power, all that water once again came rushing back downstream, and the wood and steel that it carried with it from the bridges and other structures that it had ripped apart were being used as battering rams by the water to destroy and tear down even more buildings. As all this rubbish passed through the city again, it tore at the foundations of the bridges built far above the water and soon they too fell apart and came crashing into the river to join the other debris on its way down the river to where the Thromins met the Nefacarious Sea. There the entire river delta was beginning to look like a massive junkyard that spanned for miles and miles on the deposits of sand and soot that had been built up over the years.

As crews and crews of people spent hours in the freezing rain and the heavy winds, trying to pump the water off the streets and out of the buildings, an earthquake rumbled through the city, shaking loose everything that had lost its strength in the water. Some of the crew members, and other people out trying to save their homes and city, lost their footing, and several hundred people were pushed down the river with the rest of the debris.

The Darklands City residents didn't know where to go or what to do. All around them, torrential water flowed through their city at a dangerous pace, and above them, a storm raged with such velocity that it left them with no way out.

As hurricanes do, this hurricane spawned several tornadoes. They touched down all over Darklands City.

This seemed like a night that could never happen.

Earlier that evening, in the little village of Volkstag, Tye and Anna sat on the porch and watched the sunset. Tye's head swooned as he and Anna had just discussed the Fountain of Blood and the death of the son of the Great Emperor. Never before had he heard anything like this, and he found it hard to believe that anyone would go to such extremes just to meet the demands of justice. He knew what it was to lose someone in death, but to willingly give up someone you loved to death for someone else, who probably wasn't even going to care anything about the sacrifice made, or the intensity of the gift...Tye could not even imagine the kind of person that could do this. He tried to imagine the Great Emperor and what kind of a ruler he must be. As he sat there, staring up at the sunset, he heard a distant scream that startled him out of his own thoughts and back to the mountains in front of him. The scream seemed to come from behind the mountains in front of the house.

Just after the scream, Tye heard a low rumbling, but he could not tell what it was. Soon he could see black clouds billowing up over the side of the mountain. They stacked up until they could finally reach over the mountain. As soon as they could get over the mountain, they shot across the valley so fast that it was like night and day. Almost immediately the entire valley sat underneath them, and they hung ominously in the sky. Tye noticed something strange about these clouds—

they seemed to have small bubbles coming out of the bottom of them. And they were black. Black as any cloud Tye had ever seen before. He looked over at Anna. Out of reflex, before he even had a chance to think, he helped Anna out of her seat.

"We've got to get out of here," he told her.

She looked up at him with a helpless look in her eyes, one which made Tye's heart heavy. It was so tender and so frightened, he wanted to protect her, to take care of her, but something told him that there was nothing he could do. He hoped against hope that she would be all right.

As they were moving off the porch and into the house, Tye watched as a long black funnel, shaped like a finger, made its way toward the ground. With it came the noise of a hundred jet airliners. As it descended, three or four littler funnels followed and rode along the side of the bigger one. The twister touched the ground and threw debris everywhere. Then it howled and shrieked as it moved across the valley.

Tye hurried Anna into the house and down into the basement. They sat in the corner huddled together, fighting back every urge to let their fear take the best of them. Tye tried to remain calm, especially for Anna's sake. She said very little to him at the time, but almost as if she sensed that everything would be okay, she took his hand and squeezed it reassuringly.

The tornado bounced again and again from one side of the valley to the other, making it even more destructive than if it had been on a plain. Unable to get out of the valley, it twisted and turned from one mountain to the other, looking for some other place to go. This only made the magnitude of the twister even more deadly. Soon it managed to blow itself out, and as quickly as it started, it stopped.

Tye and Anna sat in the basement, listening to the silence. It was so beautiful. Anna looked over at Tye. He couldn't see her in the darkness, but he could hear her breathe a sigh of relief.

"Are you all right?" he asked.

"I'm fine," Anna replied. "I'm still here."

As she spoke those words, the earth below them began to reel and sway. Again Tye felt a sudden sense of terror surge through his body. They sat quietly, fearing that in the darkness they might stumble into something or find themselves under a weak part of the floor above them. It seemed like hours to the two of them, even though it was only a minute, that the ground once again steadied itself, and the silence returned. Outside they could hear the screaming of children and doors and windows being slammed as they opened and shut for their owners running in and out of their houses, trying to cope with the sudden onslaught of nature's fury.

Anna lit a candle on the fireplace, and then looked over at Tye. "My son," she said through a shaky voice. "This has got to be a sign. A sign that life as we know it is coming to an end."

Tye returned Anna's gaze. Something about Anna's words rang true. He could tell deep inside that she was right, and that news was all the more disconcerting to him. "Oh god," he pleaded. "I don't think my heart can take too much more of this."

16

Once again Darklands City called an emergency meeting of all city officials, and among those called was Rhend. Because of the structural damages to the City Building, and because of the threat of danger from city residents, city officials could not meet in the City Building. Instead they met in secret, out of town and away from the confusion and the anger of the people. Max was there to represent the interests of his factions in the matter as well. It was now no secret that Max was involved deeply in the politics of the Darklands.

The intensity of the mood in the room could have been measured with a thermometer. Tempers were short, dispositions foul. Words flew and voices raised higher both in intensity, and in pitch. At first it was all Mr. Myer could do to get, and keep, everyone's attention. They were all shaken and dazed over the events of the night.

Once Mr. Myer did succeed in getting everyone settled, he quickly began the job of officiating the meeting. Step by step they tried to piece the evening together, piece by piece and event by event, but there was no explanation for what had happened. They went over every scenario, they checked every book, they went back over every type of document that had ever recorded any such phenomenon, but even the most outrageous of tabloids did not compete with what had just happened. There was no such thing as a hurricane developing in just a few hours, and then slamming onto the shore only a few hours after that. It wasn't possible, not even in a fantasy. So whenever one council member brought up anything regarding possibilities, someone else would disagree, and then a fight would begin again. It wasn't long before the meeting got out of hand.

Days had passed, and the city officials were still meeting in secret, still trying to resolve this latest crisis. Information was slow in coming, and when it did come in, it was sketchy at best. Tempers were hot, supplies were low, and answers didn't exist. For the first time in the history of Darklands City, the city officials were no better off than the residents that they had looked down on in contempt for so many years. Since the night of the hurricane, the tornadoes, and the earthquake, they too had lost everything, and they found themselves fighting for their lives.

Nobody knows how serious the fighting might have become, but Max interrupted it. He stood up out of his chair and walked to the head of the conference table where he stood behind Mr. Myer. Once he had everyone's attention, he addressed the members of the council.

"The news that is coming back to us is very disturbing," he told them. "So instead of all this bickering, I suggest that we find a way to get past all this and figure out what we're going to do about the problems at hand."

They all quieted down, and Mr. Myer opened a file folder

literally packed beyond capacity with all kinds of documents.

"Ladies and gentlemen," he said in a very serious tone. "I'm afraid things have gotten very bad here lately."

That was an understatement, and everyone there knew it.

"But," Mr. Myer went on. "Things are about to get a lot worse." He looked around the room, again very seriously. His look alone was beginning to frighten everybody else. "News has come back to us that Wildy is still alive."

A strange chill went through the room. Nobody could explain why, but this news cut them deeply, and their emotional state suddenly went further into upheaval. Was it fear? Was it hate? Was it sorrow? Nobody knew for sure what they were feeling, only that whatever it was, it was uncomfortable for them, and that terrified them. And they hated those feelings, almost more than they hated Wildy.

"I'm afraid the news gets even worse," Mr. Myer said. "We believe that what has happened in the past few days and weeks happened because of some sort of dealings that he made with certain occult factions. We believe that he has made a pact with..." Mr. Myer wasn't sure that he wanted to say what he was about to say. It just didn't seem possible. Again, it was like reading some made-up story, but when he looked over at Max, Max seemed sure that this was not the case. What Mr. Myer was about to say, Max believed to be true. So Mr. Myer continued his thought. "The Prince of the Air, or his most commonly known name...Draygon."

Another chill went through the council, even worse than the one they had just experienced when they heard the news that Wildy was alive.

"Where are you getting this information?" another one of the council members asked, hoping that it was all a lie, made up by some unreliable source.

Mr. Myer looked over at Max. Max took his cue and filled them in on what he knew.

"One of our agents in the Darklands came across Wildy and some of his friends several hundred miles from here. Up in the mountainous areas of the northern Darklands. This source tells us that they saw Wildy kneeling before an altar and calling on the name of the being we know as the Prince of the Air."

"But we all know that this Prince of the Air doesn't exist," another council member put in. "Does he?"

"Whether he exists or not," Max said, "Something strange is happening. Everyone in this room, and indeed, this city, has just lived through a night that could only happen by some supernatural force."

Silence lingered in the room for several minutes. Nobody knew how to respond. If this information about Wildy was true, how were they going to stop him? If he could do this kind of damage in the Darklands, what defense did they have against him? How were they going to counter his attacks on them? It was like a really bad dream. The type of nightmare where one would have to be on the verge of insanity to even conceive such a notion. Yet everyone there was wide awake, and the people standing in front of them and presenting them with this information were very serious.

Max went on. "I know this is hard for you to hear, but you've got to. Wildy has done exactly what we feared he might do. Only worse. He has now begun to assemble a new gang, an army if you will, and they're growing in numbers rapidly. Only now he works with another young boy. They seem to have teamed up. The boy travels with Wildy, and he seems to be very strong in the occult. It is possible that it was this boy that introduced Wildy to this sort of power. Whatever the case, though, together they are forming another rebel gang, and they have become powerful. You have seen it at work in the Darklands. Wildy is announcing his presence in the Darklands."

"That's all we need," Rhend shouted. "Another gang led by Wildy... Only this time he's got a partner? And he's sold his soul to some fictitious being know as the Prince of the Air? And with that power he's found a way to control the elements? What are you, crazy? First of all, let me point out that we have reliable sources that say that he always works alone."

"Would that reliable source be you?" one of the council members teased.

Rhend said nothing regarding the comment. He simply glared at the lady, then continued.

"Nobody in the world is more power-hungry than Wildy... Secondly, no matter what anyone says, we all know that there is no such thing as a 'Prince of the Air,' just as there is no such thing as some 'Great Emperor.' Those are myths that have never been proven. And even if there were such a person, you can't tell me that Wildy would openly claim to be a follower. Nobody would believe him, and worst of all, nobody would take him seriously, and Wildy couldn't live with that."

"Like it or not, Rhend," Max said, "these things are true. There is such a thing as Prince of the Air, and there is a Great Emperor. Secondly, Wildy has been known to make alliances on occasion if it served his purposes. Thirdly, where do you go if you're looking for the ultimate power? Well, if you can't get it legitimately, and we know that the Great Emperor would never support Wildy, then you must go to the ultimate source of evil. And that would be the Prince of the Air... Furthermore, Wildy is not openly calling on the Prince of the Air, he's calling him by another name. A name that he wants us to believe is just the opposite of the Prince of the Air."

"And what might this name be?" Rhend asked coldly. He hated Max, and he especially hated it when Max showed him up in front of anyone, which Max seemed to love doing.

"That other name might be—and is—the Warrior," Max replied.

The name hit Rhend like a slap on the face.

"How do we know all this?" Rhend continued questioning.

"One of our agents has been following a coven operation up in that area for months now, trying to build up evidence of its existence, so that they could be legally and rapidly disbanded. While he was working undercover in this particular coven Wildy and his newly formed gang stormed into the coven and announced that they were taking over. They called on some demonic being, and before anyone knew what was going on, all those in that meeting were dead. We also received reports that he put himself in good graces with Draygon by slaughtering several professed followers of the Great Emperor in their fortress several miles north of here."

A strange sensation came over Rhend. It was almost as if he had gone completely numb. It seemed as if he were watching himself from across the room, not really standing there talking to Max, or in the room at all. He cautiously and quietly sat down in his chair. When he sat down, it was all he could do to hold himself up without completely falling out of his seat.

"As you can see," Max said softly, "these are grave times. We must do what we can to rid ourselves of this scourge. We must call upon the Great Emperor for help."

Everyone sat in silence for the longest time. Nobody knew what to say.

Max looked around the room with a very serious look on his face.

"But the only way that the Great Emperor will help us," he said, "is if we eliminate those that are his enemies. The Darklands needs peace. And the only way to bring peace to this land is to rid ourselves and the Great Emperor of these renegades."

"How are we going to know who's who?" One council member asked.

"We've thought about that," Mr. Myer put in. "We're going to revamp the identification system and strongly enforce it. Unwavering and without mercy."

17

Rhend surveyed the damage at the coven. Max's information had been right. Whatever happened here was severe. He saw the bodies scattered throughout the clearing, he could see dried blood on the rocks and in the dirt, and he noticed the ripped and torn clothes along with other debris scattered all over the ground. He saw the remains of the alter, which looked as if it had been torn apart.

A strange sensation filled Rhend as he stood there looking around. It was obvious that nobody had been up here since the night of the attack, yet Max knew about it, and his information seemed to be correct. How did he know so much?

He turned to Borgie. "How did Max know about all this?" he asked.

"I don't know!" Borgie confessed. "Max knows many

things, and nobody knows how."

"You know you're a traitor, don't you?"

Borgie said nothing. He looked at Rhend with a blank stare. Eventually, he did rebut. "I ain't no traitor," he said.

But Rhend couldn't worry about that right now. Night was quickly falling, and he had to hurry. He and Borgie took the bodies and piled them together, along with their clothes and other debris scattered throughout the clearing. Then they soaked them in lighter fluid and lit them on fire. Rhend had to be sure that no one else ever found out about this place. After that, they stacked the rocks back in place to re-form the alter, then they carefully reconstructed the pentagram and glued the candles back together with the wax from the other candles. Once they put everything back in order, they lit the candles and set them on the four corners of the alter.

When everything was ready, Rhend knelt before the alter.

He called upon his guide in the spirit realm. For several hours nothing happened, and Rhend started getting angry. He screamed and cursed and kicked at the alter. Finally he took a knife from his pocket, sliced open his wrist, and let the blood drain down on the alter. After only a few moments, there was a shard of a dark black light that hovered just above the alter. Then it materialized into a birdlike creature and lowered itself onto the alter. It had the body of a vulture, with a long neck and face like a snake, claws for feet, and fangs for teeth. Its eyes were huge round spheres, and they moved independently from each other within its head. It hovered just above the alter, its neck coiling and sliding around rest of its body, and its head swinging from side to side. It spotted the blood and lapped it up greedily.

The sight of this creature terrified Borgie, and he quietly but quickly found a place to hide somewhere away from the open area of the coven.

"Why have you called me?" it hissed when it had finished with Rhend's blood.

"How could you have made a pact with Wildy?" Rhend demanded sharply.

The creature slapped Rhend with its wing, then stuck its snakelike face in Rhend's face, opening wide its mouth to expose the large fangs that dripped poison mixed with blood.

"What right have you to question what we, your leaders, do?"

Rhend quickly apologized and changed his tone of voice. Then he explained to the creature that what he really wanted to know was why they had picked Wildy. "Why Wildy?" he asked.

The creature swung its snakelike neck from side to side.

"I did not make the pact with Wildy," it said. "And I do not tell the master how he must rule his domain. He chooses whom he will choose."

Then the creature's eyes began to swirl, and his body rocked back and forth rhythmically. It put its face just in front of Rhend's face. Rhend quickly became mesmerized by it, and his head and body began to follow that of the creature.

"You want ultimate power?" the creature asked in rhythm with its movements. "Then you must kill Wildy and take your place with the master."

Then the creature pulled back sharply, and it felt to Rhend as if a rubberband had snapped in his face. With a quick jerk, he was released from the hypnotic gaze of the creature and he fell backward onto the ground.

"Wildy will not rule the Darklands, I will!" Rhend shouted as he jumped up. "Wildy will die first."

The creature hissed and laughed, and then whispered, "You want power...?" And with that, it disappeared.

18

The sun shined brightly over the countryside, and its warmth bathed the four young people as they made their way to the other side of the mountain. They had wanted to put as much distance as they could between themselves and the coven.

On the other side of the mountain, they spotted a small village down in the valley. It sat on what used to be a river, but now it was merely a dried up riverbed.

All of their clothes were nearly worn completely through, so they decided it might be okay to risk a trip into town to pick up supplies, mainly clothes. They had done quite well living off the land, as far as food went, but their clothes and shoes were not meeting the demands of their new life style. And the land did not offer anything to take care of those particular needs.

They all suspected that going into town might be risky, and none of them knew what to expect once they got there. They didn't know if any of the villagers would recognize them. Wildy had no idea what to expect anymore. He didn't know if Darklands City thought him dead or alive. They talked it over and decided that this was something they needed to do. The three boys had some money on them. Akeshia had been stripped of everything, so she had only the clothes she had managed to scavenge off the bodies back at the coven.

They knew that it might not be safe in the village, so they worked out a plan ahead of time. They talked about how they should approach the town and the people in it. They also talked about what to do should something go wrong and they were recognized. They made a plan to get in and out of town quickly and quietly.

As they neared the foot of the mountain, they decided that it would be better if only a couple of them went in to buy the supplies, and the other two would lay low and scope out the rest of the town, gathering any information they could. Wildy and Akeshia were chosen to go into the store and pick up the supplies, while Rusty and Michael would wander about the area.

Wildy's clothes were still bloodstained from the night at the Fountain of Blood, and he knew that this made him stand out. He tried to be as inconspicuous as he could, but he knew that he wasn't exactly an average small-town boy. His hair was long and ratted, his clothes were torn, and his face was scruffy and hard. If anyone should meet him on the street, they would immediately cross to the other side and he knew this. So when they arrived at the store, he carefully maneuvered in and out of the clothes racks, avoided all mirrors, and stayed as far out of sight as he possibly could. Every time someone came into the shop, Wildy would hide in the back.

This was the first time Wildy had ever gone into an establishment alone, without the express purpose of robbing someone. He didn't like having to sneak around. It was a completely different feeling for him, and he missed the power he had over everyone in Darklands City. Even so, he was still glad to be off the streets of Darklands City. He didn't miss the gangs, the violence, and the loneliness he felt while on the streets. Now that he had met someone who loved him, and who believed in him, he couldn't imagine going back to what once was. Now he would stand by the Warrior by choice, not just because he didn't know where else to go or how to get back. For the first time, he was a part of something, and that felt good to him.

Akeshia picked out several pairs of jeans, some all purpose shirts, some heavy duty shoes, and took them up to the counter. While the lady clerk added up the prices, Wildy moved toward the door. The lady quoted the price to Akeshia, and she laid the money on the counter. The lady just looked at her. Her continued stare made Akeshia uncomfortable.

"May I see your identification?" the lady asked.

"What identification?" Akeshia asked.

"All citizens of the Darklands must have identification to either buy or sell in the Darklands. That's how we know if..." She noticed Wildy inching toward the door. "Oh my god," she said, "You're one of them!" She looked at them hard for a moment, and then suddenly screamed. Her husband came in from a back room to see what was wrong.

"They don't have the identification!" she screamed hysterically. "They're Warriorites!"

Her husband looked them over, and then he looked over at Wildy. He studied his face for a moment, then immediately backed against the wall.

"Please don't hurt us," he pleaded. "Take what you want, but please don't hurt us."

The man's wife pushed the clothes into Akeshia's hand and pleaded with them to leave the store. Akeshia put some money on the counter, but the woman wouldn't take it. Akeshia left the money on the counter, took the clothes, and took Wildy by the arm, ushering him outside.

Once they were on the street, they were met by Rusty and

Michael. They found a quiet place where they could be alone and talk. Rusty had a newspaper in his hands, and he showed it to Wildy and Akeshia. Michael was really shook up, and he could hardly speak.

The paper told about a new identification procedure that everyone in the Darklands must submit to, or they would not be allowed to do any business. This included simple things, from buying groceries to selling merchandise of any kind. It warned that breaching this new law would result in prison.

The paper said that this was a last resort because of the newest threat to the Darklands. It told the story of the battle in Darklands City between the two gangs, and then it said that Wildy had survived. Underneath that, it said that Wildy was involved with outright worship of the Prince of the Air. It was the Night of the Storm that marked the solidification of this alliance. The paper continued by listing crime after crime that Wildy and his gang, the Venomites, had supposedly committed. It warned that Wildy was "wanted, dead or alive, preferably dead," and that there were large sums of money offered toward the deliverance of Wildy or any of his cohorts to the Darklands officials. Then the paper made a very grave claim; it said that until Wildy and his group were eliminated, events like the Night of the Storm would become commonplace.

Wildy could not deny most of the crimes mentioned because he had committed so many that he had no way of knowing if he had really done them or not. Even so, he was sure they had to be making most of it up. They were making him out to be almost a demon, a creature more evil than he could have been even as the city's most notorious gang leader.

The paper went on to say that Wildy was extremely dangerous, and that anyone who saw him should get out his way and inform the authorities immediately. But it also noted that killing him would be acceptable, if one could do so without risk of losing him. And the line that really hit Wildy hard was, "If you opt to kill him, be sure to kill anyone else that might be with him."

Wildy stared at the paper. In the city there was always someone around him, and he had nothing to fear. Now there were only four of them, and he knew they didn't stand a chance. But what really got to him was that these three were innocent. They hadn't done anything, but now, because they were associated with him, they would be considered his accomplices, and therefore criminals. They would have the same price hanging over their heads simply because of him.

He looked at Rusty. Rusty had quietly moved the paper out of Wildy's grip and was putting it away. Something was troubling Rusty and Wildy could see that, but Rusty would say nothing about it. Wildy tried to coax it out of him, but Rusty wouldn't speak of it. Quickly Michael pulled the paper out of Rusty's hands and handed it back to Wildy.

"He didn't want you to see this."

Wildy looked back at the paper. There was another whole section that he hadn't even noticed. In this section, he read about him and his new partner. In order to become as powerful as he was attempting to become, he had teamed up with a young man known only as Rusty. Rusty was a master at the craft of the black art and had a very high standing with the powers of darkness, as he had been trained in them all his life. It was for this purpose, according to the paper, that Wildy had left Darklands City in the first place—to search Rusty out. Together he and Wildy had entered into this new and bizarre pact. Again it referred back to the Night of the Storm. It referred back to that night so many times that even Wildy was starting to be afraid of a possible reoccurrence. That's why officials had set up the identification procedure and the strict policy against any Warriorites. "Warriorites are outlaws," they warned, "and outlaws will not be tolerated in the Darklands."

Wildy looked at Rusty. He knew what Rusty was feeling. He sensed the fear and the overwhelming sensation of sorrow behind Rusty's eyes, even though Rusty didn't say anything. Rusty wouldn't talk about it, and Wildy wouldn't make him.

"We've got to get out of here," Wildy said, handing the paper back to Michael.

They crept around some of the buildings and worked their way out of the town, doing their best to stay out of plain view. But there were a couple of blocks in which they had to walk right through the center of town before they could get into a more secluded area. As they were walking down the street, a young man about their age started following them. He was trying to be inconspicuous, but they were aware that he was behind them.

He finally approached them. "I know you," he said quietly to Wildy.

Wildy grabbed him by the throat and ducked into an alley.

"One word and you're dead," Wildy said. "Now, here's what we're going to do: We're going to walk out of town, and you're coming with us. Got that?"

The young man was completely taken off guard by this behavior, and he shook his head yes. He knew better than to put up a fight. They quickly made their way out of town, Wildy's arm gripped tightly around this young stranger's neck. And with his other hand, Wildy held the boy's arm behind his back to guarantee his cooperation. Once they were far enough out of town, Wildy turned the boy loose.

"Now I suggest you get out of here and don't look back, got that?"

The guy again shook his head.

"I got it," he said, "but don't you want to know how I know you?"

"I know how you know me," Wildy said, taking the newspaper from Michael and holding it up for him to see. "This."

"Well, that too," the boy said, but it was someplace else. I was outside the coven the night of your battle. I saw you and this other guy (he pointed to Rusty) take on those people. That was the girl they were going to sacrifice." He pointed at Akeshia. Then he noticed the look that everyone was giving him—a sort of terrified look that one of them might have escaped, and that he might be following them.

"Don't worry," he assured them. "I'm not one of them."

"Then what were you doing there?" Rusty asked.

"Well," the boy told them, "I was camping with some friends, and we heard a noise. So we went over to see what it was. And we saw what happened. There's been a real problem with those guys around here, so we all knew what was going on. They have been stealing our animals and killing them, using their blood for their sacrifices. They take what they want, and if anyone opposes them, they cast spells on them, and strange things happen. Lately, people have begun to disappear. Especially children. Nobody knows where these people meet, and nobody wants to. So when we saw them at the coven, we were scared to death—we tried to get out of there without making any noise or tipping them off that we were there. Then we saw you guys come into the circle. We saw that big hideous demon, and we saw you fight them. I watched you hew down every last one of them. We ran away because we weren't sure who you were, but I know now."

"How do you know?" Rusty asked.

"Well I don't really know who you are, but I know you're not with that other group. I know you're here for a reason." He spoke to Wildy. "Nobody like you winds up way out here in the middle of nowhere unless there was something really big going on. We've all heard about what happened in Darklands City, and now you're out here. There are several young boys who live in this area who were just dying to get into your gang when you were leading it." Then he addressed Rusty. "And when you held your sword above your head and called on the name of the Warrior, I watched what happened. I saw a flash of light, and I felt the earth move, and I saw what happened to those people. That was power. Power like I've never seen before in my life. I've had a few days to think that night over, and I think something powerful is happening. I don't know who the Warrior is, but I heard you call on him, and I saw what happened. I tried calling on him to find out who he is, and what he wants, and how I might find out more about him, and now here you are."

"Look," Wildly told him. "You don't have any idea what you're even getting into."

"I know that," the guy replied. "But I'll bet you didn't either."

He looked around at everyone. "I can't explain it," he said. "Do you know what it's like to be drawn by something, and you just can't figure out why?"

"As a matter of fact, we do," Wildy told him. "Believe me, we do."

"My name's Thomas," the guy said, holding out his hand to shake.

Rusty carefully explained to him all the things that had recently happened to them and the possible cost of that sort of a commitment. Thomas understood, but was not swayed by the horror stories.

"Whoever this Warrior is," Thomas said, "he must be incredibly powerful. I can't imagine what happened on the mountain that night, but it has terrified everyone in the valley. People can't stop talking about it. For the first time in centuries a Tornado touches down and rips apart the valley. A river that used to run right through town now runs several miles to the east. I have to know more about this Warrior. I just have to."

Rusty wasn't exactly sure of how to inaugurate Thomas into the group, so he had Thomas kneel down on one knee, and then Rusty placed his sword on Thomas' right shoulder.

"Thomas," he said, "you have now volunteered to become one of the warriors. The commitment you are making is a serious one. We have told you everything that we know about this involvement, and yet you choose to belong. Therefore, we cannot deny you membership. But to be one of the warriors, you must be willing to pledge your life to him. Completely, and without regard to anything else. This means you will live for him, and you will die for him. Whichever he may allow you to do. Do you agree to these conditions?"

Thomas agreed, and Rusty initiated him into the brotherhood.

Once Thomas was initiated, he told the others to wait for him while he went back into town to pick up some things.

Wildy was suspicious of this, so they told him they would meet him back there in a couple of hours. Wildy thought that that way they could be on the lookout for any kind of an ambush.

Two hours later, the sun had begun to set over the mountains. Akeshia and the three boys were getting nervous. Wildy decided he would go down and wait for Thomas, and the others would hang back. That way if it was a set-up, they could get out of the area. Wildy was a very competent fighter, so he figured he had a better chance out there than anyone else.

Sure enough, when Thomas came into view, there were at least a dozen people behind him. He was waving and pulling a cart behind him.

Wildy approached him cautiously, with his hand on the hilt of his sword.

"It's okay," Thomas kept screaming. "Don't worry. These guys want to join as well." He approached Wildy. "These are some of my friends. I told them what happened on the mountain, and who you are, and they want to join too. I explained to them everything you explained to me. They are willing to make that commitment."

Some of the people with Thomas were young kids who had earlier wanted to run away to the city and join with Wildy while he was still terrorizing the streets of Darklands City. When they heard he was there, they were immediately ready to follow. Wildy had a very serious talk with each one of them and explained to them that this was not what it was in Darklands City, and that this time the whole game plan was different. They weren't out there for themselves now, and this wasn't a game of power to them, but all power was of the Warrior. Even with this, they were all willing to follow Wildy and the Warrior.

Rusty swore each and every one of them in. Some seemed very young to Rusty, and others had to be much older than he or Wildly, but all were ready to leave everything behind and follow the Warrior.

Wildy helped Thomas unload the cart and put everything in bundles so that it would be easier to carry the stuff up the mountain. Then they broke up the cart and buried any remaining traces of it in the ground by some trees.

Thomas had thought of everything. He had clothes, food, cooking utensils, medical supplies, and a few other odds and ends. He had also managed to find an old scroll containing the holy words of the Prince of Light. It was something he had found years ago, but he had never thought anything of it. In fact, he had completely forgotten about it until that night at the coven.

As they carried the things up the mountain, Thomas told them some of the news he had picked up while he was in town. The biggest story was that news of Wildy's presence in the little village had spread like wildfire, and that the town's folk were holding a special emergency meeting to decide what to do about him. Thomas explained to the group that the townspeople had sent word to the authorities of the Darklands and Darklands City to inform them that Wildy was in the area; they wanted them to send some reinforcements before things got out of hand.

To Wildy, this news wasn't anything new. He was used to being an outlaw and being hunted. But to Rusty, this was devastating. He had never in his life done anything that he could get in this kind of trouble for. He was always very careful of that. Yet now, he was a wanted man. He was helping to lead a group of rebels, and he was deliberately defying authority. And to make matters worse for Rusty, he was taking other innocent people and making them outlaws as well. He thought back to Dr. In. What if he was leading his people to the same kind of fate, just like Dr. In did?

More importantly, why were these people so willing to follow? Didn't they question anything that they were doing? Did they understand the commitment they were making? Was he going to lead them well? Rusty tried to work through all this. All the way up the mountain, he didn't say a word. He could not get Dr. In and the fortress out of his mind.

Wildy, on the other hand, had thoughts of his own. Thoughts of the danger he was putting these other people in. Because of him, these people were willing to put their lives on the line. By following him, they would be treated the same way that he would be if they were ever caught, but they hadn't done anything. He looked up toward the sky, hoping the Warrior would give him some sort of sign. Something that would indicate to him that he was or was not doing the right thing. Was this what the Warrior meant when he said, "Find all those that will follow...?" He too said nothing as they walked up the mountain.

Akeshia noticed that they were both extremely quiet, and she suspected that it had something to do with the new responsibility that they were taking on. She did her best to keep the attention of the others off of Wildy and Rusty and onto other things, which was a tough job, due to the popularity of Wildy. But she somehow managed to pull the focus away from them.

19

That night, while he slept, Thomas had a dream. He dreamt he was taken on a journey, and that journey began at the foot of a tall and foreboding mountain. The mountain was so high and looked so frightening that his heart trembled. In the dream, he began to ascend this mountain slowly, ever so slowly. He was alone, and behind every boulder was every fear he had ever had, every dark deed he had ever done, and every dark thought he had ever thought. At last he had to face every one of them. Although he didn't actually see anything but shadows, he knew what each and every one of them was, and every one of them weighed heavily on his mind as he continued to climb.

Higher and higher he climbed, never daring to look behind him. Every boulder held some dark secret behind it, and every secret held some dreaded fear of being discovered, of being exposed. The fear of the secrets kept him from looking behind the boulders, but as he passed by, all the darkness behind them seemed to jump onto his back and cling to him. With the added weight of each one, the going got tougher and tougher, and his climb up the mountain took longer and longer. He would have stopped, but something at the top kept calling him, closer and closer. He didn't know if it was a voice, a feeling, a whisper, or the wind, but whatever it was, it terrified him. Either way, forward or backward, he had to face this terror. But the strongest sensation pulled him forward.

When he reached the top, he noticed that it opened up onto a stone plain that spread several yards in all directions. On the plain was a large stone table, and from that table, blood flowed out to the gutters, then over the cliffs below. Thomas approached the table cautiously. When he reached the table, he was instantly pulled into it.

He thrashed around, desperately trying to pull himself out of the blood, but it seemed almost as if a weight had been tied to his feet. Then suddenly he noticed a body in the table with him. The sight of the body terrified him. He tried to get away, but a hand from the body reached out and pulled him back into the table. He started screaming as loud as he could, but no one could hear him. There was no one anywhere near, and he knew that. He looked back at the body, and this time it was still. He crawled to one side of the table to get as far away from it as he could. His mind began to imagine that the body was looking at him, although he knew that wasn't possible because it was dead. Yet another look at the body revealed that the eyes were open.

He sat still. He didn't dare move. He didn't dare breath. He didn't know what to do. It seemed to him that those eyes were staring directly at him, but he couldn't tell for sure. Was this person dead, or wasn't he? The eyes. Those eyes seemed to be looking at him, directly into him, as if the man were alive. Perhaps he was undead. This thought made Thomas panic. Once again he rushed to get out of the fountain, but again it seemed as if the body held on to him.

As the eyes continued to look on, everything that had attached itself to Thomas on his way up the mountain was now in direct sight. For the first time in his life, Thomas could see those dark deeds, and hear those dark secrets, and look directly on every dark thought that he had ever had. They were staring at him face to face, and he could barely breath under the weight of them. It was like a force on his chest that seemed to overpower him. Then, suddenly, he heard a terrifying scream.

The scream that he heard was his own. He tried with all his might to open his eyes, and when he did so, he sat up like a bolt. With his eyes opened, he saw a dim fire and several people gathered around him. He tried to crawl away from them, continuing to scream for help. Then Akeshia's voice began to calm him.

"It's okay," she said. "Thomas, it's okay."

Wildy and Rusty held him firmly as he sat there trying to catch his breath.

He looked up at Akeshia, trying to catch his breath and fight back a reservoir of tears and emotions that had suddenly come rushing to the surface, much like the way he had shot up in bed. He noticed that the fire he saw was the fire in the camp, and the people gathered around him were those of his friends. He sat back with his back against the wall of the cave. His clothes were soaked in sweat, and everyone around him had a very concerned and worried look on their faces.

"It was only a bad dream," Akeshia said softly. But her face still showed worry.

"I guess it was," Thomas breathed. "A horrible nightmare."

He took the back of his hand and wiped it across his forehead. He noticed that it was awfully wet and sticky for just sweat, so he held it up to his face and looked at it. He was alarmed at what he saw. He looked down at his sweat-soaked clothes. They were not soaked in sweat after all—they were soaked in blood. He jumped up.

"What's going on?" he shouted. "What's happening?"

"Tell us what happened," Rusty said, holding him down and trying desperately to calm him. "Maybe that will help us figure this out."

Thomas had a feeling of fear in his stomach and legs that seemed to paralyze him. He was numb with fear, and his body seemed to be floating off the ground. His mouth was so dry that he could barely talk, but somehow, through many tears and desperate attempts to catch his breath, he was able to relate the whole dream to the rest of the them. They all listened closely, sensing his terror and feeling his fear.

After Thomas' story, there was a moment of insanely tense silence as everyone waited for some kind of answer.

"You've been to the Fountain of Blood," Wildy told him. "That dream you had was real. I know; I've been there. It's a terrifying place at first, but when you look back on it, it's the most incredible thing you'll ever see."

"He's right," Rusty replied. "And the body you saw was that of the Warrior." Then he looked at everyone else. "What Thomas has experienced is the Warrior's initiation into his covenant. This is how he is choosing to bring into his covenant those who will really be his. If you truly want to be his, you too will face—and submit—to the Fountain of Blood. I don't know how, I don't know when, but everyone here will face it if they haven't already. Be prepared."

After Rusty finished, they sat around the fire and talked. Everybody was afraid to fall back to sleep. But one by one they all began to drop off. Thomas was the last one. He fought it and fought it, but soon his eyes started getting too heavy to stay open. He stood up and walked outside, but it soon became apparent that he was not going to be able to stay awake much longer. Something pulled and pulled at his eyelids until he could no longer hold them open.

When he finally did fall asleep, he was immediately back at the top of the mountain and in the Fountain of Blood. As he sat there in the blood, he looked at the body again. This time it looked peaceful, and its eyes were shut. He could feel the blood drowning every one of those dark deeds and secrets and thoughts that had somehow attached themselves to him on his way up the mountain. When at last it was time to go, he stepped out of the table and started down the mountain and the path below. He climbed down slowly, and this time the boulders and rocks were just that—boulders and rocks. They carried no more fears, no more darkness, and no more regrets. Instead, they carried hope and courage and comfort. As he passed by them, they reached out to him and grabbed him around the heart, and he felt his spirits lift with the weightlessness of them all.

At the bottom, he met the man he had seen in the fountain. At first he was afraid. He thought the man was dead. But the man put out his hand and took hold of Thomas' hand, comforting him.

"You have faced the Fountain of Blood. You no longer belong to the Darklands. All your darkness has been bathed away from you in my blood. You are free from them. But you are now an enemy to the Darklands, and you will be called to fight the powers that own them. But do not fear; I will give you weapons, and you must train yourself to use them." Then he looked deep into Thomas' eyes. "You are welcome here, and I will supply you with everything you need. In me you will want for nothing." Then he picked Thomas up and threw him into a lake nearby.

Thomas felt the water sweep over him, and soon was completely emerged in it. As he went down deeper and deeper, he could feel himself becoming clean—his clothes, his skin, and, most importantly, his soul. But he continued to sink, deeper and deeper, and he wondered if he was going to drown. Still, down and down he went.

He sat up and rubbed his eyes, looked around him, and noticed that he was again in camp. It was early morning and everything was quiet. No one else was awake yet, and the fire had burned out. So he laid his head back down. When he did, his arm hit something. It felt somewhat like steel, but it was also like electricity. It didn't hurt him, but it made his whole body tingle when he touched it.

He picked it up and looked at it. It was a sword. The same sword that Rusty and Wildy had used during the massacre at the coven. The same sword that the Warrior had given him in his dream at the bottom of the mountain, by the lake. He looked around the camp and noticed that everybody else had one too; he assumed that they had also visited the Fountain of Blood during the night.

That morning Rusty explained to them the story behind the Fountain of Blood and the reason that they all had to visit it.

Once Rusty was alone, he thought to himself that the Warrior must be choosing the army. The Warrior himself was handpicking this army, even though they were recruiting them. And the Warrior was picking them carefully. This gave Rusty comfort. He wasn't going to be a Dr. In. It wasn't him that was making the decisions, and Rusty could see that now. He smiled to himself and breathed a sigh of relief. "Thank you," he whispered into the air where he thought the Warrior might be.

Rusty didn't know what lay ahead, but he got the idea that the Warrior was preparing them for something. But now he knew that the Warrior was behind them after all.

20

Several nights had passed since the newcomers joined Wildy, Rusty, Michael, and Akeshia, and in that small amount of time, the newly formed band of Darklands rebels had already seen and heard many strange things.

It had also been several weeks since Tye had met Anna and begun his studies under her. Their studies were kept secret because of the new laws regarding involvement with the Warriorites, so Tye kept mostly to himself when out of the house. The people in his village were becoming more and more suspicious of the Warriorites and the mountain in which the Warriorites had last been spotted.

Stories of the massacre at the coven had trickled down, and as usually happens when a story is told and retold, it became more and more embellished upon until the story itself was more than the actual event. And this particular version of the story made Wildy and his partner look like some supernatural punks that single-handedly destroyed hundreds of people with some form of black magic. The people of the Darklands were convinced that this little gang was practicing witchcraft and magic that had never been known to man before, and the Darklands officials were doing everything in their power to encourage this belief.

Now there were people more powerful than those of the coven, and that thought scared the villagers like no other thought could. With a little help from Darklands officials, Darklands residents began to suspect that Wildy and this other guy, whose name, they were told, was Rusty, the one who called down the fire from heaven, were trying to destroy them and build up a power more incredible than those that had gone before. And circumstances seemed to back up that belief, the earthquake, the dried-up riverbed, the scream in the night that had caused the freakish weather, which had caused the Nefacarious Sea to suddenly lash out.

One night, just before sunset, Tye and Anna watched a thick black cloud that seemed to hover over the mountain's summit.

"What do you think it is?" Tye asked.

"I don't know," Anna responded, and she clutched her holy book even tighter.

Tye noticed this behavior and felt a strange feeling creeping over his body. What was it about that cloud that scared him so much? Worse yet, what was it that had Anna so upset? Were they in for another horrible episode? Was the weather going to go freakish on them again?

"We should get inside right away," Tye said nervously.

"Perhaps you're right." Anna had a hard time moving her tired old body out of the chair on the porch. Tye gently helped her out of the chair and into the house. Her face was pale, and she clutched him like never before.

"What's wrong?" Tye asked, becoming more and more

frightened by the minute. "Is it that cloud?"

"I don't know," Anna said. "There's something hanging in the air. Something I have never felt before."

"They sat inside by the fire and watched in silence. Anna's breathing was slow and laborious. Tye was afraid and held her hand tightly.

"I don't think I'm going to be able to weather this storm," she said silently.

Tye felt a chill run through his body. He looked deep into Anna's eyes. "What are you talking about?" he asked.

Anna said nothing, and Tye was afraid to ask any more questions, so they sat there in silence.

Soon after Tye and Anna had noticed the cloud, it moved slowly down the mountainside, descending like a fist that slowly began to open up, exposing what looked like long, chilling black fingers—fingers like that of death itself. Slowly they stretched out across the mountain, then crept down its side and toward the base and the valley below it. As it stretched out farther and farther, it enveloped everything in its path with an unpierceable darkness. Soon the cloud had completely covered the mountain and started approaching the villages at its base.

Behind the black hands, a headlike shape with piercing red eyes followed. Those eyes seemed to see through everything. The sight of this frightened and alarmed the villagers, and they locked themselves in their homes, hoping to escape this terror.

Anna and Tye watched as well, helpless. Anna held Tye's arm even tighter.

"I never had children," she whispered.

This seemed to Tye like an odd time to bring up something like this, but he said nothing and allowed Anna to speak her mind.

"It had always been my hope," Anna went on, her voice shaking, "that I would someday have children of my own. Children that would grow up to be healthy young people such as yourself." Then she said nothing.

"Why didn't you have children?" Tye asked, wanting to break the tension that seemed to hang in the air and in every corner of the house.

"We never could. My husband Simeon and I were never able to have them. We asked many times of the Great Emperor and the Prince of Light, but I guess it was not to be in this life. My Simeon was killed many years ago by a band of hoodlums as he was crossing the mountain pass into town." Tears filled her eyes, and Tye felt her sorrow. He looked at her closely for several minutes.

"So you do know my pain," he whispered, with tears in his eyes.

"Yes, I do," Anna whispered back. "And someday, you must find a way to forgive Wildy. I had to forgive Simeon's attackers. It was hard, I admit, but when I did, my soul was set free. And when you forgive Wildy, your soul, too, will be free. Free from the hate, free from the anger, and free from the pain."

They sat in silence. Tye thought over Anna's words. How could she have forgiven someone who did such a horrible thing to her, taking from her the most precious possession in her life? How could anyone forgive that? How could he forgive Wildy? But he didn't have much time to think about it.

Soon the thick blackness had covered the village. Every fire in every fireplace extinguished itself, every candle burned out, every window and door flew open, and a terrifying chill filled the air. Every resident of the villages soon felt those fiery red eyes coming into their homes and slowly looking around, studying every corner and every inch of their dwellings. They tried to hide, but the eyes saw everything. In particular, these eyes were especially keen in the dark, and the residents had no recourse for this unseen terror. They were prisoners of this darkness that, instead of hiding them, only made them vulnerable and completely helpless.

Children wanted to cry and scream, but their parents held them tightly, gripping them around their mouths so that they would not be able to utter any sound, fearing that any sound would only give them away. Even the animals were restless. They howled, bayed, snorted, pranced around, and ran in circles, as if they themselves recognized this danger and were trying to escape it somehow.

Eventually, the darkness did lift and move away from the village. Nobody knew where it went, and nobody was sure whether or not it was gone for good. Tye took Anna's hand to reassure her, but it was hard and cold. He looked over at her, and her body sat lifeless in the chair. He looked into her face, and it seemed to glow. This was not the Anna that he had seen just before the darkness struck. Instead of fear, her face radiated hope and peace. She looked almost more beautiful than Tye had ever seen her look. He held her hand for hours and cried bitterly. He loved Anna, and now she was gone.

That night, nobody slept. Everyone sat in total darkness while outside the animals continued to pace and grunt and snort all through the rest of the night.

21

Four funerals took place over the three-day span following the night of the cloud. They were mostly elderly people who had probably suffered heart attacks during that darkness. Anna was one of them. Hers was the last funeral to be held, and her parting was marked as a sign. A sign that the events in the Darklands had gone beyond what anyone could have even thought. Everyone in Volkstag knew that Anna was a spiritual woman, and her death during that night only served as a bad omen.

Tye watched silently as they placed Anna's body into the ground. He could not describe the emptiness inside of him. He vowed he would never let anyone close to him again, and his anger at losing so many close loved ones was building in intensity every minute. All he could think of while they placed Anna's body in the ground was how angry he was at everyone being taken away from him like this. He wanted to scream, and the more he thought about it, the angrier he became, until he suddenly felt the urge to go screaming through the countryside and beat himself against anything that got in his way, just so that he could alleviate some of the anger. But he was a level-headed guy; he planted his feet firmly and watched helplessly as they threw dirt on Anna's grave.

As he was watching this, trying hard to control his emotion and clear his head, he noticed that some of the others of the village were talking about him and looking over at him. Tye had no idea what they were talking about, and he wasn't sure he wanted to find out. Why would everyone be talking about him? In all his time in Volkstag, he had kept quiet, he had laid low, just as Anna had recommended that he should. He feared they might be planning to hand him over to the authorities, so he turned and headed toward Anna's house. He would pack up his only belongings, mostly the books that Anna had given him, and he would get out of town. He decided that he would go farther up into the mountains where it might be somewhat safer for him—away from the governments of the Darklands.

He was still several feet down the driveway yet when he saw several men going through the house. Fearing what that might mean, he ducked behind some trees. He watched in silence for several minutes, when suddenly he was hit on the back of the head.

When Tye awoke, he was in a jail cell, and some of the men from the house were looking over him. As soon as he was awake, they set him up, but because he was still a little lightheaded from the bump on his head, they leaned him against the wall. When he was stable, they started to question him. One man in particular stood out.

"What's your connection with this woman you were living with?" he asked Tye.

Something came over Tye, and he suddenly felt that the

less he said, the better off he might be.

"I worked for her," Tye responded. He knew that this wasn't the whole truth, but it was the truth.

The man threw Tye against the wall of the cell. "You're lying!" he screamed. "We know that you've been doing something there, now what was it?"

"I just worked for her," Tye persisted.

The man grabbed him again, and this time he threw him against the bars where he held Tye by his hair. "I'm not going to keep asking this question," the man said. "Either you tell me everything that was going on in that house, or you'll die the most horrible and painful death you've ever imagined." Then the man turned to some kid behind him. "Borgie!" the man barked.

"Yes, sir," the boy answered.

"Give me your gun."

"But Rhend, sir," the boy said. "If you kill him, we might not find out where he is."

Rhend impatiently slapped Borgie across the face. "I know that," he said. "Now give me your gun."

Angrily Borgie placed the gun in Rhend's hand. He was furious, embarrassed, and humiliated, but he didn't dare do anything with all Rhend's men gathered around. So he took out his anger on Tye.

Rhend aimed the gun at Tye's knees. "Either you tell me what you were doing with that lady, or you lose a kneecap. Now I know you're tied in with Wildy somehow, and I want the truth. I want to know everything you know."

A wave of terror swept over Tye. He began to sweat and pant, and it was all he could do to keep himself from crying. He knew that to cry would only make this man angrier, and that could be deadly. So he said nothing.

Borgie grabbed him by the face and beat his head against the cell bars several times, but Tye still said nothing. Then Borgie kicked Tye's feet out from under him, and when Tye fell to the floor, Borgie grabbed him by the hair and pulled him back onto his feet. Once again, he slammed him into the wall.

Tye's face was bleeding pretty bad now, and he could hardly stand. Rhend pointed the gun at his knees and pulled the trigger. Tye screamed and fell to the floor. He lay there in fear, waiting for the pain to begin. But there was no pain. Instead, sheer pandemonium among the rest of the men. Somehow Rhend had missed and hit one of the other men. The man screamed in pain as he fell to the floor, and Rhend screamed in anger.

"That does it!" Rhend screamed. "You're dead! I'm going to kill you in the most horrific way I can think of. You will beg me to let you die, but I won't. I'm going to keep you alive just so I can torture you."

He walked over to the other side of the room and banged his fists on the wall of the cell. Then he became strangely calm. He turned around and looked at Borgie.

"Borgie," he said.

"Yes sir," Borgie responded.

"I meant what I said about you being a traitor."

He turned the gun on Borgie and shot him in the stomach. Borgie doubled over in pain.

"I just wanted to let you know I never forget."

Then he raised the gun a little and shot Borgie in the head.

Everyone else in the room moved away from the body, fearing that any wrong move would bring the same consequences on them.

Tye didn't know what to do. He sat there, dead still, hoping that Rhend wouldn't see him. Very quickly, and as quietly as possible, he curled himself up, hoping to pull himself out of sight. Rhend did see Tye, though, and he resumed his anger. He crossed over to Tye, and pulled him up to his feet, and threw him back on the floor. He hurled insult after insult, and he threatened Tye with some of the most horrible things he could think of.

As he was speaking, he was beating Tye with the butt of the gun. Again and again he brought the butt of the gun against Tye's head. Tye curled up to protect himself, which only made Rhend angrier. Again and again he kicked Tye in the ribs, in the back, in the legs. Every part of Tye's body was either being kicked or hit with either the gun or Rhend's fists. The rest of the men derived some sort of pleasure out of this, and they too joined in the game.

Tye looked up and saw one of the boys that he had seen looking over at him and whispering at Anna's funeral. Tye didn't have a lot of time to think about it, though, as Rhend would not afford that possibility. He couldn't even think of why this guy stood out, while no one else did. This boy screamed and yelled with everyone else, but he kept looking at Tye with the strangest expressions. Then he moved to an area just behind the rest of the group, but where Tye could still see him, and started making hand gestures and mouthing something to him. It looked to Tye like he was saying, "Hang on," but Tye couldn't tell for sure. Nor could he understand why this boy would be saying something like that to him.

Soon everything went black for Tye and the voices disappeared. He could no longer hear or feel anything.

Tye suddenly found himself walking near a river. A closer look revealed that it was the river just outside of his jail cell, only now it was flowing with water. It was early in the evening, and he could barely make out a figure, but he could tell that somebody was walking toward him. He couldn't see who it was, yet he felt very anxious and uneasy about meeting him. Soon the figure came into view, and Tye almost died when he saw who it was. It was Wildy.

Tye felt a sudden surge of anger and hatred well up within him. He wanted to attack Wildy, he wanted to kill Wildy—he stared hard at him but neither of them moved. Wildy held Tye's gaze for a very long time, but Wildy neither said nor did anything.

Then, in almost a whisper he said, "I'm sorry."

Tye stared angrily at him, then lashed out, "You're sorry?" he screamed. "What if you were me? What if all this had happened to you? What if you had to live with the damage you've caused to all those you've come in contact with?

Would you be merely sorry then?"

Wildy looked at him quietly for a moment, then he spoke. "I will. Think about the time in which we live. I will be on your side. Everything that I have done to others will be done to me."

Something about these words and the way Wildy said them struck a nerve in Tye's heart. He could see real pain on Wildy's face, and when he looked into Wildy's eyes, he saw something else. He wasn't sure what, but he had seen it in his own eyes several times before on his journey to Volkstag. It was that light that he noticed in his eyes after having met the Prince of Light on the streets of Darklands City. He remembered how many times he would look at his reflection in the water and notice that look. That look that seemed to signify something else alive and beyond the surface of the face.

Tye began to weep. Suddenly he didn't want Wildy to go through what he had been through. He didn't want Wildy to feel the pain that he had felt. He put his arms around Wildy and cried. "I hope it doesn't," he said. "Pray for forgiveness."

"I have," Wildy said quietly. Then he looked at Tye with the look of an innocent child, one that had done wrong and was trying to make things right with its parent. "Will you forgive me?" Wildy asked.

Tye thought and thought. This was the toughest question ever put to him, and he couldn't answer it.

A voice from behind him whispered, "And yet you cannot bear for him to suffer your pain. You have forgiveness that you do not even know."

Tye turned around to see the voice, but there was nobody there. He turned back around to face Wildy, and Wildy also was gone. He was standing there alone. The wind began to shake him and call his name. It shook him harder, and as it shook him, he started to feel pain. It created pain in every joint and every muscle of his body.

Tye jumped uncontrollably, like he had been startled, and woke up. Something grabbed his chest and gently pushed him back down. At the same time, something clamped over his mouth so that he could not make a sound. He lay there for several minutes, not knowing what to do next. Then he rubbed his eyes and looked around the room. He wasn't near a river now, he was in his cell, lying on a cot. He had no idea how he got there or what had happened to Rhend or the others. There was one guy standing over him—the guy that had been trying to communicate with him earlier. When Tye saw this boy, he jumped to get out of his way. This caused him tremendous pain, pain that seem to run parallel with every movement that he attempted to make. The guy sensed this, and he gently held Tye still. Then he bent down close to Tye's ear and whispered, "It's okay. I'm not going to hurt you." Tye fell back on the bed. That was so good to hear, even though he wasn't sure if he could believe it.

"What is it?" Tye asked through the boys hand. He moaned. Just the movement of speaking caused him great pain.

The boy quickly shushed him again, then he moved his hand away from Tye's mouth. He got down on his knees and pulled his face close to Tye's. "We've got to be quiet," he whispered. "I'm here to get you out."

"Where's everybody else that was here? Where's that man with the gun?" Tye whispered.

"The man with the gun has a name. It's Rhend. Trust me, you don't ever want to meet him again. As far as everyone else is concerned, I've drugged them. I've drugged everybody here," the boy told Tye, "but you're an important prisoner. They're keeping close watch on you."

He carefully and gently helped Tye stand up. As soon as he stood up, all the blood rushed out of Tye's head and he could hardly stand. His head hurt so bad that he couldn't even hold it up. Once he had recovered from the initial shock of standing, they moved toward the door. Tye could feel every step, and the pain reverberated through every pore of his body. His head ached so bad that he couldn't see, and he was so dizzy that he couldn't walk. Even leaning on this stranger, Tye was unable to move.

"I'm sorry," Tye whispered. "I don't think I'm up to this. You better get out of here before that drug wears off. I'll be okay in here."

"Sure you will," the boy said. "Just look at you now. Imagine another day of this." As soon as he said that, he picked up Tye and carried him out of the building and down away from the village toward the riverbed. At the riverbed, they were met by several other people, and together they helped this boy carry Tye up the mountain and deep into the forest where they could be safe for the moment. There they set Tye down on some moss, covered him with some blankets, built a fire close by, and set up a camp.

"My name is Mark," the boy said. "We're all really sorry about this morning. We weren't talking about you in the way that you thought we were; we were talking about how to approach you. We knew what was happening—we knew about the break-in on your house. But we knew that if we got too close, or if we said anything to you, they would know that we were involved, and that would end all our chances. The only thing left to do was wait and see what they were going to do to you, and then break you out of jail."

Tye tried to raise his head up and look at them, but he wasn't able to keep it up. Mark placed his hand under Tye's head and held it there so that Tye could look at them directly.

"Why?" Tye asked.

"You lived with her, you studied under her, and rumors say that you've actually met the Warrior face to face. We want to meet him too. We want to be in on this. But we need a leader, and you're the one."

"How can I be the one?" Tye asked. "I know very little about him. Only enough to know that he takes leadership very seriously."

"But you know him," Mark replied. "The rest of us know only what's going on in the Darklands. We know about the signs of the judgment of the Great Emperor, but we don't understand why."

"You'll be criminals," Tye told them.

"I already am," Mark responded. "I just pulled you out of jail."

"What if I make a mistake? Something that could cost you your life?"

"We'll watch out for each other, but we need someone to explain it all to us. Or to at least get us started." He looked long and hard at Tye. "Look," he said, "If you're looking for an excuse not to do this, there's plenty of them. But the bottom line is, we need you, and we're willing to help you in any way we can."

Tye looked at Mark. "You're right," he said, "There are plenty of them." He leaned back, and Mark gently laid his head down on the ground. Tye lay there for several moments and didn't say anything. Finally he spoke. "Okay," he said, "I'll do it."

Mark smiled, took off his coat, and gently placed it under Tye's head. Then he covered Tye with another blanket.

"You just rest," Mark said. "You'll be okay. We'll take care of everything for now, and when you're ready, we can get started."

Tye looked up at him. This was so unusual. He didn't know any of these people, and he was usually rather shy, but he hurt so bad that he couldn't really feel out of place, so he laid his head back and went to sleep.

22

Time had begun to take its toll. As the days went by, things continued to get worse. Events in the Darklands had gone beyond anything imaginable. The planet seemed to be spinning out of control, and nobody could understand why. More and more strange things began to happen. Fire fell from the sky, hail the size of small animals destroyed the countryside. Things had become critical, and the Warriorites were being blamed for everything. Wildy and Rusty had become the two most infamous people throughout the Darklands, and their names struck terror into the hearts of every Darklands resident.

Instead of the usual quiet most of the Darklands villages had grown up with for generations, things around them had suddenly been thrown into utter chaos. To cope with this sudden surge of supernatural activity, everything else came to a stop. Businesses closed, and homes were boarded up tight to protect their owners from any kind of sudden attack. All travel between villages was temporarily restricted except for official business only, and that would be handled only by the proper authorities. No one was to move until something could be done. But this cure created problems of its own.

Because nobody could travel, medical, food, and clothing supplies stopped coming in. This had so many adverse effects on the villagers of the country that a state of emergency had to be declared.

The people of the valley were frightened like they had never been in their entire lives. They had stopped sleeping because of fear. They had stopped eating and drinking because of the lack of supplies. They had stopped treating the sick because of lack of medicine. All these problems combined drove the morality rate of the people into the basement and the mortality rate through the roof.

The most frightening thing in the world had become the mountain and its Warriorites. Their infamy soon spread throughout the Darklands.

One day several of the Warriorites went out on a hunting trip. They were following a particularly large deer, and the buck ended up taking them near the foot of the mountain instead of going into the woods which would be typical for the animal. When they reached the foot of the mountain, they decided they had better not go any further, and they let the deer go. But while they were returning back to the campsite, Rusty suddenly spotted something out of the corner of his eye. Carefully he went over to check it out.

It was a fire, a small fire about his height. It burned in a single column, but it didn't burn on anything. As the group approached it, it moved. They followed it and attempted to get a little closer again. Again it moved. Closer and closer it moved to the plain and to the village. Wildy wanted to turn back, but Rusty thought that it was a sign from the Warrior and that they had to follow it. So they did.

In the village, the children were playing, and the adults were going about their business trying to find ways of taking care of themselves and their families. Things were as normal as they could be under the present circumstances, and everyone tried to keep themselves busy. Because of the ban on travel, people were not allowed to come to this village and view the mountain, but there were certain daredevils that had to see what it was like, and who would risk everything to get a look. They traveled mostly at night, with the only light being that of the moon—a method of travel that was very dangerous for a number of reasons, but because of all this activity, the village had become more and more populated, which just added more stress to the already tired and run-down population.

A crippled young boy in his late teens hobbled across the village square. To him, every step was a major effort. Because each step was so hard and complicated, he had to stop and rest every four or five. His feet were in severe pain, and every step he took felt like someone had set them on fire. He would step, then wince, then rest, and then step again. Occasionally he would be bumped by a passerby or a child at play. He would wince and try to pretend that everything was okay. His feet had been like this most of his life. He had been told by his physician that he should give up walking all together, even more now that he couldn't get the pain medicine that Ryan so desperately needed. Yet Ryan was desperate to walk, and he refused to give up what little walking he was able to do. He worked his way over to a stump in the middle of the square and sat down. Then he set his crutches down beside him and shifted several times to try to get comfortable.

The boy's name was Ryan, and as he was going through this ritual to find the position that would cause him the least amount of pain, a man in a dark cloak came up behind him, picked up his crutches, and walked away. Ryan screamed after him to bring them back, but the man disappeared. Frustrated, Ryan put his head in his hands and placed his elbows on his lap.

As he was sitting there, a girl came running into the square, screaming frantically, "The Warriorites are coming this way, and they're coming fast."

Pandemonium broke out, and people began running everywhere, trying to find a place to hide. For the most part it was every man for himself, so Ryan was left alone and defenseless. He looked desperately for his crutches, but they were not there. In panic, he dropped down to the ground and started to crawl as fast as he could. He cried out for help, but no one responded. They were all too worried about themselves. While they did trip over him, kick him, and step on him as they tried to get away, not one of them stopped to help him.

He hadn't crawled very far before the Warriorites were upon him. When he saw them, he became more frantic and tried crawling faster. Rusty noticed him and went over to help him. Ryan cowered as Rusty approached, like a puppy who was about to be hit, and screamed, "Please don't hurt me! Please don't hurt me!" Then he began to cry.

Rusty squatted down close to Ryan so that he could talk to him. "It's okay," he said softly. "We're not going to hurt you." Then he looked at Ryan closely. "Can you walk?"

"No," Ryan responded.

Rusty picked up Ryan and set him back on the stump. Ryan struggled to break free, but Rusty had plenty of strength, and he would not lose Ryan. Akeshia quickly sat down next to him to comfort him.

"It's okay," she said. "We're not going to hurt you." She held his hand to assure him. "What's your name?" she asked.

"Ryan."

Akeshia gently put her arm around him. "Ryan, don't be afraid. Nobody's going to hurt you. I promise."

Ryan looked up at Rusty and Wildy and the rest of the group.

"Well, don't look at me," Wildy protested.

"We're not going to hurt you, Ryan," Rusty conferred.

Ryan breathed a sigh of relief. "They say you're...," then he decided not to go.

"It doesn't matter what they said," Rusty told him. "We're really not what they say."

"What happened to your legs?" Wildy asked him.

"I had an accident," Ryan told him.

"What kind of accident?" Wildy asked again.

"I slipped on some stairs."

Rusty looked at Ryan for a minute like he was trying to figure something out. Something was going on in his mind. He was beginning to see something, and he wasn't sure what. Nothing like this had ever happened to him before, so he had no idea of what to do. Then he said almost as if he knew it as a fact, "That's what you've been telling everyone, but what really happened?"

Instantly Ryan became very uncomfortable. "I don't understand."

Rusty squatted back down to Ryan's level and gently put his hands on Ryan's arms, looking him in the eyes. "I know it's a painful memory," Rusty said softly, "but you've got to tell me."

Tears filled Ryan's eyes. "How did you know?" he asked.

"The Warrior knows," Rusty told him.

At the name of the Warrior, Ryan's legs kicked. Rusty looked down at Ryan. They both had felt it, and if Ryan had been scared before, he was terrified now. Not knowing what else to do, he told them his story—the truth about what happened to his legs.

"When I was five, my mother got angry with me for crying so she slapped me across the legs. All that did was make me cry harder because it hurt, so she started kicking me in the legs. She kicked them, and when I still wouldn't stop crying, she started hitting them with a broom handle. She hit them over and over and over again as hard as she could for several minutes. And I've never been able to walk since then."

"And they covered it up by telling everyone you fell," Akeshia said with a hint of shock and anger in her voice.

Rusty was right. The memory of this was incredibly painful, and Ryan wept uncontrollably. He didn't want to cry in front of anyone so he buried his head in his hands and tried to hide. Akeshia sensed this, but she also knew that it was important that he face this memory that, for some reason, the Warrior had brought up, so she turned him a little toward herself, held him close to her, and comforted him. He felt that she really loved him, and he felt safe in her arms and free to cry. So there he released all the years of this pent-up memory.

Rusty too began to cry, but he did not say why.

"Isn't there anyone in the Darklands who likes children?" Wildy asked.

This time Rusty moved his hands from Ryan's arms to his legs. "Ryan," he said, "the Warrior knows the pain you have suffered over the years. He has also watched the abuse your mother has brought on you, and he has been compassionate toward you. That little 'accident' almost killed you. You spent weeks in critical care, but the Warrior spared your life."

"For what?" Ryan asked bitterly. "To give her something to do for the next few years?"

"The Warrior has intervened many times in your life," Rusty told him. "You are not able to see that, and I know it's hard to believe. But to show you what you mean to him, I now bring to you a gift from him."

"A gift?" Ryan asked.

"Ryan?" Rusty asked. He paused, and then he went on. "Would you like to walk?"

Everyone of the Warriorites stared at Rusty, even Akeshia. Nobody knew what he was about to do. They wondered if he might be acting a little impulsively, yet nobody interrupted him.

"Do you want to walk?" he asked Ryan a second time.

"I'm afraid," Ryan told him.

"There's nothing to be afraid of," Rusty told him, and he held out his hand. "Here, take my hand."

Ryan took Rusty's hand, and Rusty pulled him to his feet. Then he said to Ryan "It is with joy and love that the Warrior offers you back the use of your legs."

Ryan almost fell back, but suddenly he felt a twinge in his legs. It was as if they had been asleep for a long time, and now they were waking up. He felt them tingle and at first he couldn't move because of the tingling but soon he managed to get his balance, and there he was, standing. He started screaming, "I'm standing, I'm standing!" Then he began to jump and run and walk. He jumped up on the stump and jumped back down. He ran around the group and hugged each and every one of them. He got to Rusty, and once again he began to weep, but this time it was tears of joy.

"My legs," he said, "they work again." He hugged Rusty and thanked him. For several minutes he hung on to Rusty and cried, and then thanked him some more. Then he asked if there was a way to thank Rusty, but Rusty told him that he could not repay what was given as a gift—a gift, not from Rusty, but from the Warrior. Ryan began to get a clear look at what the Warrior was really like, and he wanted especially to thank him. So he asked if he could join the Warriorite army as thanks to the Warrior.

"We're outlaws," Wildly told him. "There's a lot of people trying to get rid of us...permanently. Yet people aren't the worst of it. Draygon is. He's relentless. Are you ready to be hunted like some animal, to be continually watching your back, to be up against powers that are so terrible you could never imagine anything worse? Are you ready to die, Ryan?"

Wildy's voice was serious, and Ryan felt afraid.

"He's right, Ryan," Rusty said. "If you join the Warrior's army, you become an enemy of Draygon and his entire domain. That includes the Darklands, the residents of this village, your family and friends, and the supernatural forces at work in the Darklands as well."

"The Warrior made me whole," Ryan told him. "I sense something inside of me. I feel like a kettle that's about to boil over. I must follow. I must meet the Warrior."

One of the Warriorites brought Ryan a sword.

"Then you will meet the Warrior," Rusty told him, and he held out the sword to him. "Place your hands above mine on the sword." When Ryan did so, he continued. "Ryan, you are accepted as one of the Warriorites. You have equal the privileges and responsibilities of anyone in the Warrior's army. You will meet the Warrior, but only in the way that he will reveal himself to you personally. No one here can tell you how that will be or when it will take place, but he will try you and determine your heart. Are you willing to submit to this testing and to give your total loyalty and devotion to the Warrior?"

"I am," Ryan said.

Rusty released the sword. "The Warrior will test your statement and your loyalty. You are now a Warriorite. Master this sword, it is your only weapon from now on, and your only defense."

While the rest of the gang welcomed Ryan into the group, a young mother carrying a small baby in her arms approached Rusty. She was timid and afraid, but desperate enough to chance approaching him.

"Please sir," she said quietly. "My baby is very ill. I think she's going to die. I've done everything I can. The doctor can't treat her because of the ban on travel, and we can't get her the medicine she needs. We've tried everything we have, and it's been no good. I saw what you did with that boy..." She began to weep. "Please, can you help?"

Rusty felt his heart go out to her, and he wanted so bad to do something. He took the small child in his arms and held her close.

"What's the baby's name?" he asked.

"Carrie," the mother told him.

Rusty looked lovingly down at baby Carrie.

"Carrie," he said, "in the name of the Warrior, you will be well."

The baby cooed, stretched out her hands, and smiled as big as she could. Then she reached up and took Rusty's nose to play with it. Rusty kissed her on the cheek, played with her hands, tickled her a little bit, and then gave her back to her mom.

"Carrie is going to be just fine," he told her.

The mother put her hand on Carrie's forehead. Sure enough, the fever had broken and the color had returned to Carrie's face. Carrie's mother wept and took her baby. She hugged Rusty and thanked him.

Suddenly the entire group was surrounded by people who were sick and needing help. Old people with arthritis, doubled over from the pain, young people with diseases, scrapes that wouldn't heal, illness that wouldn't go away because there was no medicine in the village. Even people with terminal illnesses, heart problems, and more. All these people approached the Warriorites, hoping to be made well, and they weren't disappointed. Neither were the Warriorites. That day, every Warriorite was able to effectively pass on the Warrior's gift of health to anyone that asked.

Despite all this, many of the town's people were angry and wanted revenge on the Warriorites for the events in their villages and on their planet. They felt that it was with the power of Draygon that these people were healing and doing all these miraculous things. From that day forward, the town became sharply divided over the Warriorites. Some stood behind them and believed that they really were people of the Prince of Light, and others hated them and plotted their destruction.

23

It had been a long day. Everyone in the group had been mobbed by many people looking for relief from their various illnesses all day long. They were pressed, pushed, and just plain worn out. Now they were looking forward to getting away from the village and back up the mountain where, hopefully, everything would be somewhat quieter.

As they headed up the mountain, Rusty noticed that Wildy was not with them. He checked around, then asked everyone else in the company if they had seen him, but nobody had in quite a while. They hadn't even noticed him leave. Rusty was now very concerned, so he went back to look for him and had the rest of the group hang back outside the village while he, Michael, Akeshia, and Thomas went in to see if they could find Wildy. He hoped against hope that

Wildy wasn't in some sort of trouble.

As soon as they were near the village, they heard a noise that sounded like people screaming and shouting. They followed the noise to the other side of town to an old farmhouse outside of the village, and near to the back of a barn. Behind the barn, they noticed a lot of people gathered so they crept up to the outside of the group and attempted to blend in without being noticed. Several of the people were holding torches and hurling insults as well as stones and sticks, clumps of dirt, and anything else they could get their hands on toward something in the middle of them. Rusty got in closer to see what they were screaming at. He saw immediately what it was, and the minute he did, his heart went sick. They had Wildy, and they had him in the middle of the circle standing on a small step ladder with a noose tied around his neck, and the other end of the rope tied to a tree, and they were about to kick the ladder out from under him any minute.

One man up in front, who appeared to be the leader of the posse, screamed to the people: "We will no longer allow this punk to terrorize our children, our families, our village, and our countryside with his evil and vile practices. We do not allow devil worshippers here. Let us see how well his rebel gang functions without him! And as soon as we're done with him, they will collapse right into our hands." Cries and screams of agreement went up from everyone in the group. Then he raised his hands triumphantly, and the townspeople began chanting, "Kill the devil worshipper…kill the devil worshipper!" This crowd was thirsty for blood, and it showed in their venomous command for Wildy's death.

The man turned to Wildy and looked him right in the face. "I got you!" Rhend spat. "I got you. You never thought I would. You slimy scum. You vile little…I got you and now I'll make you pay for everything you've done to me. I'll make you suffer like no human being has ever suffered before. I'll take you apart piece by piece, and when I'm done, I'll take your body back and frame it in my den. I'll be the one who killed the infamous gang leader." Then he punched Wildy in the side, slapped him in the face, and punched him again. He'd almost killed Wildy before the rope even had the chance to.

Rusty motioned to Akeshia and Michael and Thomas to meet him outside of the area where the townspeople could neither see nor hear them.

"They must have grabbed him while we were distracted with everything else," Akeshia said once they were out of range.

"More than likely," Rusty said. "But we've got to get him out of there."

"How?" Michael asked.

"I don't know yet," Rusty said, "But we've got to do something. I won't let him die like this." He turned and ran toward the group. Michael grabbed him.

"I know how you feel, Rusty...," Michael said.

"No you don't!" Rusty whispered loudly. "Do you see what they're doing to him? And it's my fault. I should have been paying attention. How could I be so stupid? My god, what kind of leader am I if I can't even keep track of my own partner? I should have been watching out for him."

Akeshia moved in carefully, placing herself between Rusty and the crowd. "It's all of our faults," she said. "But if we don't act carefully, then we could wind up making it worse and every one of us could end up just like him. Let's approach this situation cautiously."

Rusty knew that this was best and agreed.

They snuck back into the middle of the group and positioned themselves just on the inside, where the people had formed a circle around Wildy, and then they put themselves almost in a square, taking up four corners inside the circle where they would be hidden by the first row of people. They had their swords tucked very close to them so as not to give themselves away.

Akeshia saw the old man and woman who owned the store that she and Wildy were in. They were screaming right along with everybody else, so she made sure to stay out of their sight. She looked up at Wildy to see how he was doing. His face was emotionless; he just stared into the middle of the group of people and said nothing. They had taken his sword, and his hands were bound tight behind his back. Judging by the bruises on his face, he had been severely beaten. He stumbled and staggered and swayed, and he could barely stand on the ladder. At one point, he lost all his strength and fell, and the only thing holding him up was the rope around his neck. When that happened, Akeshia almost gave herself away, when out of reflex she jumped to help him. Fortunately she caught herself before she went too far. After that, she sent a message up to the Warrior.

"Please," she whispered. "Please don't let him go like this. Please rescue him."

At that moment Rhend kicked the ladder out from under Wildy. Out of instinct, Rusty grabbed his sword. The others did the same and followed Rusty's lead. They held the swords toward Wildly. When they did, a bolt of lightening shot down from the sky and hit Rusty's sword. From there it deflected onto the other four swords at the same time. Then the bolt went from the swords to the center of the group and hit the rope, severing it, and Wildly fell to the ground. Then the bolt went up the rope, into the branch, and throughout the tree. The tree grew brighter and brighter, until suddenly it exploded.

Rusty hadn't noticed before, but when the tree started glowing, he could make out several of the shapes that he had seen the night of the coven. Gross and hideous, they had been pushing the townspeople to destroy Wildy. As the tree grew brighter, they began to smoke and burn. They cried out in pain, but there was nothing they could do. When the tree exploded, these creatures suddenly disintegrated into puffs of screaming smoke as they ascended above the crowd and then vanished into the night.

Rusty ran to Wildy and pulled him to his feet. The rope had been completely burned off his body, but he himself wasn't burned anywhere. The five of them stood and faced the crowd, which was in such a state of shock by what had just happened that all they could do was stand and watch. Rusty raised his sword above his head, and the others followed his example.

Rhend started screaming and yelling insults and obscenities. "I'll get you," he screamed out, "if it's the last thing I do!" Then he lunged at Rusty.

A bolt of energy emanated from the swords and hit him square in the chest. He screamed and fell on his back. As he lay there motionless, his skin split down the middle, then slowly began to curl back around the rest of his body. Lying just below the skin was an evil and grotesque demon. She came out of the man and stared wildly at them. "You'll pay for this!" she screamed. "You'll pay." Then she lunged at them, but again another bolt of light shot out from the swords and this time it sent her into the air where she was caught by a whirlwind of fire and pulled away. As she was swept away, her screams haunted the countryside. The townspeople watched in terror as they heard her blood-curdling cries of anguish and anger. They offered little resistance after that and opened a path for the Warriorites to pass through.

Those villagers who weren't part of the posse, but were with the Warriorites at the time of the miracles, heard the noises and screaming and came to see what had happened. When they saw the demons and their demise, many of them believed in the Warrior and joined the band of Warriorites.

Akeshia looked to see the extent of Wildy's wounds and discovered they were quite severe. His face was beaten hard like she had suspected, but also his back and his stomach were ripped open and bleeding profusely. His eyes and mouth were puffy and swollen and his hair was matted with blood. He had been beaten, kicked, and slapped, and had lost a lot of blood in the process. Quietly to herself, Akeshia wept for him.

Rusty and Michael walked on either side of him and all but carried him back up the mountain. All the way up the mountain Rusty cried to himself. As Wildy's partner, he knew he had failed. He let them get Wildy. All the way up the mountain he apologized to the Warrior. He couldn't forgive himself for what he had allowed to happen.

Wrapped up in these thoughts, Rusty barely said anything. Occasionally Wildy would make a groaning noise, or something that sounded like it, and Rusty would quickly ask him if he was okay, but other than that, not a word.

At the campsite, Akeshia took some water from the lake, heated it over a fire, and took a piece of cloth and cleaned Wildy's wounds. Once she had cleaned them, she bandaged them as best she could, then prepared him a bed and put him in it. He was tired and sore and could barely move, so he didn't put up much of a fight. When he lay down, he sent everyone away except for Rusty.

"Rusty," he spoke so softly that Rusty almost couldn't hear him.

"What is it?" Rusty asked.

"If I don't make it through the night," he said, "promise me you won't give up." Then he looked directly into Rusty's eyes. "I never really thought you'd make it, and I never guessed you'd turn out like this, but the Warrior has made you very powerful... Promise me you won't give that up... I only say that because I know what you've been through. I know how things like this hurt you. Keep caring. Remember, the Warrior knows what's best... Promise?"

Tears filled Rusty's eyes. "I promise," he said.

"One more thing?" Wildy asked.

"What is it?" Rusty replied.

"I saw you crying when you were talking to Ryan. Was your dad like his mother?"

"Sometimes," Rusty said, then he began to cry from the memories.

"Somehow I knew that," Wildy said.

Wildy closed his eyes. His breathing was slow and shallow and at times it seemed like he stopped breathing altogether. In fear Rusty would nudge him or place his head over Wildy's chest to make sure he was still breathing, or he would place his hand over Wildy's heart to make sure it was still beating. Rusty didn't sleep at all that night. He sat by

Wildy and watched him closely all through the night. As he kept his vigil over Wildy, Rusty also continued asking the Warrior for help, that he would heal Wildy like he had healed those people in the village.

Sometime in the middle of the night Akeshia came to relieve Rusty, but he wouldn't leave. So she sat down next to him. For a long time neither of them said anything. Finally Akeshia broke the silence.

"I'm really sorry, Rusty," she said.

"It's not your fault," Rusty told her. "It's my fault. I should have been paying attention. I got so excited about Ryan walking, and the little baby getting well, and all the other things that happened in that town, that I didn't pay attention. I should have noticed something. I let them do this to him."

Akeshia placed her hand on his shoulder. "Forgive yourself, Rusty. There are some things that are out of our control no matter what we do. This was one of them."

All that night, Rusty and Akeshia watched Wildy closely. In the morning Wildy was alive, but he was still very sore and hardly able to move. Rusty still refused to leave Wildy, so Michael and Akeshia took care of the business of the Warriorites for him.

As the days went by, Wildy began to get his strength back, and it became apparent that he was going be okay. By this time Rusty was in such bad shape that they were starting to worry about him, so they had to demand that he get some sleep.

Soon after that, Wildy was up and about, functioning as normal. His bruises were healed, and he felt just like new. He couldn't prove it, but he was absolutely certain that it was the Warrior that had pulled him through.

24

Tye looked around him carefully. He couldn't shake the thought that he was being followed. *I'm getting paranoid*, he thought, and then looked around the room carefully. How could he tell? There must have been hundreds of people all around him. He checked to see if he could notice anything unusual. He didn't notice anything, so he continued walking. Again the feeling came over him, and again he looked around the room. But still he saw nothing. Perhaps he was being too obvious.

So this was the City Building. Of all the years Tye had lived in Darklands City, he had never been inside. He'd heard all his life that it was big, but now that he was inside, it was really big, and he could not get over the magnificence. The first ten floors were nothing but row after row of restaurants, shops, and markets of every kind imaginable. It was like one giant shopping mall. All the shops and businesses ran around the outside parameters of the building, and on the inside was a large open space where one could stand and look up into the huge structure of the building. Glass elevators, three on each wall, moved up and down at an almost dizzying speed. In the center of the whole building, large cliffs of rock and dirt reached up into the rafters of the ceiling, and a waterfall made its way down from the tenth floor to a pool below. The pool was also made of dirt and stone, and Tye almost felt as if he were out in some sort of modern meadow. The water was crystal clear and looked as if it were at least a story deep. Tye thought he could see a whole other level under the pool, but he couldn't be sure.

He stood at the foot of the waterfall, watching the water cascade into the middle of the City Building. *What an incredible building*, he thought to himself. Then suddenly that feeling came back—the feeling that he was being watched. He didn't like this feeling at all. He lowered his head to about chest level and looked around his arms and shoulders to see behind him. Still he could not make out anyone specifically looking at him. He took a deep breath. *I'm just paranoid*, he told himself. *With all these people here, I'm bound to feel like someone is watching me.* He leaned over to get a better look in the pond. As he looked down deep into the water, he noticed something he hadn't noticed before. There were fish swimming around in it. Very big fish. *No, those aren't fish...those are sharks.* Tye took a deep breath. *They put sharks in a pool inside a shopping mall? What kind of people do that?* Then suddenly Tye noticed another face staring up at him. He spun around to see who it was, and before he could say anything, a hand grabbed him around the back of the head, pulled him close to a girl's face, and she kissed him. He struggled to break free of the girl's grasp, but she had caught him completely off guard, and she held him there tightly no matter how he struggled.

"Who are you?" he gasped as soon as she let him go.

She placed her finger on his lips tenderly and looked him directly in the eye.

Now that Tye had a good look at her he noticed that she was indeed a very beautiful girl. She had long dark hair that hung down to the middle of her back, alive with curl. Her skin was dark and soft, and her figure...Tye couldn't take his eyes off her. She was the most beautiful woman Tye had seen in a long time. Her face had a sort of tough look, but it didn't threaten Tye. Instead it seemed somewhat gentle behind that tough exterior. She seemed to Tye like she was definitely the type of woman that could take care of herself in just about any situation.

But why did she kiss him like that? Did he know her from somewhere? Had she mistaken him for someone else? Or was this her way of picking up dates? He had certainly never had this kind of a response from any girl in his life. Girls of her beauty usually never gave him a second glance.

She looked into his eyes for several moments; her eyes darted back and forth as she studied his face. "You *are* Tye?" she asked.

"Yes," Tye responded.

"I'm Sam."

Tye looked at her. "You're Sam?"

"It's short for Samantha," she told him. "I get this all the time. Most people are a little shocked to see that I'm a female."

"But why did you kiss me?" Tye asked.

She took him by the hand. "It's less suspicious that way. People will think we're dating, and they won't suspect anything."

"But shouldn't we be meeting in secret?" Tye asked.

"It's too dangerous," Sam told him.

They walked around the building, looking into the shops and holding hands like they were in love. Tye enjoyed holding her hand, but this whole procedure confused him. Why were they going to such lengths to look like lovers? Sam watched a couple of kids playing, and then joined in the game.

The kids seemed to really enjoy her. Tye watched her closely. She really was beautiful. But he had much more important things on his mind. Yet he was glad when she took his hand again. He held it like he was really in love.

Soon they stopped at one of the restaurants and picked up something to eat. They took it with them back down to the waterfall, sat on the ledge, and ate. As they ate, Sam looked deep into Tye's eyes.

"What is it?" Tye asked her.

"You don't look like the kind of guy who could be a criminal," she bluntly told him.

Tye suddenly became very uncomfortable and started to squirm.

"It's okay," she told him. "I know who you're with."

Tye looked at her. He hadn't given anyone that information. He didn't know what to say or how to respond to her.

"Look," she said to him again, "don't worry. Your secret's safe with me. I promise."

"Shouldn't we go somewhere else and talk?" Tye asked.

"It's okay," she said. "The sound of the water will cover us talking. We're less conspicuous that way."

Tye's paranoia took over again. How did he know that he could trust her? What if she was setting him up? With those questions on his mind, he pulled away from her. She sensed Tye's concern, pulled him to his feet, and held him close to her. Then she again kissed him. This time Tye felt her stick something in his back pocket. It felt like a wallet. "Everything you requested is in there," she whispered in his ear. "Your new ID, your work orders, and your security clearance. You report for work right after lunch. You're on the top floor. Floor one hundred and ninety-six. There's a special elevator at the end of the corridor that leads away from the waterfall. Look around for it ahead of time and don't look like you don't know where it is. Under no circumstances do you act like you don't know what you're doing. Lunch is over in about a half-hour; I suggest you use that time to familiarize yourself with everything in the building. Find the corridor to the elevator, and then walk around some. That way you won't look suspicious. Once you get to the top floor, talk to the receptionist. Her name is Sneau (pronounced snow). She will take you around." Then she handed him a magazine. "Read this," she demanded, "and then throw it in the incinerator. It's right over there." She pointed toward a large bin in the corner near one of the less traveled corners of the building. "Nobody will take anything out of there—that's where they dump the grease and other chemicals from the restaurants. Make sure you're casual about it, and try not to be seen. I'll be by to pick you up after work. Then I'll give you everything you'll need. But for now this will do you. Meet me here. And remember, I got you in, but the rest is up to you." Then she turned and left.

Tye stood there quietly. He didn't know what else to do. Sam certainly knew how to make him feel at ease around her. He enjoyed her approach. It was nice being able to talk to someone. He had been forced to lay low ever since he entered the city, and he had gotten very lonely. He swallowed hard and walked around the building like she had told him. He saw the corridor. It was hard to spot at first, buried back behind the waterfall, but Tye managed to find it. As he passed by the hallway, he noticed that it stretched as far back as he could see. He had some time to kill until it was time to report to work, so he walked back around and sat down on one of the benches away from the water where he could hear better.

As he sat there, finishing his lunch and reading the magazine Sam had given him, another gentleman sat down next to him. They sat there for several moments, neither of them saying a thing. Tye looked over the magazine. The first two articles in it were the most boring articles he had ever read. He couldn't even decipher what they were talking about. It seemed to be some sort of technical magazine, but for what Tye could not make out. Finally the guy next to Tye started to make conversation.

"I never thought they'd get this thing stabilized after the earthquake," the man said.

Tye looked at him. He wasn't exactly sure what the man

was talking about, but he had to say something. Something that seemed somewhat intelligible.

"Well," he said carefully, "you work at it, and you'd be surprised what you can do."

"Good thought," the guy responded. Then he turned to Tye and held out his hand to shake. "My name's Lyle. I work on 136."

At first Tye wasn't sure what he meant, but he quickly pieced it together. Of course it occurred to him that he didn't know what his new name was, and he had to quickly scramble to make one up. "Lenny," he said quickly, and he shook Lyle's hand. "One hundred ninety-six."

Tye watched as the color suddenly drained completely out of Lyle's face. His eyes darted back and forth, and he quickly looked around the room to see if anyone was watching. Then he stared at Tye for a moment and withdrew his hand.

"I'm sorry," Lyle said softly. "I didn't know. I really didn't. Please don't tell anyone. Usually, nobody from there comes down here. I had no way of knowing. Please don't say anything." His eyes had a look of terror as he begged Tye not to tell anyone.

"I won't say a thing," Tye assured him. "I promise."

Lyle looked at him. "Thank you," he said and quickly picked up his things and left. Tye was once again alone. Why did Lyle act like that? What was it that Tye said?

He opened up the magazine again. When he got to the third article, he could see what it was Sam wanted. The magazine had been disguised as a technical magazine, but inside he noticed that the magazine carried information pertaining to Darklands City and the leaders. It told him about the City Building, about its history, and about some of the city's leaders. He also found a little insert that had been slid into the middle of the magazine. The insert told him his name, his age, his date of birth, and everything else Tye would need to know when questioned. He almost laughed when he read that he had a code six security clearance. *What the heck is a code six security?*

• • •

Soon it was time for Tye to head upstairs to his first day on the job. He moved cautiously down the corridor. As he continued farther and farther down, the corridor began to turn corner after corner, one after the other, and it slanted downwards. Tye felt as if he were in some sort of maze, and he didn't understand why the floor continued to descend when he was supposed to be going up.

He looked around him and saw cameras everywhere, monitoring the hallways. They were hanging from the ceiling and coming out of the walls. There wasn't a single area that a camera could not see. Tye knew that he had better play it cool, so he stuck his hands deep into his pockets and continued as casually as he could down the hall, corner after corner.

Soon the hall began to fill with people, most of them soldiers. They moved around the hallway, all looking at him like they suspected him of something. Tye deliberately slowed his pace, so as not to give them the impression that he was in a hurry, and thus arouse their suspicions any more than they already seemed to be.

He finally came to a large metal door. It loomed over him like some sort of iron vault, waiting like a trap for anyone foolish enough to think they could outsmart it. The door had all sorts of electrical devices running across it, and Tye could only guess what they were for. To the right of the door, a metal box with a light blinking erratically on and off caught his attention. Tye could see that it was the security lock. Now was the time to see if he could really trust Sam. He pulled the wallet out of his back pocket and found a security card. He swallowed hard. Perhaps Sam was right, maybe he wasn't the criminal type. Until recently, he had never in his life done anything illegal. The only thing he ever did that landed him in jail was to know Anna. And up until he met Rhend, he didn't even know that was a crime. He thought about turning back, but then thought better of it. After all, with all these cameras and these people watching him, someone might get suspicious; he could wind up in more trouble than he already was in. No, he was committed to it, and he had to go through with it. And whatever happened from this point, he had to take it as it came. He took a deep breath and ran the card through the slot on the top of the electric box.

The box chirped and beeped, and then let out an ear-piercing screech. Tye froze. It was the wrong card, and he was caught. He wanted to run, but he could not move.

Then door swung open, almost knocking Tye against the wall. One of the guards at the long desk near the door saw this and laughed to himself, then went back to his work. "Must be a rookie," the guard said under his breath. Tye stood in the doorway for a couple of moments until he realized that the screech was just the door alerting him and everyone else in the room that his card had been accepted. His relief was so great that when he finally let out his breath, he almost passed out in the doorway from the lack of oxygen in his brain. He pulled his card out of the box and entered the next room. The door closed behind him with a heavy bang.

He looked around the room. It was beautiful. It had posh carpet wall to wall, and was beautifully decorated with elegant furniture. Expensive portraits hung on the walls, and large lofty plants gave the room a certain...he didn't quite know how to put it, but it was like he had walked into a mansion. To Tye's right as he entered the room, huge glass doors spanned the entire length of the wall. A closer examination of the glass revealed that the glass was scored around bars that ran through the glass and made the walls impenetrable. Guards roamed the room, watching everything.

Everywhere he looked he saw cameras, electronic boxes like the one on the door, and armed guards—many armed guards. Judging from the tight security, he guessed that this must be where the dignitaries entered and exited the building. The sight of all this brought back to Tye exactly who he was, and what it was he was doing, and again, a shot of panic ran through his body.

At that moment he heard sirens approaching. They grew louder and louder as they approached, until they were deafening. Again he thought he was caught. He fought as hard as he could to keep his feet firmly planted on the floor, afraid that the slightest movement might bring about some serious repercussions. He turned around to see a motorcade approaching. The cars pulled up to the front door, and every guard in the building mobilized. A long black limo pulled up, and several very distinguished people stepped out of it. The entourage made their way in front of Tye and to the elevator. One of the guards ran his card through the box, and the elevator opened.

Damn! he thought angrily to himself. *My nerves are shot, and this stuff keeps happening.*

Once everything had quieted down, Tye once again headed toward the elevator. He ran the card once again through the electronic sensor. The sensor beeped and blinked, then screeched. The elevator doors opened, and Tye walked in.

The elevator was huge. It was like stepping into a small room. The floor was carpeted, there were pictures on the walls, glass on the ceiling, it was well lit, and there was a small couch and a chair inside, so that one could sit and enjoy the ride one hundred and ninety-six floors into the sky.

The elevator attendant/guard looked over at Tye. "What floor, sir?" he asked.

Tye looked over at him. He couldn't believe it. Even the elevator attendant was a guard, and he was as fully armed as everyone else.

"One hundred ninety-six," Tye said, almost in a whisper.

The guard punched a series of buttons, and the doors closed. Tye was glad he was the only person in the elevator. As soon as the doors closed, he felt a sudden thrust, and it felt as if he were being sucked through the door. The elevator began to move at a speed that made Tye sick.

All the way up to the top, Tye found himself being closely watched by the elevator attendant/guard. He couldn't help but wonder what this meant. Did the attendant watch everybody like this, or was it something Tye was doing? Maybe it was the way he looked. Tye became very self-conscious, and the guard didn't seem to mind that Tye knew he was staring.

I'm just being paranoid, Tye thought again, and he did his best to ignore the attendant. Although the couch and chair were there to sit on, Tye thought better of it. He wasn't sure of the protocol there, and thought it best to stand. He looked over at the elevator attendant again. This time he looked down at the name tag. The guard had a silver and gold bar that hung smartly on his shirt pocket. The name imprinted on the bar said "Timothy."

While in the elevator, he went over everything he had read in the magazine in his head, trying to make sure he didn't miss anything. His new name was Matthew Ryan. He quickly rehearsed all the information provided to him. His age, his qualifications, and his job description. Matthew...what kind of a name was Matthew? Any information that he wasn't sure of, he would remember and make a note of, and when he got a chance he would find a quiet place and look over his ID cards again.

The elevator slowed to a stop, and Tye felt his stomach drop as it did. *This elevator ride is going to be tough getting used to,* he thought.

"Here you are," Timothy spoke at last. Express, all the way up to the top."

The doors swung open, and Tye could not believe what he saw. This did not look like an office at all, but a palace. Large scarlet drapes hung on the windows from floor to ceiling. Immense pillars spanned the space between the floor and ceiling. The floor was marble, and broken only by soft pathways of carpet that led from one hallway to the other.

Tye approached the receptionist. "Are you Sneau?" he asked.

"Can I help you?" she responded.

"Personnel sent me...Sam."

Sneau looked up at him and smiled. "Certainly." Then she caught him off guard with her next question. "Are you Sam's new boyfriend?"

Tye didn't know how to respond. He looked at Sneau carefully before saying anything. Her eyes seemed to be searching his face, looking for something. He searched her face for some kind of hint as to what he should say. But Sneau's face gave no such information. This could have been a trick question. "Well," he said shyly. "We've been seeing each other, but I didn't realize that it was official."

"Well you know, Sam," Sneau laughed nervously, "she does seem to move things along."

"That she does," Tye laughed back.

Sneau's eyes softened, and the muscles in her face relaxed. Her body posture took on a softer air to it, and she took Tye by the arm. She led him through the front office and through the halls into the heart of the 196th floor. She detailed his job as a page boy and what that required. He would be asked to run messages from these offices to other offices on the floor, in the building, and possibly throughout Darklands City. He would do research for officials in the building if asked; he could be called on to run errands, and he could even have to deliver meals when meetings got long and arduous. He was at the beck and call of every official on the floor. Sneau pointed out to Tye that the only people on this floor were the highest ranking in the city, and that they were to be treated with the utmost respect. She left nothing out, but explained everything very carefully to him, in great detail. After explaining something to Tye, she would make him repeat it back to her. The tone in her voice was very serious, and moment by moment as he talked with her, he became more and more aware that he had embarked on a very serious and dangerous mission. But Sneau never came out and said anything regarding Sam or his real mission. Everything was treated very formally, and the only thing Sneau really talked about was the job. She carefully pointed out specific rooms, such as the library which contained all the official documents of Darklands City, and the records room where records were kept on citizens, both alive and dead. Following her lead, Tye never brought anything up. He made it a point to take great care in watching everything around him at every moment so that he might prepare himself for any situation.

Sneau announced to him that they were almost done with the tour, and that it would be time for Tye to take his position. She made it as clear to Tye as she could that in his job, he had little or nothing to say. He was to listen and do, and that was it. Never question anything. This was a top-secret job, and any deviation of one's duties could result in immediate termination of both job and life.

Tye swallowed hard again. This day was not at all the type of day that he would like to repeat. All this fear was exhausting.

They were making their way to the front of the room again, down one of the long and dark hallways. While they were passing one of the rooms, a large double door swung open, almost hitting Tye in the face. He quickly jumped back and waited for the door to close. The door closed, and a man looked back at Tye.

"Did I hit you?" he asked.

"No, I'm fine," Tye said politely, not wanting to offend anyone his first day on the job.

The gentleman looked over at Sneau. "Is this a new employee?" he asked suspiciously.

"Yes, sir," she responded. "He's been sent up from personnel. He's a new page boy."

The man looked hard at Tye. His eyes were piercing and powerful, and they seemed to see things that the ordinary person might not notice. There was something about them that Tye did not like. Tye hated to think it, but he saw something suspicious, almost like what he saw in Rhend's eyes back in the jailhouse in Volkstag. But as uncomfortable as Tye was, he didn't dare blink. He planted his feet firmly on the ground and held the man's gaze. There was something very strange about this man, and Tye sensed that he must be very powerful by the way Sneau acted around him. She seemed to get very quiet and reserved, and even afraid. But Tye continued to hold his gaze. The man seemed to approve of Tye's stance. Soon a smirk crossed his face, then he broke out into a full smile.

"Personnel sent you up?" he asked Tye.

"Yes, sir," Tye replied.

"And what did you do before that?" the man asked.

Tye shot a glance out of the corner of his eyes to Sneau. She was cool, but he could tell that she was nervous. He didn't know what to say. This was not something he had talked over with Sam, and he hadn't had the chance to go over it with Sneau. In his mind he asked the Warrior to help him out. *Please*, he thought. *Help me come up with something to say.* Then suddenly he blurted out without even thinking, "I worked downstairs in the mall."

What a stupid thought! he said to himself. He knew that he was dead for sure. How could he have said something like that? He looked over at Sneau, and she didn't look too happy with that answer either.

"You worked down in the mall?" the man shouted. "Personnel sent a storekeeper up here?"

His stare turned icy, and Tye didn't know what to do. He continued to hold the man's gaze. Again he sent up a message to the Warrior to bail him out. And again, almost as if something had a hold of his mouth, he blurted out. "Personnel knows me, and they have known me for years."

Again he wanted to kick himself for what he just said, but the man's expression suddenly changed again, and this time it was hard for Tye to figure out.

"They do?" the man questioned.

"Yes, sir," Tye replied.

The two looked at each other a while longer. Tye hoped the man didn't ask any more questions, because he didn't have any more answers. He didn't even know what he was doing now.

"How do they know you?" the man asked again.

Tye could feel his body turning numb. This was not the time to improvise. What should he do? Again he sent a silent plea up to the Warrior. This time he begged the Warrior to help him out. But this time nothing responded. He could not think of anything to say. So he stood there, feeling stupid and saying nothing.

"You can tell me!" the man snapped. "I've got code six clearance."

Code six clearance! Tye thought. *So that's what code six clearance is.* He looked at the man again, and this time said quietly and as politely as possible, "As do I, sir."

The man gave him a strange look.

Sneau seemed to pick up on something, almost as if she knew what it was Tye was doing, even though Tye himself didn't. Then the man looked over at Sneau. He could see the recognition on her face.

"He's a plant?" the man asked her.

"He's dating Sam," Sneau said to him.

The man laughed. "You lucky devil, you," he grinned. Why didn't you just say so in the first place? But then, I know why." Then he put both his hands on Tye's shoulders. "You follow orders very well. Never tell anyone who you are, no matter who it is, or what's at stake. I like you; you've got guts. What's your name, son?"

"Matthew," Tye said quickly, remembering his new name.

"Well, Matthew," the man said, "I like your style. You're too good to be a lowly page boy. From now on, you will work with me."

Tye heard Sneau take a deep breath, but he dared not look over at her, so he kept his eyes fixed on the man in front of him.

"You will be my personal liaison. I'm swamped with work, with the peace summit coming up, and I could really use the help. And you have the clearance, so you've been briefed in all this." Then he looked over at Sneau. "Call down to personnel and tell them to find a new page boy, and that I will be taking Matthew."

"Yes, sir," Sneau responded. She quickly excused herself to take care of the gentleman's bidding. As soon as she was gone, the man put his hand on Tye's shoulder, and ushered him into the room.

"Follow me, Matthew," the man said.

"Yes, sir," Tye responded.

"Oh, by the way," the man said, "you can call me Max. Just Max."

25

Tye sat alone in Max's office. It was late in the night, early in the morning. He pulled one of the large high-back chairs that Max kept for guests near to the windows and looked out over Darklands City. It looked so different from up here. Up here he was where the power was; this was where the games were played, and this is where life or death were nothing but numbers and statistics, and they meant less than out there on the streets. He looked at his watch. It said 3:30 A.M. *My god, it's late*, he thought. *If I don't get some sleep I'm going to be exhausted in the morning.* He set the book he was reading down in his lap and rubbed his eyes. He had been working with Max for several weeks now, and in that time he had made it a point to learn everything he could about the Darklands hierarchy of power. He spent every bit of free time in the library or with any books that he could get. Yet he still didn't know what to do. The lists of people and the rules of the game seemed so confusing to him.

He had come to work in the City Building so that he could gather information, so that he could find unused ID numbers and make them available to the Warriorites and others who weren't able to get one for one reason or another. In short, he was a spy. It was his job through a series of contacts to keep the Warriorites informed of everything that was going on in Darklands City. But Tye refused to think of himself as a spy, fearing that this might cause him to make a mistake somehow. If he thought of himself as Matthew, he felt he stood a better chance of protecting his alias.

He thought back to the last night back at the camp with Mark and his new friends. With the news of the new identification procedures, many Warriorites and others who didn't make it into the good graces of the government were starving. They couldn't buy food, they couldn't buy clothes, and they couldn't even buy medicine. Tye decided on his own to leave the group and move into Darklands City to find a way to get ID numbers and information to the Warriorites throughout the Darklands. Everyone else in the group tried to talk him out of it, but Tye had to do something. He couldn't just stand back and watch these people starve or go without clothing or other basic necessities of life, or worse, to die because they were unable to buy medicine or medical help.

Once Tye's new friends realized that there was no way they were going to talk Tye out of his plan, they agreed to help him out; if he could get the information to them, they would run it to the Warriorites.

Tye thought about where he was now. It must have been the Warrior who had put him there. He came to the City Building to be merely a page boy, and now he was in a place where he could really do some good. He had started out as a page boy, but instead he became the personal runner for the most powerful man in the Darklands.

But Max was always hovering over him like a mother hen

over her chicks. Sometimes it was almost impossible to do what he came to do. He sent a mental message up to the Warrior. *If I could just have some time*, he said. *Some time away from Max so that I can get some things done*. But he never said anything out loud, knowing how dangerous that would be. Tye made it a rule not even to talk to himself. That way he would never give away anything unwittingly.

Suddenly he became aware of another presence in the room. He quickly spun around in his chair, and there was Max sitting behind his desk, watching Tye.

"I didn't hear you come in," Tye said, once he caught his breath.

"Well you looked so peaceful," Max said.

Tye turned and looked back out the window.

"It's different out there this time of night isn't it?" Max asked him.

"It's not so chaotic," Tye said.

"Looks are deceiving," Max replied.

For several moments neither of them said anything. Tye had gotten used to being with Max, so he wasn't as nervous anymore, but he was constantly on guard, more so with Max around than ever.

"I see you're doing some reading," Max questioned.

"Got to stay on top of things if you're going to stay on top," Tye answered.

"You've got a lot of drive, Matthew," Max said. "It'll take you a long way in life. Just be careful not to become overzealous."

Tye wasn't sure if that was a threat, a warning, a suggestion, or really what Max was getting at, but he took it in stride and merely shook his head. Again there was silence for several minutes.

"What do you know about the Warriorites?"

Max's question caught Tye completely off guard.

"The who?" he asked more out of reflex than anything.

"Surely you've heard of the Warriorites?" Max questioned suspiciously.

"Yes, sir, I have," Tye whispered, looking out the window. "I get really jittery when people talk about them."

Max got up from his desk, grabbed a chair, and moved it next to Tye's in front of the window. He sat there quietly, looking out for quite some time. Tye couldn't help but notice that Max looked edgy. The color had left his face and he looked nervous. Was he afraid of something? Had the Warriorites done something? He had heard of the episode in the little village and the murder of Rhend. Everyone in the underworld had heard of Rhend's disappearance. It had been a struggle for Max, but in the name of the mayor, Max seized all Rhend's holdings and kept them from being taken over by someone else.

Tye also thought it strange that Max had all the power. He was really nobody in the greater scheme of things, but yet everybody feared him, including Tye. *Mr. Myer is just a figure-head*, Tye thought to himself. *That's the way power works. But how in the world did I wind up working for Max?*

Max's voice suddenly rocketed Tye back out of his thoughts. "Do you believe in the Warrior, Matthew?" he asked.

Tye looked over at him. "I'm not sure," he said.

"How about Draygon?" Max asked again.

"Well," Tye replied cautiously. "I know that something is behind all this. But isn't it possible that a lot of this is fabricated? You know how rumors start. Something gets said, and then as it's repeated, the details get changed little by little, until the story isn't anything like the actual event. Isn't it possible that these Warriorites made up their name, and that they murdered Rhend, and that they do all these killings, and that they rely on the rumors and stories of supernatural carryings on to keep the people afraid for their lives, and then use that fear to control them?"

Max looked closely at Tye. "Surely you can't be that cynical," he said quietly.

"I don't know," Tye said. "I just find that enemies of the common folk are often fabricated, overblown fantasies created by an uneducated mind with too many myths and legends running around unchecked by any real scientific understanding or basis of reality."

"You are that cynical," Max laughed. "Yet the Warriorites give you the jitters."

Max looked over at Tye, but Tye only continued looking out the windows.

"The Warriorites are extremists," Tye said.

"That's possible," Max said, still smiling. But then he suddenly got very serious. "Listen, Matthew," he said, and his voice seemed to tremble. "I've got to go to a meeting tomorrow. A very important meeting. Mr. Myer will be running things while I'm gone, and I want you to keep an eye on everything he does. He's a greedy and stupid man, and I shouldn't be surprised if he doesn't try something. Everybody here knows who you are, so use that power if you have to."

"Shouldn't I be going with you?" Tye asked.

"No, I'm afraid not." Max's voice trailed off into the darkness. "This is one meeting that I must attend alone. Absolutely nobody else can know about it." Then he gave Tye a very serious look. "Is that clear?"

"Yes, sir, it is," Tye responded.

"I like you, Matthew," Max responded. Then once again he got very quiet. For several hours they both sat there, saying very little, locked up in their own private worlds. Tye would have given anything to know what had Max so quiet, but he kept silent. Max seemed to enjoy the company, so Tye sat there as long as Max did.

Then, early that morning, before the sun had come up, Max suddenly shook himself and got up out of the chair.

"Well," he said at last, "I'd better get going. Remember, Matthew."

Tye put his hands to his lips and made the motion of turning a key to lock and seal them. "My lips are sealed," he said.

"Good," Max responded. "We don't want Mayor Myer getting any delusions of grandeur."

"God forbid," Tye joked.

Max looked at him for a couple more minutes, then opened the door and left. Tye turned back to the window and watched the sun come up over the River Thromins. He had some time. How much time he didn't know, but he had some time. As soon as the sun was up, he immediately went to work.

26

As soon as Max arrived at his destination, he was immediately ushered into a long dark hall by two guards. The hall was extremely long, and the ceiling was high and lofty. The floor was made of cobblestone, delicately pieced together, and the walls were made of large stones stacked upon each other one by one and cemented together with mortar. There were massive pillars along the sides of the hall and in the center of the hall supporting the weight of the ceiling. The ceiling was covered with gothic paintings and strange symbols that not even Max could recognize. The hall was beautifully decorated and elegant. But despite its beauty, the air in the room was cold and musty and the hall was vast and unfriendly.

From the hall, Max and his guides entered a room guarded

by several hundred elegantly dressed guards, as guards go. They wore black pants with golden seams that ran up the outside of their legs and black and gold shirts inlaid with silver warlike designs. From their right shoulders a silver cord hung down and across their chests and tucked neatly into the seams of the lower breast on the left-hand side. From their left shoulders, scarlet capes hung about halfway down their backs and tucked into the seams of the lower right-hand side of the shirts. Beautiful swords hung in sheaths along their sides. They were in top physical shape, and they stood as still as stone statues. Their eyes didn't blink, and it looked to Max like they weren't even breathing. They were truly impressive to look at, but they were nothing to be reckoned with. They were hard and cold, and never thought twice about doing their masters bidding, regardless of what that might be. They would brutally torture and kill their own brother, or father, or mother if they were ordered to do so.

The room was more like a long dark corridor than an actual room. Beautiful tapestries depicting fierce and brutal battles lined the wall, scarlet draperies hung from the pillars, and a coat of arms decorated the ceiling. The room was divided in half by a narrow piece of red carpet that ran the length of the room. On either side of the carpet, long marble tables stretched lengthwise toward the front of the room. They were tall and solemn, like in a courtroom. Behind the tables were rows of wooden high-back seats, carved with strange figures and shapes. The chairs were filled with people in long red and black robes and solemn faces. The room looked like a courtroom, and these people looked like the jury.

At the front of the great hall, several steps made their way up to a large platform, and sitting on that platform was the most magnificent throne. The arms of the throne were lined with beautiful gems, and it also had a high back with the same strange carvings, only these carvings were laced with gold. Expensive cloth lined the seat. The throne was heavily guarded. Six of the most powerful guards stood around the throne on the platform. The only light in the room was provided by hundreds of candles burning throughout the hall. The light from the candles flickered and sputtered as the air currents in the room carelessly batted the flame around from side to side. The light cast eerie shadows as it fluttered from side to side with the whim of the air around it.

Two guards met Max and his escort at the entrance to the room. They took Max by the arms and escorted him down the long dark corridor until they were standing in front of the platform at the bottom of the stairs. Max could feel the eyes of all those people behind the benches as the guards half-led, and half-dragged him down the narrow, carpeted pathway to the front. In this darkness, Max could not make out the faces of those at the marble tables, so he had no way of knowing what expressions they might bear, whether pleased or cold. But from their silence and the forcefulness of his escort, this was not to be a pleasurable visit.

The guards brought Max to the bottom of the stairs and forced him down on one knee before the monarch on the throne. From here, Max could see the man on the throne. The man wore a crown that rose several inches above his forehead. He also wore a white robe with gold inlays around the hem of his feet and his hands. The gown draped around the monarch's feet as he sat there, looking down on Max. He looked like he was very old and frail, almost as if he might break if he had to move too quickly, but at the same time his eyes were frightening and powerful, and they seemed to bore right into Max. He may have looked fragile, but he had a power Max could not even imagine, and Max could see it in the eyes.

As Max stared at the man, Draygon entered the room. He was unseen by anyone there, but his presence was felt nonetheless. He walked up to the front of the room, perched atop of the throne, and glared down at Max. Max could not see Draygon, but he suddenly felt something horrible and powerful just beyond his reach, and he became very frightened.

"You called for me, sir?" Max bowed humbly.

"Did we not commission a task of you?" the man asked him.

"The task you commissioned of me, I have completed. I obtained for you the Darklands. I've obeyed your orders in handling affairs of state, and I've kept you completely anonymous," Max replied with a shaky voice.

"That you have," someone from the other side of the room spoke out. "But there is still the problem of the young man, Wildy, and his Warriorites. You were to abolish this menace from the face of the earth. Now he's grown in power once again, and with this young sorcerer, Rusty, his power has grown stronger than ever."

"I am doing all I can think of," Max replied. "We've made them outlaws, we've put high prices on their heads, and we've authorized their deaths at any cost. We've created intricate identification procedures so that they cannot do anything without being able to identify themselves properly. Yet they continue to grow in numbers." Max was pleading, doing everything he could to shift the blame off of himself and onto something or someone else, but this did little to impress either the monarch on the throne or anyone else in the room.

"This Warrior and his followers are enemies of the Great Emperor and of the Darklands. Find them or it will be your life!" the monarch on the throne said fiercely to him.

"But, sir...," Max started to say, but that's as far as he got. No sooner had he started to protest than Draygon dropped down on the throne and entered the monarch's body. With a sudden surge of power, the monarch stood up, walked down to Max, and slapped him across the face.

"There are no excuses!" Draygon snapped as he slapped Max again. "You were commissioned to do a job, and I will tolerate no less than their complete annihilation from the Darklands. Then he took the monarch's body and sat him back down on the throne. "Now leave my presence, and do not return until you bring us news of the deaths of Wildy and his companion, Rusty."

Max could not believe the difference in the physiology of the monarch. He had suddenly become very powerful. He stood up out of the chair. Max didn't really have a lot of time to think about it, though, as the monarch once again spoke to him.

"We now wish to demonstrate to you that we are not playing some child's game, but we are indeed serious." Then the monarch looked at someone behind Max. "Guard," he called out. "Have this man beaten, and then thrown out of this court."

As soon as he finished with his command, Draygon again left the body of the monarch and took his perch above the throne. The monarch's body again became frail and still.

Draygon had no sooner finished speaking than the guards were upon Max. They grabbed Max by the arms and ripped off his shirt. Max begged and pleaded for mercy, but all his pleas fell on deaf ears. Two guards continued to hold him by the arms, and another guard flogged him. There was great pleasure in the voices of the guards as they brought the whip down again and again on Max's back. Most of the time, their aim seemed a little off, and the whip would wrap around and cut Max's stomach. Max could not help but think that it was on purpose that the guard continued to miss. Lash after lash made its way down Max's back and legs. He screamed out in pain, but this only seemed to excite everyone in the room, especially Draygon, who egged the guards on. He laughed viciously and threw himself around the room, screaming with the rage that consumed him.

Soon the beating was over; Max was physically picked up and carried out of the hall by the two guards. They lifted him up like they were carrying a book and tossed him about as far once they were out of the hall.

Max stood in the courtyard and stared back at the hall. His back and shoulders and legs and stomach were oozing with blood, so he washed himself off in the fountain outside in the courtyard. The courtyard was heavily guarded, he could see, and these people were not the type of people that Max was willing to take too much risk with. He now wished that he wouldn't have taken the job, but it was too late. He had, and now he had to live with the consequences. It all seemed so wonderful at first. Ultimate power of the Darklands, lots of money, and anything else he wanted... But now someone else was pulling the strings, and it could cost him his life.

When they threw him out of the hall, one of the guards had thrown Max's shirt back to him so Max took it, dipped it in the fountain, and cleaned himself off. His stomach wasn't so hard to get to, and his legs he could get to with some difficulty, but his back was a whole different matter. With the amount of pain that he felt all through his upper body, it was nearly impossible for him to reach behind and gently pat off the blood, which by now had begun to dry and clot. So every time he did reach behind him, the wounds would again open, and then they would start bleeding all over again. It was almost useless for Max to even try to clean them off.

Tye and Sam drove along the country road together on the pretense of going on a picnic. The sun was high above them, the day was warm, and the air seemed almost motionless. But despite the beautiful weather and the pleasant day, neither Tye nor Sam were speaking to each other.

Tye turned the car onto the little road and pulled off near a quiet little campsite out of the way from everything else. Meanwhile, Sam rifled through some documents trying to get them all in order. There were a few people at the little camping area, but for the most part it was quiet. Tye pulled the car into the parking lot, and they pulled their gear out of the car and carried it over to a quiet and shaded little place near the river.

They were near the Feldspiz (Feld shpits) River, which ran south from the Alnon mountains and joined the River Thromins only about ten miles downstream.

When they found a cozy little spot, somewhat secluded by trees yet still visible to passersby, they laid a blanket down on the ground and set up for their picnic. Sam pulled some plates and other utensils out of a basket they had brought, and they sat down to eat.

Sam handed Tye a plate of food, and he took it from her. But instead of eating, he played with it. He swirled it around and around with his fork, all the while looking aimlessly over the river, not really paying any attention to what he was doing. Sam looked at him compassionately.

"Look!" she said finally, pulling Tye out of his daze. "I'm sorry. I didn't know things would go this far. I never meant to hurt you. I was trying to protect you. To protect us, and it seemed that the safest way for us to be inconspicuous was to pretend that we were lovers."

"It's not your fault," Tye whispered toward the river. "I should have better control over my emotions. That's all."

"You're a nice guy...," Sam started to say, but Tye stopped her.

"Don't say that. Do you know how many times in my life I've heard that line?"

"I'm sorry," Sam said again.

Tye continued looking over the river. *How could I be so stupid?* he asked himself. He knew that what he was doing was dangerous. Yet he allowed himself to fall for Sam. *It's that we've been working so hard and so close*, he thought to himself. *It's okay*, he continued. *You've survived worse than this.*

His thoughts were soon interrupted by approaching footsteps. He looked up to see Mark. Tye hadn't seen Mark since the night he decided that he would return to Darklands City several weeks ago. Mark was one of his biggest supporters once he realized what it was Tye was doing. He also knew that Mark was a runner for them, but he never thought he'd get the chance to see Mark again. He was so shocked and elated that he almost gave himself away, but said nothing.

"Excuse me," Mark said politely, "but I brought out my food, and then I noticed that I forgot to bring any sort of plates to eat off of. You wouldn't happen to have a couple extra paper plates would you?"

"Certainly," Sam smiled sweetly toward him. Then she reached into the bag and pulled out a couple of plates with some documents sandwiched between them. "Take care," she said to him. "These things are incredibly sensitive."

"No problem," Mark said to her. "I'll take the utmost care with them. Then he turned to leave. He looked over at Tye. "How do you do, sir?" he asked as he passed.

Tye crawled up close to Sam. "That was our contact?"

"I thought you knew that," Sam answered.

"I knew that he was running for us, but I never thought I'd see him again." Tears tried to fill his eyes, and he fought hard to hold them back. Sam saw this, and she took him by the hand and held it close to her. "For the past few months I've been too busy to realize how vulnerable I am. But everything is in such turmoil. I've never been so afraid as I have been recently..." He looked into Sam's eyes. "What puzzles me is this. If you don't believe in the Warrior, then what are you doing fighting for him?"

"I'm not fighting for him," Sam said. "I'm fighting to do something about all those innocent people that are dying out there. This Warrior claims to love his people, yet he allows these horrible events to take place in his so-called domain."

Tye looked at her. He saw a side of her that he had always seen since he met her, but he was just able to put words to it.

"You really do care about those people very much," he said to her, squeezing her hand. "You're a very compassionate person. You don't know it, but that's one of the traits of the Warrior."

Sam looked over at him, but said nothing for several minutes. "I know nothing of the Warrior," she said. "I only fight to bring down this oppressive government. I'm fighting to end the tyranny that beats down and destroys helpless and innocent people."

"You fight with the Warrior," Tye said. "You just don't know it."

"That I don't know," Sam whispered. "But I know that your cause is against the government, and that I will fight for." Then she looked away. "I cannot believe in a supreme being who says he loves, yet he allows men like my father to destroy millions of innocent people."

"Your father?" Tye asked.

"Max," Sam answered.

Tye suddenly felt something shoot through his body like a bullet. He shot up to his feet and walked a little way away from her. Then he turned around and walked back to her. "You mean to tell me that Max is your father?" he whispered close to her ear.

"I thought you knew that," she whispered back. "How do you think you wound up working for him personally? When Sneau told him we were dating, he took you under his wing. That's how you got this gig."

"How did you find out about that?"

"He told me. Over dinner."

"You had dinner with him?" Tye almost shouted.

"Keep you voice down," Sam whispered back. "And yes. I have dinner with him often. How do you think I know so much, and how do you think I got you into the system?"

Tye turned and faced the river. He didn't know what to do. Sam approached him and stood in front of him. She placed her hands on his arms and they looked each other eye to eye for several moments.

"I know you're afraid," Sam said. "I understand that. I'm afraid too. I know that my father would have no qualms about killing me if he ever found out about what I'm doing. All my life I have watched my father beat and intimidate, and ultimately destroy, anyone who dared to get in his way. He is a violent and evil man. I've been afraid of him all my life. Right now he thinks that I do nothing but run around and spend his money. That's what he wants. He wants me out of his way, and as long as that's what he thinks, then we're safe. That's how I've been able to get you and your group into the system." She looked deep into his eyes. "I know you're afraid, but I would never hurt you. Never. You're the sweetest, most tender and tragic person I have ever met."

Tye let down every one of his defenses. He could no longer fight the tears welling up inside of him, and he broke down crying. Sam held him close to her for several minutes. Then she sat back down on the blanket and held out her hand toward Tye. Tye took her hand and sat down next to her. Then he laid his head in her lap, and she ran her fingers through his hair. Tye had years of tears built up, and he let them all go here. He didn't care. He couldn't take this charade anymore. His nerves were shot, his life was empty, and he had nowhere to turn. Except Sam. Soon he looked up at Sam, and she looked back at him.

"When I said you were a nice guy," she said, "I didn't mean it."

"Oh?" Tye question.

Sam continued looking at him. "Oh, what the hell!" she said. "I love you! But I'm afraid too. I don't want to lose you. I don't want to have you taken away from me. My life is dangerous, and I'm just this close to losing it."

Tye looked up to her. "It doesn't matter," he said. "We're both living on the edge. If we stay together as long as we can, then we will always have that—those few days or weeks we are able to spend with each other. All I want is to have you as long as I possibly can. And if I have to say good-bye to you soon, at least I will have had you briefly. That would be easier to take than never having had you at all."

They embraced and held each other for what seemed like hours.

"We'll find a justice of the peace, and we'll do it tomorrow. But we won't tell my father," Sam said at last.

"Max," Tye said quietly. "My father-in-law."

Max returned to his office later that night, enraged. He called a very private emergency meeting with Mr. Myer.

Max could hardly move, and he sat as still as he could in his chair so as not to give away to Mr. Myer that he was in pain. "This Warrior thing is out of hand," he yelled over to Mr. Myer. "You were told that the one condition for your continued power in the Darklands was simply that you were to deal with this situation, and what are you doing about it?"

"Look!" Mr. Myer shouted back. "I'm doing everything I possibly can, but these people are crawling out of the woodwork. Every time we turn around, there's a new group of them forming somewhere in the Darklands. How do you deal with that?"

"A volcano buried one of the cities on the southern border," Max said quietly.

"I know that," Mr. Myer replied.

Max stood up out of his chair and walked around to Mr. Myer, hoping this would intimidate him a little.

"This planet is falling apart because of these punks, and you've done nothing to stop it!" Max was once again shouting.

"I'm doing everything I can," Mr. Myer shouted back. "I'm doing everything I possibly can."

Max gave Mr. Myer a strange look, and he continued to look at Mr. Myer that way for several moments.

"Maybe you are," Max said. "Maybe you are doing all you can, and that just isn't good enough." He grabbed Mr. Myer around the neck and dragged him to the window. He kicked the glass out with his feet, then threw Mr. Myer off the one hundred and ninety-sixth story of the City Building.

Mr. Myer screamed and tried to hold on to Max, but he was taken by surprise and wasn't able to get a good grasp on anything. He clutched and clawed at Max to try and stop his fall, but Max overpowered him, and Mr. Myer fell to his death. Max watched him fall, and then he crossed back over to his desk. His life was on the line, and he wasn't going to lose it because of some incompetent like Mr. Myer.

He sat there in the darkness for several minutes, looking out the broken window. He could tell by the wet feeling all down his back and arms and legs that he was bleeding again, and the pain that accompanied it seemed almost unbearable.

Tye passed by the open door and looked in on Max.

"Are you okay?" Tye asked.

"Matthew," Max said, "you're still here."

"You told me to keep an eye on Mr. Myer," Tye told him, "and he's still here."

"You do your job very well," Max said. "You're very thorough. However, I'm afraid you won't need to be looking after him anymore. He's left us permanently." Max looked toward the broken window, and Tye followed his gaze. "It seems that Mr. Myer has committed suicide."

"I understand," Tye said.

"Take care of things, will you, Matthew?" Max asked. "Make sure that he gets a proper burial. One that no one will ever find."

Tye nodded quietly to Max. "I'm on it immediately," he said.

"I knew you would be," Max said. He got up and walked toward his private bathroom. Tye couldn't help but notice that he seemed to be walking rather stiffly, and that his shirt was soaked in something, but he dared not ask about it. He quietly walked outside of Max's office and into the hall. Once in the hallway, he took a deep breath and leaned against the wall.

He suddenly felt very sick to his stomach. His head was spinning and his body had gone numb. He thought he might throw up, but he knew he'd better not. A move like that might upset Max if he found out about it, so Tye took a couple of deep breaths, then moved down the hall to the elevator where Timothy was still on duty.

"Finally going home, sir?" Timothy asked.

"No, not really," Tye said, and sat down on the couch.

Darklands City was strangely quiet that night. Tye stood along the banks of the River Thromins in a very secluded, industrial area of the city. He could hear police sirens far behind him and other noises of the street that he could not identify. He wished that he could make sense out of the lunatic life style he had suddenly moved into.

He stood there listening to everything around him. But

aside from the very distant police siren and the occasional other noises that Tye could not identify, there was no sound. He constantly looked around him, making sure no one was looking. As he stood there, he tried hard to feel something, something for Mr. Myer, some sort of remorse for what had just happened. But he could not. Mr. Myer was very much responsible for the serious turn of events in the Darklands, and somebody simply did to him what he had indirectly done to thousands, possibly millions, of other people.

I'm numb, Tye thought. *Nothing seems to matter anymore.*

He watched carefully as two men, police officers, took Mr. Myer's body, placed him in a squatting position, wrapped it up tightly in plastic, then in canvas, and put tape around him. They then put him in a high metal drum used for sealing contaminated liquids. They put several sandbags in the bottom of the barrel and filled it with some horrible-looking, foul-smelling liquid chemical. The scent burned Tye's nose and made him nauseous as he breathed it in. He tried to block it out by holding a cloth over his nose, but that didn't seem to do much good.

The officers finished sealing the barrel and rolled it down a dock that stretched several feet over the water and out onto a boat that had been tied up at the end of the dock. They motioned Tye to join them, then they took the boat into the middle of the river and dumped the barrel over. The barrel splashed as it hit the water, and then sank. The sound of the water closing over the drum made Tye's heart sick. *What kind of game was he mixed up in?*

He looked around him to see if anyone might be looking.

"Don't worry about being seen," one of the officers told him. "Nobody ever comes out here. It's safe, trust me."

Tye stared into the darkness. There were no streetlights, and except for the small lantern on the bow of the boat, he could barely see his hand in front of his face. *Oh my god!* he thought. *I've become one of them!*

He motioned the officers to take him back to the shore.

27

Several days later, after Max had a chance to heal, he mobilized the police, the military, and everyone who was able to serve on the force. In his pain and anger, Max lost his sense of caution and declared all-out war against the Warriorites. Max knew the mountain with which the battle of the coven had taken place, and based on all the information coming back to him, he suspected that they had set up some sort of base camp there.

Tye found out about it and tried to get the information to Wildy and Rusty. But for some reason he couldn't find anyone to get the information to them. As a last resort, he called an emergency meeting with Mark. Instead of meeting somewhere out of town, they met in the mall. Tye recognized that this was dangerous, but somehow he had to get the information to Rusty and Wildy quickly lest they be cut off and not able to escape. And with Max so obsessed with this, Tye was on call nearly twenty-four hours a day.

Mark and Tye sat down to dinner together near the water fountain and began chatting. They tried to keep everything on a superficial level for as long as they could. Even when they got down to serious business, they tried to speak to each other in an informal way so that anyone watching would have no reason to suspect anything.

"There's nobody left who can take this," Mark said. "Everyone's gotten out of town. Mr. Myer's 'suicide' has put a stop to people coming and going into the city. It's even more dangerous now than ever."

Tye thought for a minute. He couldn't leave them out to die like that. Somebody had to tell them. "Then I must go," he said.

"Don't be crazy," Mark said. "You've done more here than anyone. It's too dangerous for you to leave. There's still much you can do."

"But I can't leave them to die," Tye said, "and I can't expect someone else to do it."

"You have to expect someone else to do it," Mark told him. "We're fighting for a cause…remember?"

Tye took a drink of his water and looked down into the pool. The sharks were swimming peacefully after having just been fed.

"I'll go," Mark said.

Tye spat his water out, then quickly cleaned it up. "Are you kidding?" he asked.

"I'm the only one left," Mark said, "and somebody has to tell them. I'll do it."

Tye looked at him. He admired Mark. He had since he met Mark in the jailhouse in Volkstag. Mark was a man of courage, with a strong desire to fight—which might have played into why he didn't want to let Mark go. But Mark was right. Somebody had to go, and there was still much Tye could do working for Max.

"All right," Tye conceded. "You go. But take care."

"I will," Mark said. He stood up and shook Tye's hand. "By the way, I understand congratulations are in order."

"Thank you," Tye said, standing up to see Mark off.

"Does Max know?" Mark asked.

"He knows," Tye said, but he's too obsessed with the Warriorites to give it any mind. As long as I keep her busy and out of his way, that's all that matters to him." He looked hard at Mark, then extended his hand again to shake. "Take care," he said quietly.

"You too," Mark said. "Hopefully we will see each other again. If not here, then in the Warrior's kingdom."

"Yes, definitely," Tye said.

They shook hands again and departed.

28

As soon as Mark arrived with the news of Max's planned invasion, Rusty quickly sought the holy scrolls and went back into his memory to see if he could come up with any sort of game plan. They sought the Warrior for his advice, but there was no answer. Wildy didn't know if they should stay or go. They tried every way they could think of to reach a decision, but there seemed to be no answer from the Warrior. At Rusty's advice, since they hadn't gotten anything else from the Warrior, they decided that the risk of leaving was too great, and that they should stay put until they heard otherwise.

Days went by, and the activity in the valley increased. Spies from the Warriorite party went out continually into the valley, gathering any information they could. Information like when the day of the attack might be, how many of them would be arriving, what the plan of battle was; but these answers didn't come. Security was so tight around the whole operation that nothing leaked out.

To Rusty, things were looking more and more desperate. He sought the Warrior with more and more earnest, but still he heard no word. He knew it was insanity to stay there and face those odds when they did have a better chance in the mountains where they had become familiar with the terrain and survival, than they would in the countryside where they were totally exposed and unfamiliar with the area. He was also concerned about trying to leave with so many people down at the bottom of the mountain. Any attempt to escape now might mean capture for certain. So they waited. But Rusty had them move the camp as far up the mountain as they could. Farther and farther up they moved, and while they waited, they practiced and practiced with their swords. They set up dueling matches, they simulated battles, and they sharpened their skills. By keeping themselves busy, they were able to put the fear out of their minds, and the increased physical exercise helped keep alive the hope that each in turn would be able to face the insurmountable odds.

Rusty quickly sent out word informing all other franchises to stay where they were and keep themselves hidden. It wouldn't be safe for anyone to attempt to help. But soon, with the increased amount of people, it was clear they were cut off from the rest of the world. Tye tried to get in with supplies and information, but he was not able to. They were sealed in by Max and his army. And Mark was trapped with them as well. He had gotten in, but he wasn't able to get out. They were trapped and all alone. Rusty hoped that the messengers he had sent out to their franchises had left in time and arrived safely at their destination, and that no one would be walking into this trap.

Early one morning, a small but high and thick black cloud settled just on the peak of the mountain. It sat there ominously, not moving. The wind was blowing slightly, and the

Warriorites could hear it as it swirled around the top of the mountain, but the cloud didn't move.

Late into the morning, at the foot of the mountain, the massive army began to assemble itself for attack. The spies that had been sent out earlier ran up the mountain, warning everyone that the army below was attacking. The Warriorites took their rehearsed attack positions, everyone's hearts pounding. Rusty tried once more to contact the Warrior, but still there was nothing.

He didn't know if he had made a wise decision or a foolish one. He didn't take his new position as a leader of this group lightly, and this whole event was tearing him up inside. But it was too late to do anything else. What made this especially difficult for him was that all these people trusted him and put their lives in his hands. At his advice, they stayed, and under his suggestion, they all hoped for some sort of miracle. Again he thought of his former leader, Dr. In, and hoped to god that he wasn't doing the same thing to these people that Dr. In did to his.

All was silent for several hours.

As the sun reached high noon, the army below them began to move. The sound of the their marching shook the earth. There were so many gathered there that it literally looked like the entire valley below the Warriorites was moving toward them. Closer and closer the massive army marched.

Rusty swallowed hard. Now he was sure he had made a mistake. There was no way they were ever going to be able to take on this many people. Once again, he sent word to the Warrior.

"I don't know if you're listening," he said, "but there's no way we're going to win this one unless you do something fast. You never left me any instruction, so I did what I thought would be best. And that was to stay put until we got some form of instruction from you. Why haven't you said anything? Did we do the right thing? If it was just me, I wouldn't care. But these people are with me as well, and I care about them. Please help us."

The first row of marchers reached the bottom of the mountain, and the minute their feet touched its base, the cloud hovering at its summit exploded like a six-hundred-megaton nuclear bomb. It sent a wind so hard and so fast and so sudden down the mountain that the band of rebels were thrown face down into the dirt and buried several feet into the ground. When the wind hit the bottom of the mountain, it had so much energy that every person there was literally blown miles away. There was nothing left in the valley below. Not a single tree, not a single structure, not a single living thing. The villages were buried so deep in the ground, they would never be dug up. It looked like a holocaust. What had become the dried-up riverbed from the night of the earthquake was now covered over and buried under dirt. There was so much dirt thrown about that the ground in the valley raised about ten feet higher than it used to be.

Then as quickly as it had come, the wind died and the cloud was gone.

The Warriorites lay where they had been blown into the ground for several minutes, not daring to move. Eventually they dug themselves out, stood up, and looked out over the valley below. A sense of awe filled the air. Rusty looked up to the sky and whispered a little thank you toward the Warrior, yet deep in his heart he hurt for those who had been on the other end of this catastrophe.

29

When they looked around the valley, they could see nothing but dirt. The cloud was gone, the sun was bright. Everything looked exactly as it had a few moments ago. Only the landscape looked different. As Rusty stood there and looked around at the devastation, he suddenly felt something pushing him up the mountain. He looked over at Wildy, and he could tell that Wildy felt it too.

"We need to get back up the mountain," Wildy said.

They cut short their celebration and quickly headed up to camp. An hour later, they were all eating around the opening of the cave, talking about the events that had just transpired, when all of a sudden, everything went black. It happened so fast that everyone jumped up, thinking someone had turned out the lights. But there were no lights; they were outside.

They looked up at the sky, but there was no sun. They couldn't even see the glimpse of an eclipse. The sun had just disappeared.

"What's going on?" Thomas asked.

Akeshia grabbed Wildy.

"Are you still there?" she asked.

"I'm here," he told her. "But how about everyone else? We need to do a roll call and find out if everyone else is still here."

They did a roll call, and everyone was there. The only explanation Rusty could give them was no explanation. But he did remember reading something in the holy scrolls about certain references to the sky going dark and other supernatural phenomenon, and he thought that this might be one of them. Even so, this didn't make the experience any more comfortable.

When night came, the stars came with it, and they were glad to see some light after many hours of darkness. The stars shined brightly for a couple of hours, then all of a sudden they began to drop from the sky and fall toward the Darklands. The Warriorites ran for cover, fearing that they might be hit by some of them. Hundreds of thousands of them fell toward the planet with lightning speed. When they hit the Darkland's atmosphere, they burned brightly and lit up the night sky. The sight of them was eerie and sent chills through everyone in the camp.

That night nobody slept. They were too frightened and too turned around to sleep. So they spent another sleepless night sitting in silence around the campfire, waiting and watching to see what would happen next.

For Max, the darkness brought with it even more than fear and uneasiness.

As he sat at his desk high atop the City Building, going over some paperwork and taking care of city business, everything outside suddenly went dark. He jumped up and looked out the window, thinking that somebody must have covered it with something, but the window was clear. The city had gone completely dark. Not a trace of the sun could be seen.

Suddenly every streetlight, every lighted sign, and every other form of manufactured light in Darklands City came on. Max looked at it, thankful that at least there was some form of light. But then that all went black. One by one, but very quickly. It was almost as if a black cloud had suddenly dropped itself on the planet. An even stranger darkness seemed to cover the city. Max could not identify it. He was used to darkness, as most of his work was done in it, but this darkness had a strange scent to it, like flowers, or perfume, a sweet perfume, but to Max the smell was horrible. He hated the stench. It made his nostrils burn and his eyes water, and the more he breathed it in, the worse it became. As the scent entered his body, it filled his every pore, and he began to hurt. Then every muscle, every joint, and every nerve began to hurt, and the pain began to build in intensity. Soon it had become unbearable. He ran to the medicine chest and found a vial containing pain medication. He thought that might help, but the pills he took proved to be no help against the growing sensation of pain. He took more and more of the medicine, but still nothing. His pain soon became so excruciating that it seemed to leak out of his entire body.

As the pain grew, Max became more and more frustrated. *This has to be the work of the Warriorites*, he thought. *What else could it be?* Despite all of his efforts against these wretched rebels, he was still unsuccessful at bringing their terror to an end. He not only had to contend with their outright rebellion against the government, but these supernatural things. His life seemed miserable. His superiors were hovering over him, threatening him, and beating him, and despite all that he had done, the people of the city were ready to revolt, and all around, no matter how many of the Warriorites he killed, they kept multiplying. Under the influence of such intense pain, which only seemed to magnify his thoughts of despair, Max gave up and swallowed the entire bottle of pain medicine. This seemed like the only way out. If he didn't do it to himself, then his superiors would. And their way would be more painful. He knew that no human being alive could survive the amount of medicine he had just taken, so he pulled up one of the chairs near the window and awaited his death. At least now he would be out of the Darklands. Now he would be through with this crazy war and leave the problems to someone else...but death did not come.

In despair, Max decided to try something else. Perhaps these pills weren't as potent as they said they were. Or possibly there was nothing he could do that would take this pain away, so he crossed over to the window to jump. That would be final enough. That would kill him...but he could not get that far. Just short of the window he fell to the floor, and despite every effort he made to move closer, either by crawling or pulling himself up off the floor, that's where he lay for several hours. He cursed Wildy and the band of Warriorites, but he could do nothing else, not even die.

He lay there on the floor for hours, but nothing changed. Soon he could manage to get his body up off the floor. When he did, he ran around the room in rage and tried once again to throw himself out the window. He could not. Every time he got near the window, his body became limp, and he could not control it. Max could do nothing to his satisfaction, not even kill himself.

In the great hall, the monarch sat on his throne and looked out over the candle-lit room. As he did, a sudden wind came up throughout the room and blew out every flame. There was no light in the building. The guards scrambled to find some form of light, but they could not. They lit match after match, but no light would exist in this darkness. Not even the artificial lights brought in as an emergency alternative would burn. Nobody could see, and everybody kept running into each other.

The room was in total darkness. But this darkness was different than the darkness the monarch and his court were used to. The great monarch loved darkness. He thrived on it, he lived for it, and all his deeds were done in it. But this darkness was unfamiliar to him.

As the monarch and the rest of his court sat in this darkness, a strange cloud entered the room, carrying with it the scent of flowers and sweet perfume. As the monarch breathed it in, his entire body began to stiffen with pain. The pain continued to build and build with every breath, until it had become so intense that he started gnawing on his tongue, trying to stop it. Soon he had cut his tongue with his teeth and had severely chewed it up trying to stop the pain, but nothing would work. Blood ran down his face and stained his beautiful white gown with gold inlays. But the pain did not go away. The pain continued for hours, and as the pain worsened, everybody's anger toward each other grew and grew, and their anxiety about life built until none of them could even face life anymore. It wasn't long before everyone in the room started thinking of suicide. The guards turned on one another, trying to destroy themselves. The court of rulers tried to take their own lives, but it could not be done. No matter what the soldiers did to each other, they could not die. They only added to the pain that had already grown beyond the human ability to endure. Not since the beginning of time had pain been felt like this. All the torture in the world combined would not compare to the pain felt by the occupants of this room. And nobody there could take his or her own life.

With each passing moment, the pain continued to build in intensity. As the darkness increased, the pain increased also. The monarch vehemently spat out curses over Max and the Warriorites. But that did not stop the pain. He looked for Draygon, but Draygon was not there. There was no explanation for this darkness, although the monarch knew where it had come from, and he cursed the Prince of Light as well.

But the harder he cursed, the worse the pain became. He wanted revenge. Revenge on the Prince of Light. And he would seek his revenge through the Warriorites.

30

Max was again summoned to the hall of the monarch and his court. He trembled as he entered that great hall, full of the most powerful men and women in the planet Darklands. He knew that they were unhappy with him, so he cautiously approached the throne and bowed low.

Again Draygon was present, and he sat perched above the monarch. The monarch looked down on Max with disgust, but for the longest time nothing was said. The silence made Max extremely uncomfortable, but he dared not be the first to break it. At last the monarch did speak.

"You have failed us," he spoke.

"Please," Max pleaded. "I have done the best that I could."

"You were to save Darklands City from the brink of

destruction and bring them under our rule. You were to trample underfoot any form of rebellion in the country, and you were to bring the countries of the Darklands together under one rule—ours. And instead, Darklands City remains in violent turmoil. The rebellion of the Warriorites has all but consumed this planet, and the countries that were to unite under our rule have become bitter enemies."

All around him Max could hear the mumbling and murmuring of the rest of the gathering.

"There is something supernatural going on," Max said. "It's almost as if the Great Emperor is doing this."

The man on the throne suddenly became very angry. He threw his scepter at Max, and it hit him across the face. Max reeled from the pain.

"Don't you ever say that to me again!" the man shouted.

Then he pulled his frail body off the chair. Draygon saw him, then descended into the body of the monarch. He walked down to Max, grabbed him around the collar, and pulled him to his feet.

"You are no longer needed here," Draygon sneered. "Your useless life is even more useless to us now."

Two guards approached Max and grabbed him by either arm. Max kicked and fought, trying to break free, but these men were too powerful for him. They carried him off to a prison cell somewhere in the basement of the Great Hall, where they kept him overnight. All that night Max paced the floors back and forth, begging and pleading the guards to let him go, but the guards were not convinced.

The next morning when the monarch returned for Max, he was taken into a small chamber and placed in a chair where the guards tied him down hand and foot. Max begged and pleaded for them to set him free, but his pleas fell on deaf ears. They merely gagged him to keep him quiet. As they tied him down, Max struggled desperately to break free. He could see the monarch sitting just opposite him. Behind him were several other people who Max assumed must have been the unseen rulers behind the marble tables. They had all gathered outside the chamber and were watching him.

As soon as Max had been tied down, the soldiers left the room. For a very long time, all was silent. Max began to cry.

Soon another man entered the room carrying a syringe full of liquid. Max tried to fight, but he had been tied down so well that he couldn't move even the slightest little twitch. The man with the syringe stuck the needle in Max's arm and injected the liquid. After that he removed the gag from Max's mouth, then he left the room.

At first Max felt nothing, but soon he felt his entire body warming up. Then he got hot. Then he began to shake. Soon he could hardly breath, and he went into convulsions. Every muscle in his body twitched and wrenched so hard that even though the chair was bolted to the floor, it moved with the force of the convulsions. After that, Max started drooling profusely and throwing up all over himself. He screamed in pain, and his screams reverberated around the room and carried down the corridors of the building and out into the courtyard.

Max was convulsing so hard now that the leather straps and bindings that held him were starting to rip and come undone. He had beaten his hands so hard on the arms of the chair that they had started bleeding, and blood was pouring down from them like water. Blood came out of his nose and his mouth, and even through his tear ducts and out his eyes. One of the straps around his arm came loose, and Max started beating himself uncontrollably with the free hand. It would hit him and the chair as it flailed around out of control.

Soon Max took one final gasp and his body stiffened up. He was dead.

Even after his death, Max's body continued to vibrate and convulse for several minutes.

Everyone in the other room sat in silence for several moments. Once Max's body stopped twitching, they applauded, and then left the room one by one. As soon as everyone was out of the room, the guards returned and untied Max's body from the chair. Max's body was so stiff that they had to break the bones in his arms and legs to get the body into a moveable position. Then they took the body and tossed it into an incinerator.

31

It was almost three o'clock in the morning, and Tye wondered why Max had not returned from his meeting. He should have been back by then. Tye sat in Max's office wondering what could be the matter. As he went over in his mind the work he needed to finish by tomorrow, he heard a knock at the door. Then the door opened, and Tye turned around to see Timothy, the elevator guard, enter the room with four other guards behind him. This was the first time Tye had ever seen Timothy outside of the elevator.

"What is it?" Tye asked, not knowing what to think.

"Could you come with me, sir?" Timothy asked.

"Why?" Tye asked again. "What's wrong?"

Timothy carefully reached around and touched his gun which hung in a holster on his waist, in such a way as to point out to Tye that he meant business. "No questions," Timothy said in an almost threatening tone of voice. "Please come with us now."

Tye swallowed hard, and without saying another word, he followed Timothy out the door while the other four guards walked along beside and behind him. Together they all moved toward the elevator. Tye looked around the room. There was a foreboding feeling about the room now.

They ushered him into the elevator, and four of them stood in front of the door while Timothy stood in back and kept an eye on Tye. Tye sat down on the couch. *What the hell*, he thought. *It's my last chance.* He looked up at Timothy, searching his face for some sign of what was going to happen to him. But Timothy's eyes revealed nothing. He stared coldly at Tye, his face hard. There was no glimpse of emotion whatsoever. Timothy's eyes seemed indifferent to Tye, but he noticed something else behind them. Something that Tye couldn't identify or recognize. He thought to himself that he could run as soon as the elevator doors opened, but then decided better of it. After all, they'd shoot him down. But then that might be better than torture. Suddenly the thought of torture ran through his mind. What would they do to him? His palms started sweating, and his breathing became more and more shallow. He felt his face turning red, and his body tingled, then turned numb. He was caught. Why else would they be taking him? They were arresting him.

The elevator doors opened, and Tye was hurried out of the elevator and into an armored car. He couldn't help but notice that his captors looked a little nervous. The more nervous they looked, the more nervous he became. He got a sick feeling in his stomach, one like he might vomit. He began talking to himself, trying to calm himself down, trying to hold himself together.

Once in the car, they drove off into the city. But they drove around and around, down one street, and then into another. They did this until Tye was completely lost.

Soon they came to a stop at a secluded area near the river

Thromins. Once there, Tye was taken out of the car and ushered into an area of thick underbrush. When they arrived in the thicket, Tye could see the forms of three other people. One of them looked familiar. Then he heard a voice.

"Tye, is that you?"

It was Sam's voice.

"It's me," he said back.

Sam ran to him, and they embraced. Then Tye turned and looked back at Timothy.

"What's happening?" he asked. "Why were we brought here? Are we in trouble?"

Timothy looked around, and then spoke in whispers, fearing he might be heard.

"Sorry about the melodramatics," he said, "but we had to be safe."

"What's wrong?" Tye asked.

"Max is dead," Timothy said abruptly. "He was killed early this evening, and the people that killed him are taking over. Even now they are arriving at the City Building. Darklands City is no longer safe. You can do no more there. These people are ruthless, and everyone tied in with Max will be removed—violently...and permanently."

Tye looked over at Sam. It was dark, and he couldn't read the look on her face. She held his hand, but he didn't notice anything different in her grip. Then he looked back at Timothy.

"Don't think of staying," Timothy said, almost reading his mind. "Your work is done. You cannot help your people anymore."

Those words stunned Tye.

"You mean you knew?" Tye asked.

"I work in the elevator," Timothy said. "I see the habits of just about everyone on the 196th floor... Now you must go. There's a small boat tied up to some underbrush down by the river. Get in it and paddle out of here. Take great care. Follow the south side of the River Thromins, and then take one of the tributaries. Get as far away from this city as you can."

Tye shook Timothy's hand. When they were done with the shake, Tye still couldn't let go of Timothy's hand, he was so grateful.

"I hate to leave you here," Tye said to him.

"You must," Timothy replied, pulling his hand away.

Tye embraced Timothy and hugged him. Timothy didn't respond, but Tye didn't care. He wanted to somehow thank Timothy for saving his life. Soon he pulled away and took Sam's hand. Together they walked down to the shores of the river. They found the boat just like Timothy had said they would, carefully crawled in, and then paddled out into the water. Tye had to be very cautious as he maneuvered the boat since the currents in the River Thromins could be very dangerous. Especially at night.

Sam said nothing all that night, and Tye wished that he could find a way to comfort her.

When morning arrived, they had traveled several miles up one of the tributaries. Tye noticed that they were deep into the forest by now and decided that this might be a good place to pull ashore. They broke the boat up into pieces and buried it, then started their journey on foot. Tye looked over at Sam.

"Are you okay?" he asked.

Sam said nothing at first, so Tye took her hand and they walked on a little further. Then Tye stopped and looked Sam directly into her eyes. He said nothing to her at first, but only looked at her.

"I love you," he said at last. "I really love you."

"And I really love you too," she said to him. Then she took both of his hands in hers and looked deep into his eyes. "I understand now more than I ever did."

"About what?" Tye asked.

"About you, about the Warrior, about the Warriorites, and about the Darklands," Sam said.

Tye looked at her and smiled. "The Warrior's really a wonderful person once you get to know him."

After that they walked farther inland, saying nothing to each other for a long time. Soon the path began to take them up, up into the mountains, up into seclusion, where hopefully nobody would find them. As they walked farther and farther, they began to feel somewhat better about their chances of survival.

Finally Sam turned to Tye. "My father was an evil man," she said in a matter-of-fact tone. "He destroyed others, and now someone did it to him." Then she fell silent again.

Tye tenderly put his arm around her as they walked, and she held him close like she was afraid to let him go. He kissed her on the head and ran his fingers through her hair. He loved her, and he was glad that they had met. And if he had to run for his life, it felt good to have someone like her with him.

32

The small remnants of the once enormous Warriorite army gathered around a mound of dirt outside the campsite. Tears filled their eyes as Rusty quietly spoke, "And so we commit another body to the ground to rest until the Warrior returns to claim him. We all knew the cost, even Ryan. And he was willing to sacrifice his life for the Warrior. We now add him to the thousands of Warriorites who have fallen to Draygon and his forces, and to the Darklands and their forces, and we cling to the hope that the Warrior is soon going to prevail. We comfort each other with those very words. We loved you, Ryan." He could no longer hold back his tears. "I hope to see you soon."

For several minutes they all stood there silently staring at the mound of dirt that was now Ryan's resting place before returning tearfully back to camp. In the darkness, and in their anguish, they could hardly see where they were going and tempers were short as they bumped into each other.

The monarch had been true to his word. He and his forces, combined with Draygon and his forces, waged an all-out war against the Warriorites, and this time they seemed to be winning. The group that had once reached numbers too numerous to count throughout the planet Darklands had rapidly dwindled down to a precious few. The battle had become ferocious, and the onslaught was taking its toll on the Warriorites. Ryan was the latest victim of the violent war between the powers of the Darklands.

After the burial, Rusty and Wildy took care of things around the camp and made sure all the business was taken care of, then they went off to talk.

"I'm tired of burying people, Rusty," Wildy said angrily. "I'm sick of death, I'm sick of people dying. I hate this place, I hate this planet, and I hate everything that's happened to us so far." He noticed the expression on Rusty's face. "I can't help it," he went on. "I'm really angry."

Michael approached Wildy and Rusty, and when he got their attention, he began to express his concern. And he wasn't quiet about it, so everyone in camp heard him.

"What's going on, Rusty?" he asked. "What's happening?"

"These are the final days, Michael," Rusty told him. "The days of the great and severe battle. They told us about it in the fortress."

"I remember hearing about that," Akeshia commented, "but there were so many theories. Nobody could agree on what was really going to happen."

"Well, here we are," Rusty said. "And it's happening. And not like any of us had planned."

"So where's the Warrior in all this?" Wildy asked.

"Who do you think is behind all this?" Rusty returned.

"You mean it's not Draygon?" Michael asked.

"This is judgment," Rusty stated. "The Great Emperor is judging the Darklands.

"Well he's judging us too," Wildy said.

"He never said we'd be special," Rusty reminded them. "But we're not being judged. None of his judgment has come upon us. It has only affected us."

Mark looked around him. He had been trapped with Wildy and Rusty since he risked his life to get them the information that Max was planning an all-out war against them. He picked up his water canister and took it over to the lake to get some water to drink. He dipped the canister into the lake, then put the canister up to his mouth to take a drink. Instantly he spat it back out onto the ground. He spat and spat. The others watched him, wondering what he was doing.

"What's the matter, Mark?" Wildy asked.

"There's something wrong with the water," Mark told him. "It's warm and thick, and it smells."

Rusty crossed over to him and took the canister from his hand and dumped out the contents near the fire to see if he could detect what was wrong with it. In the firelight they could make out something that looked like blood. It was blood. He dropped the canister, and the blood flowed out onto the ground.

Rusty went over to the lake and touched the water. Everyone else had gathered around to see.

Wildy felt the water in his hand, held it up to his nose, and smelled it. It smelled horrible. Then he put just a little bit on his tongue. Like Mark, he spat and spat, trying to get the taste out his mouth. He felt like vomiting, the thought of it was so nauseating. "The water's turned to blood," he announced finally.

A strange feeling went through everyone there. How could something like this happen? An entire river flowing with blood... They would all die of thirst. What could they drink if the water was blood? Mark was the first voice his concern.

"Great!" he said. "We're all going to die of thirst."

"How could that happen?" Wildy asked.

"The Warrior will provide for us," Rusty told them. "He always has up to this point."

"He's provided for some of us, but for some of us he hasn't," one voice spoke out.

"Maybe it's supposed to happen like this," another voice joined in. "Like everything else that's happened so far."

"You mean the Warrior brought us out here to die, to wind up like everyone else," Mark snapped.

Wildy pulled Rusty aside.

"What are we going to do?" he asked. "Food rations are low, moral is low, and now we can't drink the water. That means that we're all going to die. Or worse, these people are going to revolt and kill us."

Rusty looked hard at Wildy.

"Have we ever gone without anything before?" he asked Wildy.

Wildy said nothing. The Warrior had taken very good care of him since he left the city, and now was not the time to start doubting.

As he thought about Rusty's comment and his response to it, he suddenly noticed that the voices around him had stopped. He looked around to see why and noticed that everyone was looking up at something in the sky. He followed their gaze. There where the moon was supposed to be, a giant red ball hung ominously in the sky, like it was proclaiming some sort of doom over the land.

"We're as good as dead!" Mark spat bitterly.

Wildy snapped out of his trance, grabbed Mark by the collar, and shook him pretty hard. Then he pulled Mark out of the circle of people and took him someplace more private. Once they were out of earshot of everyone else, Wildy pulled Mark up close to him so that they were looking eye to eye. Wildy spoke slowly and deliberately, and his voice was very threatening.

"One more word out of you," he told Mark, "and you'll be eating your teeth! You got that?"

Mark instantly backed down.

Once Mark backed down, Wildy relaxed also and let go of Mark's collar.

"So what's with you lately?" Wildy asked Mark. "You were the one that risked your life to bring information during the time we were under siege. You were the one that stuck around through thick and thin, and now you're falling apart."

"I don't know," Mark responded. "I feel let down. I've done everything I can for you and the Warrior. I've given him my life, and look at what I get in return. Look at this life. I would just like to think that the Warrior cared a little more about what's going on here."

"We all knew what we were getting into," Wildy told him. "The Warrior made it very plain to every one of us that things like this might happen. And that they would happen to each one of us. Nobody's special here."

"I know that," Mark replied, "but he didn't tell us that he was going to go off and leave us all alone. I always thought he would be with us."

Those words hit Wildy pretty hard because they were some of his own feelings. Only he had never dared to express them, not even to himself. He looked into Mark's eyes and could see his own hurt and apparent abandonment staring back at him. He held Mark close for several moments, something that he had never done before, but he knew Mark's pain, and he wanted so much to give back a little of what Mark had given them.

"I know how you feel," he told Mark. "But don't give up. Hold on to what the Warrior said and believe that he will never leave us. It's our only chance of survival."

Mark held Wildy in return and wept. "I will," he said.

Rusty stepped in to ease the tension in the rest of the group.

"Bring me a canister," he said.

Everybody looked at him like he was crazy, but he insisted so they gave him one. He instructed them to fill it from the lake. At first they weren't going to, but again Rusty insisted. So Mark went down to the lake and filled it, then brought it back to him.

"What are you doing?" Wildy asked him.

Rusty said nothing to Wildly, but took the canister and held it high in the air.

"The Warrior has promised that he would provide us all the things that we have need of," he proclaimed. "And so in the name of the Warrior, I drink."

He brought the canister to his mouth and took a long drink. Everyone else in the camp fought back the urge to vomit. Just the sight of this made their stomachs sick.

After Rusty had drunk, he held the canister up near the fire and tilted it so that the contents of the canister would spill out. And what spilled out was water. The others shouted with excitement and relief. They all ran like children to a fountain on a hot summer day and filled their canisters. They were delighted when, once they pulled the canisters out of the lake and consecrated the contents to the Warrior, the canisters were filled with water. A flood of excitement poured over them. They all laughed, slapped each other on the back, and celebrated. Wildy looked over at Mark, and they smiled at each other and clanked their canisters together as a toast. But no sooner had they done this than the ground below them began to rock back and forth. The earth around them shook hard, and then parts of it began to give way. Again, the mood suddenly went from celebrating to panic, and they fell to the ground, screaming in fear.

33

The moon shined large and full, like a giant red ball in the sky, casting an eerie red glow in the night. The Warriorites had fallen asleep outside by the campfire, and although they had posted guards to keep watch at all times, they still felt uneasy, and nobody slept very well. Many of them tossed and turned and drifted in and out of sleep. The truth was, none of them had slept well in days, and no matter how tired they got, sleep continued to allude them.

This night, as the night wore on, a strange sleep fell over them that even the posted guards found themselves unable to fight. They sensed that they were starting to drift into sleep very rapidly, and they tried everything in their power to stay awake, but they soon lost the battle and went to sleep.

Off in the distance, a small light—white, blue, gold, and

the size of a bird—approached the top of the mountain, hovered over some trees, and then slowly and gracefully made its way down the mountain toward the campsite. It landed outside of the camp, in the outer glow of the fire. Once it landed, it straightened itself and grew in height. It began to take on a new form, the form of a beautiful woman. Her hair was long and flowing, and it hung down past her waist, and it was so white that it glowed. It was full and feathery, and it seemed to dance in the eerie moonlight. She wore a long flowing gown that wrapped itself delicately around her and seemed to hover just above the ground. It was decorated in a light greenish white silk, and it sparkled with glitter. Her slender and poised form stood about six feet tall, and she carried a very gentle nature about her, a grace that could soothe even the most savage and uptight of beings. She was beautiful in every way imaginable. She stood outside the campsite and quietly called to Wildy.

At first Wildy heard his name being called in a dream. In his dream he could hear a low soft voice calling him to come, but no matter where he looked, he could not find it. As he searched, he woke himself up looking for whatever voice had called his name. He woke up slowly, and sleepily looked around. His eyes had not yet had time to focus, so he laid his head back down on the ground. Then he heard the voice again. He sat up again and looked around him. He could see the small band of Warriorites, all of them asleep on the ground. He noticed that the guards had also fallen asleep, but in his dreamlike state, he didn't think too much of it. He noticed the figure standing just outside the campsite, calling to him. His eyes were blurred from drowsiness, and he could barely make out the form at first, but as he continued to stare at her, he noticed her beauty and her grace.

"What are you?" he asked.

"I am Angel," she replied in a voice that seemed to resonate like the sweetest music.

Wow, Wildy thought. *A real angel.*

She held out her arm to him and began to motion him to

her with her hand. Her long fingers moved slowly and gently as she moved them one by one toward her, calling to him. Her fingernails were painted with soft white that seemed to leave traces of light when she moved them in an upward motion beckoning to Wildy.

"Come to me, Wildy," she whispered, "I bring a message from the Warrior."

The Warrior, Wildy thought. *Finally.*

He was mesmerized by Angel, and he could not take his eyes off her. Slowly he got up and walked toward her. He had a hard time moving, and he seemed so tired. His body still seemed to have that slow and sluggish feeling that one gets while dreaming the kind of dream where one finds himself going somewhere, but can never get there because of the weight of his body. And what little movement he is capable of making, he does with much effort, and the going grows intensely laborious.

Rusty, on the other hand, tossed and turned like he was having a nightmare. His body was covered with sweat, and he had kicked the covers off of himself and almost tossed and turned right out of the area he was sleeping in. He panted and gasped for breath, and then suddenly sat up straight in bed, facing opposite Wildy. He rubbed his eyes and tried to catch his breath. Once he had managed to bring his breathing down to a pace that he could control, he tried to comfort himself and calm himself down mentally. *It was only a bad dream*, he thought. Only it wasn't really a dream, it was more like a feeling. A horrible feeling that something unseen was out there, waiting in the darkness. Even now that he was awake, the feeling was still there. He couldn't understand it, so he rubbed his eyes again to see if he really was awake. He was, but the feeling was still there, and he couldn't shake it.

Then he heard Angel call to Wildy. He'd heard that voice. That was the voice in his dream. He spun around to see Wildy laboriously walking toward the most beautiful woman he had ever seen in his life. He was stunned by her beauty, but at the same time a sensation of fear came over him that seemed to send the skin on his entire body crawling over itself trying to find a place to hide.

"Who are you?" he shouted out.

Wildy stopped and looked back at Rusty. His eyes were glazed over, and it seemed as if no one was really behind them at all.

Angel turned her attention toward Rusty and spoke to him.

"Rusty," she whispered in her musical voice, "I have a message from the Warrior. Come, I must deliver it unto you."

Rusty couldn't explain it, but something about her made him quiver.

"You're not from the Warrior," he said.

"Why do you say that?" she asked.

"There's something evil about you," he shot back, not even knowing why he had said that.

"How can that be?" She sounded hurt that Rusty didn't believe her, and her voice sweetened even more. "How can I be evil?"

"I don't know," Rusty said. "I don't know, but I can feel it!"

Angel's voice softened even more, and she began to talk in musical patterns that slowly put Rusty into a trance.

"You know you can't trust your feelings," she whispered.

"I know that, but..."

"But what?" Angel whispered. Then she pulled out a small green bag that had been hanging around a gold band tied around her waist and held it delicately in her hands. "You know that the things of the Warrior are much deeper than you."

"I know, but..."

"You've never ever seen me before; how could you possibly know if I was a good person or a bad person so soon after meeting me?"

Something in Rusty moved and caused him to snap out of his trance. He shouted out, "The Warrior reigns in the Darklands!"

Angel was a little taken aback, but she held her composure.

"What?" she asked.

"The Warrior reigns in the Darklands!" he said again.

"Yes," she said, "but..."

Rusty shouted, "Say that you worship him! Say that your loyalty is to him and to him only. Bow your knee to him right now."

As if it would be possible, Angel's voice grew even sweeter.

"Now Rusty..."

This time Rusty screamed it out at the top of his lungs.

"Say you worship the Warrior. Bow your knee to him and acknowledge that he is your king. Worship him right now, in front of us!"

His voice had gotten so loud that it woke up everyone else in the camp. Rusty's scream had startled them, so they all jumped up and looked around to see what was happening. They took one look at Angel and her incredible beauty and were taken in by it. Nobody there could take their eyes off her.

Angel tried to calm Rusty down, but Rusty continued yelling at her.

"You can't do it! If you were truly of the Warrior you would have no reservations about bending your knee to him, even in front of us. You would live to worship him. You would bow to him with great joy. You would invite us to join you in your worship. You're not from the Warrior, you're from Draygon. You can't worship the Warrior because of your hatred and your fear of him. You aren't of us!" Then he shouted out to everyone in the group. "Draw your swords. Prepare to rid ourselves of this foul being full of the stench of Draygon!"

Some of them drew their swords, but most were reluctant even to get that far. They couldn't take their eyes off Angel. Rusty drew his sword and held it high above his head. Angel reached into the small bag she had been holding and pulled out a handful of a green, glitterlike substance and spread it into the air. Slowly it began to cover the air around the campsite. As the Warriorites breathed in its sweet fragrance, it slowly began to paralyze them so they fell to the ground. Even Wildy found himself on the ground. Rusty's sword dropped so that the tip of it touched the ground, but he managed to hold on to it. Angel then focused her attention on Wildy.

"Wildy," she said in a hurt tone, "you don't believe that horrible lie, do you?"

"You're so beautiful." Wildy's voice was so hoarse now that he could barely talk. He just whispered through parched lips. Her beauty had consumed him so that he couldn't even think clearly.

"And how could anything so beautiful be bad?" she asked in such a way that she took all suspicion off of her.

"I don't know," Wildy said.

"It couldn't," she said firmly. "Come here, Wildy, and I will show you my beauty. Come to me, and I will take you with me, and together you and I will go and meet the Warrior. He has a special message for you... Come with me."

Again she motioned with her hand for Wildy to come to her, and this time Wildy could not resist her. He painfully pulled himself up off the ground and struggled toward Angel. Rusty screamed after him to stop, and that it was a trap, but Wildy only kept on going, not noticing Rusty's warnings.

Angel continued to motion to Wildy, and he moved closer and closer to her. Rusty tried to move but he couldn't. He shouted out, "In the name of the Warrior!" and suddenly found himself able to lift his sword up off the ground. He stood up and painfully moved toward Angel. He caught up with Wildy and yelled to him, "Wildy! It's a lie. She's not an angel," he shouted, trying to stop Wildy.

But Wildy didn't listen. So Rusty pushed Wildly over, so that he fell to the ground and could not get back up. Then Rusty walked over to Angel.

"You can't have him!" Rusty screamed. "In the name of the Warrior, you can't have him!"

Angel fell back at the name of the Warrior, but she quickly regained her composure. She looked Rusty in the eyes and her eyes began to dance back and forth in a soft, steady motion that soon had Rusty under their spell. He couldn't take his eyes off her eyes, and her voice seemed to lull him into a strange feeling of almost unconsciousness.

"Come here, Rusty," she whispered.

Rusty approached her.

"Who is this person you speak of?" she asked.

"He's the Warrior," Rusty said, fighting hard to keep himself from falling deeper under her spell.

"Is he real?" she asked.

"Yes," Rusty replied.

"Are you sure?" she asked again.

Rusty's sword dropped a little.

"I think so."

"Don't you know?" she asked him, her voice becoming smoother and quieter.

Rusty's sword dropped a little further.

"He says he is."

"When was the last time you saw him?"

Rusty thought for a moment. It seemed like so long ago.

"I don't remember."

Angel whispered in his ear.

"You don't remember because he's a fairy tale."

"Fairy tale," Rusty repeated to himself, now completely under her spell.

"He's a myth," Angel went on.

"A myth." Rusty barely said the words audibly. His hands released the sword, and it dropped to the ground. As soon as it hit the ground, Angel moved in on him. She grabbed him around the shoulders and held him up to her chest like he was a rag doll. Then she held his head to her shoulder and looked up toward the moon. Large hideous fangs grew out of her mouth, and she bit deep into his neck. As she held him there, she ripped and tore his flesh and severed his jugular vein. Rusty struggled desperately to break free, but to no avail. His blood ran down Angel's body and stained her clothes. She lapped it up like a dog going to a bowl of water after a hot day in the sun.

Wildy fought desperately to break free from the spell she

had put him under. He tried and tried to get his arms and legs to move, but they wouldn't. He had no control over his body at all. He reached toward his sword, but he couldn't move, so he cried out.

"Please, Warrior, please help me."

His arm swung clumsily and touched his sword. He pulled it out of his sheath. When his hands touched it, he felt its power rush through his body, and he jumped up and held it in the air. He called to the others, and they somehow got hold of their own swords, then they joined Wildy and held their swords toward Angel. The power of all their swords focused toward her at once, broke the spell, and they were able to think clearly and move again.

"Stop!" Wildy shouted.

Angel pulled away from Rusty, and his body fell to the ground. She looked at them, this time not the beauty that had completely mesmerized them only moments before, but instead with eyes bugged out, her face hideously deformed, and hair that was long and stringy (and she barely had any in her head). Her teeth were so deformed that they looked like long sharp points in her gums and head, her hands were wrinkled and withered, and her fingernails spun in a spiral in front of her fingers. She looked up at Wildy, her face and clothes stained with Rusty's blood.

"Get out of here!" Wildy screamed. "In the name of the Warrior, get out of here!"

He and the others charged at her. Angel screeched loudly, laughed a hideous and foul laugh as proclamation that she had won, and ran off into the woods.

Wildy ran over to where Rusty's body lay and knelt down beside it to hold it in his arms. Rusty's neck and parts of the side of his face were completely shredded, and he lay in a pool of his own blood. His body was limp and lifeless in Wildy's arms.

"Rusty?" Wildy cried. "Rusty?"

He shook Rusty, but there was no response.

"Come on, Rusty," he said, and this time, for the first time in his life, he cried. And he didn't try to stop the tears. "Please, Rusty, please say something! Anything! Yell at me for being so stupid, call me an idiot! Please, I know that I am, I know it! Rusty?"

Akeshia put her head on Rusty's chest and listened. Then she felt his pulse.

"He's dead," she whispered.

Frantically Wildy grabbed Rusty again and shook him.

"Come on, Rusty, wake up!"

Michael gently took Wildy's arms and held them. He looked Wildy in the face and whispered, "It won't do any good, Wildy," he said. "He's dead."

Wildy jumped up and grabbed Michael around the nape of the neck and began to shake him instead.

"He can't be dead!" Wildy screamed. "Do you hear me? It's my fault! I should be dead, not him!"

Wildy again broke out into uncontrollable sobs.

"I killed him. It's my fault."

"It's everyone's fault," Michael said. "He told us to draw our swords. If we all would have listened... If we would have fought with him, he would have been okay. But we made him go against her all by himself. We're all to blame."

"How could the Warrior let this happen?" Wildy asked. "What kind of person is he that he would let an innocent person suffer for the stupidity of everyone else? This was Rusty...the first person to believe me. He left everything for the Warrior. He lost everything for the Warrior. His family, his friends, his home...and now his own life. Only he lost his life because of me, not because of the Warrior. He lost everything... How did he know who she was? Why did he do it? Why did the Warrior let this happen to him, when *he* was innocent?"

Akeshia put her arm around Wildy, and he put his head on her shoulder and cried.

"The Warrior didn't let this happen to him," she said. "We did."

"But why couldn't she have gotten me?" Wildy sobbed.

"Why couldn't she have gotten me like I deserved?"

He went over to Rusty's body and held it in his lap. Then he slowly rocked back and forth for several minutes, not saying anything. He ran his hands through Rusty's hair, he held Rusty's body close to his. He held Rusty's hand and rocked some more. For several minutes he did this. Nobody knew what to do. Akeshia motioned them all away for a while until Wildy could work this out. Rusty's face and shoulders soon became wet with Wildy's tears. He looked down into Rusty's lifeless face.

"We'll fight it to the end," he said. "I promise. We'll do it for you. I know that's what you would do." He thought about what he just said. "That's what you did," he added.

34

Only a few minutes had passed since Rusty had given his life for his friend Wildy. Everyone in camp was in mourning, and a strange heaviness hung over them. This was their leader, the one who stayed alive for them to take care of them. They had hurt over the other losses, but Rusty was always the one who seemed to understand best the ways of the Warrior. He made the ancient stories come alive for them, and when he talked about the Warrior, or the Prince of Light, they seemed to be able to understand so much better. They had always had his wisdom to lead them and to help them with their decisions, but now he was dead, and it was his grave this time that they were digging. This was the most tragic night any of them had ever experienced thus far.

They had laid Rusty's body on a stone slab while they

went several feet away to dig his grave. As they were digging, The Warrior wearing a hood and cloak crept over to the table and looked down at the body of Rusty. He ran his hands through Rusty's hair and held him for a moment. Tears fell down his face and landed on Rusty's face, mixing with the dry blood. He then picked up the body of Rusty and carried it away. Akeshia saw him and called out.

"That man's got Rusty," she screamed.

Everyone else ran after the man to try and catch him, but it was no good. He was gone.

"It's no use," Akeshia said hopelessly. "We've totally lost him now."

"How are we going to explain this one to the Warrior?" Wildy asked. "It's not enough that we killed him, that we lost him in life, but we've lost him completely. Right down to his body." Then he walked over to the stone slab and kicked it.

"Damn it!" he screamed. "Damn it!" he screamed again. Then he started to kick at anything he saw, and then he started hitting things, screaming, and cursing, trying to work out his anger. Michael went to stop him, but Akeshia held him back.

"He needs to work this out," she said.

The rest of them held each other and wept. This loss was even greater than the first. Now they had completely lost Rusty.

When Wildy finally did calm down, tears once again filled his eyes.

"Rusty," he said, looking into the sky. "Wherever you are, I'm really sorry."

35

The Warriorites had managed to cry themselves into a troubled sleep. Everyone, that is, except Wildy. He tossed and turned and thrashed about in his bed. The harder he tried to sleep, the further sleep went from him. Late into the night, or early in the morning, he wasn't really sure, he gave up on trying to sleep and got up to walk a little way away from the campsite where he could be alone and talk without being heard.

He looked up toward the sky, not knowing where else to look. He hoped that wherever the Warrior was, he was listening to him right now.

"There's nothing left, sir," Wildy said, looking up into the sky. "We fought hard for you, we tried, but we lost it all…" He again burst out into tears. "Even Rusty. I loved him. He was like a brother and a friend. And I'm the one that killed him. It's because I let my guard down...and then he put his life ahead of mine."

Wildy sat in silence for a while and wept. When he began speaking again, his voice sounded so loud in the darkness that he had to bring it down to a whisper.

"There's hardly anyone left," he said helplessly. "They're all dead... I've seen more people die since I started fighting for you than I did when I was out on the streets of Darklands City leading gang wars...only here, we were supposed to win...weren't we?"

He half-hoped to hear nothing. But there was something inside of him that wanted desperately to know whether or not he was going to win, or die like his friend Rusty. Half of his hope came true. He heard nothing. He wasn't sure that he was even getting through, but he decided, for Rusty's sake, he would finish the cause that Rusty so strongly believed in.

"We did what we were told...," Wildy continued, not really sure if he was being heard by the Warrior at all. "I've never really known what it was like to love and care for someone, and before you know it, everyone I've learned to care for is gone...dead. I'm sick of death, and I'm sick of putting bodies into the ground, and I'm sick of losing friends...and their bodies. Do you know what it's like to lose someone you love?" This time he really hoped for an answer. He listened carefully for several minutes, hoping that the wind might whisper something to him, or that something out of the night would respond. But again, there was nothing.

"Please say something," Wildy pleaded. "Anything. Tell me what to do, where to go from here. Tell me you're disappointed with me, tell me I let you down, tell me anything... Did you leave us here to fight Draygon on our own? If so, I think we ought to know."

Again he searched the night sky, still hearing nothing.

"Well," he conceded, "we lost. And for all it's worth, I'm sorry..." Then he added passionately, "I really am."

36

Somewhere in the middle of the Darklands, nobody really knows where, a giant black hole hovered over the surface of the planet like a black and empty, ravenous cavern, which ruthlessly sucked and pulled all forms of life into it. Once it reached the earth, the hole would envelop and encase all life with death, and with the stench of death. Then it would trap them in the dark and dank caverns that ran like a maze under the planet's surface. Once any form of life found itself sucked into the powerful grip of this black hole, it could never again be released, nor would it ever live again.

The black hole cared nothing for status, position, or influence—man, woman, child, or beast. Nobody was safe from its powerful and eventual grasp. Death roamed the planet freely and continually, and everyone unlucky enough to meet him was stolen away, and in their place, Death left the empty frame of their body where life once was. Death could strike anywhere, and at any time, without warning. Sometimes he would come quickly, without any warning, and sometimes he took his time, slowly and painfully destroying his prey.

The maze of caverns and dirt, where Death kept his catch as trophies to his supreme rule, was so concentrated that no light had ever penetrated its dense black interior...except one light. No one who had ever entered the black hole, or the dark caverns, had ever left...except once.

At the very core of this black hole loomed the Fortress of Death.

The Fortress of Death was a powerful stronghold that held the high distinction of Draygon's ultimate conquest. Everyone on the Darklands would eventually end up there, and once inside, it was impossible to break out. Nobody could escape it. There was no need to set up guards to protect it from invaders, there was no need to fortify the fortress to keep anyone from escaping, and there was no need to recruit newcomers. There was only one way out, and for the longest time, Draygon held that key. But although he no longer held the key, he still had no worries of escape, because the bearer of the key was the only one with the power to escape death, and nobody else up to date had been able to do so...except one...the bearer of the key.

Death was everyone's destiny. Good or bad, right or wrong, righteous or wicked, every living thing must die. And when they did, they would end up here. Nothing in the world could change that. And when death did find his victims, they were placed in this dank fortress with no hope of escape.

The fortress stood several stories in the air and reached out for miles in every direction. It had four walls made of cold, uncut stones cemented together. Surrounding the fortress, a strange thick liquid flowed like molasses, only it was a strange combination of black and poison green. It was called the River of Death, and the fort was built in the middle of this river.

The River of Death was miles wide and impassable. It was not possible to swim in this water because the currents were too strong. It wasn't possible to sail or boat across it, because of its density and thickness. Nothing could move in its thick and gummy surface. It flowed like mud and its massive size and weight made it like quicksand. It flowed through and around and under the Fortress of Death.

Underneath this Fortress of Death and the River of Death were millions of caverns and tunnels and caves that wound their way into total emptiness. They went on and on, almost forever, and every one of them reeked of the death that dwelled there. Every cavern there was filled with dead bones and rotting flesh. No one, not even Draygon or his men, ever went into these caverns. They were reserved specifically for the residents of the Darklands who had once been Death's prey. Once Death had feasted on their life's essence, he would throw them into the caverns. There they would rot and decay in the stench and foul air, never to exist again. Their death would be complete.

The Fortress of Death was run by none other than Death himself, directly under the leadership of Draygon. Draygon was the only person on the face of creation that Death answered to.

Death was the epitome of all lifelessness. He had no flesh, only a dark cloak that he wore to cover his skeletonlike body. He stood about nine feet tall if he ever stood up straight, but he hunched at the shoulders and neck so that he stood only about seven feet tall. Despite his seemingly frail existence, he was the most powerful being under Draygon. He was also the cruelest and most heartless. He didn't care if he took children away from parents, parents away from children, he didn't care if he separated husbands and wives, lovers or close friends. Nor did he care how he took them, or who it hurt. Sometimes he would grab his victims suddenly and without warning. Other times he would torture them and painfully drag out their departure from the Darklands. He had a constant and vacuous thirst for life and the essence of life, and he ravenously devoured every little drop of it he could find. His insidious hunger led him to every corner of the Darklands, looking for every ounce of life he could devour. No one could defeat him, or outsmart him, or simply escape him. Nor could they comprehend his incredible power and its significance in the ultimate struggle between Draygon and his enemy, the Prince of Light.

Only one person had ever gone into the Fortress of Death, faced death and Draygon, and come back out again—the only person to ever face Death and win. And that was the Prince of Light, in a surprise attack. But the surprise *was* the surprise, because he didn't come unannounced. For thousands of years before he came, he announced his coming. His prophets spoke about it, and they wrote about it, and it was passed on from generation to generation that this Prince would enter the world of the Darklands and face Draygon and Death. And when the Prince of Light did arrive, he was heralded by all his followers of the Great Emperor's kingdom. Only those mortals of the planet Darklands had no idea who he was, nor did they care. Among Draygon and his followers, every being of the Prince of Light's entourage announced his coming, and much ado was made over his arrival. This approach puzzled Draygon. It seemed strange to him that the Prince of Light didn't seem to be doing anything at all to hide the fact that he was coming to do battle. This plan was hard for Draygon to comprehend. He had read all the prophecies, and he had heard all the legends. The Great Emperor did not seem to be interested in hiding his strategy for winning back the right to lay claim to the Darklands. He even published it through his prophets and commanded that they write down everything he told them about how he planned to win back Darklands. So when the Prince of Light did arrive on the planet, Draygon followed him everywhere, hounding him, pestering him, taunting him, trying to establish his game plan, and to find a way to destroy him. Draygon somehow thought that if he could pull the Prince of Light into the Fortress of Death, then he would win this battle.

Late one night, he and all his forces went out against the Prince of Light with just that purpose in mind: to bring the Prince of Light into the fortress. Only the prince went willingly, without putting up a fight. He allowed Draygon to beat him, torture him, and then to murder him. The son of the Great Emperor murdered by one of his own beings, and the Great Emperor didn't do a thing to intervene. This strategy confused Draygon, but he wanted nothing more than to rid himself of this enemy, and the thought of having him dead obsessed Draygon's every move. He sent Death personally, to hold the prince captive underneath the caverns, and he and Death kept a constant vigil for several days. Draygon held the only key to the fortress and the caverns below it, and he guarded it with his own life. He entrusted it to no one, not even Death himself. Once he had locked the Warrior away, Draygon paced the hard stone floors day and night, clutching the key tightly in the palm of his hand.

Once in the fortress, the Warrior remained silent and still, dead and motionless. Unknown to Draygon, the Prince of Light's blood began to flow from his body and slowly make its way through the cracks in the Fortress of Death. It flowed through literally every dank and dark tunnel of the fortress, and then collected in one place at the very heart of the darkness. It gathered there and waited, building up pressure and intensity with every passing moment. Then suddenly, unexpectedly, the Prince of Light burst out of the dark chasms, vibrating with life. He took Draygon by surprise, overpowered him, and stole his key. With that key, he stole away Draygon's power over death, and his ability and his right to hold those souls there as prisoners. Then the Prince of Light catapulted out of the black hole with such a force that it sent every one of Draygon's allies skyrocketing out of control. They scrambled and clattered to find a place of security. The Prince of Light had broken Draygon's power at its core, and now he could come and go as he pleased, even into the Fortress of Death. Then the prince presented the key as a trophy to his father, the Great Emperor.

The blood of the Prince of Light that had been spilled during the massacre by Draygon and his people and had been pooling up and building pressure under the Fortress of Death, began to bubble and gurgle and steam like a boiling cauldron. When the prince shot out of the chasm, his blood suddenly spewed forth like a geyser, and it shot up from the caverns below through the heart of the Fortress of Death, up through the ground and high into the sky. The earth around the fortress suddenly broke loose and shot up into the air with the pressure of the blood. Then it fell and collected itself together to form a high mountain where the image of the Prince of Light remained as a symbol to all, mortal and supernatural, good and evil, that the Prince of Light had defeated Draygon and won the right to lay claim to the planet Darklands.

The Fountain of Blood told all Darklands residents the story of their dilemma and of the requirements for the Great Emperor to fairly and justly claim the Darklands people as his own. Anyone who bathed in the Fountain of Blood became detestable to Death, and although he could still steal away their essence, and that life within them, he could not hold them. Because their life and the essence of their life were completely drenched in that blood, Death's stomach would not be able to hold them. His stomach was too sensitive for that. And although he continued to devour them, they only gave him brief satisfaction, and then he became sick immediately after devouring them. But he was addicted to the life essence, and therefore he could not stop. This way the Prince of Light made his existence detestable and painful.

Those that had bathed in the Fountain of Blood were also detestable to Draygon because they were constant reminders of his battle with the Prince of Light and his failure to hold the Prince of Light captive in his most powerful stronghold. So his anger against any one of the Warrior's followers burned even hotter than that anger which he felt toward other Darklanders.

This was a bitter defeat for Draygon and his second-in-command, Death, but despite the devastating effect it had on his kingdom and on his reign as ruler of the Darklands, he continued to push Death to destroy as many Darklands residents as he could. And because Death's unquenchable thirst for life matched Draygon's unquenchable thirst for blood, the two of them feasted on blood and life like sharks over a kill.

Several stories in the air, above the River of Death, on the very top level of the Fortress of Death, Draygon made his headquarters. It was a large hall with cold marble floors, pillars, and arches that spanned across the ceiling. The floor led up to a stairway that covered one entire side of the room and those stairs led up several more feet to a high platform. This platform stretched across the side of the room and reached several feet farther out over the River of Death, stretching several feet farther than the rest of the building. The walls on that ledge were completely glass on three sides, and from this place Draygon could see literally all of the Darklands.

He sat in a large high-back black chair that spun around on a shaft. The chair was nestled comfortably in the middle of the platform where he could easily look through any window that he wanted.

Today he sat quietly, looking out into the darkness that seemed to completely cover the Darklands. Wildy, Akeshia, and Mark were brought into the hall by Draygon's forces. The three kicked and fought every step. The guards brought them into the hall and held them at the bottom of the stairs. One of the guards announced their presence.

"My lord," he said, "we have the last of the rebels."

Draygon said nothing for several moments; he simply continued staring out into the Darklands. Eventually he dismissed the soldiers who bowed low to him and left. Still he sat silent. At last he spoke. There was anger in his voice, but he kept it under control so that it was low and calm. Underneath though, he seethed with hate for these three.

"So this is all that's left of the infamous Warriorites," he sneered. "The gang who roamed the countryside holding all of the Darklands in terror. A group of people too numerous to count, now down to three..." He pounded his fist down on the arm of his chair and shouted. "Three!" He looked hard at the three standing in front of him. "Your Warrior has set you up," he proclaimed triumphantly. "Pity it had to come to this."

For a long time nobody said anything, but Wildy spoke at last. "I still choose to follow him," he said.

Draygon stood up out of his chair, walked to the end of the platform, and looked hard at Wildy. "Go back to the streets where it's safe, Wildy," he said.

Wildy looked him straight in the eye. This time he wasn't afraid of Draygon. He wasn't afraid to look him in the eye, and he wasn't afraid to die. And he had been with the Warrior so long, that win or lose, he wasn't giving up now. He had too much invested, and he was going to finish what he had committed to. "The only place I'll ever be safe," he responded, "is fighting you."

Draygon looked over to the back wall and stared up into the darkness.

"Well, then," he said. "I guess you're about as safe here as you'll ever be." He paused for a minute, and then continued. "I see your Warrior hasn't taught you much."

"He taught me how to deal with you," Wildy sneered with contempt.

Draygon's face flushed red with anger. He screamed out at Wildy, "Am I some mere mortal that you can speak to me so?"

He pointed his hand at Wildy, and Wildy was knocked to the floor. His body began to vibrate like thousands of volts of an electrical current was running through it. Akeshia and Mark moved in to help him but were kept out by some unseen forcefield. Despite every effort, they were continually thrown back and away from Wildy, and every time they hit the forcefield, they felt the same pain that Wildy did. Eventually

Draygon stopped, and Wildy lay on the floor, trying to catch his breath. Draygon walked down the stairs and approached Akeshia and Mark.

"Safe you will never be," he said as casually as if he were talking about the weather. "But I will give you a chance to save your lives. If you will renounce the Warrior and join with me and my forces, I will let you live."

"We will never bow to you," Akeshia spoke. "Never."

Draygon's expression was hard to judge. Akeshia looked him firmly in the face, but she could not read what his next move might be. She looked so hard at him that her eyes defocused and she could see only a few feet in front of her own face.

Draygon looked at her for several moments. Moments that seemed to Mark to be longer than he could take. But finally Draygon spoke. Again, his speech was casual, with little emotion. "Very well then," he said. "Die."

He held out both his hands toward Mark and Akeshia, and they fell to the floor as Wildy had earlier, writhing and screaming in pain. A blue lightninglike bolt came from every one of Draygon's fingers, and they would throw and pull and hold the two, moving them in every imaginable direction, but never letting them go. Wildy jumped up to help them, but was thrown out by the forcefield. Again and again and again he tried, but the field could not be broken.

Suddenly Mark screamed out. "Okay!" he screamed. "Okay!"

Draygon stopped and looked at him.

"You win!" Mark cried. "I'll do it." He pulled himself up off the floor to look at Draygon, but he was barely able to keep eye contact.

Akeshia was barely able to move, but she managed to pull herself to a sitting position and looked up at Mark. "Mark, no," she pleaded.

"Do what?" Draygon asked Mark.

Mark hesitated for a moment. He struggled hard with what he was about to do. His head was screaming at him not to do it. He almost decided not to, but suddenly Draygon jolted him again.

"You'll what?" Draygon said, jolting him.

Still Mark could say nothing as he struggled desperately with his decision.

"You'll what?" Draygon asked again, this time getting more impatient. He jolted Mark even harder than before.

At this point Mark had had it. Where was the Warrior, and how could he let Draygon do this to him? He resolved himself to go through with it. "I'll renounce the Warrior!" Mark screamed, still flinching from all that his muscles had been through.

Wildy stood up and faced Mark, looking him in the eyes. Mark was not able to return Wildy's gaze.

"The Warrior set us up, Wildy!" Mark announced bitterly. "He stood by while one by one we were killed off. He set us up! Even Rusty. Well, I'm not going to die!"

Draygon looked over at Akeshia.

"How about you?" he asked. "Do you want to live, or die as another one of the Warrior's little scapegoats?"

Though she couldn't even pull her body off the floor, Akeshia remained firm in her conviction.

"Though he himself were to destroy me, I will trust him with everything that I've got," was her proclamation.

"Have it your way," Draygon said, and he held both hands toward her. Again the blue lightninglike bolts of energy began to cover every area of her body. She screamed in pain and writhed on the floor.

Mark cried and turned his head. He felt like he had betrayed her, and he couldn't watch her die like this. Wildy, on the other hand, continued trying to get to her. His body was in such intense pain as he pushed and pushed against the electrical forcefield, yet he refused to give up. He kept calling her name and reaching for her. He'd approach the forcefield, and it would throw him back. Then he'd approach the forcefield again, and it would throw him back again. He would run to the back of the room and then run at the forcefield as hard as he could. He was getting exhausted, and every muscle in his body was twitching from all the electricity, but he would not give up.

Neither did Draygon. He continued his barrage against Akeshia until finally her body lay motionless on the floor. Wildy ran to her and held her, limp and lifeless in his arms. He stroked her hair and cried, calling her name softly, but she did not answer.

"You don't have to suffer like this," Draygon told him. "Let Akeshia be a lesson to you."

Wildy became consumed with anger. He set Akeshia's body down an the floor and stood up to face Draygon, his eyes burning with hate. "You know damned good and well I'd never bow to you." He spat, trying to control his rage.

Draygon grabbed Mark by the throat with his hand and began to choke him. He lifted Mark just a few feet off the ground so that Mark could get no leverage. Mark struggled and struggled to breathe, but he could not break Draygon's grip.

"You can save his life," Draygon said to Wildy. "It's simple. Just say the words."

"Wildy, help me," Mark managed to squeak out.

Wildy was torn inside. A good leader always put himself before the rest of his people, and therefore he would give his life to save that of one of his followers. Yet to deny the Warrior was expressly forbidden by the Warrior himself. He dared not. They all knew that death was a possibility. The Warrior was very clear about that. But still, now that it was really happening, and real emotions entered into the picture, it changed the shape of everything.

"I can't do it, Mark," he said at last. "I must remain true to the Warrior."

Mark made a gesture to Wildy. Draygon gave one final snap of Mark's neck, and Mark's body went limp. Draygon let go of Mark and his body fell to the floor in a huddled mass. Wildy crossed over to where Mark's body lay.

At that moment, he became aware of another presence in

the room. He looked over to the door and could see a figure in black. It was Death, and he was approaching the bodies. As he passed Wildy, Wildy felt the air suddenly grow cold, and the stench of Death's clothes and his breath nearly made him vomit. Death approached Draygon at the foot of the stairs and bowed low.

"Forgive me, master," he hissed, "but I smelled the sweet, savory aroma of rotting dead flesh."

Draygon's face became alive with an evil pleasure.

"Death, my friend," he said. "Your talents amaze me. Receive these two into Sheol, and feast to your heart's content."

Death bowed low again and approached the bodies. He had to wrestle Mark's body out of Wildy's grip. Death placed his bony finger in Wildy's side, just under his rib. The pain was excruciating, and when Wildy grabbed his side, Death took the two bodies and carried them out of the room.

When he could breath again, Wildy got up and faced Draygon.

"Go ahead, Draygon," he panted. "Do whatever you want. But someday the Warrior *is* coming back, and he's going to smear your ass all over this planet."

Draygon controlled his anger, but he was dangerously close to allowing it to surface.

"My," he said, "such a display of emotions. You are strong. But not to worry, I can break you." He snapped his fingers to illustrate this point.

Draygon swung his hand to the side and Wildy sailed across the room and landed on the floor. Then Draygon held out both his hands and Wildy began to vibrate under the blue electricity. This time Draygon's anger was in full force, and he violently began to throw Wildy all over the floor with the electricity.

"Do you renounce the Warrior?" he screamed.

"Never!" Wildy screamed back. "Never."

Draygon stopped. He thought for a moment. "Perhaps pain isn't convincing enough," he said.

He walked back to his chair and looked out over the Darklands. Wildy lay on the floor trying once again to catch his breath. Every muscle in his body ached severely as it twitched uncontrollably. All over his body were massive bruises. His head ached and pounded, and he could barely move. Every movement that he did make brought him severe pain.

"Perhaps you would like to see what's left of your little rebellion?" Draygon asked.

"It doesn't matter," Wildy said, painfully pulling himself off the floor. "The Warrior knows what he's doing."

"Perhaps," Draygon said. "Or perhaps you were never intended to win this war after all."

"He didn't desert me," Wildy said.

"I never said he did," Draygon retorted. "But take a look. See for yourself what's out there."

The pain Wildy felt as he walked up the stairs to the platform was excruciating, and he took a long time getting up there. Once there, he crossed to one of the windows and looked out into the darkness. Suddenly images of the Darklands began to flash on the windows, and Wildy could see them almost as if he were there; he could see every detail of the landscape, every movement, and every inch of the planet. Several of those pictures were the mounds of dirt near their old campsite and pictures of bodies lying and rotting on the countryside. Draygon taunted him with these pictures.

"Look at all your friends, Wildy. Look at their dead bodies rotting in the ground. Lifeless and deserted. You see, the Warrior's presence is nowhere in the Darklands. Only death lives here... And what about your friend Rusty? He's dead too. And that's all your fault. You killed your best friend."

Pictures of Rusty filled Wildy's head, and he had to fight hard the urge to cry at what he had done to his friend. Draygon sensed this and used it to his advantage.

"The only one left alive out of your little rebellion is you," he taunted. "But it should be the other way around. It should be you lying in Rusty's place. Wherever that is. But you don't know where that is, do you? Of course not, you lost the body."

Draygon's voice began to grow more and more angry. "Your friends lie stinking up the countryside, and you still hold to that silly notion that the Warrior hasn't deserted you? The Warrior saved your life in the beginning only to get your hopes up and watch you die in the end. He knew as well as I that you would never escape me. That I would eventually destroy you. How is it that someone who claimed to be victorious could just disappear without a trace? Just like that? Why doesn't your Warrior just pop along and claim his victory? I know why. He's lost, that's why. He knew he would lose, so he left you alone to deal with me."

Suddenly pictures of Wildy's every activity before he met the Warrior began to flash across the window. Wildy watched deed after deed, enlarged and run before him in moving pictures. Some of these things Wildy could not even watch. He winced as he saw them.

Wildy said nothing, but a sense of hopelessness began to wash over him like a river over a waterfall. He felt his anger surge, and the words of Draygon began to reach their intended mark in Wildy's mind. Briefly he entertained Draygon's thoughts. Draygon sensed this, and with an evil gloating he pushed Wildy even harder.

"Yes," he gloated. "I sense your anger...your despair... good... Let them rise, Wildy, let them grow inside you... stronger... Let them consume you...you're loosing hope... there is no hope...you're angry at the Warrior...let that anger turn to hate... Yes, just like that...you hate the Warrior...you hate him for leaving you, for hurting you, for lying to you...for killing Rusty...surrender to it, Wildy, you cannot escape it. You hate him for calling you to follow, only to disappear. And most of all, you hate you for all those evil deeds that you have done. All those innocent people you hurt. All those lives you took. How could anyone have done what you've done and not be bothered by it?"

Wildy had given up hope. He couldn't watch anymore.

He knew that Draygon was right, that he really was a terrible person, and that he was foolish to think otherwise. Then another thought crept across his mind. He remembered the words of the Warrior the night he met him. He remembered when the Warrior addressed Draygon about the Fountain of Blood. Then he remembered visiting the Fountain of Blood for himself and sitting there next to the body of the Warrior. At that moment, the screen suddenly went blood red, and Wildy could no longer see anything else. And though he could not see Draygon at that moment, he sensed something come over him for just a split second.

Something suddenly came over Wildy. An intense anger, a fierceness, and he lunged at Draygon with full force. "Go to hell, Draygon!" he screamed. As he lunged, an invisible forcefield blocked him and threw him back. He lunged again. This time the forcefield threw him down the stairs. Draygon stood up and followed him.

"Yes, Wildy," he proclaimed triumphantly. "Let that anger consume you..." He took in a deep, self-satisfied breath. "Think of Rusty, whom you let die... You killed the only person you ever dared to trust."

Again Wildy lunged at Draygon in a rage, and again this forcefield threw him back onto the floor. Just as he landed, he heard someone call his name. The voice sounded familiar...but it couldn't be...he was dead. He turned to look, and he saw someone standing in the room just in front of the door. It was Rusty, and behind him were several hundred men and women, all Warriorites.

Wildy and Rusty ran to meet each other and embraced ecstatically.

"I thought you were dead," Wildy said as he held Rusty and cried.

Rusty looked over at Draygon.

"The Warrior knew of your plans at the campsite that night, so he used that opportunity to send me underground so that I could continue what he knew you would try to squelch. You thought I was dead. I was, but the Warrior gave me life.

He rescued me from the Fortress of Death and retrieved me, and I continued working in the Darklands. Only you weren't looking for me because you thought I was dead. Your cohorts knew about it, but they wouldn't report it to you out of fear for themselves. What you meant for my evil, the Warrior turned to my good." Then Rusty pointed behind him. "There are still remaining Warriorites in the Darklands," he proclaimed. "Besides these with me here, there are literally thousands of men and women and children hidden away from you throughout the Darklands. The Warrior has still won."

"Not quite!" Draygon snapped. He raised his arms, and, one by one, all those people who had come in with Rusty quickly fell to the floor dead. Rusty and Wildy and Draygon were the only ones left standing. "You people are too quick to assume. Did it ever occur to you that you're just pawns in the Warrior's struggle for power?"

"And you're just a pet," Rusty added, "that the Warrior lets out of its cage now and then, but you're never allowed to leave the yard."

Rusty's statement infuriated Draygon so that he violently swung his arm to the side, and Rusty went flying through the air. Again his body lay motionless on the floor.

"Be sure to thank the Warrior for giving me a second chance to kill you," Draygon said in a rage.

Wildy crossed over to him and began calling his name. Rusty got up off the floor.

"What are you doing?" Draygon asked.

"You can't kill me now," Rusty said.

"Don't be so sure," Draygon sneered.

Again Death entered the room and bowed low before Draygon.

"Death, my friend," Draygon said. "You can't still be hungry?"

"Famished, master," Death replied. "I smell more rotting flesh."

"Very well, then," Draygon said. "Go, feast on life's essence. Gorge yourself. And for desert, I have two very special treats for you. You will eat them alive. Slowly and painfully, draining every ounce of life out of them, little by little. At least you will enjoy a feast today."

Death began to drool and lick his skeletal face. "I can taste their life fluids in my mouth now, master. I can taste the life draining out of them. I cannot wait. Please, I must have them now."

"Then now it is," Draygon told him. "Feast, my friend. And I shall watch with great pleasure."

Death approached Wildy, and the two stood face to face. Death held out his arms and fanned his cloak. Then he came at Wildy, laughing and hissing. When he reached Wildy, he stuck his hand deep in Wildy's chest. Wildy felt Death's cold hand moving around inside of him, and he could feel his breath becoming shorter, his head becoming dizzy, and his heart beginning to slow down. He tried to move, but he could not. He was paralyzed. Death grinned and salivated all down the front of himself. Then he put his mouth up to Wildy's chest, and began to drink the blood as it flowed from the fountain of Wildy's heart. Wildy could feel his life flowing away from him. Slowly he could feel his life being drained from his body and becoming one with Death.

Suddenly, something filled the air. At first it was hardly noticeable, but soon everyone was aware that there was a sound—a single note, but it began to build. Louder and louder it grew. Soon other voices joined in, all taking on harmonies to that one single note. The song grew so loud that they could barely hear anything else over it or the voices that were singing it. It was a beautiful song, and it seemed to come from everywhere at the same time. From above them, from below them, from around them, but also from inside of them. These voices hit so many harmonies that it almost didn't seem possible. There weren't enough notes on a musical scale to match those harmonies.

As the song went on, Wildy felt life returning to him. As if by confirmation that something powerful was happening, Death suddenly took his hand out of Wildy's chest and fell to the floor. After that, a thick cloud rumbled and pulsated and rolled across the floor. It smelled like a sweet perfume, and as it touched the bodies that had fallen there, they came to life and stood up, including the body of Akeshia. Draygon watched in horror. As beautiful as the song was to Wildy and Rusty and the rest of the Warriorites there, it was not to everyone else. It was creating such pain in Draygon and Death that they held their hands hard across their ears trying to keep the song out. It did no good. The song seemed to sink into every pore and work its way into every muscle and every nerve of every person or being in the room.

"Death," Draygon screamed, "take these, destroy them!"

"I'm losing my power, master!" Death screamed back over the noise. "All those that I have devoured until now are churning in my stomach. I cannot hold them down."

"You must!" Draygon screamed back at him. "You must not let them go!"

Death fought hard to hold onto his victims, but suddenly he began to vomit all those that he had ever devoured before. His stomach wrenched in pain, and from it every soul that lay in every cavern of the Darklands, both good and bad, were thrown out of his stomach and onto the floor. Then something whisked them away onto the plain that surrounded the Fortress of Death. Draygon watched with terrified eyes as the bowels of the fortress itself emptied right in front of him.

Soon the caverns were completely empty, and Death vibrated in painful convulsions from losing everything in his stomach. His hunger was now at an epidemic. Even after he had brought up all the contents of his stomach, it still continued to constrict violently, like he had the dry heaves. Then he began to vomit blood—the Warrior's blood. He screamed in pain and tried to stop but it was no use. He just vomited even harder.

The black hole around the fortress suddenly began to close in on itself tighter and tighter as it became more and more dense. It was like a million tornadoes all at once, and it screamed and pulled and twisted until it imploded and then exploded into a great ball of light and energy that shot all throughout the Darklands, and then around the universe itself, shattering the other black hole that kept the Darklands secluded from the rest of life.

Rusty screamed out over the music. "Death," he screamed, "where is your sting? Grave, where is your victory?"

Death screamed and fell on his face.

The windows shattered outward, and a shard of light shot into the room. The light grew and grew and filled the room. Then the light pushed up against the roof and the walls of the building until they suddenly blew off, and everyone in the room could see clearly outside into the Darklands. All the souls began to assemble themselves on the sides of the River of Death. Everyone except for Wildy, Rusty, and Akeshia, and the group that had accompanied Rusty into the room. Death was empty now, and every resident of the Darklands that had ever lived in its history now stood on the side of the river. All over the Darklands those that had sacrificed their lives for the Warrior came up out of their graves and stood up and watched the scene that was before them. And those that had survived stood alongside them that had died.

Anna was there, Tye was there, Ryan was there...everyone that had lived and worked for the Warrior.

Off in the distance, a small black cloud rolled across the sky at a speed that seemed almost impossible to watch. It grew and grew and grew until it covered the whole sky. Lightning flashed across the sky, and the air was moving with electricity. Millions of bolts of lightening all seemed to be flashing at the same time, as far as the eye could see. The lightning shot like an arrow across the sky. The clouds rolled back on both sides and a pathway made of cloud stretched from the sky down to the fortress. A blast of music began to play, with several million voices and instruments. It was a triumphant song, and it seemed to cover not just the Darklands, but the entire universe.

The cloud stopped, and all was quiet for a moment. Then suddenly there was an explosion that rocked the planet, and the Fortress of Death blew to pieces. Wildy and Rusty watched as several beings emerged from the upper layer of clouds, caught them in midair, and set them on the ground near the River of Death. Death and Draygon fell, and once they did, they fought desperately for their very lives in the murky river.

The beings were spectacular, unlike anything the Darklands had ever seen before. They stood about twelve feet tall, with powerful bodies. Their feet looked like some form of a white hot metal that glowed and reflected the light around them. Something that looked like lightening covered their bodies. Only this lightning flashed with all the colors of the rainbow. It flashed and shot back and forth, but the lightning never left the form of the beings themselves.

The faces of these beings were incredible. They glowed like pure white lillies against the background of all the color that defined their forms. Their hair was long, white, and blue like lightning, and it seemed to flow behind them like long hair in a strong wind. Instead of just glowing, their hair also seemed to jump and crawl and spin like it was playing chase with itself.

These beings picked the Warriorites up in their massive arms like they were picking up little dolls, only they were gentle and they didn't hurt anybody. When they set them down on the riverbank, they said nothing, but there was a strong element of joy on their faces. They looked like they were smiling and laughing and singing all at the same time.

Then out of the cloud again was another funnel cloud like a tornado. Only this was triple the size of any of the other funnels that had been swirling around just a few minutes ago. It descended with a deafening roar, and when it touched the ground, it sent anything in its way miles from it. Again, these beautiful beings whisked away any Warriorites in its path so that they were safe from any danger.

The tornado touched the ground and held there for several minutes. Then it slowly lifted back into the clouds, but it left behind a most magnificent structure. The structure, or building, was miles long, miles wide, miles high, and it was made of light. It was also transparent so that everyone there could see inside of it. Although the walls were strong and impenetrable, there was the distinct impression that it was nothing but a blast of color. Every wall, every part of this building, including everything in it, was like crystal.

Inside the building on two opposite sides were rows and rows of benches and high-back chairs similar to those in a courtroom, only beautiful and majestic instead. At the very front of the building were steps that led up to a high platform. Leading up to the platform was a long corridor. The entire building shined like a jewel. The most precious and expensive gems and stones made up everything in this building. The purest diamonds made up the pillars, and living, breathing marble made up the floor. The chairs were uncut pearls, and the platform was pure gold.

Behind the first of the beings out of the clouds were four more, even more different from the first. Although they too seemed made of light, electricity, and color, they were much more powerful and unique than the first beings. Instead of having feet, they had wheels that spun madly inside of one another, so that they could go in any direction without having to turn. They also had four different heads, each one facing a different direction. Each head acted on its own, yet in conjunction with the rest of the body, and each head had the shape of a different beast. They had the face of a man, the face of a lion, the face of an ox, and the face of an eagle. They each had wings that seemed to touch and join with the wings of the other being, and they were all carrying something on their shoulders.

As they descended further, the Warriorites could see that they were carrying a throne, a majestic throne made of sapphire and white gold and yellow gold, more magnificent than anything any ruler had ever hoped to sit in. All the colors now bouncing around the atmosphere were reflected in the throne, intensified, and thrown back into the air with great force.

The most amazing thing about the throne was the person sitting on it. He was the Great Emperor himself, who seemed to outshine even the sun. His presence was awesome, like being in the middle of a bolt of lightning, and it was so intense and electrifying that it seemed to virtually draw the energy out of every mortal there, and they could no longer stand.

The beings ascended to the giant hall and set the Great Emperor's throne on the platform of gold.

Then another voice sounded throughout the Darklands, and every resident of the planet heard it loud and clear. "Now is the time for the judgment of every inhabitant of the Darklands," it said. "Now every man, woman, and child will stand before the Great Emperor." As the voice spoke, a parade of other creatures descended from a pathway in the clouds and took their seats in the great hall. There were virtually millions of them. They all looked just like the residents of the Darklands, only their bodies were much more defined, and they lacked any physical flaws whatsoever. They were heightened in stature, every muscle in their bodies was tuned to perfection, their skin and hair were alive and vibrant, and in every way imaginable, they looked more attractive than any Darklander ever did. They were leaders of all the other planets and universes that expanded beyond the planet Darklands and the black hole that held it secluded from them. They belonged to those worlds that still lived within the law of the Great Emperor, who had been watching the saga of the Darklands throughout the ages, but had never taken part in the rebellion. All of creation, every form of life in every corner of every universe, no matter how remote, had watched the events as they unfolded on this planet. Now they were allowed finally to touch the planet's surface, but they could only touch the ground in the Great Hall and nowhere else. There they would preside as the jury in this judging of the Darklands, while the Great Emperor would preside as the judge.

Once everybody had taken their places, the trial began. Everyone in the Darklands watched from outside the Great Hall, but everyone that stood before the Great Emperor was alone inside the Great Hall with the jury and the Great Emperor.

One by one, every person stood before the Great Emperor. The monarch and his court were the first ones brought. These powerful men who had ruled the Darklands so brutally now stood before the one in whom they claimed the right to rule. Every one of them stood naked and exposed before the Great Emperor. The monarch was the first to stand there.

"In my name," the Great Emperor thundered, and his voice seemed to work on every frequency of sound so the lowness of his voice seemed to rattle the entire planet, and the highness of his voice seem to resonate out of the sky. "You abused and destroyed those who had been placed under you. Your evil deeds had no limit. You did not plead the case of the fatherless to win it. You did not defend the rights of the poor. Instead you murdered the fatherless and oppressed the poor. You took advantage of those under you, and you misled the Darklands. I will avenge myself and those that you have oppressed. You will die slowly and painfully, and all those whom you have oppressed will watch you die."

The monarch, a once powerful man, became a whimpering baby begging for mercy, but the Great Emperor would show none. It would be done to him as he had done to everyone else around him. Max watched with great pleasure as the monarch begged and pleaded for his life, and as the Great Emperor had the monarch thrown out of his court naked, a shell of the man he once was, or thought he was.

Soon Rhend was brought forward. He was also naked, and so frightened that he had defecated all over himself. He kicked and screamed and begged to be left alone. He was thrown down onto the floor at the bottom of the golden platform. He lay motionless for several minutes, hoping that he would not have to look up and face the emperor, but by some force, he was compelled to look into the Great Emperor's eyes.

The Great Emperor looked hard at Rhend for several moments, and Rhend squirmed trying to get out of the gaze. But that was not possible.

Another being came forward with a very large book,

containing the life and deeds of Rhend, and they were all read aloud. Everything that Rhend had done in secret, every deal he had made and word that he had spoken was recorded in this book. As the being read off the pages one by one, Rhend watched in horror as all these deeds were projected onto some sort of screen and broadcast all over the Darklands. Rhend was filled with embarrassment as he watched, and he knew that everyone else in the world was watching at the same time. He hated the Great Emperor for embarrassing him, and he wished there were some way that he could get even.

Soon the reading was over, and again the Great Emperor looked hard at Rhend. Rhend was trying to back up by sliding across the floor, but he could not move. So he continued pushing at the floor with his arms, going nowhere.

The Great Emperor spoke. "Rhend," he said. "According to the records you have spent your life pursuing nothing but self-gain and power. You have trampled the weak and inflicted pain on the powerless."

Suddenly the being holding the records cried out in a loud voice for all of the Darklands to hear. "Let it be known," he called out, "that the man, Rhend, has been weighed in the scales of justice, and has been found wanting."

Rhend was then carried out of the hall and thrown outside, kicking and screaming, trying to get out of the grasp of his captors. When he was thrown outside of the Great Hall, he began screaming and cursing. He looked around for something to wear, but could find nothing. He tried to find someplace to hide, but there was nowhere to hide. He was exposed to the world, along with the monarch and his court, and they stood there like someone sentenced to die and robbed of any dignity.

Mr. Myer was up next. He too was thrown before the Great Emperor naked and defenseless. It was such an irony. The one thing Myer desired more than anything in life was wealth. Now he was in the midst of the most incredible wealth any creature could ever imagine, and he could have nothing.

His book was also brought before the Great Emperor and

the jury and read aloud before the Darklands. The jury listened and watched intently. They were there to attest to the fact that every decision the Great Emperor would make regarding the guilt or innocence of any Darklander would be fair and just. And by the time Mr. Myer's file had played, it was obvious to all that he too was found wanting.

The announcement was made to that effect, and he also was thrown out of the Great Hall and into the Darklands outside.

Then Dr. In was brought forward, naked as well.

The emperor chastised him for his deception at the Fortress of Light, for claiming the name of the Prince of Light, for flagrantly throwing around his name, and yet not living according to his standards and principles, but merely making up the rules so that they would suit his own needs.

Dr. In knew what was happening, and he begged for mercy, but none would be found. Then he too was thrown into the Darklands with the others.

Then another man was brought forward. When Rusty saw him, he cried out and wept bitterly.

"Dad," he screamed. His father heard Rusty's scream and turned to see him standing outside of the judgment hall. Tears filled his eyes as he looked over at Rusty. Then he turned back to the Great Emperor.

Rusty watched silently as the deeds of his father were read aloud and projected throughout the Darklands. Despite all the abuse and the violence of his father, his double standards, and his love for the praise of men, he was still Rusty's father, and Rusty loved him. To see this slowly tore Rusty apart, and he could no longer watch. He turned away.

Wildy and Akeshia took Rusty in their arms and tried to comfort him. Nobody said anything. They held each other close and tried to provide him the support he would need to get through this, his most painful trial ever. Rusty's father was lost forever. He would never see him again. This thought was too much for Rusty.

When the file was through playing on Rusty's father, the

Great Emperor looked down on him with disgust. "You used my name to manipulate and control and abuse the precious child and wife that I placed in your care," he said. "You cared more for your own reputation than you did for your own family. Only now the entire world and all those that have gone before you can see the type of man you really are, and your reputation is lost. You can do nothing to hide it now, and you will die in your shame." Then he had Rusty's father thrown out of the Great Hall along with everybody else.

As Wildy was with Rusty, trying to comfort him, something caught his eye. It was a young man looking at him. The young man was Tye, and for some reason, he knew who Tye was. He also knew what he had done to Tye and to his family. He cautiously approached Tye, but he said nothing for several moments. They looked at each other in silence. Then Wildy broke down and wept.

"I'm sorry," he sobbed. "I'm so sorry. I didn't mean to cause you this much pain."

Tye looked at him. It was just like the night he saw Wildy in his dream, and he felt love for Wildy. Tye took Wildy and hugged him, then spoke quietly, "I forgive you."

They heard another voice that said, "And I forgive you too."

They both looked around, and there was Tye's sister, Diana. She was beautiful and had a delicate and gentle nature about her. Tye immediately ran to her and embraced her, and they wept. Soon they were joined by their father and their mother. Once they were all together, Tye introduced them to Sam.

Wildy held back and allowed the four of them to get to know one another again and to meet the newest member of the family. They were all alive and together again.

Deep in Wildy's heart, he was saddened. It was hard for him to watch this reunion. It only made him feel more isolated and alone. But he was very happy for them at the same time. He wished that he had a family, or someone that he could be this close to. This was a thought he never really dared allow himself to have most of his life, but now that things were finally over for the Darklands, he wished he had someone to share it with.

Eventually, Diana approached Wildy. "Looking back from here," she said, "it doesn't seem so bad. Everything's brand new here, including my life." With that, she held Wildy and they wept some more.

Soon though, Wildy heard his own name called.

He trembled and approached the Great Hall. As he approached, his clothes were somehow stripped from his body, and he too was naked. Then, as he entered the door of the Great Hall, he was met by the Warrior. The Warrior looked at him and smiled.

"Fear not," he said, and he took a robe that seemed to Wildy to be made out of the same kind of light that every one of the beings around him was wearing.

The Warrior took the robe and placed it on Wildy. Once the Warrior wrapped it around Wildy, it sealed itself and wrapped itself snugly around his body. Wildy could feel it as it began to cover him. It vibrated with electricity and made him feel so alive. The robe tingled all over his body.

The Warrior walked Wildy down the hall to the Great Emperor. It was the longest walk Wildy had ever taken in his life. He was afraid like he had never been afraid before. When he reached the throne of the Great Emperor, Wildy could sense the force around the emperor. It was so strong. He seemed to be made of energy—so much energy that his essence sucked every little bit of energy right out of Wildy. He no longer had any control over his limbs, and he fell to his face.

The Great Emperor smiled at Wildy, and although Wildy couldn't see the smile, he could feel the smile on his back. He could feel the emperor's eyes as they looked down on him. They were not hostile eyes, but tender and compassionate. Then suddenly he noticed that he was being lifted up off the floor by some unseen force. And before he could figure out what was happening, he was again standing before the Great Emperor.

THE WARRIOR

The emperor looked at him and smiled. "I can see by your clothing that you have the seal of my son. Do not be afraid." Then Wildy's book was opened and his deeds were read aloud. But much to Wildy's surprise, only positive deeds were recorded. None of those horrible things that Wildy knew so well that he was guilty of were ever read. Wildy looked up to the emperor, wondering why none of those were mentioned. Those that he had murdered on the streets, the crime he had taken part of, and in some cases spearheaded...Diana... And the worst of all in his mind, losing Rusty to the demon that dreadful night...

"Those deeds no longer exist," the Great Emperor said softly, jarring Wildy out his thoughts. "Every one of those deeds has been drowned in the Fountain of Blood, and your are free of them. "Wildy," he said again, "you were not called to win any war, you were called to bring all those that would, to come to a knowledge of the Warrior. That you have done well. I commend you. You have fulfilled your task...I am proud of you. And as for your friend (he pointed toward Rusty), you are forgiven."

Wildy felt his heart burst with joy at those words. He was forgiven. And not only that, but he was complimented and commended for his work, and by none other than the Great Emperor himself. The Great Emperor had one more thing to say to Wildy. "Wildy, no longer will you be known by that name, but instead you have earned another name. A new name that I will give you, and you shall forever be known by that name. A name that represents not who you once were, but who you have become and who you are now."

The Great Emperor looked behind Wildy and called Rusty forward.

Rusty approached the throne, and when the Great Emperor saw Rusty, he cried.

"I know of your tears," he said. "I know of your pain. But you will not be an orphan. You too have done your job well. You have made me proud." He looked over Rusty's shoulder toward someone behind him. "Bring them in," he said.

A man and a woman who had been standing in the wings were brought forward. And after them followed Akeshia, Michael, and Ryan. The Great Emperor spoke to them. My dear friends, Anna and Simeon, you have long wanted children of your own, and you have loved and cared for many that were not yours. But in your world, children of your own were not to be. Well now I give you your very own family. Four boys and a girl."

"This is your new family," he said to Rusty, Akeshia, Michael, and Ryan. And then he looked at Wildy. "This is the family you wanted. Wildy, deep down you used to yearn for a family of such. I have watched with great interest your relationship with Rusty, and how like brothers you two have become. So I give you each other. You are now brothers by blood."

Then he looked back over at Anna. "My dear Anna," he said. "You never lost faith in me, you will be together always, and nothing will ever again tear you apart. And you will be young forever."

As the Great Emperor spoke those words, the lines and wrinkles lifted from Anna's and Simian's face, and they were young again. Young and in love.

Anna and Simian thanked the emperor, and then took Wildy, Rusty, Michael, and Akeshia in.

One by one, every human being on the planet faced the Great Emperor. Nobody really knew how long this took, because time seemed to have stood still. But it was a significant amount nonetheless.

Max was brought up.

Sam watched from the side as Max approached the Great Emperor. For the first time in her life she was able to see the real state of her father, and she was able to see that the Warrior really did demand justice, and that her father would know and experience what he had done to others. This gave her an even stronger love for the Warrior.

Max himself could not get over the shock of finding out that Tye (whom he called Matthew) was a Warriorite. He was very angry that he never picked up on this all the time that Tye worked for him.

Soon Sam was called.

She approached the throne, clothed in a white gown. The Great Emperor looked down on her and smiled as one by one the deeds of her putting her life on the line for the Warrior and his cause were read aloud. "You were reluctant at first," the Great Emperor told her, "but only because you did not understand me. But you did fight the cause of the poor, and you did fight the cause of the oppressed, you did fight for my cause. And once you knew me, you joined my cause for justice and life. Welcome to my home."

Eventually, the man who sold the Darklands over to Draygon at the beginning of time was made to come forward and to look at what his deed had done to the Darklands. He was devastated and would not have survived it, but the Warrior stood by him every minute and strengthened him to go through it. When it was over, the Great Emperor extended his hand toward him and forgave him. Then all the residents of the Darklands who were now part of the Great Emperor's kingdom extended their applause, signifying that they forgave him as well.

Then Draygon himself was called forward, and he and all his men were brought into the hall before the Great Emperor at the same time.

Draygon tried to escape but he was brought by beings so powerful that even he could not escape their grasp. They brought him in and set him before the Great Emperor. The Great Emperor said nothing for several minutes, he merely looked at Draygon with a hard, firm stare. Draygon could not hold his gaze. He was trembling so strongly that he almost could not stand up, and this continued silence was driving him crazy. He had known that this day would eventually come, but he had buried himself deep in his hatred and his determination to destroy the Darklands people before the Great Emperor caught up with him. Now that the time was here, he was more terrified than he ever imagined he would be. Exhausted and frightened, he collapsed like a leaf in front of the Great Emperor and the Warrior.

Eventually the Great Emperor did speak, and when he did his voice seemed to swell and fill the whole room. To Wildy and Rusty it was tender and beautiful, but to Draygon and Death, it was cruel and deafening and painful. "Draygon," the Great Emperor said, "I have allowed you to rule, and to demonstrate your form of government. A government that consisted of stealing, lying, and outright destroying the things that I loved the most just to put yourself in a position of power. You have proved that your government does not run on justice, or love, or compassion, only that you have nothing but contempt for those under you. And now your government will be no more. I will no longer tolerate your vial, evil practices. Your time has come to an end." Then he looked over at Death. "You and Death will be no more. Death, you too will die, but you will die on a full stomach. I offer you one last feast before you go. Your master. You will devour him, and then you too will die."

Death was ravenous, and he trembled from hunger. He had lost everything else he had in his stomach. He had no loyalty, only hunger. He approached sheepishly at first, and Draygon tried to fight, but he no longer had the power. He was like a little whimpering child, helpless and defenseless. For the first time in Draygon's life, he was staring death in the face, and now he would know what that was like. And death would be slow and painful for him, like so many that had died that same way because of Draygon's evil regime. Now he knew their fear, and that fear gripped him. He would cease to exist forever, and that thought terrified him. He fell on his face before the Warrior and begged for mercy. He cried out, "Please, mighty Prince, Lord of heaven and earth, Son of the Great Emperor, please have mercy on me." But there was no mercy for the merciless. Wildy couldn't help but notice how different he looked now. For years, he had been handing out death, and now death had come to him, and he was afraid of it.

The entire Darklands watched as Death devoured Draygon,

the same way he tried to devour Wildy. He cupped his hands in Draygon's chest near his heart, and then slowly drained every ounce of life fluid out of him. The entire Darklands watched, some in silent fear, and some in joy for the end. When Draygon's body fell lifeless to the floor, he was thrown into the River of Death where he sank further and further into the mire.

Those of Draygon's minions, who had all been rounded up from the four corners of the Darklands, were present at the arrival of the Great Emperor and now they were forced to watch their leader die. This brought great pleasure to them, because they hated him so much. But it also brought fear to them as well, because once he was dead, they too would die. They tried to escape, but they also were detained by the forces of the Great Emperor. One by one, they were all brought before the Great Emperor where they begged and pleaded for their lives, which included bowing down to the Prince of Light and proclaiming him as the king of all creation. But there was no mercy for them, and they were thrown into the River of Death.

When this was all completed, the Great Emperor focused his attention on the residents of the Darklands, those that had chosen to ignore his warnings, and to destroy the people that he had called to him. The old man and lady from the little store in the village were there. Those at the mob the night of Wildy's lynching were there, and many more. Everyone there knew why they were there, and they also knew that they had made that decision to be there. Some were glad to be there. Not that they were glad to die, but their contempt for the Warrior made it so that they could not stand to be in his presence. Some wished they had chosen not to be there. Rusty's parents, Dr. In, the residents of the Fortress of Light, Mark. But whatever the reason, they trembled in fear of the pain and death that was before them.

The Warrior turned his focus on Mark. Mark was brought forward, and the Warrior spoke to him. "Mark," he said tenderly, "you were never set up. It was never intended for you to lose. You knew from the beginning that your life might be required of you. I kept nothing from you. I told you it would be difficult, and you agreed to that sacrifice when you accepted the call. Your acceptance of that call was your agreement. I never asked anything from you that you didn't agree to, or that you wouldn't be able to handle."

Mark's eyes filled with tears, and he wept bitterly. He knew what the Warrior said was true, but now it was too late to change what was already done. The Prince of Light had Mark thrown into the River of Death with everyone else at the judgment. There were tears in his eyes as he did so.

When Tye saw this, he wept also. Sam took him by the hand and tried to console him, but to Tye it was like losing a brother. Of all people, he thought Mark would be the one to stand for the Warrior at all cost.

It was obvious to everybody at the judgment hall that the act of judgment on the corrupt and vile of the Darklands hurt the Great Emperor deeply, but he was, after all, just and fair, and he had provided every opportunity for those people to be saved from it. He also knew that anyone that didn't like him in the beginning would not like him now and would resent his form of government—one that ran on fairness, love, and respect for others.

This being done, the Great Emperor spoke again. "Bring Death to me."

Death was brought before him, and then he too was thrown into the river. When he reached the river, it swirled around him like a whirlpool, then all bunched together and sank deep into a large pit, disappearing into nothing. Then fire, like the lava of a volcano, only much more intense, swept across the Darklands. It moved slowly at first, and then quickly it covered the entire planet. The Fortress of Death was also was destroyed. All those in the Great Hall rose off the ground and floated on the fire like a boat on a lake.

Explosions of fire began to break out all over the Darklands. Volcanoes erupted, throwing lava miles into the air. The earth shook and the ground opened up and lava came rushing to the surface. The heat was so intense that soon particles of air began to catch fire, and the fire would dance throughout the atmosphere. All the water on the planet began to evaporate, but because of the heat, it burned up before it could get very high up into the atmosphere. Soon the entire sky began to fall in a fiery mass and hurl itself toward the Darklands. The fire reached higher and higher into the air, until the entire universe was burning with the heat and flames. Giant planets exploded and fell and were sucked up by the fire and hurled toward the Darklands. Comets and stars exploded into brilliant flares of fire, and then disappeared. Soon the boundaries of the universe itself caught fire and burned away. The last to go was the black hole that had sealed the Darklands from the rest of the universes that existed beyond it. It caught fire, and like a tornado, swirled its way toward the planet, and then dropped into the swirling mass of fire that was now the planet Darklands.

With those boundaries gone, the Darklanders could see everywhere else in the universe. And those residents of the other universes watched with amazement the final ending of the dark planet that they had been allowed to only watch for so many years.

The River of Death was the first to catch fire, and all those in the river were suddenly screaming in pain and agony. They were being burned alive, which was the most terrible way to go. Rusty looked down and saw his parents. He screamed and cried and threw himself on the floor and wept. Nobody could comfort him now from the pain that he was feeling. He wept so hard that his body vibrated. Wildy didn't know what to do and was afraid that Rusty might not be able to take too much more.

Soon everything and everyone in the Darklands and the universe was completely destroyed, and nothing of the planet or the universe remained. And then when the fire was done with its purification of the Darklands, it too ceased. And as the lava began to cool, it began to harden.

The Prince of Light approached Rusty, picked him up,

and held him close. Rusty cried and cried, and the Prince of Light didn't stop him.

Then the Prince of Light pulled Rusty away from him a few inches so that he could look Rusty in the eye. With his thumb, he wiped away the tears from Rusty's face. He looked directly into Rusty's eyes and said, "The time of weeping is over. The time of sorrow and of death is over. From this time forward there will be no memory of them."

At first Rusty said and did nothing, but soon he looked up at the Prince of Light with a look of confusion, and then his countenance began to change. His face began to take on an odd transformation, and then he smiled and looked back at the Prince of Light. He had forgotten, so completely that he didn't even understand what it was that the Prince of Light was telling him that he would forget.

He and the Prince of Light embraced strongly.

"I'm so glad you're here with me," the Prince of Light said. "I love you so much."

"And I'm glad to be here," Rusty told him.

Then Rusty turned to Wildy. Rusty thought that they had been brothers all their lives, and he had no knowledge that the man and woman standing next to him were his new parents and not his real parents from birth.

"Mom, Dad," he said to Anna and Simian. "I'm glad that at least you made it. At least the family is all together."

As Wildy watched all this, he thought how odd it was, but he didn't know how to respond to it. Then the Prince of Light looked at him and smiled. Wildy suddenly realized that his recollections of the Darklands were getting hazy. He was uncomfortable with this at first and tried to remember everything he could, but soon he too forgot.

Previous recollections of the Darklands were completely erased from every survivor, and every resident of the Great Emperor's kingdom. Only the scars of the Fountain of Blood remained on the Prince of Light as a reminder that rebellion brought nothing but pain. This reminder would act as a deterrent to a rebellion ever happening again.

As soon as things had settled down, the Great Emperor looked out into the darkened wasteland. Then the news spread throughout the Great Hall that the emperor was going to create a planet, and everybody gathered to watch.

The Emperor held his hands in the air and called out to the sky. Off in the distance a light shined down on the darkness where the planet used to be. Then water fell out of the sky and cascaded like a waterfall into the riverbed where the River of Death, only moments ago, used to flow. The water sparkled like seltzer water, alive and vibrant. Everyone present could see it bubble, gurgle, churn, and chatter to itself as it flowed with such life and vibrancy. As it touched the banks and flowed around and through the Darklands, life began to grow. Green grass, animals, plants. The most amazing life ever imagined.

Then they all looked up and saw as stars began to pop out of the sky, comets began to whiz by them, and planets began to take on new orbits around a new sun. There were big planets and small planets. Some as big as two or three planets, and some the size of moons. They all found their own orbit around their sun. And every resident of the Darklands could watch at any time. It was truly a spectacular sight. Everything was recreated, on a much grander scale than anyone there could have imagined.

Then the Great Emperor returned his attention back to those who had chosen him. A great feast was prepared for them, and they gathered around to eat and to celebrate being rescued by the Great Emperor. That part of their memory they would retain forever. They ate and drank and got to know one another. Nobody really knew how long this took, but it seemed to have gone on for years. Although it really didn't matter any more as time had ceased to exist in the Great Emperor's realm.

Wildy, Rusty, Tye, Sam, Akeshia, Michele, Ryan, Thomas, and the rest of the old gang of Warriorites, as well as some new friends they were making, went off exploring in their new home. They met and made many new friends, and they searched out every area of the new kingdom that they could find. Soon Rusty and Wildy were in a wrestling match on the green turf. It was soft and cushiony, and they seemed almost to bounce off of it.

After the feast was over and everyone had plenty of time to get to know one another, the Great Emperor himself spent time visiting with each one of them, and they could spend as much time with him as they desired. There was no time in this new land that the Great Emperor had renamed the New Lands.

As for the Warrior, no longer would he be called the Warrior, for the war was over, forever. From then on, he would be known as the Prince of Light. And everyone in the New Lands would honor him above all for his sacrifice for their lives.